Tapping the Dream Tree

By Charles de Lint from Tom Doherty Associates

Tapping the
Dream Tree

Charles de Lint

TOR®

A Tom Doherty Associates Book
New York

TAPPING THE DREAM TREE

Copyright © 2002 by Charles de Lint

This book is printed on acid-free paper.

Edited by Terri Windling

A Tor Book
Published by Tom Doherty Associates, LLC
175 Fifth Avenue
New York, NY 10010

www.tor.com

Tor® is a registered trademark of Tom Doherty Associates, LLC.

ISBN 0-312-87401-4

Printed in the United States of America

0 9 8 7 6 5 4 3 2

Copyright Acknowledgments

To the memory
of Jenna Felice

You'll be missed
more than you could ever know.

Contents

Author's Note

When I sat down to write the first Newford story (that was "Timeskip," and I didn't know that's what I was doing at the time), I never imagined that twelve years later I'd be sitting down to write an introduction for a fourth collection of these stories. Needless to say, I'm GRATEFUL that others enjoy visiting this place as much as I do, allowing me the indulgence of regularly checking in on the characters to catch up on the gossip and see who's new in town.

This time out, as in *Forests of the Heart* and *The Onion Girl*, a few of the stories take us a little farther afield from Newford's familiar streets to the hills north of the city. It's not that there aren't stories left to tell in the city itself, it's just that some took me down more rural roads.

For those of you interested in chronology, these stories all take place before the events in *The Onion Girl*.

* * *

I realize that in each of these short story collections I've thanked a number of people (often the same ones from book to book) and some of you might be getting tired of reading the list of names. But their contributions are important, so please acknowledge them with me. I would like to especially thank:

My wife, MaryAnn, who came up with the title for this collection. She has a gift for fine-tuning and asking the right questions, both of which help to keep the creative juices flowing;

My long-time editors Terri Windling and Patrick Nielsen Hayden, and all the wonderful folks at Tor Books and at my Canadian distributor H. B. Fenn, with a special thanks to Irene Gallo, who has done such a fabulous job with her design work on my books at Tor, and to Tom Doherty, who continues to support these short story collections of mine;

My friends Rodger Turner, Charles Vess and Karen Shaffer (without whom there'd be no seven sisters, wild or otherwise), Pat and Jon Caven, Andrew and Alice Vachss, Anna "Many Names" Young and Julie Bartel (who will always be Her Julieness), Charles Saunders, Paul "Possum" Brandon and Julie Hinchliffe, Glenn Elder (he really is older, I don't care what the birth certificates say) and Lorraine Stuart, Joanne ("wine and chocolat") Harris, John Adcox, Lisa ("I could be a crow girl") Wilkins, and Jane Yolen (for many things, but here it's for introducing me to the work of her poet Joshua Stanhold);

The individual editors who first commissioned these stories: Larry Segriff, Peter Crowther, Lisa Snelling (thanks for letting me play on your Ferris wheel), Martin H. Greenberg, Bill Schafer, Russell Davis, Alan Clark, Liz Engstrom, Steve Savile, and John Helfer;

And of course you, my readers, steadfast in your support, which is much appreciated.

*   *   *

Lastly, some notes on a couple of the stories. In "Big City Littles," Sheri's story of the Traveling Littles is adapted from an Appalachian story detailing the origin of Gypsies; I found my version in *Virginia Folk Legends*, edited by Thomas E. Barden. Thanks to Charles Vess for introducing me to this delightful book. And in its initial publication, *Seven Wild Sisters* was dedicated to the red rock girls, Anna Annabelle and Her Julieness, and it still is.

* * *

If any of you are on the Internet, come visit my home page at www.charlesdelint.com.

—Charles de Lint
Ottawa, Autumn 2001

Tapping the Dream Tree

Ten for the Devil

"Are you sure you want off here?"

"Here" was in the middle of nowhere, on a dirt county road somewhere between Tyson and Highway 14. Driving along this twisty back road, Butch Crickman's pickup hadn't passed a single house for the last mile and a half. If he kept on going, he wouldn't pass another one for at least a mile or so, except for the ruin of the old Lindy farm and that didn't count, seeing as how no one had lived there since the place burned down ten years ago.

Staley smiled. "Don't you worry yourself, Butch."

"Yeah, but—"

Opening the passenger door, she jumped down onto the dirt, then leaned back inside to grab her fiddle case.

"This is perfect," she told him. "Really."

"I don't know. Kate's not going to be happy when she finds out I didn't take you all the way home."

Staley took a deep breath of the clean night air. On her side of the road it was all Kickaha land. She could smell the raspberry bushes choking the ditches close at hand, the weeds and scrub trees out in the field, the dark rich scent of the forest beyond it. Up above, the stars seemed so close you'd think they were leaning down to listen to her conversation with Butch. Somewhere off in the distance, she heard a long, mournful howl. Wolf. Maybe coyote.

"This *is* home," she said. Closing the door, she added through the window, "Thanks for the ride."

Butch hesitated a moment longer, then sighed and gave her a nod. Staley stepped back from the pickup. She waited until he'd turned the vehicle around and started back, waited until all she could see was the red glimmer of his taillights through a thinning cloud of dust, before she knelt down and took out her fiddle and bow. She slung the case over her shoulder by its strap so that it hung across her back. Hoisting the fiddle and bow up above her shoulders, she pushed her way through the raspberry bushes, moving slowly and patiently so that the thorns didn't snag on her denim overalls.

Once she got through the bushes, the field opened up before her, ghostly in the starlight. The weeds were waist high, but she liked the brush of stem and long leaf against her legs, and though the mosquitoes quickly found her, they didn't bite. She and the bugs had an understanding—something she'd learned from her grandmother. Like her music.

The fiddle went up, under her chin. Tightening the frog on the bow, she pulled it across the strings and woke a sweet melody.

Butch and Kate Crickman owned the roadhouse back out on the highway where Staley sat in with the house band from time to time, easily falling into whatever style they were playing that night. Honky-tonk. Western swing. Old-timey. Bluegrass. The Crickmans treated her like an errant daughter, always worried about how she was doing, and she let them fuss over her some. But she played coy when it came to her living accommodations. They wouldn't understand. Most people didn't.

Home was an old trailer that used to belong to her grandmother. After Grandma died, Staley had gotten a few of the boys from up on the rez to move it from her parents' property on the outskirts of Tyson down here where it was hidden away in the deep woods. Strictly speaking, it was parked on Indian land, but the Kickaha didn't mind either it or her being here. They had some understanding with her grandmother that went way back—Staley didn't know the details.

So it was a couple of the Creek boys and one of their cousins who transported the trailer for her that winter, hauling it in from the road on a makeshift sled across the snowy fields, then weaving in between the older growth, flattening saplings that would spring back upright by the time spring came around again. There were no trails leading to it now except for the one narrow path Staley had walked over the years, and forget about a road. Privacy was absolute. The area was too far off the beaten track for hikers or other weekend explorers, and come hunting season anyone with an ounce of sense stayed out of the rez. Those boys were partial to keeping their deer, partridge, ducks and the like to themselves, and weren't shy about explaining the way things were to trespassers.

Round about hunting season Staley closed up the trailer and headed south herself. She only summered in the deep woods. The other half of the year she was a traveling musician, a city girl, making do with what work her music could bring her, sometimes a desert girl, if she traveled far enough south.

But tonight the city and traveling was far from her mind. She drank in the tall night sky and meandered her way through the fields, fiddling herself home with a music she only played here, when she was on her own. Grandma called it a calling-on music, said it was the fiddle sending spirit tunes back into the otherworld from which it had first come. Staley didn't know from spirit music and otherworlds; she just fancied a good tune played from the heart, and if the fiddle called up anything here, it was that. Heart music.

When she got in under the trees, the music changed some, took on an older, more resonant sound, long low notes that spoke of hemlock roots growing deep in the earth, or needled boughs cathedraling between the earth and the stars. It changed again when she got near the bottle tree, harmonizing with the soft clink of the glass bottles hanging from its branches by leather thongs. Grandma taught her about the bottle tree.

"I don't rightly know that it keeps unwelcome spirits at bay," she said, "but it surely does discourage uninvited visitors."

Up in these hills everybody knew that only witches kept a bottle tree.

A little farther on Staley finally reached the meadow that held her trailer. The trailer itself was half hidden in a tangle of vines, bookended on either side by a pair of rain barrels that caught spill-off from the eaves. The grass and weeds were kept trimmed here, not quite short enough to be a lawn, but not wild like the fields along the county road.

Stepping out from under the relative darkness cast by the trees, the starlight seemed bright in contrast. Staley curtsied to the scarecrow keeping watch over her little vegetable patch, a tall, raggedy shape that sometimes seemed to dance to her music when the wind was right. She'd had it four years now, made it herself from apple boughs and old clothes. The second summer she'd noticed buds on what were supposed to be dead limbs. This spring, the boughs had actually blossomed and now bore small, tart fruit.

She stood in front of it for a long moment, tying off her tune with a complicated knot of sliding notes, and that was when she sensed the boy.

He'd made himself a nest in the underbrush that crowded close up against the north side of her clearing—a goosey, nervous presence where none should be. Staley walked over to her trailer to lay fiddle and bow on the steps, then carefully approached the boy's hiding place. She hummed under her breath, a soothing old modal tune that had first been born somewhere deeper in the hills than this clearing. When she got to the very edge of her meadow, she eased down until she was kneeling in the grass, then peered under the bush.

"Hey, there," she said. "Nobody's going to hurt you."

Only it wasn't a boy crouching there under the bushes.

She blinked at the gangly hare her gaze found. It was undernourished, one ear chewed up from a losing encounter with some predator, limbs trembling, big brown eyes wide with fear.

"Well, now," Staley said, sitting back on her haunches.

She studied the animal for a long moment before reaching carefully under the branches of the bush. The rabbit was too scared or worn out—probably both—to do much more than shake in her arms when she picked it up. Standing, she cradled the little animal against her breast.

Now what did she do with it?

It was round about then she realized that she and the rabbit weren't alone, here in the clearing. Calling-on music, she thought and looked around. Called up the rabbit, and then something else, though what, she couldn't say. All she got was the sense that it was something old. And dangerous. And it was hungry for the trembling bundle of fur and bone she held cradled in her arms.

It wasn't quite all the way here yet, hadn't quite managed to cross over the way its prey had. But it was worrying at the fabric of distance that kept it at bay.

Staley had played her fiddle tunes a thousand times, here in her meadow. What made tonight different from any other?

"You be careful with this music," Grandma had told her more

than once. "What that fiddle can wake in your chest and set you to playing has lived over there behind the hills and trees forever. Some of it's safe and pretty. Some of it's old and connects a straight line between you and a million years ago. And some of it's just plain dangerous."

"How do you know the difference?" she'd asked.

Grandma could only shake her head. "You don't till you call it up. That's why you need be careful, girl."

Staley Cross is about the last person I expect to find knocking on my apartment door at six A.M. I haven't seen her since Malicorne and Jake went away—and that's maybe three, four years ago now—but she looks about the same. Straw-colored hair cut short like a boy's, the heart-shaped face and those big green eyes. Still fancies those denim overalls, though the ones she's wearing over a white T-shirt tonight are a better fit than those she had on the last time I saw her. Her slight frame used to swim in that pair.

I see she's still got that old army surplus knapsack, hanging on her back, and her fiddle case is standing on the floor by her feet. What's new is the raggedy-ass rabbit she's carrying around in a cloth shopping bag, but I don't see that straightaway.

"Hey, William," she says when I open the door on her, my eyes still thick with sleep. "Remember me?"

I have to smile at that. She's not easy to forget, not her nor that blue fiddle of hers.

"Let's see," I say. "Are you the one who went skinny-dipping in the mayor's pool the night he won the election, or the one who could call up blackbirds with her fiddle?"

I guess it was Malicorne who told me about that, how where ravens or crows gather, a door to the otherworld stands ajar. Told me how Staley's blue spirit fiddle can play a calling-on music. It can call up the blackbirds and open that door, and it can call us to cross over into the otherworld. Or call something back to us from over there.

"Looks like it's not just blackbirds anymore," she tells me.

That's when she opens the top of her shopping bag and shows me the rabbit she's got hidden away inside. It looks up at me with its mournful brown eyes, one ear all chewed up, ribs showing.

"Sorry looking thing," I say.

Staley nods.

"Where'd you find it?"

"Up yonder," she says. "In the hills. I kind of called him to me, though I wasn't trying to or anything." She gives me a little smile. " 'Course I don't try to call up the crows either, and they still come with no nevermind."

I nod like I understand what's going on here.

"Anyway," she goes on. "The thing is, there's a boy trapped in there, under that fur and—"

"A boy?" I have to ask.

"Well, I'm thinking he's young. All I know for sure is he's scared and wore out and he's male."

"When you say boy . . . ?"

"I mean a human boy who's wearing the shape of a hare. Like a skinwalker." She pauses, looks over her shoulder. "Did I mention that there's something after him?"

There's something in the studied casualness of how she puts it that sends a quick chill scooting up my spine. I don't see anything out of the ordinary on the street behind her. Crowsea tenements. Parked cars. Dawn pinking the horizon. But something doesn't set right all the same.

"Maybe you better come inside," I say.

I don't have much, just a basement apartment in this Kelly Street tenement. I get it rent-free in exchange for my custodian duties on it and a couple of other buildings the landlord owns in the area. Seems I don't ever have any folding money, but I manage to get by with odd jobs and tips from the tenants when I do a little work for them. It's not much, but it's a sight better than living on the street like I was doing when Staley and I first met.

I send her on ahead of me, down the stairs and through the door into my place, and lock the door behind us. I use the term "lock" loosely. Mostly it's the idea of a lock. I mean I'm pushing the tail end of fifty and I could easily kick it open. But I still feel a sight better with the night shut out and that flimsy lock doing its best.

"You said there's something after him?" I say once we're inside.

Staley sits down in my sorry excuse of an armchair—picked it out of the trash before the truck came one morning. It's amazing the things people will throw away, though I'll be honest, this chair's had its day. Still I figured maybe a used-up old man and a used-up old chair could find some use for each other and so far it's been holding up its end of the bargain. I pull up a kitchen chair for myself. As for the rabbit, he sticks his head out of the cloth folds of the shopping bag and then sits there on the floor looking from me to Staley, like he's following the conversation. Hell, the way Staley tells it, he probably can.

"Something," Staley says.

"What kind of something?"

She shakes her head. "I don't rightly know."

Then she tells me about the roadhouse and her friend dropping her off near home. Tells me about her walk through the fields that night and finding the rabbit hiding in the underbrush near her trailer.

"See, this calling-on's not something I do on purpose," she explains when she's taken the story so far. "But I got to thinking, if I opened some door to who knows where, well, maybe I can close it again, shut out whatever's chasing Mr. Rabbitskin here."

I raise my eyebrows.

"Well, I've got to call him something," she says. "Anyway, so I got back to playing my fiddle, concentrating on this whole business like I've never done before. You know, being purposeful about this opening doors business."

"And?" I ask when she falls silent.

"I think I made it worse. I think I let that something right out."

"You keep saying 'you think.' Are you just going on feelings here, or did you actually see something?"

"Oh, I saw something, no question there. Don't know what it was, but it came sliding out of nowhere, like there was a door I couldn't see standing smack in the middle of the meadow and it could just step through, easy as you please. It looked like some cross between a big cat and a wolf, I guess."

"What happened to it?" I ask.

She shakes her head. "I don't know that either. It ran off into the forest. I guess maybe it was confused about how it got to be here, and maybe even where here is and all. But I don't think it's going to stay confused. I got only the one look at its eyes and what I saw there was smart, you know? Not just human smart, but college professor smart."

"And so you came here," I say.

She nods. "I didn't know what else to do. I just packed my knapsack and stuck old Mr. Rabbitskin here in a bag. Grabbed my fiddle and we lit a shuck. I kept expecting that thing to come out of the woods while we were making our way down to the highway, but it left us alone. Then, when we got to the blacktop, we were lucky and hitched a ride with a trucker all the way down to the city."

She falls quiet again. I nod slowly as I look from her to the rabbit.

"Now don't get me wrong," I say, "because I'm willing to help, but I can't help but wonder why you picked me to come to."

"Well," she says. "I figured rabbit-boy here's the only one can explain what's what. So first we've got to shift him back into his human skin."

"I'm no hoodoo man," I tell her.

"No, but you knew Malicorne maybe better than any of us."

"Malicorne," I say softly.

Staley's story notwithstanding, Malicorne had to be about the damnedest thing I ever ran across in this world. She used to squat in the Tombs with the rest of us, a tall horsey-faced woman with—and I swear this is true—a great big horn growing out of the center of her forehead. You've never seen such a thing. Fact is, most people didn't, even when she was standing right smack there in front of them. There was something about that horn that made your attention slide away from it.

"I haven't seen her in a long time," I tell Staley. "Not since we saw her and Jake walk off into the night."

Through one of those doors that Staley and the crows called up. And we didn't so much see them go, as hear them, their footsteps changing into the sounds of hoofbeats that slowly faded away. Which is what Staley's getting at here, I realize. Malicorne had some kind of healing magic about her, but she was also one of those skinwalkers, change from something mostly human into something not even close.

"I just thought maybe you'd heard from her," Staley said. "Or you'd know how to get a hold of her."

I shake my head. "There's nobody you can talk to about it out there on the rez?"

She looks a little embarrassed.

"I was hoping I could avoid that," she says. "See, I'm pretty much just a guest myself, living out there where I do. It doesn't seem polite to make a mess like I've done and not clean it up on my own."

I see through what she's saying pretty quick.

"You figure they'll be pissed," I say.

"Well, wouldn't you be? What if they kicked me off the rez? I love living up there in the deep woods. What would I do if I had to leave?"

I can see her point, though I'm thinking that friends might be more forgiving than she thinks they'll be. 'Course, I don't know how close she is to the folks living up there.

I look down at the rabbit, who still seems to be following the conversation like he understands what's going on. There's a nervous look in those big brown eyes of his, but something smarter than you'd expect of an animal, too. I lift my gaze back up to meet Staley's.

"I think I know someone we can talk to," I say.

The way William had talked him up, Staley expected Robert Lonnie to be about two hundred years old and, as Grandma used to describe one of those old hound dogs of hers, full of piss and vinegar. But Robert looked to be no older than twenty-one, twenty-two—a slender black man in a pin-striped suit, small-boned and handsome, with long delicate fingers and wavy hair brushed back from his forehead. It was only when you took a look into those dark eyes of his that you got the idea he'd been a place or two ordinary folks didn't visit. They weren't so much haunted, as haunting; when he looked at you, his gaze didn't stop at the skin, but went all the way through to the spirit held in there by your bones.

They tracked him down in a small bar off Palm Street, found

him sitting at a booth in the back, playing a snaky blues tune on a battered old Gibson guitar. The bar was closed and, except for a bald-headed white man drying beer glasses behind the bar, he had the place to himself. He never looked up when she and William walked in, just played that guitar of his, picked it with a lazy ease that was all the more surprising since the music he pulled out of it sounded like it had to come from at least a couple of guitars. It was a soulful, hurting blues, but it filled you with hope, too.

Staley stood transfixed, listening to it, to him. She felt herself slipping away somewhere, she couldn't say where. Everything in the room gave the impression it was leaning closer to him, tables, chairs, the bottles of liquor behind the bar, listening, *feeling* that music.

When William touched her arm, she started, blinked, then followed him over to the booth.

William had described Robert Lonnie as an old hoodoo man and Staley decided that even if he didn't know a lick of the kind of mojo she was looking for, he still knew a thing or two about magic—the musical kind, that is. Lord, but he could play. Then he looked up, his gaze locking on hers. It was like a static charge, that dark gaze, sudden and unexpected in its intensity, and she almost dropped her fiddle case on the floor. She slipped slowly into the booth, took a seat across the table from him and not a moment too soon since her legs had suddenly lost their ability to hold her upright. William had to give her a nudge before she slid farther down the seat to make room for him. She hugged her fiddle case to her chest, only dimly aware of William beside her, the rabbit in its bag on his lap.

The guitarist kept his gaze on her, humming under his breath as he brought the tune to a close. His last chord hung in the air with an almost physical presence and for a long moment everything in the bar held its breath. Then he smiled, wide and easy, and the moment was gone.

"William," he said softly. "Miss."

"This is Staley," William said.

Robert gave her considering look, then turned to William. "You're early to be hitting the bars."

"It's not like you think," William said. "I'm still going to AA."

"Good for you."

"Well," William said. "Considering it's about the only thing I've done right with my life, I figured I might as well stick with it."

"Uh-huh." Robert returned his attention to Staley. "You've got the look of one who's been to the crossroads."

"I guess," Staley said, though she had no idea what he meant.

"But you don't know who you met there, do you?"

She shook her head.

Robert nodded. "That's the way it happens, all that spooky shit. You feel the wind rising and the leaves are trembling on the trees. Next thing you know, it's all falling down on you like hail, but you don't know what it is."

"Um . . ." Staley looked to William for guidance.

"You've just got to tell him like you told me," William said.

But Robert was looking at the shopping bag on William's lap now.

"Who've you got in there?" he asked.

Staley cleared her throat. "We were hoping you could tell us," she said.

William lowered the cloth sides of the bag. The rabbit poked its head up, raggedy ear hanging down on one side.

Robert laughed. "Well, now," he said, gaze lifting to meet Staley's again. "Why don't you tell me this story of yours."

So Staley did, started again with Butch dropping her off on the county road near her trailer late last night and took the tale all the way through to when she got to William's apartment earlier this morning. Somewhere in the middle of it the barman brought them a round of coffee, walking away before Staley could pay him, or even get out a thanks.

"I remember that Malicorne," Robert said when she was done. "Now she was a fine woman, big horn and all. You ever see her anymore?"

William shook his head. "Not since that night she went off with Jake."

"Can you help me?" Staley asked.

Robert leaned back on his side of the booth. Those long fingers of his left hand started walking up the neck of his guitar and he picked with his right, soft, a spidery twelve-bar.

"You ever hear the story of the two magicians?" he asked.

Staley shook her head.

"Don't know what the problem was between them, but the way I heard it is they got themselves into a long-time, serious altercation, went on for years. In the end, the only way they were willing to settle it was to duke it out the way those hoodoo men do, working magic. The one'd turn himself into a 'coon, the other'd become a coonhound, chase him up some tree. That treed 'coon'd come down, 'cept now he's wearing the skin of a wildcat." Robert grinned. "Only now that coonhound, he's a hornet, starts in on stinging the cat. And this just goes on.

"One's a salmon, the other's an otter. Salmon becomes the biggest, ugliest catfish you ever saw, big enough to swallow that otter whole, but now the otter's a giant eagle, slashing at the fish with its talons. Time passes and they just keep at it, changing skins—big changes, little changes. One's a flood, the other's a drought. One's human, the other's a devil. One's night, the other's day. . . .

"Damnedest thing you ever saw, like paper-scissors-rock, only hoodoo man style, you know what I'm saying? Damnedest thing."

The whole time he talked, he picked at his guitar, turned the story into a talking song with that lazy drawl of his, mesmerizing. When he fell silent, it took Staley a moment or two to realize that he'd stopped talking.

"So Mr. Rabbitskin here," she said, "and that other thing I only caught half a glimpse of—you're saying they're like those two magicians?"

"Got the smell of it to me."

"And they're only interested in hurting each other?"

"Well, now," Robert told her. "That'd be the big thought on their mind, but you've got to remember that hoodoo requires a powerful amount of nourishment, just to keep the body up to fighting strength. Those boys'll be hungry and needing to feed—and I'm guessing they won't be all that particular as to what they chow down on."

Great, Staley thought. She shot the rabbit a sour look, but it wouldn't meet her gaze.

"Mr. Rabbitskin here," she said, "won't eat a thing. I've tried carrots, greens, even bread soaked in warm milk."

Robert nodded. "That'd tempt a rabbit, right enough. Problem is, what you've got here are creatures that are living on pure energy. Hell, that's probably all they are at this point, nothing but energy gussied up into a shape that makes sense to our eyes. They won't be eating food like we do. So far as that goes, the way they'd be looking at it, we probably *are* food, considering the kind of energy we've got rolling through us."

The rabbit, docile up to now, suddenly lunged out of William's lap and went skidding across the smooth floor, heading for the back door of the bar. William started after it, but Robert just shook his head.

"You'll never catch it now," he said.

"Are you saying that rabbit was feeding on me somehow?" William asked.

"I figure he was building up to it."

Staley stared in the direction that the rabbit had gone, her heart sinking. This whole situation was getting worse by the minute.

"So these two things I called over," she said. "They're the hoodoo men from your story?"

Robert shrugged. "Oh, they're not the same pair, but it's an old story and old stories have a habit of repeating themselves."

"Who won that first duel?" William asked.

"One of 'em turned himself into a virus and got the other too sick to shape a spell in reply, but I don't know which one. Doesn't much matter anyway. By the time that happened, the one was as bad as the other. Get into that kind of a state of mind and after a while you start to forget things like kindness, decency . . . the fact that other people aren't put here in this world for you to feed on."

Staley's heart sank lower.

"We've got to do something about this," she said. "I've got to do something. I'm responsible for whatever hurt they cause, feeding on people and all."

"Who says it's your fault?" Robert wanted to know.

"Well, I called them over, didn't I? Though I don't understand how I did it. I've been playing my music for going on four years now in that meadow and nothing like this has ever happened before."

Robert nodded. "Maybe this time the devil was listening and you know what he's like. He purely hates anybody can play better than him—'specially if they aren't obliged to him in some way."

"Only person I owe anything to," Staley said, "is my grandma and she was no devil."

"But you've been at the crossroads."

Staley was starting to understand what he meant. There was

always something waiting to take advantage of you, ghosts and devils sitting there at the edge of nowhere where the road to what is and what could be cross each other, spiteful creatures just waiting for the chance to step into your life and turn it all hurtful. That was the trouble with having something like her spirit fiddle. It called things to you, but unless you paid constant attention, you forgot that it can call the bad as well as the good.

"I've been at a lot of places," she said.

"You ever played that fiddle of yours in one?"

"Not so's I knew."

"Well, you've been someplace, done something to get his attention."

"That doesn't solve the problem I've got right now."

Robert nodded. "No, we're just defining it."

"So what can I do?"

"I don't know exactly. Thing I've learned is, if you call up something bad, you've got to take up the music and play it back out again or it'll never go away. I'd start there."

"I already tried that and it only made things worse."

"Yeah, but this time you've got to jump the groove."

Staley gave him a blank look.

"You remember phonograph records?" Robert asked.

"Well, sure, though back home we mostly played tapes."

Robert started to finger his guitar again, another spidery twelve-bar blues.

"Those old phonograph records," he said. "They had a one-track groove that the needle followed from beginning to end—it's like the habits we develop, the way we look at the world, what we expect to find in it, that kind of thing. You get into a bad situation like we got here and it's time to jump the groove, get someplace new, see things different." He cut the tune short before it could resolve and abruptly switched into another key. "Change the music.

What you hear, what you play. Maybe even who you are. Lets you fix things and the added bonus is it confuses the devil. Makes it hard for him to focus on you for a time."

"Jump the groove," Staley repeated slowly.

Robert nodded. "Why don't we take a turn out to where you've been living and see what we can do?"

I call in a favor from my friend Moth who owns a junkyard up in the Tombs and borrow a car to take us back up to Staley's trailer. "Take the Chevette," he tells me, pointing out an old two-door that's got more primer on it than it does original paint. "The plates are legit." Staley comes with me, fusses over Moth's junkyard dogs like they're old pals, wins Moth over with a smile and that good nature of hers, but mostly because she can run through instrumental versions of a couple of Boxcar Willie songs. After that, so far as Moth's concerned, she can do no wrong.

"This guy Robert," she says when we're driving back to the bar to pick him up. "How come he's so fixed on the devil?"

"Well," I tell her. "The way I heard it, a long time ago he met the devil at a crossroads, made a deal with him. Wanted to be the best player the world'd ever seen. 'No problem,' the devil tells him. 'Just sign here.'

"So Robert signs up. Trouble is, he already had it in him. If he hadn't been in such a hurry, with a little time and effort on his part, he would've got what he wanted and wouldn't have owed the devil a damn thing."

Staley's looking at me, a smile lifting one corner of her mouth.

"You believe that?" she says.

"Why not? I believed you when you told me there was a boy under the skin of that rabbit."

She gives me a slow nod.

"So what happened?" she asks.

"What? With Robert? Well, when he figured out he'd been duped, he paid the devil back in kind. You can't take a man's soul unless he dies, and Robert, he's figured out a way to live forever."

I watch Staley's mouth open, but then she shakes her head and leaves whatever she was going to say unsaid.

" 'Course," I go on, "it helps to stay out of the devil's way, so Robert, he keeps himself a low profile."

Staley shakes her head. "Now that I can't believe. Anybody hears him play is going to remember it forever."

"Well, sure. That's why he doesn't play out."

"But—"

"I'm not saying he keeps his music to himself. You'll find him sitting in on a session from time to time, but mostly he just plays in places like that bar we found him in today. Sits in a corner during the day when the joint's half empty and makes music those drunks can't ever forget—though they're unlikely to remember exactly where it was that they heard it."

"That's so sad."

I shrug. "Maybe. But it keeps the devil at bay."

Staley's quiet for a while, doesn't say much until we pull into the alley behind the bar.

"Do you believe in the devil?" she asks before we get out of the car.

"Everybody's got devils."

"No, I mean a real devil—like in *the Bible*."

I sit for a moment and think on that.

"I believe there's good in the world," I tell her finally, "so yeah. I guess I've got to believe there's evil, too. Don't know if it's the devil, exactly—you know, pointy horns, hooves and tail and all—but I figure that's as good a name as any other."

"You afraid of him?"

"Hell, Staley. Some days I'm afraid of everything. Why do you think I spent half my life looking for oblivion in a bottle?"

"What made you change?"

I don't even have to think about that.

"Malicorne," I tell her. "Nothing she said or did—just that she was. I guess her going away made me realize that I had a choice: I could either keep living in the bottom of a bottle, and that's not living at all. Or I could try to experience ordinary life as something filled with beauty and wonder—you know, the way she did. Make everyday something special."

Staley nods. "That's not so easy."

"Hell, no. But it's surely worth aiming for."

William drove, with Staley riding shotgun and Robert lounging in the back, playing that old Gibson of his. He worked up a song about their trip, a sleepy blues, cataloguing the sights, tying them together with walking bass lines and bottleneck solos. Staley had made this drive more times than she could count, but all those past trips were getting swallowed by this one. The soundtrack Robert was putting to it would forever be the memory she carried whenever she thought about leaving the city core and driving north up Highway 14, into the hills.

It took them a couple of hours after picking Robert up at the bar to reach that stretch of county road closest to Staley's trailer. The late afternoon sun was in the west, but still high in the summer sky when Staley had William pull the Chevette over to the side of the road and park.

"Can we just leave the car like this?" William asked.

Staley nodded. "I doubt anybody's going to mess with it sitting here on the edge of Indian land."

She got out and stretched, then held the front seat up against the dash so that Robert could climb out of the rear. He kicked at the dirt road with his shoe and smiled as a thin coat of dust settled over the shiny patent leather. Leaning on the hood of the car, he cradled his guitar against his chest and looked out across the fields, gaze tracking the slow circle of a hawk in the distance.

"Lord, but it's peaceful out here," he said. "I could listen to this quiet forever."

"I know what you mean," Staley said. "I love to travel, but there's nowhere else I could call home."

William wasn't as content. As soon as he got out of the car, a half-dozen deerflies dive-bombed him, buzzing round and round his head. He waved them off, but all his frantic movement did was make them more frenzied.

"What's the matter with these things?" he asked.

"Stop egging them on—all it does is aggravate them."

"Yeah, right. How come they aren't in your face?"

"I've got an arrangement with them," Staley told him.

They weren't bothering Robert either. He gave the ones troubling William a baleful stare.

" 'Preciate it if you'd leave him alone," he told them.

They gave a last angry buzz around William's head, then zoomed off down the road, flying like a fighter squadron in perfect formation. William followed their retreat before turning back to his companions.

"Nice to see some useful hoodoo for a change," he said.

Robert grinned. "It's all useful—depending on which side of the spell you're standing. But that wasn't hoodoo so much as politeness. Me asking, them deciding to do what I asked."

"Uh-huh."

Robert ignored him. "So where's this trailer of yours?" he asked Staley.

"Back in the woods—over yonder."

She led them through the raspberry bushes and into the field. Robert started up playing again and for the first time since they'd met, Staley got the itch to join him on her fiddle. She understood this music he was playing. It talked about the dirt and crushed stone on the county road, the sun warm on the fields, the rasp of the tall grass and weeds against their clothes as they walked in single file towards the trees. Under the hemlocks, the music became all bass and treble, roots and high boughs, the midrange set aside. But only temporarily.

When they reached the bottle tree, Staley glanced back. William gave the hanging bottles a puzzled look, but Robert nodded in apparent approval. His bottleneck slide replied to the clink of glass from the bottle tree, a slightly discordant slur of notes pulled off the middle strings of the Gibson.

The bluesman and Grandma would've got along just fine, she decided.

Once they came out from under the trees, they could walk abreast on the shorter grass. Robert broke off playing when Staley gave her scarecrow a little curtsey by way of greeting.

"How well do you know that fellow?" he asked.

Staley smiled. "About four years—ever since I put him up."

"The clothes were yours?"

She nodded.

"And you collected the wood for his limbs?"

She nodded again. "Why are you asking all these questions?"

"Because he's halfway alive."

"You mean the branches sprouting?"

"No, I mean he's got the start of an individual spirit, growing there in the straw and applewood."

Staley regarded the scarecrow in a new light. Now that it had been pointed out, she could feel the faint pulse of life in its straw breast. Sentient life, not quite fully formed, but hidden there as surely as there'd been a boy hidden in the raggedy hare she'd lost in the city.

"But, how . . . ?" she began, her voice trailing off.

Robert turned in a slow circle, taking in the whole of the meadow. Her trailer, the vegetable garden.

"You've played a lot of music in here," he said. "Paid a lot of attention to the rhythms of the meadow, the forest, how you and your belongings fit into it. It's got so's you've put so much hoodoo in this place I'm surprised you only ever called over those two feuding spirits."

William nodded. "Hell, even I feel something."

Staley did, too, except it was what she always felt when she was here.

"I thought it was home I was feeling," she said.

"It is," Robert said. "But you've played it up so powerful it's no wonder the devil took notice."

Staley shot a glance at her scarecrow, which made Robert smile.

"Oh, he's more subtle than that," he told her. "He's going to come up at you from the backside, like pushing through a couple of feuding spirits to wreck a little havoc with the things you love." He gave her fiddle case a considering look. "You know what you've got to do."

Staley sighed. "Jump the groove."

"That's right. Break the pattern. Don't give the devil something he can hold on to. Nothing's easier to trip a body up than habits and patterns. Why do you think the Gypsy people consider settling down to be so stressful? Only way they can rest is by traveling."

"You're saying I should go? That I've got to leave this place?"

Robert raised an eyebrow. "You a Romany girl now?"

"No."

"Then find your own groove to jump."

Staley sighed again. Intellectually, she understood what Robert was getting at. But how to put it into practice? She played the way she played because . . . well, that was the way she played. Especially here, in this place. She took the music from her surroundings, digging deep and deeper into the relationships between earth and sky, forest and meadow, her trailer and the garden and the tattered figure of the scarecrow watching over it all. Where was she supposed to find a music still true to all of this, but different enough to break the pattern of four summers immersed in its quiet joys and mysteries?

"I don't know if I can do it," she said.

"You can try," Robert told her.

"I suppose. But what if I call something worse over?"

"You didn't call anything over. Those spirits were sent."

Staley shook her head. "This fiddle of Grandma's plays a calling-on music—I can hear it whenever I play."

"I don't deny that," Robert said. "But you've got to put some intent into that call, and from what you've been telling me, you didn't intend to bring anything over last night."

"So when those blackbirds gather to her fiddling," William said, "it's because she's invited them?"

Robert shrugged. "Crows and ravens are a whole different circumstance. They live on the outside of where we are and they learned a long time ago how to take advantage of the things we do, making their own hoodoo with the bits and pieces we leave behind."

That made sense to Staley. She'd never deliberately called up the blackbirds, but they came all the same. Only not here. That was why she'd always thought it was safe to play whatever she wanted around the trailer. She'd see them from time to time, mostly going after her garden, or sneaking off with a bit of this or that for their nests, but they didn't gather here. The closest roost was out by the highway.

She glanced at Robert to find his gaze on her, steady but mild. She wanted to say, How do I know the devil's not being so subtle that he's persuading me through you? But they'd been talking long enough. And whatever else Robert was, she doubted he was the devil.

Kneeling on the grass, she cracked open her fiddle case. Took out her bow, tightened the frog, rosined the hairs. Finally she picked up the blue spirit fiddle her grandmother had given her and stood up again. She ran a finger across the strings. The E was a touch flat. She gave its fine-tuner a twist, and tried again. This time all four strings rang true.

"Here goes nothing," she said, bringing the fiddle up under her chin.

"Not like that," Robert told her. "Dig a little with your heart before you start in on playing. You can't jump the groove until you know where it's at."

True, she thought.

William gave her an encouraging nod, then walked over to the trailer and sat down on the steps. After a moment Robert joined him, one hand closed around the neck of his guitar, damping the strings.

Staley took a breath and let it out, slow. She held the fiddle in the crook of her arm, bow dangling from her index finger, and closed her eyes, trying to get a feel of where the meadow was today, how she fit into it. She swayed slightly where she stood. Toe on heel, she removed one shoe, then the other, digging through the blades of grass with her bare toes until she was in direct contact with the earth.

What do I hear? she thought. What do I feel?

Woodpecker hammering a dead tree limb, deeper in the woods. The smell of grass rising up from by her feet. Herbs from the garden, mint, basil, thyme. The flutter and sweet chirps of chickadees and finches. A faint breeze on her cheek. The soft helicopter approach of a hummingbird, feeding on the purple bergamot that grew along the edge of the vegetable and herb beds. The sudden chatter of a red squirrel out by the woodpile. Something crawling across her foot. An ant, maybe. Or a small beetle. The hoarse croak of a crow, off in the fields somewhere. The sun, warm on her face and arms. The fat buzz of a bee.

She knew instinctively how she could make a music of it all, catch it with notes drawn from her fiddle and send it spiraling off into the late afternoon air. That was the groove Robert kept talking about. So where did she go to jump it?

The first thing she heard was what Robert would do, bottleneck slides and bass lines, complicated chord patterns that were both melody and rhythm and sounded far simpler than they were to play. But while she could relate to what his take would be—could certainly appreciate it and even harmonize with it—that music wasn't hers. Following that route wouldn't be so much jumping her own groove as becoming someone else, being who they were, playing the music they would play.

She had to be herself, but still play with a stranger's hand. How did a person even begin to do that?

She concentrated again on what this place meant to her, distilling the input of sounds and smells and all to their essence. What, she asked herself, was the first thing she thought of when she came back here in the spring from her winter wanderings? She called up the fields in her mind's eye, the forest and her meadow, hidden away in it, and it came to her.

Green.

Buds on the trees and new growth pushing up through the browned grasses and weeds that had died off during the winter. The first shoots of crocuses and daffodils, fiddlehead ferns and trilliums growing in the forest shade.

She came here to immerse herself in a green world. Starting in April when the color was but a vague hue brushing the landscape through to deep summer when the fields and forest ran riot with verdant growth. Come September when the meadows browned and the deciduous trees began to turn red and gold and yellow, that was when she started to pack up the trailer, put things away, ready her knapsack, feet itchy to hit the road once more.

Eyes still closed, she lifted her fiddle back up under her chin. Pulling her bow across the strings, she called up an autumn music. She put into it deer foraging in the cedars. Her scarecrow standing alone, guarding the empty vegetable and herb beds. Geese flying in formation overhead. Frosts and naked tree limbs. Milkweed pods bursting open and a thousand seeds parachuting across the fields. Brambles that stuck to the legs of your overalls.

She played music that was brown and yellow, faded colors and grays. It was still this place. It was still her. But it was a groove she didn't normally explore with her music. Certainly not here. This was her green home. A green world. But all you had to do was look under the green to see memories of the winter past. A fallen tree stretched out along the forest floor, moss-covered and rotting. A dead limb poking through the leaves of a tree, the one branch that didn't make it through the winter. The browned grass of last autumn, covered over by new growth, but not mulch yet.

And it wasn't simply memories. There were shadowings of the winter to come, too, even in this swelter of summer and green. She wasn't alone in her annual migrations south, but those that remained were already beginning their preparations. Foraging, gathering. The sunflowers were going to seed. There were fruits on the apple trees, still green and hard, but they would ripen. The berry bushes were beginning to put forth their crop. Seeds were forming, nuts hardening.

It was another world, another groove.

She played it out until she could almost feel a change in the air—a crispness, dry and bittersweet. Opening her eyes, she turned to look at the trailer. Is this what you meant? she wanted to ask Robert. But he wasn't there. She took bow from strings and stood there, silent, taking it all in.

Robert and William were gone, and so was the summer. The grass was browned underfoot. The fruit and leaves from her scarecrow's apple limbs were fallen away, the garden finished for the year.

What had she done now? Called up the autumn? Lost a few months of her life, standing here in her meadow, playing an unfamiliar music?

Or had she called herself away?

She knew nothing of the otherworld except for what people had told her about it. Grandma. Malicorne. A man named Rupert who lived in the desert, far to the south. Beyond the fact that spirits lived there who could cross over into our world, everything they had to say about the place was vague.

Right now, all she knew was that this didn't feel like her meadow so much as an echo of it. How it might appear in the otherworld.

The place where the spirit people lived and her fiddle had come from.

Grandma had told her it was a place sensible people didn't go. Rupert had warned her that while it was easy to stray over into it, it wasn't so easy to leave behind once you were there.

How could this have happened? How—

Movement startled her. She took a step back as a hare came bounding out of the woods to take refuge under her trailer. A moment later a large dog burst into the meadow, chasing it. The dog rushed the trailer, bending low and growling deep in its chest as it tried to fit itself into the narrow space. Giving a sudden yelp, it scrabbled away as a rattler came sliding out from under the trailer. The snake took a shot at the dog, but the dog had changed into a mongoose, shifting so fast Staley never saw it happen. The mongoose's teeth clamped on the rattler, but it, too, transformed, becoming a boa constrictor, fattening, lengthening, forcing the mongoose's jaws open, wrapping its growing length around the smaller mammal's body, squeezing.

Staley didn't need a lot of considering time to work out what was going on here. Maybe she'd fiddled herself over into the other-world, but it was obvious that also she'd pulled those two hoodoo men along with her when she'd come.

"Hey, you!" she cried.

The animals froze, turned to look at her. She was a little surprised that they'd actually stopped to listen to her.

"Don't you have no *sense*?" she asked them. "What's any of this going to prove?"

She looked from one to the other, trapped by the dark malevolence in their eyes and suddenly wished she'd left well enough alone. What business of hers was it if they killed each other? She'd gotten them back here where they belonged. Best thing now was that they forgot she ever existed.

For a long moment she was sure that wasn't going to happen. It was like playing in a bar when a fight broke out at the edge of the stage. The smart musician didn't get involved. She just stepped back, kept her instrument safe, and let them work it out between themselves until the bouncer showed up. Trouble was, there was no bouncer here. It was just the three of them and she didn't even have a mike stand she could hit them with.

She didn't know what she'd have done if they'd broken off their own fight and come after her. Luckily, she didn't have to find out.

The mongoose became a sparrow and slipped out of the snake's grip, darting away into the forest. A half second later a hawk was in pursuit and she was on her own again. At least she thought she was.

A low chuckle from behind her made her turn.

The newcomer looked like he'd just stepped down out of the hills, tall and lean, a raggedy hillbilly in jeans and a flannel shirt, cowboy boots on his feet. There were acne scars on his cheeks and he wore his dark hair slicked back in a ducktail. His eyes were the clearest blue she could ever remember seeing, filled with a curious mix of distant skies and good humor. He had one hand in his pocket, the other holding the handle of a battered, black guitar case.

"You ever see such foolishness?" he asked. "You think they'd learn, but I reckon they've been at it now for about as long as the day is wide."

Staley liked the sound of his voice. It held an easygoing lilt that reminded her of her daddy's cousins who lived up past Hazard, deep in the hills.

She laughed. "Long as the day is wide?" she asked.

"Well, you know. Start to finish, the day only holds so many hours, but you go sideways and it stretches on forever."

"I've never heard of time running sideways."

"I'm sure you must know a hundred things I've never heard of."

"I suppose."

"You new around here?" he asked.

Staley glanced back at her trailer, then returned her gaze to him.

"In a manner of speaking," she said. "I'm not entirely sure how I got here and even less sure as to how I'll get back to where I come from."

"I can show you," he told her. "But maybe you'd favor me with a tune first? Been a long time since I got to pick with a fiddler."

The thing that no one told you about the otherworld, Staley realized, is how everything took on a dreamlike quality when you were here. She knew she should be focusing on getting back to the summer meadow where Robert and William were waiting for her, but there just didn't seem to be any hurry about it.

"So what do you say?" he asked.

She shrugged. "I guess. . . ."

I'm already feeling a little dozy from the sun and fresh air when Staley begins to play her fiddle. It doesn't sound a whole lot different from the kinds of things she usually plays, but then what do I really know about music? Don't ask me to discuss it. I either like it or I don't. But Robert seems pleased with what she's doing, nodding to himself, has a little smile starting up there in the corner of his mouth.

I can see his left hand shaping chords on the neck of his guitar, but he doesn't strum the strings. Just follows what she's doing in his head, I guess.

I look at Staley a little longer, smiling as well to see her standing there so straight-backed in her overalls, barefoot in the grass, the sun glowing golden on her short hair. After a while I lean back against the door of the trailer again and close my eyes. I'm drifting on the music, not really thinking much of anything, when I realize the sound of the fiddle's starting to fade away.

"Shit," I hear Robert say.

I open my eyes, but before I can turn to look at him, I see Staley's gone. It's the damnedest thing. I can still hear her fiddling, only it's getting fainter and fainter like she's walking away and I can't see a sign of her anywhere. I can't imagine a person could run as fast as she'd have to to disappear like this and still keep playing that sleepy music.

When Robert stands up, I scramble to my feet as well.

"What's going on?" I ask him.

"She let it take her away."

"What do you mean? Take her away where?"

But he doesn't answer. He's looking into the woods and then I see them, too. A rabbit being chased by some ugly old dog. Might be the same rabbit that ran off on us in the city, but I can't tell. It comes tearing out from under the trees, running straight across the meadow toward us, and then it just disappears.

I blink, not sure I actually saw what I just saw. But then the same thing happens to the dog. It's like it goes through some door I can't see. There one minute, gone the next.

"Well, she managed to pull them back across," Robert says. "But I don't like this. I don't like this at all."

Hearing him talk like that makes me real nervous.

"Why?" I ask him. "This is what we wanted, right? She was going to play some music to put things back the way they were. Wasn't that the plan?"

He nods. "But her going over wasn't."

"I don't get it."

Robert turns to look at me. "How's she going to get back?"

"Same way she went away—right?"

He answers with a shrug and then I get a bad feeling. It's like what happened with Malicorne and Jake, I realize. Stepped away, right out of the world, and they never came back. The only difference is, they meant to go.

"She won't know what to do," Robert says softly. "She'll be upset and maybe a little scared, and then he's going to show up, offer to show her the way back."

I don't have to ask who he's talking about.

"But she'll know better than to bargain with him," I say.

"We can hope."

"We've got to be able to do better than that," I tell him.

"I'm open to suggestions."

I look at that guitar in his hands.

"You could call her back," I say.

Robert shakes his head. "The devil, he's got himself a guitar, too."

"I don't know what that means."

"Think about it," Robert says. "Whose music is she going to know to follow?"

The stranger laid his guitar case on the grass and opened it up. The instrument he took out was an old Martin D-45 with the pearl inlaid CD MARTIN logo on the headstock—a classic, prewar picker's guitar.

"Don't see many of those anymore," Staley said.

"They didn't make all that many." He smiled. "Though I'll tell you, I've never seen me a blue fiddle like you've got, not ever."

"Got it from my grandma."

"Well, she had taste. Give me an A, would you?"

Staley ran her bow across the A string of her fiddle and the stranger quickly tuned up to it.

"You ever play any contests?" he asked as he finished tuning.

He ran his pick across the strings, fingering an A minor chord. The guitar had a big rich sound with lots of bottom end.

"I don't believe in contests," Staley said. "I think they take all the pleasure out of a music."

"Oh, I didn't mean nothing serious. More like swapping tunes, taking turns till one of you stumps the other player. Just for fun, like."

Staley shrugged.

"'Course to make it interesting," he added, "we could put a small wager on the outcome."

"What kind of wager would we be talking about here?"

Staley didn't know why she was even asking that, why she hadn't just shut down this idea of a contest right from the get-go. It was like something in the air was turning her head all around.

"I don't know," he said. "How about if I win, you'll give me a kiss?"

"A kiss?"

He shrugged. "And if you enjoy it, maybe you'll give me something more."

"And if I win?"

"Well, what's the one thing you'd like most in the world?"

Staley smiled. "Tell you the truth, I don't want for much of anything. I keep my expectations low—makes for a simple life."

"I'm impressed," he said. "Most people have a hankering for something they can't have. You know, money, or fame, or a true love. Maybe living forever."

"Don't see much point in living forever," Staley told him. "Come a time when everybody you care about would be long gone, but there you'd be, still trudging along on your own."

"Well, sure. But—"

"And as for money and fame, I think they're pretty much overrated. I don't really need much to be happy and I surely don't need anybody nosing in on my business."

"So what about a true love?"

"Well, now," Staley said. "Seems to me true love's something that comes to you, not something you can take or arrange."

"And if it doesn't?"

"That'd be sad, but you make do. I don't know how other folks get by, but I've got my music. I've got my friends."

The stranger regarded her with an odd, frustrated look.

"You can't tell me there's nothing you don't have a yearning for," he said. "Everybody wants for something."

"You mean for myself, or in general, like for there to be no more hurt in the world or the like?"

"For yourself," he said.

Staley shook her head. "Nothing I can't wait for it to find me in its own good time." She put her fiddle up under her chin. "So what do you want to play?"

But the stranger pulled his string strap back over his head and started to put his guitar away.

"What's the matter?" Staley asked. "We don't need some silly contest just to play a few tunes."

The stranger wouldn't look at her.

"I've kind of lost my appetite for music," he said, snapping closed the clasps on his case.

He stood up, his gaze finally meeting hers, and she saw something else in those clear blue eyes of his, a dark storm of anger, but a hurting, too. A loneliness that seemed so out of place, given his easygoing manner. A man like him, he should be friends with everyone he met, she'd thought. Except . . .

"I know who you are," she said.

She didn't know how she knew, but it came to her, like a gauze slipping from in front of her eyes, like she'd suddenly shucked the dreamy quality of the otherworld and could see true once more.

"You don't look nothing like what I expected," she added.

"Yeah, well, you've had your fun. Now let me be."

But something her grandmother had told her once came back to her. "I tell you," she'd said. "If I was ever to meet the devil, I'd kill him with kindness. That's the one thing old Lucifer can't stand."

Staley grinned, remembering.

"Wait a minute," she said. "Don't go off all mad."

The devil glared at her.

"Or at least let me give you that kiss before you go."

He actually backed away from her at that.

"What?" Staley asked. "Suddenly you don't fancy me anymore?"

"You put up a good front," he said. "I didn't make you for such an accomplished liar."

Staley shook her head. "I never lied to you. I really am happy with things the way they are. And anything I don't have, I don't mind waiting on."

The devil spat on the grass at her feet, turned once around, and was gone, vanishing with a small *whuft* of displaced air.

That's your best parting shot? Staley wanted to ask, but decided to leave well enough alone. She gave her surroundings a last look, then started up fiddling again, playing herself back into the green of summer where she'd left her friends.

Robert's pretty impressed when Staley just steps out of that invisible door, calm as you please. We heard the fiddling first. It sounded like it was coming from someplace on the far side of forever, but getting closer by the moment, and then there she was, standing barefoot in the grass, smiling at us. Robert's even more impressed when she tells us about how she handled the devil.

After putting her fiddle away, she boils up some water on a Coleman stove and makes us up a pot of herbal tea. We take it out through the woods in porcelain mugs, heading up to the top of the field overlooking the county road. The car's still there. The sun's going down now, putting on quite a show, and the tea's better than I thought it would be. Got mint in it, some kind of fruit.

"So how do I stop this from happening again?" Staley asks.

"Figure out what your music's all about," Robert tells her. "And take responsibility for it. Dig deep and find what's hiding behind the trees—you know, in the shadows where you can't exactly see things, you can only sense them—and always pay attention. It's up to you what you let out into the light."

"Is that what you do?"

Robert nodded. " 'Course it's different for me, because we're different people. My music's about enduring. Perseverance. That's all the blues is ever about."

"What about hope?"

Robert smiled. "What do you think keeps perseverance alive?"

"Amen," I say.

After a moment, Staley smiles. We all clink our porcelain mugs together and drink a toast to that.

Wingless Angels

Christina's not particularly happy and I don't blame her. If it wasn't for me, we wouldn't be hiding behind this Dumpster in back of the Harbor Ritz, trying not to breathe while these freaks keep getting closer and closer to where we're pressed up against the wall, pressed up so tight the bricks are leaving imprints on our skin. The sound of approaching footsteps is faint but distinct, hard leather brushing the concrete. I thought everybody did rubber-soled shoes these days, but what do I know?

Of course Christina's got to take some of the heat for this—if it wasn't for her, we wouldn't have been out on the streets tonight, sticking our noses in where they don't belong. But I'm the one who didn't take any of this seriously. Turns out my idea of how the world works is so off-base I've put a serious crimp into the question of our continued well-being. But, really. Life's complicated enough without adding monsters to the equation. Or whatever these things are.

One thing I know, they're ugly as sin. I pulled a couple of stretches in county, back in my impressionable youth, and, trust me, I know ugly, but correctional services never locked up anything like this. They smell like a sewer, great hulking creatures that remind me of neither rodents nor reptiles so much as something in between. Greasy-haired, with long narrow faces. Eyes like slits, lit by some inner hunger. Muscles corded and bulging under the thin fabric of their cheap suits, yet they move as delicately as ballerinas, a murderous *bourrée* in perfect demi-pointe.

There's five or six of them—I never stopped to take an exact head count—and they're strong. Scary strong. Earlier tonight, I saw one of them pull apart the iron railings of a fence the way you or I might tear cardboard, and I swear, from the way those long noses of theirs keep twitching, they're tracking us by smell.

"Oh, man," Christina breathes in my ear. "If they—"

I put a finger across her lips, but it's too late. The footsteps stop.

It starts with a roll of undeveloped film, nothing special, Kodak 100, black and orange metal canister with plastic at either end, we've all seen them a hundred times before. Baxter and I are leaving a Williamson Street diner when I spy it in the gutter, peeking out from behind a fast food wrapper, like it's shy, or embarrassed to be seen in such company. Trash offends me, and since there's a waste container provided by the city conveniently close at hand, I pick them both up. The wrapper goes directly into the trash can, but I hesitate with the film canister.

"Whatcha got there?" Baxter asks.

I hold it up between my forefinger and thumb to show him. "Nothing. Some garbage."

"You should get it developed."

I shrug. "What for?"

But I stick it in my pocket all the same and then promptly forget about it until a week or so later when I'm looking for a phone number I jotted down on the back of somebody's old business card. Organization isn't one of my strong points. I have an electronic organizer which'd be really useful if I could ever get it together to actually input some information. As it is, it only serves as a glorified calculator, though I did manage to set the time and date when I bought it.

Anyway, I'm looking for this number, trying to remember what I was wearing that day and going through the pockets of pretty much anything I've had on over the past couple of weeks, when I come across the film canister. I put it aside while I continue my search, finally tracking the card down in the jumble on my dresser top where I dump the detritus that hangs out with the lint in my pockets. I make the call, then have another look at the film canister. What the hell. I run it by Kiko's Kwick Print where my friend Christina works.

Last week, she was a blonde. Today she's got a kind of raggedy pageboy, black and shiny as a crow's feather. It suits her better than the long blonde hair did. Brings out the character in her eyes, big and warm as a summer's day, an appealing mix of blues and greens and hazel browns. But she's wearing the frumpiest dress, one of those old-fashioned belted affairs that looks more like a housecoat, white with faded yellow polka dots and it's not closing properly in the front, showing way too much cleavage. Christina does all her shopping in the thrift stores, but the day she bought this dress she wasn't rolling sevens. 'Course I don't tell her that.

"I didn't even know you had a camera," she says as she writes out my order.

"I don't."

I'm finding the dress distracting.

"My face is up here," she says.

"Sorry. It's just . . ."

"Are you coming on to me?"

She's teasing, but I catch something unfamiliar in her manner, like she wouldn't mind if I was. We've been friends a long time, but not like that. I hit on her when we first met, but she was going with some guy and it's not something I ever really think about anymore. Whenever one of us doesn't have a commitment, the other one does. You know the scene.

"Depends," I tell her. "Are you seeing anyone?"

I'm trying to remember her last boyfriend. Dan? Don?

"Depends," she gives me right back. "Do you want me to be?"

There's a long heartbeat of silence that swells there in between us, a moment that could go either way. In the end, we put it on hold, something to consider. Christina smiles.

"So where'd you get the film?" she asks.

"I found it on the street and I guess curiosity just got the better of me today."

Her smile gets a little wider, more knowing.

"Yeah," she says. "Like that's never happened before."

I can't help it. I'm like the cat that's just got to know everything.

She hands me my claim ticket.

"Maybe I'll call you sometime," I say. "We could go for dinner, take in a show or something."

"Maybe I'll call you."

And she does, a few hours later, but she hasn't got cozying up on her mind.

"Sammy," she says. There's an odd quality to her voice. It takes me a few moments to realize it's anxiety. "These pictures . . ."

"What about them?"

"They—I can't explain over the phone. You have to see them."

I understand what she means when I swing by Kiko's a little

later. It's the date stamps on the photos. They start off normal enough, last month, last week, but then they head off into the future, the red numbers marking off days and times that haven't happened yet.

"Must've been a defective camera," I say.

I never have understood the need some people have to document the exact moment they took each shot.

Christina shakes her head. "Look at the pictures."

I'd been flipping through them, a catalogue of some boring tourist's mementos of their trip to the big city, but stopped looking at the actual images when I twigged to the screw-up with the date stamps. Now I return my attention to the pictures.

It takes me a moment to see what she means because you don't spot them at first. They aren't pretty when you do. Ugly monster-men, slinking around in the shadows. Kind of an *X-Files* take on finding Waldo. Like the shot of St. Paul's, long view including the rose window and bell tower. Pay attention and you see the freak standing back there where darkness pools in the cathedral's arches. Once you twig to their presence in one, you can pick them out in each of the others, doing their creepy thing. I wonder who's filming a bad B-movie in town this week when I get to the last couple of shots on the roll.

This is sick stuff. There's a group of the freaks in these, a couple holding down some guy while the others do things to him I wouldn't wish on my worst enemies, and some of them seriously deserve it. Like the guy who keeps repoing my car.

"We have to do something," Christina says. "Report them to the police."

I shake my head. "And say what? We're talking big time con job here. I mean, check them out. These guys don't even look human."

"I think that's supposed to be the point."

"What? That there are monsters hiding among us?"

I do a Vincent Price impression, stentorian tone and all, but Christina ignores it.

"I don't know about monsters," she says. "But guys running around in costumes killing people is serious business." She hesitates a beat, then adds, "They are costumes, right?"

"Well, I'll tell you this. They're not real boogie men."

The pictures put a lie to that, but we both know what they can do with special effects in the movies these days.

"Except," I add, reluctantly, "who takes pictures of a murder and then leaves the undeveloped film around for anyone to find? And if someone was taken apart the way they did that guy, it'd be in all the papers."

"What if it hasn't happened yet?" she says.

She puts her finger on the date stamp of the last one. It's a week away. Okay, six days, if you want to get anal about it.

I shake my head. "Come on."

"But what if?" she says. "You hear about weird stuff like this all the time."

"Only in the tabloids and on TV," I say. "Real life's got a whole other take on something like this."

"But—"

"We don't even know who these people are supposed to be."

"We should try to find out. If it can save somebody's life . . ."

I want to repeat, nobody's in danger, this whole thing is a bad joke, but she looks so upset and serious I figure the least I can do is go through the motions and check it out. Give her a little peace of mind.

"I know some people who claim to have the inside track on this sort of thing," I tell her. "You know, the weird and the wooly. I'll see what they can tell me."

"You think I'm nuts."

I smile. "But not dangerously so."

I bundle up the photos and negatives and stick them back into their envelope.

"How much do I owe you?" I ask.

"It's on the house."

"Thanks."

She's still looking upset. She also needs another button at the top of that dress.

"You know," I tell her, lifting my gaze to those eyes of hers. "When I first heard your voice, I thought you were calling to ask me out."

I can tell that helps ease the bad way she's feeling.

"I guess this must be my lucky dress," she says.

"So you busy tonight?"

She nods. "But I'm free tomorrow. Anything in particular you'd like me to wear?"

Point for her.

"Surprise me," I tell her.

And she does.

When I come by to pick her up the next night, she meets me at her door in this slinky black vinyl affair that's clinging to everything that it's not pushing into a more interesting shape.

"You like?" she asks.

I'm not going to tell her I feel we should be going to some seriously hip club where they probably wouldn't even let us in instead of this little Italian restaurant over in Crowsea where I've made reservations. I'd prefer her in jeans and a blouse, but I have to admit there's something fascinating about what she's wearing. How often do you actually see anyone poured into a dress like this outside of a fashion spread?

"I picked it up as a joke," she says. "I just wanted to see that look on your face, but now I feel like an idiot."

"I like," I assure her.

She puts on a jacket over the shiny vinyl and we head off for the restaurant in her car. I hoofed it to her apartment since my own wheels got repoed again this afternoon. Story of my life. I don't mean to fall behind on my payments, but that's the downside of walking the straight and narrow. These days I do legwork for a couple of lawyers, take on a few odd jobs on the side, all legit. It leaves me scrambling some weeks, but it sure beats doing time. Hell, pretty much anything beats doing time.

"Did you have any luck with your friends?" Christina asks after the waitress has brought us our drinks.

"Yes and no," I say, and then I tell her about my day.

Newford's got more than its fair shake of the gullible, not to mention the usual cadre of psychics and charlatans waiting on the sidelines to relieve them of their hard-earned cash. Sometimes it seems that no matter where you turn you're hearing about séances and oracular readings, spiritual this and mystical that, not to mention whole shelves devoted to books and magazines on the same topics in the local B & N, revealing mysteries, explaining the unknown, half of them laying it all out so you can do it yourself, in the privacy of your own home, a little quality time spent with the ghosts and the goddesses. There must be something in the water here because sometimes it seems that people in this city will believe any damn thing.

But at least most of the ones I know who're into the weird and the wacky also know when to leave the hoodoo at home. In other words, they can make like normal people when need be. It's only when they're open for business that they put on the spooky voices and do their mystical thing.

But today when I set out looking for the usual suspects with their business in mind, I keep coming up with a losing hand. Bones, Christy, the Prof, nobody's in their usual haunts until I finally track down Father Sully in Jimmy's Billiards, corner of Vine and Palm. He's not my first choice, an alcoholic ex-priest I only know by reputation, but I'm running out of options.

Sully's got something of the insect about him, he's all arms and legs with big, buggy eyes and hair that stands up like so many antennae or centipede's legs. He's already half-cut and it's barely mid-afternoon. But I want to do good for Christina, play it straight and give this deal a fair shot, so I sit down on the bench beside him, buy him another shot of whiskey with a beer chaser, tell him about my problem to the accompaniment of the click and clatter of billiard balls making their way around the tables and into the pockets. It doesn't take much to get him going. It never does with these guys.

"They're angels," he says when I show him the pictures.

Maybe I should have held out for one of the others. Christy's friend the Prof, maybe. When I called, his housekeeper was expecting him back any time.

"Angels," I repeat.

He nods. "Good shot," he tells a player at the table near us when he sinks a tough shot. "Wingless angels," he adds, turning back to me. "And don't ask them to sing—it'll just break their hearts. It's very distressing, as I'm sure you can imagine. They get all maudlin and homesick, which isn't a pretty sight. Mind you, they're never a pretty sight, are they?"

"Can you tell me something that actually makes sense?" I ask.

"They sing like angels, but they can't fly," he tells me. "Chose the wrong side when the war raged in heaven and now they're living down below with the rest of the sinners. Lucifer's boys."

I *really* should've held out for one of the others.

"See," he goes on, alcohol heavy on his breath as he leans closer to me, "sometimes they walk among us, but they can't ever have what we have."

"Which is?"

"A shot at getting back upstairs."

"So what're they doing here?" I have to ask.

He shrugs. "You know, the usual thing. Taking in the sights, a little R & R, leading us into temptation."

"And the guy they're killing?" I say, pointing to the last couple of pictures.

"Hasn't happened yet—at least not according to these dates. Why do people date stamp their photographs anyway? Can't they remember when they took them?"

So we have something in common. Why isn't that a comfort?

"Beats me," I tell him.

He nods, returns his attention to the game at the table.

"So what should I do?" I ask, not expecting any more sensible an answer to this than I've gotten so far. He doesn't disappoint me.

"You mean to stop them from killing the man?"

I nod.

Sully gives me a drunkard's grin. "Ask him what he did to tick them off."

"And I would find him how?"

"Use your intuition." He taps his temple with a forefinger. "Go out walking with the intent of finding him and you will. If you concentrate on what you're looking for, fill your head with it, nine out of ten times, whatever you're looking for will come to you. That's what Jesus would do."

"I don't remember anything like that in the Bible."

Maybe that surprises you, that I've read the Big Book, but when you're doing time and other material is scarce, it turns out to be a

pretty good read. These days I do a lot of reading—it keeps me out
of trouble.

"That's one of the things that didn't make it into the texts,"
Sully says. "But everybody knows it."

Right. Like everybody knows about these wingless angels, I suppose. But I can't be too hard on the old guy. I mean, I'm the one
who came asking.

"Thanks, Sully," I tell him. "You want another drink?"

"I believe that would be in order. Long conversations make for
dry throats."

I leave him with his drinks, absorbed in the game once more.

"Let's try it," Christina says when I finish my story.

All I can do is look at her across the table, and I'll admit that's
not hard on the eyes, even with the vinyl dress, but I can't believe
she's taking any of this seriously.

"Sully's a drunk," I tell her.

"You said he was a priest."

"*Ex*-priest, as in no more."

"He knew what they were, straightaway."

"He *said* he knew what they were. There's a big difference. I
could make up as good a story. I mean, really. Angels?"

"Come on," she says, those big eyes of hers just drawing me in.
I'm going to tell her no?

I have to tell you the truth here. What I said before was only
partly true. We are only friends, but I've always had a thing for her.
Who wouldn't? She's smart and pretty and she's got a heart as big
as the sky is wide. When she turned me down, back when we first
met, I took it at face value and settled for being pals. Funny thing is,
I like having her for a friend. I never had a woman for a friend
before and it's an experience I'd recommend. For one thing, I come
away from our conversations with things to think about, and let me

tell you, that doesn't happen around the guys I know. Before I knew Christina, I never gave a whole lot of thought to what we've been doing to the world, what we do to each other. I minded my own business and asked others to do the same. But how hard is it to clean up after yourself or to look out for someone worse off than you are?

So being friends is good, and I don't want to lose that. But if she wants to take it to another level, I'm not going to complain.

See, anyone I'm going to be serious with in the romance department, we've also got to be friends. I don't want to end up like my parents who could barely tolerate each other. I want it to mean something, us being together. I want us to look forward to being together, instead of thinking up excuses as to why I've got to get out of the apartment, just to get some breathing space. That was always the old man's line. He couldn't breathe around Ma and us kids.

So would I go chasing down the monsters' victim for Christina, given that I don't believe either he or the uglies exist? Hell, I'd go look up Lucifer, slap him silly and damn the consequences, if that'd make her happy. Which is how we end up wandering the streets long past midnight, and where I blow it because I can't keep my mind—my intent, as Sully put it—on this victim. When I'm not thinking about Christina, I'm thinking about these monsters, how good the costumes were in the pictures, the time that had to have gone into making them, the way they set up the shots, and the next damn thing you know, we've got them chasing us down Williamson to the waterfront and all my doubts go out the window. Because whatever these freaks are, they're not make-believe.

"They must've felt us thinking so hard about their victim," Christina says when we duck into an alleyway that'll take us in behind the Harbor Ritz.

"I was thinking about them," I tell her.

She gives me a look, half angry, half scared.

"Jesus, Sammy. You brought them right to us. You weren't *supposed* to be thinking about *them*."

So she's not all that happy with me, with good reason, and I hate the way it feels, but right now we've got more serious concerns on our mind. Like staying alive.

That's when we try hiding out behind the Dumpster and you know how well that turns out.

Okay, I think. I've made a mess of things so far, but I can still make good. For Christina, anyway.

I stand up and pull her to her feet. The freaks are closing in on us, but there's still room for what I've got in mind. I tell Christina to make a run for it, I'll be right behind her, but I can see it in her eyes, she's not buying it. She knows I plan to do the hero thing and from the way she squares her shoulders, it's plain she's going to stick with me. I appreciate the gesture, but what's the point of both of us dying if the uglies might be satisfied with only one?

"Just go," I tell her.

We have to breathe through our mouths, the reek's so bad, a combination of the Dumpster and the monster boys coming for us.

Christina shakes her head. "Sing," she says.

I look at her like she's gone insane. The freaks have got us boxed in now, a semicircle of greasy long faces, eyes glittering with this weird inner glow. The smell of them is almost overpowering. It's too late for either of us to make a break. Too late for anything.

"Sing?" I say.

She nods. "Maybe we can get them going."

I try to keep myself between her and the freaks. I can see the pleasure grow in them as they savor the moment. I remember the last couple of photos on that damn roll of film I was stupid enough to pick up and get developed. They're going to have some fun with us tonight.

"You're not making sense," I tell her.

"It's like your friend the priest said."

Ex-priest, I think. And he's not my friend. He's just some old drunk who could have done a better job of convincing me these monsters are real.

"He said a lot of stuff . . ." I start to say, but Christina's not listening.

She starts in with the drawn-out refrain from "Gloria." Her singing voice is high and sweet and it breaks my heart that these freaks are going to silence it forever. But something strange happens with the monsters. They cock their heads and listen. Oh great, I think. Good choice. A hymn to their old boss. That'll win them over. But they start to sing along with her, first one, the others falling in with harmonies, and the sound is unbelievable. It's like sunrise, a cathedral sound filled with light and mystery and the great swelling feeling you get in your chest when something's just too beautiful for words.

Then I realize what Christina meant. Sully's wingless angels. Get them singing, he told me, and they'll get all maudlin and homesick. And maybe too distracted to pull us to pieces.

Christina falls silent, her own pretty singing shamed before these celestial voices. Damned if tears don't come to my eyes as their voices wash over us, echoing and bouncing throughout the alley until it sounds like a choir of thousands. I know we should be trying to slip away, but it's just too mesmerizing. Christina's crying beside me. Hell, even the uglies have tears streaming down their cheeks.

I don't know how long we stand there listening, but finally I stir. I take Christina's hand and lead her past the freaks with their honey gold voices, my heartbeat drumming wildly as we approach, then pass in between two of them. But they keep right on singing, faces lifted to the sky, tears flowing, and we just head off down the alley, walk around to the front of the hotel and walk inside. We get a hard stare from the concierge, and I can't blame him. I know how bad we look, Christina in that dress, both of us disheveled and shaky like a pair of junkies. But I give him as hard a stare back that tells him in no uncertain terms that I'll bust him in the head if he even thinks of kicking us out. He gets real busy with some papers behind his counter.

"Don't take it out on him," Christina said. "What happened to us wasn't his fault."

I realize she's right. Maybe he's an officious little prick, maybe he's just doing his job. But I can't take it out on him, my feeling so helpless before the fallen angels.

"Can you still hear them?" Christina asks.

I nod. It's all I can hear, though Christina and I seem to be alone in that. The concierge, the bellhops, the desk clerk, a couple sitting together surrounded by a small tide pool of luggage, none of them give any indication that they can hear that unheavenly chorus. My ears are ringing, like we just got back from a loud concert.

"Look," Christina says.

It's the guy from the pictures, coming in through the front door into the lobby, big as life and still alive. Of course he's not due to die for another five days, if the date stamps on the photos are to be believed. Christina gets up to meet him, tugging down the hem of her dress.

"Excuse me, sir," she says.

He gives Christina a once-over that makes me really under-stand—emotionally, as well as intellectually—how she feels when my gaze gets locked on her cleavage.

I stand up as well, feel like hitting the guy, but Christina plays mind reader again. She puts out a hand to stop me from walking past her.

"What can I do for you?" the man asks, implying there's a great deal and all of it would be pleasurable. What, does he think she's a hooker and I'm her pimp? It's that damn dress.

Christina cuts right to the chase.

"Have you had any dealings with strange beings?" she asks.

It's amazing to see the man's facade collapse, a balloon losing all its air, macho man goes flaccid.

"Are they here?" he asks. Scared now, libido forgotten. "I know we had a deal, but I just need a little more time. Do you know how hard it is to find a teenage virgin in this city?"

Christina's revulsion is plain. I don't even want to know what he needs the virgin for.

"You better start running," I tell him.

It's funny. He doesn't question us or anything—what we know, how we know it—just bolts back out the door he came in. Christina and I collapse back on our couch and let the soft cushions envelop us.

Christina leans her head against my shoulder. "What happens now?"

"You want to go out there and chance running into them again?"

She shakes her head.

"Me neither."

I dig a charge card out of my pocket. It belongs to one of the lawyers I work for, couple of grand limit. It's for expenses and normally I wouldn't touch it.

"I'll get us a couple of rooms," I say.

Christina catches my arm as I start to get up.

"One room," she says.

Of course, later I start in to wondering what happens when the monsters think of us again and that involves another visit to Father Sully. This time I bring Christina with me. She's wearing a nice flower print cotton dress, another thrift shop find, but this time it's a winner. We find Sully drinking out of a paper bag in Fitzhenry Park, doing a really lousy job of hiding what he's got in the bag. I ask him what we can do to keep the monsters from coming after us again.

"Live a good life," he tells us. "Be good people. Keep hateful thoughts out of your heart and mind. The angels will be too busy tempting sinners and following up on old bargains to even think about you again."

That'll be easy for Christina, I think, but where does it leave me? I'm not the gentlest guy in the world, though lord knows I've been trying. I figure with my luck, I'll have the uglies on my tail within a couple of weeks, though they'll have to wait in line behind the repo man since I just got my car out of hock again.

I feel Christina's fingers twine with mine and turn to look at her.

"I know what you're thinking," she says.

I never could put anything past her.

"I'll be here to keep you honest," she tells me.

Sully gives a big amen to that and I nod in agreement. Looks like I've got my own debt to his wingless angels. I just hope they don't try to collect because I don't have what could even remotely be called a decent singing voice.

The Words That Remain

"Not yet," she said. Her voice was measured and calm, calmer than she'd ever thought she'd feel when this time arrived. "Give me a little longer. Just long enough to know who I am."

But Death had not come to bargain that night and took her away.

"This place is haunted, you know," the night clerk told him.

Christy stifled a sigh. Normally he was ready to hear anybody's story, especially on this sort of subject, but he was on a book tour for his latest collection, and after today's long round of interviews, signings, drop-in visits to bookstores and the like, all he wanted was some time to himself. A chance to put away the public face. To no longer worry if he'd inadvertently picked his nose and someone had seen and made note. ("While the author's premises are intriguing, his personal habits could certainly stand some improvement.") He needed to get back to his room and call home, to let Saskia's voice remind him of the real life he led the other fifty or so weeks of the year when he wasn't out promoting himself.

But he felt he owed it to Alan, not to mention his own career, to do what he could to promote his books. Ever since the surprising success Alan's East Side Press had had with Katharine Mully, particularly her posthumous collection *Touch and Go*, the media had taken a serious interest in what Alan liked to call their contemporary myth books, said interest translating into better coverage, more reviews, and increasingly lucrative deals for paperback editions and other subsidiary rights. Alan considered Christy's and Mully's books to perfectly complement each other, rounding out his catalogue, the urban myths and folktales Christy collected telling the "real story" behind the contemporary fairy tales Mully had so effectively brought to life in her fiction.

He approached the various readings and signings with a genuine fondness for the readers who came to the events with their own stories and enthusiasms, and he made the rounds with as much good grace as he could muster toward those media types who sometimes seemed to be less interested in the actual work than they were in filling a few column inches of type, or minutes of airtime. Still, at the end of a long day, it was wearying and hard to maintain the public persona—not so much different from his own, simply more outgoing. Right now he seriously needed some downtime.

But, "Haunted?" he said.

She nodded. "Like in your books. There's a ghost in the hotel."

Christy could believe it. There'd been a mix-up with his reservations so that when he'd arrived from the airport to drop off his bags, he'd been shunted to this other, smaller hotel down the street. Truth was, he liked it better. It was an older building, its gilded décor no longer the height of fashion, furnishings worn and decidedly frayed in places, but no less charming for that. If there weren't ghosts in a

place like this, then they'd certainly drop by for a visit. It was the
kind of hotel where bohemians and punks and open-minded busi-
nessmen on a budget could all rub shoulders in the lobby. The staff
ran the gamut from the elderly man in a burgundy smoking jacket
who'd checked him in this morning to the young woman standing
on the other side of the counter at the moment. Earlier he'd heard
the big band music of Tommy Dorsey drifting from the small office
behind the check-in desk; tonight it was the more contemporary
sound of Catatonia.

Leaning against the counter, Christy made note of the woman's
nametag. Mary, it read.

At first he thought the name didn't really suit her. Mary struck
him as a calm name, a little on the conservative side, and the night
clerk was anything but, though he had to give her points for trying.
She could have been anywhere from nineteen to twenty-nine, her
frame more wiry than skinny, her chopped blonde spikes twisted
and poking up at random from her brown roots through an odd collection of clips, bobby pins and elastics. Her fashion sense was riot
grrl attempting business chic; he could tell she was about as comfortable in the sleek black skirt, white blouse and heels as he was in
a tie and jacket—it didn't feel like your own skin so much as some
stranger's. Her multiple earrings and the tattoo peeking out from
below the sleeve of her blouse, not to mention that mad hair, told
another story from the one her clothing offered, revealing part of
the subtext of who she really was.

"What sort of ghost, Mary?" he asked.

There was an old smell in this hotel, but he didn't mind. It
reminded him of favorite haunts like used book stores and libraries,
with an undercurrent that combined rose hip tea, incense, and late
night jazz club smoke.

"A sad one," she said.

"Aren't they all?"

She gave him a surprised look.

"Think about it," he said. "What else can they be but unhappy? If they weren't unhappy, they wouldn't still be hanging around, would they? They'd continue on."

"Where to?"

"That's the big question."

"I suppose."

She fiddled with something on the desk below the counter, out of Christy's sight. Paper rustled. The monitor of the computer screen added a bluish cast to her features and hair.

"But what about vengeful ghosts?" she asked, gaze remaining on the paperwork.

Christy shrugged. "Vengeful, angry, filled with the need to terrorize others. They're all signs of unhappiness. Of discontent with one's lot in life, or should we say afterlife? Though really, it's the baggage they carry with them that keeps them haunting us."

"Baggage?"

"Emotional baggage. The kind we all have to deal with. Some of us are better at it than others. You've seen them, sprinting through life with nothing more than a carry-on. But then there are the rest of us, dragging around everything from fat suitcases to great big steamer trunks, loaded down with all the debris of our discontent. Those ones with the trunks, they're the ones who usually stick around when the curtain comes down, certain that if they can just have a little longer, they can straighten up all their affairs." He smiled. "Doesn't work that way, of course. Alive or dead, there's never enough time to get it all done."

She lifted her gaze. "You even talk like a writer."

"I'm just in that mode," Christy told her. "Too many days talking about myself, going on endlessly about how and why I write what I do, where I find the stories I collect, why they're relevant beyond their simple entertainment value. It gets so that even ordinary conversation comes out in sound bites. I've been at it so much today my brain hasn't shifted back to normal yet."

"I guess you can't wait to get home."

Christy nodded. "But I like meeting people. It's just hard with so many at once. You can't connect properly, especially not with those who're expecting some inflated image that they've pulled out of my books and all they get is me. And it gets pretty tiring."

"I'm sorry," she said. "I'm keeping you up, aren't I?"

Christy had long ago realized that, in one way, ghosts and the living were much the same: most of them only needed to have their story be heard to ease their discontent. It didn't necessarily heal them, but it was certainly a part of the healing process.

"I can never sleep after a day like this," he lied. "So tell me about your ghost."

She went shy again, looking away.

"Really," he said. "Share the story with me. I've done nothing but hear myself talk these past few days. Listening to somebody else would be a welcome change."

That wasn't a lie and perhaps she could tell, because she gave him a small, grateful smile when her gaze returned to him.

"Do you believe in what you write?" she asked after a moment.

That was a familiar question from this and other tours and he didn't have to think about an answer, the rote response immediately springing to mind. He left it unspoken and traded it for a more truthful answer.

"It depends on the source," he usually said. "I know for certain that the world's a strange and mysterious place with more in it than most of us will ever see or experience, so I can't immediately dismiss elements that are out of the ordinary simply because I haven't experienced them. But by the same token, I also don't immediately accept every odd and unusual occurrence when it's presented to me because the world's also filled with a lot of weird people with very active imaginations. The trouble is, unless you experience what they have, it's difficult to come to any definitive conclusion. I will say that, for all my predilection toward the whimsical and surreal, empirical evidence makes a strong argument."

What he said to Mary was, "Yes. It might not necessarily be true for me, or for you, but if it's in one of my books, it's there because it's true for someone."

"I don't understand," she said. "Things are either true or they're not."

"I think it's more a matter of perception. Just because ninety-nine-point-nine percent of the world has decided that something like a ghost or fairy spirit can't exist, doesn't mean they're right."

"Do you really believe that?"

He nodded.

"That's not what you said on the TV interview this morning."

Christy smiled. "You watch that show?"

"Only for the how-to segments."

"But a pumpkin carving contest aimed at speed rather than quality?"

She laughed. "Come on. Don't tell me you didn't think it was funny."

"This is true. . . ."

Christy had had a hard time keeping a straight face while sitting in the green room and watching that segment on the monitor. Between the host and the three guest pumpkin carvers, they'd made such a mess that it was only through the director's clever manipulation of camera angles that his own interview hadn't appeared to be filmed in the disaster zone it had been. There'd been pulp and seeds everywhere, squishing underfoot wherever you stepped, and he was still surprised that no one had been hurt with all those flashing knives. He'd left the studio with the smell of pumpkin pulp lingering in his nose for hours afterwards.

"So why do you say what you do when you're being interviewed?" she asked. "I mean, if you really believe in this stuff . . ."

"I don't want to be dismissed as a crackpot," he told her, "because then they'll also dismiss the stories out of hand. This way, if I allow them to see that I have my own healthy skepticism, the stories get to stand on their own. We can talk about them, ad nauseum, but in the end, the words will remain. The stories will be there and taken more for their own merit, rather than being the product of some obviously deluded individual."

"Do you really think they get a fair shake because of that?"

"A fairer shake," Christy said.

She smiled. "You still talk like an author, you know."

"And you still haven't told me about your ghost."

She hesitated a moment longer, twisting her finger around one of the escaped locks of her short hair. The movement brought a stronger waft of rose hips to him and he realized it was her perfume, not tea he'd smelled earlier. From the office behind her, the CD player changed discs and Ednaswap began singing about a safety net.

"Well, the way I heard it," Mary said, "she was the daughter of the hotel's owner. Really talented and artistic, but unfocused. She could have been a painter or a poet. A singer, a dancer, a writer, a photographer. She was good at everything she tried and she tried a lot of different things."

"But?" Christy prompted when Mary fell silent.

"Her father wanted her to work in the hotel. She was all the family he had and he refused to let her go out into the world and ruin her life trying to make a living with anything so chancy. She could have just taken off, I suppose, but it was a different time. A teenage girl didn't do that in those days. Or maybe she simply wasn't brave enough. So she tried to be both. Dutiful daughter, working with her father in the family business, and the free spirit who wanted to create and experience and never settle down. But it didn't—couldn't—work."

"I knew it was going to be a sad story," Christy murmured.

"It gets sadder."

He nodded. "They usually do."

"One day," Mary went on, "she couldn't deal with it anymore, so she killed off the free spirit inside her. She called up an image of Death in her mind, you know, scythe, black hood and all—not too imaginative, but then she was trying to kill her imagination, wasn't she? So cowled Death came at her bidding and cut the free spirit out of her soul and together they buried the poor little dead thing—figuratively, of course."

"Of course."

"Over time she pretty much forgot about that spirit lying somewhere, buried deep in her memory, and the odd thing is, she did come to feel better. There was no resentment toward her father or the hotel. When she did think of that girl, she remembered her as someone she'd once known, rather than someone she'd once been. But the funny thing is—the *ghostly* thing—is that from time to time guests will see that free spirit roaming through the halls."

"But the woman never does?"

Mary shook her head.

"An unusual ghost," Christy said.

"Mmm."

"And what do you think is keeping her here?"

"Well, not vengeance," Mary said with a small laugh.

"Why not?"

"Well, if she was that sort of a person, she'd never have let herself be shut out of her life the way she was, would she? I think she's just, like you said, sad. In mourning for everything she lost. She can't go on because she never got to find out who she could be. Or maybe she just wants some recognition."

"But not from the guests."

"No. I think it'd have to be from the woman who killed her." She cocked her head to look at him. "Have you ever heard of a ghost like that?"

Christy shook his head. "But that doesn't mean she's not real."

"To me."

"And whoever else has seen her." Christy paused a moment, then asked, "I assume you have seen her?"

"I think everyone who's in this hotel for any length of time gets to see her. But most of them don't know she's a ghost."

"Now I'm really intrigued."

Mary smiled. "Use it in your next book. 'Course, I guess you need an ending to be able to do that."

"No, I just tell the stories the way I find them, anecdotal, fragmentary or complete." He regarded her for a moment. "You only know what I write from that TV show."

"I don't get into bookstores a lot. Pretty much all I read is what people leave behind in their rooms. I'm sorry."

"Don't be. I think there are far more people in the world who haven't read me than there are those who have. Or who even know who I am." He smiled. "And frankly, most of the time I'm happy to leave it that way."

"When aren't you?"

"Oh, when I'm looking at some rare first edition that I can't buy because I only have this month's rent in my bank account."

"I hear being rich isn't all it's cracked up to be."

"Did you ever hear a rich person say that?" Christy asked.

"Only when they're trying to pass as one of the proletariat."

"Now who sounds like a writer?"

Before she could respond, another of the hotel's guests approached the desk, asking if there were any messages for him.

"Thanks for the conversation, Mary," Christy said as she turned away to look.

"You, too," she told him over her shoulder. "Sleep well."

The next morning, when Christy went to the front desk to check out, he had a copy of one of his books in hand. He doubted Mary would still be on shift this morning, but thought he could at least leave a copy for her with whoever was on duty.

The morning clerk could have been Mary's mother—she even had the same name on her nametag, but there the resemblance ended. She was middle-aged, forty-something—which made her roughly his own age, he thought ruefully. Funny how you forget that you grow older along with everyone else. Medium height, not quite overweight, attractive in a weary sort of a way, short brownish-blonde hair that had started to outgrow its last cut, dressed in a skirt and blazer that appeared a little outdated.

Her taste in music, judging from the faint wisp of sound drifting out of the office behind her, ran more to the classics. Something by Paganini was playing. Solo violin. The smell of her coffee made him wish he'd ordered some from room service, instead of waiting till he got to the radio station where he was doing his first interview this morning.

"Does everyone working here have the same name?" Christy asked.

The woman regarded him with confusion.

"Your nametag," he said. "It has the same name as was on the one the clerk was wearing last night."

Now he wished he'd never brought it up. Maybe they only had the one nametag and shared it around.

"Jeremy was wearing my nametag?" she asked. She said it in the same tone she might have used if this Jeremy had been manning the desk while wearing one of her dresses.

"No," Christy said. "It was a young woman. Blonde hair, sort of punky looking—but in a nice way," he quickly added when the woman's frown deepened.

"We don't have anybody like that working here," she said. "The clerk on duty last night would have been Jeremy."

"And he'd have been at the desk here the whole time?"

"Unless it was particularly quiet. Then he might have been studying in the office in back."

Christy could see a portion of the office from where he stood. He returned his attention to the woman who was regarding him with some measure of suspicion now.

"Studying," he said.

"He's a student from the university," she explained.

Christy nodded. He knew now where this was going.

"Does your father own this hotel?" he asked. "Indulge me," he added as her look of suspicion deepened. "Please."

"My father passed away a few years ago. I'm the present owner."

"I'm sorry," Christy said. "Not that you're the owner, of course, but . . ."

"I understand," the woman said. "Can you tell me what this is all about?"

Christy shook his head. "Not really. It seems I had the most vivid dream last night."

The woman regarded him expectantly.

"I should just check out," he said.

He studied her, surreptitiously, while she completed the necessary paperwork. He could see the traces of the girl she'd been, now that he knew to look. Could almost smell the rose hips of the younger Mary's perfume.

"This is for you," he said, handing her the book when their business was done.

The suspicion returned, deepening once more when she opened it to the title page and read the inscription.

For Mary,
May you finally be recognized for who you are.
Christy Riddell

"I don't understand," she said lifting her gaze from the book to meet his. "How could you know my name before you came down to check out? And what does this mean?"

She was pointing at the inscription.

Christy could only shrug.

"It's a long, sad story," he said. "But we met once, a long time ago. I doubt you remember—you must meet so many people in this business."

She nodded.

"The inscription refers to who you were then—when we met. You told me a ghost story."

She looked down at the book again, read the title. *Ordinary Ghosts, Hidden Hauntings.*

"Like these?" she asked.

He shook his head. "No, it was a rather extraordinary ghost story, pulled out of a rather sad situation that happens more often than any of us likes to admit."

"I don't understand."

"I know. But nothing I can say will change anything, or make it any clearer. I'm sorry if I've troubled you in any way."

He nodded and turned away, walking across the lobby. He paused at the exit.

"Good-bye, Mary," he said. "I hope you enjoy the book."

"Well, I'll certainly give it a try," the woman behind the desk told him.

Christy hadn't been talking to her, but he gave her a smile. He didn't get a response from the other Mary, but he hadn't been expecting one. Nodding again, he left the hotel and hailed a cab. There were only two interviews this morning, then a signing at a bookstore. Plenty of time to think about choices made and what could come of them. Too much time, really.

But then that was what life is all about, isn't it? The choices we make and how the people we are can be left behind when we make those choices because they're no longer a part of our story. For many, not even the words remain to remind us of them. There are only all those ghosts of who we were, wandering around for anyone to see. Except ourselves.

Because we rarely see our own ghosts, do we?

As he settled in the back seat of his cab he found himself wondering about his own ghosts, how many there were, haunting the places he'd once been, those products of choices he'd made that he would never meet, telling stories he would never hear.

Many Worlds Are Born Tonight

I went down to the Beanery that night, you know, that café down in the old factory district by the canal that's more like a warehouse than a coffee bar. Big enough for a rave, but the wildest the music gets is Chet Baker or Morcheeba. Very hip place, at least this week. Nonsmoking, of course, but everything is these days. Open concept with lots of woodwork: pine floors, rustic rafters and support beams. No real general lighting, only pockets, low-hanging overhead lights illuminating tables with groups of people in earnest conversation, drinking low-fat lattés and decaf espressos, go figure. Kind of like a singles bar without the action, but I like it for that. For the anoyminity it allows me. So I'm surprised when I catch a name I haven't heard in years.

"Hey, Spyboy."

It takes me back to New Orleans, Mardi Gras. Spyboys are part of the Big Chiefs' entourages during the annual parade, the Mardi

Gras "Indians" who scout ahead for the other tribes on the march and just generally make a lot of mischief. I did my bit in the parades back in those days, but the name stuck because of another job I held before I retired: digging up dirt for the Couteau family. I'm good at secrets—keeping my own, uncovering those that belong to others. I guess I'd still be there, but I took exception to the use of my expertise. I don't mind tracking down deadbeats and the like, but it turned out that people died because of information I dug up. When I found out how the Couteaus were using me, I couldn't live with it, but you don't say good-bye to people like this.

See, I grew up wanting to be one of the good guys. Call me naïve. When I realized that wasn't happening, when I understood exactly what I'd fallen into, I had no choice but to disappear. That entailed getting out of town and staying out. Maintaining a low profile once I was gone and, most important, keeping my mouth shut.

So when I hear that name, one part of me wants to keep walking, but curiosity's always been a serious weakness. I turn to see what part of my past has finally caught up to me.

I don't recognize him right away. The lighting's bad where he's sitting, alone at a table, nursing a chai tea latté. Nondescript—your basic average joe, medium height, brown hair, brown eyes, no distinguishing features. The kind of man your gaze just slides over because there's nothing there to hold it. He's wearing a dark jacket and turtleneck.

"I heard you were dead," he says.

It's the voice I remember. That rasp, like it's working its way through a hundred years of abusing cigarettes and whiskey. Sammy Hale. Used to run numbers for the Couteaus until he got caught dipping his hand where it shouldn't. Not once, but twice. I check out his right hand where the fingers are cut off at the knuckles. It's Sammy all right.

I give him a shrug.

"I could say the same thing about you," I tell him.

"I got better," he says. Smiles.

It's enough to hook me, pull the line taut, then reel me in. He knows my weakness. I take one of the empty chairs at his table.

"Sounds like a story," I say.

"Maybe. You still in the information business?"

I shake my head, then touch a finger to my temple. "This is where it stays now. Can't sell anything anymore because that's like saying, 'Here I am.' But you know me."

He nods. "Yeah, you always had to know."

"So how'd you survive?" I ask.

Again that smile. "I didn't."

I hear a lot of stories, mostly from street people these days, and they'll tell you any damn thing. What intrigues me right now is that I remember Sammy from the old days. The one thing he never had was much imagination. Why do you think he got caught ripping off the Couteaus, not once, but twice?

I'm good at waiting. You learn more if you don't ask questions. But I can tell that's not how Sammy wants to play this out.

"So what happened?" I ask.

"I guess you could say I wandered out of the world."

"You know I'm not following you here," I say.

That smile of his plays out into a grin and then he tells me a story that even the skells hanging around outside the detox center would be embarrassed to own up to.

"Come with me," he says when he's done.

"I can't," I tell him and I walk away.

Or maybe I didn't walk away.

Maybe I hear him out and that old curiosity of mine has me follow him out of the Beanery into the night. We trade the sounds of quiet conversation and the Bill Evans Trio playing on the café's sound system for the noise of the streets, the rich smell of brewing coffee for car exhaust and the faint odor of rotting garbage. Tomorrow's pickup day downtown and all the bins are standing in a row along the curb.

Sammy keeps talking, adding details. I walk along beside him, nodding to show that I'm taking it all in.

Not that I believe him for a second.

Carnies have always been easy fall guys for mystery and trouble. People think of them with the same uneasy mix of intolerance and envy as they do Gypsies. What a life, but they'll rob you blind. Lock the doors when the tractor-trailers pull into town and the midway goes up. But what a life. Every day a different town, a whole new crowd of rubes to take advantage of. But keep your hand on your wallet and lock up your daughters.

And haunted carnivals are nothing new, either. Hell, they've got their own little category in folklore and literature, too, from Ray Bradbury to Dean Koontz. But this Ferris wheel he's talking up, it's a new one for me. It's a mechanism that doesn't make sense in the world we all inhabit, like opening a door in your house and finding it leads into a room you've never seen before. I'm haunted by the idea of his carnival ride, existing sideways to the world, a big Ferris wheel with this odd sign hanging over the entrance to the ride, "Crowded After Hours." A creaking, ancient behemoth of midway entertainment that only exists when the fair's closed down, the booths are all dark, and the carnies have closed the doors of their trailers against the night. A midnight ride where each rider is some costumed figure from nightmare or story or dream, an uneasy crowd of gargoyles and clowns and stranger beings still, like a Mardi Gras parade on a slow-spinning wheel.

There's room for Spyboy there, he tells me.

"See, you're safe on the wheel," Sammy says. "Safe from the world. Safe forever."

Maybe, I'm thinking. But are you safe from the wheel itself? Because, never mind the implausibility of it, there's something not right about this idea of chaos married to order, all these mad troubled souls doing time in the confines of their seats, the big wheel turning slowly, creaking in the mist.

"Just have a look," he says, seeing my doubt.

And I guess I will. I do. Curiosity pulling me along as we head up to the roof of the old Sovereign Building on Flood Street, just north of Kelly, in through a back door and up a stairwell until the rooftop gravel's crunching underfoot and we're standing at the edge of the roof, looking out. Sammy's eyes are shining, aglow.

"I don't see anything," I tell him.

"You have to have faith," he says. "You have to believe."

I squint and think I see something, some monstrous shape looming out of the night, clouded with mists, a wheel turning, the seats rocking slowly back and forth and all these . . . these beings on them, staring off into unimaginable distances.

"How often do we get a chance like this?" Sammy asks me.

I turn to look at him, still snared by his sincerity.

"Think about it," he says. "Every time we make a decision, we make another world. We do one thing, and we're in the world that decision called up, but at the same time, we didn't do it, so we're in that other world, too. It goes on forever, all these worlds."

"You know, you're not making a whole lot of sense," I say.

He smiles. "Just think of a world where you're not looking over your shoulder every couple of minutes, wondering if the Couteaus have finally tracked you down and sent one of their boys to deal with you."

"Eternity on a Ferris wheel doesn't really sound all that much better," I say.

"You're thinking of the outside," he tells me. "Concentrate on all the journeys you can take inside."

I shake my head. "I don't get it, Sammy. I like the world. I like being in it."

"You just don't know any different." He gives me that smile again, the kind you see on the statues of saints in a church. "In some world you've already stepped over. You're already riding the wheel and you can't imagine how you'd ever have hesitated."

"Why me?" I ask him. "Why'd you come to me?"

"We're linked," he says. "By bad blood. The Couteaus want both of us dead."

You're already dead, I'm thinking, but we've already covered that and it didn't get me any closer to understanding what he's talking about.

But I can see that ghostly wheel now, half here, so close we can almost reach out and grab one of the joints of its frame, half lost in a steaming mist.

"And besides," he says. "We're already there."

He points to a seat shared by a harlequin and something truly weird: a man with the head of a quarter moon, a blue moon, like something out of a kid's book. A man in the moon with Sammy's features. And I can make out my own features, too, under the harlequin's white makeup.

"What's with the moon head?" I ask him.

"You know," he says. "Once in a . . . I always wanted to be lucky. Different. The guy who comes and you don't know what to expect, maybe good, maybe bad, but it'll shake up your world and make some new ones because whether you like it or not, there's a big change coming. I don't want to be what I am, some loser you can't remember as soon as I walk out the door."

"I never wanted to be a harlequin," I say.

He smiles, it's like a child's smile this time, so simple and all encompassing, the whole world smiling with you.

"Spyboy was a kind of clown," he says.

"So what does that say about me?"

"That you like to see people happy. Same as me. Look at us." He points at the pair again. "Don't we make you smile?"

I'm feeling a little disoriented, dizzy almost, which is strange, though not the strangest thing to happen to me tonight. Still, I've always been good with heights, so this flicker of vertigo disturbs me, more than the wheel and Sammy's story, go figure.

"Come on," he says.

I don't know why I do it, but I jump with him, off the roof, grab hold of the wheel's frame, climb down toward where we're already sitting, Spyboy and the Blue Moon.

Only maybe I don't jump. Maybe I stand there and watch him fall, and then I go home. But I can't get it out of my head, what he told me, the way he just jumped, the height of the building, how I never heard him land on the pavement below. I wonder if someone can die twice, except there's no body this time, waiting for me when I step out of the door and into the alleyway. Maybe there wasn't when the Couteaus had him shot either.

The next day I go to work, walk in the back door of the restaurant, same as always. Raul looks up when I come in. He waits until I take off my jacket, put on an apron, start in to work on the small mountain of pots and dishes that've accumulated since I was last standing here at the sink.

"There was a guy looking for you after you left yesterday," he says.

Sammy, I think. I want to forget all about what maybe happened last night, but the thoughts keep coming back like bad pennies.

"Did he say what he wanted?" I ask, curious as to what Sammy might have said, still looking for a clue, trying to figure him out, where he went when he jumped off that roof.

Raul shakes his head. "Didn't say much of anything. He was big guy, mean looking. Talked a little like François, only not so much. Same accent, you know?"

I go cold at that little piece of news.

I'll tell you the truth, I never thought the Couteaus would bother to track me down. Where was the percentage? I didn't rip them off like Sammy, I've kept my mouth shut all along, stayed low, working shit jobs, minded my own business. But I guess just walking away was insult enough for them.

"He say anything about coming back?" I ask.

Raul shrugged. "I didn't like the look of him," he says, "so I told him you quit."

"You didn't lie," I tell him, already removing the apron.

"What's this guy got on you?" Raul asks.

"Nothing. He just works for some freaks who don't like to hear the word 'no.' He comes back, you tell him you never saw me again."

Raul shrugs. "I can do that, but—"

"I'm not saying this for me," I tell him. "I'm saying it for you."

I guess he sees something in my face, a piece of how serious this is, because he swallows hard and nods. Then I'm out the door, walking fast, pulse working overtime. There's a sick feeling in my gut and the skin between my shoulderblades is prickling like someone's got a rifle site aimed at my back.

Except the kind of boys the Couteaus hire like to work close, like to see the pain. I'm almost at the end of the alley, thinking I'm home free, except suddenly he's there in front of me, like he stepped out of nowhere, knife in hand. I have long enough to register his fish cold eyes, the freak's grin that splits his face, then the knife punches into my stomach. He pulls it up, tearing through my chest, and I go down. It happens so fast that the pain follows afterwards, like thunder trailing a lightning bolt.

And everything goes black.

Only maybe I didn't go out the back door, where I knew he could be waiting.

Maybe I grabbed my jacket and bolted through the restaurant, out the front, and lost myself in the lunchtime crowd. But I know he's out there, looking for me, and I don't have anywhere to go. I never had much of a stake and what I did have is long gone. Why do you think I'm washing dishes for a living?

So I go to ground with the skells, trade my clean jacket for some wino's smelly coat, a couple of bucks buys me a toque, I don't want to know where it's been. I rub dirt on my face and hands and I hide there in plain sight, same block as the restaurant, sprawled on the pavement, begging for spare change, waiting for the night to come so I can go looking for this wheel of Sammy's.

The afternoon takes a long slow stroll through what's left of the day, but I'm not impatient. Why should I be? I'm just some harmless drunk, got an early start on the day's inebriation. Time doesn't mean anything to me anymore, except for how much of it stretches between bottles. Play this kind of thing right and you start to believe it yourself.

I'm into my role, so much so that when I see the guy, I stay calm. He's got to be the shooter the Couteaus sent, tall, sharp dresser, whistling a Doc Cheatham tune and walking loose, but the dead eyes give him away. He's looking everywhere but at me. That's the thing about the homeless. They're either invisible, or a nuisance you have to ignore. I ask him for some spare change, but I don't even register for him, his gaze slides right on by.

I watch him make a slow pass by the restaurant, hands in his pockets. He stops, turns back to read the menu, goes in. I start to worry then. Not for me, but for Raul. I'm long past letting anyone else get hurt because of me. But the shooter's back out a moment later. He takes a casual look down my side of the street, then ambles off the other way and I let out a breath I didn't realize I was holding. So much for staying in character.

It takes me a little longer to settle back into my role, but it's an effort well spent, for here he comes walking by again. Lee Street's not exactly the French Quarter—even in the middle of the day Bourbon Street's a lively place—but there's enough going on that he doesn't seem out of place, wandering here and there, window shopping, stopping to buy a cappuccino from a cart at the end of the block, a soft pretzel from another. He finishes them slowly on a bench near the restaurant, one of those iron and wood improvements that the merchants' association put in a few years ago.

He doesn't give up his watch until it gets dark, the stores start to close down, the restaurants are in the middle of their dinner trade. I stay where I am when he leaves. It's a long time until midnight and I might as well wait here as wander the streets. I give it until eleven-thirty before I shuffle off, heading across town to Flood Street. By the time I reach the alley behind the Sovereign Building, it's a little past midnight.

I'm not sure I even expected it to be there again. Maybe, if I'm to believe Sammy, in some other world I come here and find nothing. But as I step around the corner into the alley, everything shifts and sways. I walk into a thick mist that opens up a little after a few paces, but never quite clears. The Ferris wheel's here, but it's farther away than I expected.

I'm standing in a field of corn stubble, the sky immense above me, the sound of crickets filling the air, a full moon hanging up at the top of the sky. A long way across the corn field I can see a darkened carnival, the midway closed, all the rides shut down. The Ferris wheel rears above it, a black shadow that blocks the stars with its shape. I pause for a long time, taking it all in, not sure any of this is real, unable to deny that it's here in front of me all the same. Finally I start walking once more, across the field, past the darkened booths, dry dirt scuffling underfoot. It's quiet here, hushed like a graveyard, the way it feels in your mind when you're stepping in between the gravestones.

It takes me a long time to reach the wheel. The sign's still there above the entrance, "Crowded After Hours," but the seats are all empty. The spokes of the wheel and the immense frame holding it seem to be made of enormous bones, the remains of behemoths and monsters. The crosspieces are carved with roses, the paint flaked and peeling where it isn't faded. Vines grow up and around the entire structure and its massive wooden base appears to be half-covered with a clutter of fallen leaves.

No, I realize. Not leaves, but masks. Hundreds of them, some half-buried in the dirt, or covered by the vines that grow everywhere like kudzu, their painted features flaked and faded like the roses. But others seem to be almost brand new, so new the paint looks like it'd be tacky to the touch. Old or new, they run the gamut of human expression. Smiling, laughing, weeping, angry . . .

I start to move a little closer to have a better look at them, when a man suddenly leans out of the ticket booth. My pulse jumps into overtime.

"Ticket, please," he says.

I blink, looking at him, an old black man in a top hat, teeth gleaming in the moonlight.

"I don't have a ticket," I tell him.

"You need a ticket," he says.

"Where can I buy one?"

He laughs. "Not that kind of ticket, Spyboy."

Before I can ask him what he means, how he knows my name, the mists come flowing back, thick and impenetrable for a long moment. When they clear once more, I'm back in the alleyway. Or maybe I never left. The whole experience sits inside my head like a dream.

I look up to the roof of the Sovereign Building, remembering how it was last night. The door Sammy led me through is right here in front of me. I don't even hesitate, but open it up and start climbing the stairs. When I get out onto the roof, I walk across the gravel once more to where Sammy and I stood last night. The mists are back and I can see the wheel again through them, turning slowly, all the seats filled. I watch for a long time until the harlequin and the man with the blue moon for a head come into sight. The blue moon looks at me and lifts a hand.

There's something in that hand, a small slip of paper or cardboard. I step closer to the edge of the roof and see it's a ticket. I'm so caught up in the presence of the wheel and what the blue moon's holding, that the footsteps on the gravel behind me don't really register until someone calls my name.

"Spyboy."

I don't need to hear the French accent to know who it is. I turn to find the shooter standing there. He either doesn't see the wheel, or he's only got eyes for me.

"I have a message for you," he says. "From Madame Couteau."

I see the pistol in his hand, hanging by his side. As he starts to lift it, I turn and jump, launching myself toward the seat where the blue moon Sammy is holding my ticket.

And all those possibilities open up into new worlds.

Maybe I just hit the pavement below.

Maybe I take a bullet, still hit the pavement, but I'm dead before the impact.

Maybe I reached the wheel, hands slipping on the bone joints, my scrabbling feet finding purchase, allowing me to climb up into my seat, my face falling off like a mask to reveal another face underneath, made up like a harlequin. A carnival Spyboy.

Or maybe I never went to the Beanery that night, didn't meet Sammy, turned in early and went to work the next day.

They're all possible. Maybe somewhere, they're all true.

I sit there in the gently swaying seat and look out over a darkened carnival, out past the fields of corn stubble, into the mists where anything can happen, everything is true. I remember what Sammy told me last night, though it seems like an eternity ago.

You're thinking of the outside, he told me. *Concentrate on all the journeys you can take inside.*

I have, I had, a thousand thousand lives out there. Past, present, future, they're all happening at the same time in my head. This world, all the other worlds that are born every time I made a choice, all these lives that I can journey through inside my head.

I guess what I can't figure out is, which one is really mine. Either I'm living one of those lives and dreaming this, or I'm here and those lives belong to someone else, someone I once was, someone I could have been.

I sit there beside the blue moon Sammy, the ticket he gave me held in my hand, and I think about it as the wheel takes our seat up, all the way to where the stars are whispering and the Ferris wheel kisses the sky.

The Buffalo Man

The oaks were full of crows, as plentiful as leaves, more of the raucous black-winged birds than Jilly had ever seen together in one place. She kept glancing out the living room window at them, expecting some further marvel, though their enormous gathering was marvel enough all on its own. The leaded panes framed group after group of them in perfect compositions that made her itch to draw them in the sketchbook she hadn't thought to bring along.

"There are an awful lot of crows out there this evening," she said after her hundredth inspection of them.

"You'll have to forgive her," the professor told their hosts with a smile. "Sometimes I think she's altogether too concerned with crows and what they're up to. For some people it's the stock market, others it's the weather. It's a fairly new preoccupation, but it does keep her off the streets."

"As if."

"Before this it was fruit faeries," the professor added, leaning forward from the sofa where he was sitting, his tone confidential.

"Wasn't."

The professor *tch*ed. "As good as was."

"Well, we all need a hobby," Cerin said.

"This is, of course, true," Jilly allowed, after first sticking out her tongue at the pair of them. "It's so sad that neither of you have one."

She'd been visiting with Professor Dapple, involved in a long, meandering conversation concerning Kickaha Mountain ballads vis-à-vis their relationship to British folktales, when he suddenly announced that he was due for tea at the Kelledys' that afternoon and did she care to join them? Was the Pope Catholic? Did the moon have wings? Well, one out of two wasn't bad, and of course she had to come.

The Kelledys' rambling house on Stanton Street was a place of endless fascination for her with its old-fashioned architecture, all gables and gingerbread, with climbing vines and curious rooflines. The rooms were full of great solid pieces of furniture that crouched on Persian carpets and the hardwood floors like sleeping animals, not to mention any number of wonderfully bright and mysterious things perched on the shelves and sideboards, on the windowsills and meeting rails, like so many half-hidden lizards and birds. And then there were the oak trees that surrounded the building, a regular forest of them larger and taller than anywhere else in the city, each one of them easily a hundred years old.

The house was magic in her eyes, as much as the couple who inhabited it, and she loved any excuse to come by for a visit. On a very lucky day, Cerin would bring out his harp, Meran her flute, and they would play a haunting, heart-lifting music that Jilly never heard except from them.

"I didn't know fruit had their own faeries," Meran said. "The trees, yes, but not the individual fruit itself."

"I wonder if there are such things as acorn faeries," Cerin said. "I must ask my father."

Jilly gave a theatrical sigh. "We're having far too long a conversation about fruit and nuts, and whether or not they have faeries, and not nearly enough about great, huge, cryptic parliaments of crows."

"It would be a murder, actually," the professor put in.

"Whatever. I think it's wonderfully mysterious."

"At this time of the day," Meran said, "they'd be gathering together to return to their roosts."

Jilly shook her head. "I'm not so sure. But if that *is* the case, then they've decided to roost in your yard."

She turned back to look out over the leaf-covered lawn that lay under the trees, planning some witty observation that would make them see just how supremely marvelous it all was, but the words died unborn in her throat as she watched a large, bald-headed Buddha of a man step onto the Kelledys' walk. He was easily the largest human being she'd ever seen—she couldn't guess how many hundreds of pounds he must weigh—but oddly enough he moved with the supple grace of a dancer a fraction his size. His dark suit was obviously expensive and beautifully tailored, and his skin was as black as a raven's wing. As he came up the walk, the crows became agitated and flew around him, filling the air with their hoarse cries—growing so loud that the noise resounded inside the house with the windows closed.

But neither the enormous man, nor the actions of the crows, were what had dried up the words in Jilly's throat. It was the limp figure of a slender man that the dapper Buddha carried in his arms. In sharp contrast, he was poorly dressed for the brisk weather, wearing only a raggedy shirt and jeans so worn they had almost no color left in them. His face and arms were pale as alabaster, even his braided hair was white—yet another striking contrast to the man carrying him. She experienced something familiar, yet strange when she gazed on his features, like taking out a favorite old sweater she hadn't worn in years and feeling at once quite unacquainted with it and affectionately comfortable when she put it on.

"That's no crow," Cerin said, having stepped up to the window to stand beside Jilly's chair.

Meran joined him, then quickly went to the door to let the new visitor in. The professor rose from the sofa when she ushered the man and his burden into the room, waving a hand toward the seat he'd just quit.

"Put him down here," he said.

The black man nodded his thanks. Stepping gracefully across the room, he knelt and carefully laid the man out on the sofa.

"It's been a long time, Lucius," the professor said as the man straightened up. "You look different."

"I woke up."

"Just like that?"

Lucius gave him a slow smile. "No. A red-haired storyteller gave me a lecture about responsibility and I realized she was right. It had been far too long since I'd assumed any."

He turned his attention to the Kelledys then.

"I need a healing," he said.

There was something formal in the way he spoke the words, the way a subject might speak to his ruler, though there was nothing remotely submissive in his manner.

"There are no debts between us," Cerin said.

"But now—"

"Nonsense," Meran told him. "We've never turned away someone in need of help before and we don't mean to start now. But you'll have to tell us how he was injured."

She knelt down on the floor beside the sofa as she spoke. Reaching out, she touched her middle finger to the center of his brow, then lifted her hand and moved it down his torso, her palm hovering about an inch above him.

"I know little more than you, at this point," Lucius said.

"Do you at least know who he is?" Cerin asked.

Lucius shook his head. "The crow girls found him lying by a Dumpster out behind the Williamson Street Mall. They tried to heal him, but all they could manage was to keep him from slipping further away. Maida said he was laid low by ill will."

Jilly's ears perked up at the mention of the crow girls. They were the real reason for her current interest in all things corvid, a pair of punky, black-haired young women who seemed to have the ability to change your entire perception of the world simply by stepping into the periphery of your life. Ever since she'd first seen them in a café, she kept spotting them in the most unlikely places, hearing the most wonderful stories about them. Whenever she saw a crow now, she'd peer closely at it, wondering if this was one of the pair in avian form.

"That makes it more complicated," Meran said.

Sitting back on her heels, she glanced at Lucius. He gave her an apologetic look.

"I know he has buffalo blood," he told her.

"Yes, I see that."

"What did Maida mean by ill will?" Cerin asked. "He doesn't appear to have any obvious physical injuries."

Lucius shrugged. "You know how they can be. The more they tried to explain it to me, the less I understood."

Jilly had her own questions as she listened to them talk, such as why hadn't someone immediately called for an ambulance, or why had this Lucius brought the injured man here, rather than to a hospital? But there was a swaying, eddying sensation in the air, a feeling that the world had turned a step from the one everyone knew and they now had half a foot in some other, perhaps more perilous, realm. She decided to be prudent for a change and listen until she understood better what was going on.

She wasn't the only one puzzled, it seemed.

"We need to know more," Meran said.

Lucius nodded. "I'll see if I can find them."

"I'll come with you," Cerin said.

Lucius hesitated for a long moment, then gave another nod and the two men left the house. Jilly half expected them to fly away, but when she looked out the window she saw them walking under the oaks toward the street like an ordinary, if rather mismatched, pair, Lucius so broad and large that the tall harper at his side appeared slender to the point of skinniness. The crows remained in the trees this time, studying the progress of the two men until they were lost from sight.

"I have some things to fetch," Meran said. "Remedies to try. Will you watch over our patient until I get back?"

Jilly glanced at the professor.

"Um, sure," she said.

And then the two of them were alone with the mysteriously stricken man. Laid low by ill will. What did *that* mean?

Jilly pulled a footstool over to the sofa where Meran had been kneeling and sat down. Looking at the man, she found herself wishing for pencil and sketchbook again. He was so handsome, like a figure from a Pre-Raphaelite painting. Except for the braids and raggedy clothes, of course. Then she felt guilty for where her thoughts had taken her. Here was the poor man, half dead on the sofa, and all she could think about was drawing him.

"He doesn't look very happy, does he?" she said.

"Not very."

"Where do you know Lucius from?"

The professor took off his wire-rimmed glasses and gave them a polish they didn't need before replacing them.

"I can't remember where or when I first met him," he said. "But it was a long time ago—before the war, certainly. Not long after that he became somewhat of a recluse. At first I'd go visit him at his house—he lives just down the street from here—but then it came to the point where he grew so withdrawn that one might as well have been visiting a sideboard or a chair. Finally I stopped going 'round."

"What happened to him, do you think?"

The professor shrugged. "Hard to tell with someone like him."

"You're being deliberately mysterious, aren't you?"

"Not at all. There just isn't much to say. I know he's related to the crow girls. Their grandfather, or an uncle or something. I never did quite find out which."

"So that's why all the crows are out there."

"I doubt it," the professor said. "He's corbæ, all right, but raven not crow."

Jilly felt a thrill of excitement. A raven uncle, crow girls, the man on the sofa with his buffalo blood. She was in the middle of some magical story for once, rather than on the edges of it, looking in, and her proximity made everything feel bright and clear and very much in focus. Then she felt guilty again because it had taken someone getting hurt to draw her into this story. Considering the unfortunate circumstances, it didn't seem right to be so excited by it.

She turned back to look at the pale man, lying there so still.

"I wonder if he can turn into a buffalo," she said.

"I believe it's more of a metaphorical designation," the professor told her, "rather than an actual shapeshifting option."

Jilly shook her head. She could remember the night in Old Market when she'd first seen the crow girls slip from crow to girl and back again. It wasn't exactly something you forgot, though oddly enough the memory did have a tendency to try to slip away from her. To make sure it didn't, she'd fixed the moment in pigment and hung the finished painting on the wall of her studio as a reminder.

"I don't think so," she said. "I think it's a piece of real magic."

She leaned closer to the man and reached forward to push aside a few long white hairs that had come to lie across his lashes. When she touched him, that swaying, eddying sensation returned, stronger than ever. She had long enough to say, "Oh, my," then the world slipped away and she was somewhere else entirely.

2

"I *have* resumed my responsibilities," Lucius said as the two men walked to his house a few blocks farther down Stanton Street.

Cerin gave him a sidelong glance. "Guilt's a terrible thing, isn't it?"

"What do you mean?"

The harper shrugged. "It makes you question people's motives, even when they're as straightforward as my wanting to help you find a pair of somewhat wayward and certainly mischievous relatives."

"They can be a handful," Lucius said. "It's possible we'll find them more quickly with your help."

Cerin hid a smile. He knew that was about as much of an apology as he'd be getting, but he didn't mind. He hadn't really wanted one. He'd only wanted Lucius to understand that no one was holding him to blame for withdrawing from the world the way he had— at least no one in the Kelledy household was. Responsibility was a sharp-edged sword that sometimes cut too deep, even for an old spirit such as Lucius Portsmouth.

So all he said was, "Um-hmm," then added, "Odd winter we've been having, isn't it? So close to Christmas and still no snow. I wonder whose fault *that* is."

Lucius sighed. "You can be insufferable."

This time Cerin didn't hide his smile. "As Jilly would say, it's just this gift I have."

"But I appreciate your confidence."

"Apology accepted," Cerin told him, unable to resist.

"You wouldn't have any crow blood in you, would you?"

"Nary a drop."

Lucius harrumphed and muttered, "I'd still like to see the results of a DNA test."

"What was that?"

"I said, I wonder where they keep their nest."

Stanton Street was lined with oaks, not so old as those that grew around the Kelledy house, but they were stately monarchs nonetheless. Having reached the Rookery where Lucius lived, the two men paused to look up where the bare branches of the trees laid their pattern against the sky above. Twilight had given way to night and they could see stars peeking down from among the boughs. Stars, but no black-haired, giggling crow girls. Lucius called, his voice ringing up into the trees like a raven's cry.

Kaark. Kaark. Tok.

There was no reply.

"They weren't so happy with this foundling of theirs," Lucius said, turning to his companion. "At first I thought it was because their healing didn't take, but when I carried him to your house, I began to understand their uneasiness."

He called again, but there was still no response.

"What do you find so troubling about him?" Cerin asked.

Though he had an idea. There were people and places that were like doors to other realms, to the spiritworld and to worlds deeper and older than that. In their presence, you could feel the world shift uneasily underfoot, the ties binding you to it loosening their grip—an unsettling sensation for anyone, but more so for those who could normally control where they walked.

The still, pale man with his white braids had been like that.

Lucius said as much, then added, "The trouble with such doors isn't so much what they open into, as what they can close you from."

Cerin nodded. To be denied access to the spiritworld would be like losing a sense. One's hearing, one's taste.

"So you don't think they'll come," he said.

Lucius shrugged. "They can be willful . . . not so responsible as some."

"Let me try."

"Never let it be said I turned down someone's help."

Cerin smiled. He closed his eyes and reached back to his home, back to a room on the second floor. A harp stood there with a rose carved into the wood where curving neck met forepillar. His fingers twitched at his sides and the sound of that roseharp was suddenly in the air all around them, a calling-on song that rose up as though from the ground and spun itself out against the branches above, then higher still, as though reaching for the stars.

"A good trick," Lucius said. "Cousin Brandon does much the same with his instrument, though in his case, he's the only one to hear its tones."

"Perhaps you're not listening hard enough," Cerin said.

"Perhaps."

He might have said more, but there came a rustling in the

boughs above them and what appeared to be two small girls were suddenly there, hanging upside down from the lowest branch by their hooked knees, laughter crinkling in the corners of their eyes while they tried to look solemn.

"Oh, that was veryvery mean," Maida said.

Zia gave an upside down nod. "Calling us with magic music."

"We'd give you a good bang on the ear."

"Reallyreally we would."

"Except the music's so pretty."

"Ever so truly pretty."

"And magic, of course."

Cerin let the harping fall silent.

"We need you to tell us more about the man you found," he said.

The crow girls exchanged glances.

"Surely such wise and clever people as you don't need help from us," Maida said.

"That would be all too very silly," Zia agreed.

"And yet we do," Cerin told them. "Will you help us?"

There was another exchange of glances between the pair, then they dropped lightly to the ground.

"Are there sweets in your house?" Zia asked.

"Mountains of them."

"Oh, good," Maida said. She gave Lucius a sad look. "Old Raven never has any sweets for us."

Zia nodded. "It's veryvery sad. What kind do you have?"

"I'm not sure."

"Well, come on," Maida said, taking Cerin's hand. "We'd better hurry up and find out."

Zia nodded, looking a little anxious. "Before someone else eats them all."

In this mood, Cerin didn't know that they'd get anything useful out of the pair, but at least they'd agreed to come. He'd let Meran sort out how to handle them once he got them home.

Zia took his other hand and with the pair of them tugging on his hands, they started back up Stanton Street. Lucius taking the rear, a smile on his face as the crow girls chattered away to Cerin about exactly what their favorite sweets were.

3

Jilly was no stranger to the impossible, so she wasn't as surprised as some might have been to find herself transported from the Kelledys' living room, full of friendly shadows and known corners, to an alleyway that could have been anywhere. Still, she wasn't entirely immune to the surprise of it all and couldn't ignore the vague, unsettled feeling that was tiptoeing up and down the length of her spine.

Because that was the thing about the impossible, wasn't it? When you did experience it, well, first of all, hello, it proved to be all too possible, and secondly, it made you rethink all sorts of things that you'd blindly agreed to up to this point. Things like the world being round—was gravity really so clever that it kept people on the upside down part of the world from falling off into the sky? That Elvis was dead—if he was, then why did *so* many people still see him? That UFOs were actually weather balloons or swamp gas— never mind the improbability of so many balloons going AWOL, how did a swamp get indigestion in the first place?

So being somewhere she shouldn't be didn't render Jilly helpless, stunned, or much more than curiously surprised. By looking up at the skyline, she placed herself in an alleyway behind the Williamson Street Mall, right where the crow girls had found—

Her gaze dropped to the mound of litter beside the closest Dumpster, and there he was, Meran's comatose patient, except here, in this wherever she was, he was sitting on top of the garbage, knees drawn up to his chin, and regarding her with a gloomy gaze. She focused on the startling green of his eyes. Odd, she thought. Weren't albinos supposed to have red, or at least pink eyes?

She waited a moment to give him the opportunity to speak first. When he didn't, she cleared her throat.

"Hello," she said. "Did you bring me here?"

He frowned at the question. "I don't know you . . . do I?"

"Well, we haven't been formally introduced or anything, and while you weren't exactly the life of the party when I first met you, right now we're sharing the same space somewhere else as well as here, which is sort of like us knowing each other, or at least me knowing you."

He gave her a confused look.

"Oh, that's right. You wouldn't remember, being unconscious and all. I'm not sure of all the details myself, but you're supposed to have been, and I quote, 'laid low by ill will,' and when I went to brush some hair out of your eyes, I found myself here. With you again, except you're awake this time. How were you laid low by this ill will? I'm assuming someone hit you, which would be ill-willish enough so far as I can see, but somehow I think it's more than that."

She paused and gave him a rueful smile. "I guess I'm not doing a very good job with this explanation, am I?"

"How can you be so cheerful?" he asked her.

Jilly drew a battered wooden fruit crate over to where he was sitting and sat down herself.

"What do you mean?" she asked.

"The world is a terrible place," he said. "Every day, every moment, its tragedies deepen, the mean-spiritedness of its inhabitants quickens and escalates until one can't imagine a kindness existing anywhere for more than an instant before being suffocated."

"Well, it's not perfect," Jilly agreed. "But that doesn't mean we have to—"

"I can see that you've been hurt and disappointed by it—cruelly so, when you were much younger. Yet here you sit before me, relatively trusting, certainly cheerful, optimism bubbling in you like a fountain. How can this be?"

Jilly was about to make some lighthearted response, speaking without thinking as she did too often, but then part of what he'd said really registered.

"How would you know what my life was like when I was a kid?"

He shrugged. "Our histories are written on our skin—how can you be surprised that I wouldn't know?"

"It's not something I've ever heard of before."

"Perhaps you have to know how to look for the stories."

Well, that made a certain kind of sense, Jilly thought. There were so many hidden things in the world that only came into focus when you learned how to pay attention to them, so why not stories on people's skin?

"So," she said. "I guess nobody could lie to you, could they?"

"Why do you think the world depresses me the way it does?"

"Except it's not all bad. You can't tell me that the only stories people have are bad ones."

"They certainly outweigh the good."

"Maybe *you're* not looking in the right place."

"I understand thinking the best of people," he said. "Looking for the good in them, rather than the wrongs they've done. But ignoring the wrongs is almost like condoning them, don't you think?"

"I don't ignore them," Jilly told him. "But I don't dwell on them either."

"Even when you've been hurt as much as you have?"

"Maybe especially because of that," she said. "What I try to do is make people feel better. It's hard to be mean, when you're smiling, or when a laugh's building up inside you."

"That's a child's view of the world."

Jilly shook her head. "A child lives in the now, and they're usually pretty self-absorbed. Which is what can make them unaware of other people's feelings at times."

"I meant simplistic."

Jilly wouldn't accept that either. "I'm aware of what's wrong. I just try to balance it with something good. I know I can't solve every problem in the world, but if I try to help the ones I come upon as I come upon them, I think it makes a difference. And you know, most people aren't really bad. They're just kind of thoughtless at times."

"How can you believe that? Listen to them and then tell me again how they're really kind at heart."

Jilly's head suddenly filled with conversation.

. . . why I have to buy anything for that old bag, anyway . . .

. . . hello, can't we leave the kids at home for one afternoon . . . the miserable, squalling monsters . . .

. . . hear that damn song one more time, I'll kill . . .

No, they were thoughts, she realized, stolen from the shoppers in the mall that lay on the other side of the alley's wall. It was impossible to tell their age or gender, except by inference.

. . . damn bells . . . oh, it's the Sally Ann, doing their annual beg-a-thon . . . hey, nice rack on her . . . wonder why a looker like her's collecting money for losers . . .

. . . doesn't get me what I want this year, I'll show him what being miserable is all about . . .

Jilly blinked when the voices were suddenly gone again.

"Now do you see?" her companion said.

"Those thoughts are taken out of context with the rest of their lives," Jilly told him. "Just because someone has an ugly thought, it doesn't make them a bad person."

"Oh no?"

"And being kind oneself does make a difference."

"Against the great swell of indifferent unkindnesses that threaten to wash us completely away with the force of a tsunami?"

"Is this what they meant with the ill will that laid you low?"

"What who meant?"

"The crow girls. They're the ones who found you and brought you to the Kelledys' house because they couldn't heal you themselves."

A small smile touched his features. "I remember some crow girls I saw once. Their good humor could make yours seem like grumbling, but they carried the capacity for large angers as well."

"Was that when you were a buffalo?"

"What do you know about buffalo?"

"You're supposed to have buffalo blood," Jilly explained.

He gave her a slow nod.

"Those-who-came," he said. "They slaughtered the buffalo. Then, when the People danced and called the buffalo spirit back, they slaughtered the People as well. That's the history I read on the skin of the world—not only here, but everywhere. Blood and pain and hunger and hatred. It's an old story that has no end. How can a smile, a laugh, a good deed, stand up against the weight of such a history?"

"I . . . I guess it can't," Jilly said. "But you still have to try."

"Why?"

"Because that's all you can do. If you don't try to stand up against the darkness, it swallows you up."

"And if in the end, there is only darkness? If the world is meant to end in darkness?"

Jilly shook her head. She refused to believe it.

"How can you deny it?" he asked.

"It's just . . . if there's only supposed to be darkness, then why were we given light?"

For a long moment, he sat there, shoulders drooped, staring down at his hands. When he finally looked up, there was something in his eyes that Jilly couldn't read.

"Why indeed?" he said softly.

4

When Meran returned to the living room it was to find Jilly slumped across the body of her patient, Professor Dapple standing over the pair of them, hands fluttering nervously in front of him.

"What's happened?" she said, quickly crossing the room.

"I don't know. One moment she was talking to me, then she leaned over and touched his cheek and she simply collapsed."

He moved aside as Meran knelt down by the sofa once more. Before she could study the problem more closely, the roseharp began to play upstairs.

The professor looked surprised, his gaze lifting to the ceiling.

"I thought Cerin had gone with Lucius," he said.

"He did," Meran told him. "That's only his harp playing."

The professor regarded her for a long slow moment.

"Of course," he finally said.

Meran smiled. "It's nothing to be nervous about. Really. I'm more worried about what's happened to Jilly."

The sofa was wide enough that, with the professor's help, she was able to lay Jilly out beside the stranger. Whatever had struck Jilly down was as much of a mystery to Meran as the stranger's original ailment. In her mind, she began to run through a list of other healers she could contact to ask for help when there was a sudden commotion at the front door. A moment later the crow girls trooped in with Cerin and Lucius following behind them.

"Jilly . . . ?" Cerin began.

Meran briefly explained what little she knew of what had happened since they'd been gone.

"We can't help him," Zia said before anyone else could speak.

"We tried," Maida added, "but we weren't so very useful, were we?"

Zia shook her head.

"Not very useful at all," Maida said.

"But," Zia offered, "we could maybe help her."

Maida nodded and leaned closer to peer at Jilly. "She's very pretty, isn't she? I think we know her."

"She's Geordie's friend," Zia said.

"Oh, yes." Zia looked at Cerin. "But he plays much nicer music."

"Ever so very much more."

"It's for listening to, you see. Not for making you do things."

"I'm sorry," Cerin said. "But we needed to get your attention."

"Well, we're ever so very attentive now," Maida told him.

Whereupon the pair of them went very still and fixed Cerin with expectant gazes. He turned helplessly to his wife.

"How can you help Jilly?" she asked.

"Jilly," Maida repeated. "Is that her name?"

"Silly Jilly."

"Willy-nilly."

"Up down dilly."

"I'm sure making fun of her name's helpful," Lucius said.

"Oh, pooh," Maida said. "Old Raven never gets a joke."

"That's the trouble with this raven, all right," Zia agreed.

"We've seen jokes fly right out the window when they see he's in the room."

"About Jilly," Meran tried again.

"Well, you see," Maida said, suddenly serious. "The buffalo man is a piece of the Grace."

"And we can't help the Grace—she has to help herself."

Maida nodded. "But Jilly—"

Zia giggled, then quickly put a hand over her mouth.

"—only needs to be shown the way back to her being all of one piece again," Maida finished.

"You mean her spirit has gone somewhere?" Cerin asked.

"Duh."

"How can we bring her back?" Meran asked.

The crow girls looked at Cerin.

"Well," Zia said. "If you know her calling-on song as well as you do ours, that would maybe work."

"I'll get the roseharp," Cerin said, standing up.

"Now he needs it in hand," Lucius said.

Cerin started to frame a reply, but then he looked at Meran and left the room.

"We were promised sweets," Maida said.

Zia nodded. "The actual promise was that there'd be mountains of them."

"Do you mind if we finish up here first?" Meran asked.

"Oh, no," Maida said. "We love to wait."

Zia gave Meran a bright smile. "Honestly."

"Anticipation is so much better than being attentive."

"Though they're much the same, in some ways."

"Because they both involve waiting, you see," Maida explained, her smile as bright as her companion's.

Meran stifled a sigh and returned their smile. She'd forgotten how maddening the crow girls could be. Normally she enjoyed bantering with their tricksy kind, but at the moment she was too worried about Jilly to join the fun. And then there was the stranger whose appearance had started it all. They hadn't even *begun* to deal with him.

When Cerin returned with the roseharp, he sat down on a footstool and drew the instrument onto his lap.

"Play something Jilly," Maida suggested.

"Did you say silly?" Zia asked. "Because that's not being serious at all, you know, making jokes about very serious things."

"I didn't say silly."

"I think maybe you did."

Cerin ignored the pair of them and turned to his wife. "I might not be able to bring her back," he said. "Because of him. Because of the doors he can close."

"I know," Meran said. "You can only try."

5

"I think I know now what the crow girls meant," Jilly said.

The buffalo man raised his eyebrows questioningly.

"About this ill will business," Jilly explained. "Every ugly thought or bad deed you come into contact with steals away a piece of your vitality, doesn't it? It's like erosion. The pieces keep falling away until finally you get so worn away that you slip into a kind of coma."

"Something like that."

"Has this happened before?"

He nodded.

"So what happens next?"

"I die."

Jilly stared at him, not sure she'd heard him right.

"You . . . die."

He nodded. "And then I come back and the cycle begins all over again."

Neither of them spoke for a long moment then. It was quiet in the alley where they sat, but Jilly could hear the traffic go by down the block where the alley opened into the street. There was a repetitive pattern to the sound, bus, bus, a car horn, a number of vehicles in a group, then the buses again.

"I guess what I don't understand," Jilly finally said, "is why all the good things in the world don't balance it out—you know, recharge your vitality."

"They're completely overshadowed," he said.

Jilly shook her head. "I don't believe that. I know there are awful things in the world, but I also know there's more that's good."

"Then why am I so weak right now—in this, your season of goodwill?"

"I think it's because you don't let the good in anymore. You don't trust there to be any good left, so you've put up these protective walls that keep it out."

"And the bad? Why does it continue to affect me?"

"Because you concentrate on it," Jilly said. "And by doing that, you let it get in. It's like you're doing the exact opposite to what you should be doing."

"If only it could be so simple."

"But it is," she said. "In the end, it always comes down to small, simple things, because that's the way the world really works. We're the ones who make it so complicated. I mean, think about it. If everybody really and truly treated each other the way they'd want to be treated, all the problems of the world would be solved.

Nobody'd starve, because nobody'd want to go hungry themselves. Nobody steal, or kill, or hurt each other, because they wouldn't want that to happen to themselves."

"So what stops them from doing so?" he asked.

"Trust. Or rather a lack of it. Too many people don't trust the other person to treat them right, so they just dig in, accumulating stuff, thinking only of themselves or their own small group—you know, family, company, community, whatever. A tribal thing." She hesitated a moment, then added, "And that's what's holding you back, too. You don't trust the good to outweigh the bad."

"I don't know that I even can."

"No one can help you with that," Jilly told him. "That's something that can only come from inside you."

He gave her a slow nod. "Maybe I will try harder, the next time."

"What next time? What's wrong with right now?"

He held out his arms. "If you could read the history written on my skin, you would not need to ask that question."

Jilly pushed up her sleeves and held out her own arms.

"Look," she said. "You read what I went through as a kid. I'm no better or stronger or braver than you are. But I am determined to leave things a little better than they were before I got here. That's what gets me through. And I have to admit there's a certain selfishness involved. You see, I want to live in that better world. I know it's not going to happen unless we all clean up our act and I know I can't make anybody else do that. But I'll be damned if I don't do it myself. You know, like a Kickaha friend of mine says, live large and walk in Beauty."

"You are very . . . persuasive."

Jilly grinned. "It's just this gift I have."

She stood up and offered him a hand.

"So what do you say, buffalo man? You want to give this life another shot?"

He allowed her to help him up to his feet.

"There's a problem," he said.

"No, no, no. Ignore the negatives, if only for now."

"You don't understand. The door that brought us here—it only opens one way."

"What door?"

"My old life was finished and I was on my way to the new. All of this—" He made a motion with his hand to encompass everything around them. "Is only a memory."

"Whose memory?" Jilly asked, getting a bad feeling.

"Mine. The memory of a dying man."

She smiled brightly. "So live. I thought we'd already been through this earlier."

"I would. You've convinced me enough of that. Only there's no way back."

"There's always a way back . . . isn't there?"

He didn't answer. He didn't have to.

"Oh, great. I get to be in a magical adventure only it turns out to be like a train on a one-way track and we left the happy ending station miles back."

"I'm sorry."

She took his hand and gave it a squeeze. "Me, too."

6

"Nothing's happening," Maida said.

Zia peered at the two still bodies on the sofa. She gave Jilly a gentle poke with her finger.

"She's still veryvery far away," she agreed.

Cerin sighed and let his fingers fall from the strings of the rose-harp. The music echoed on for a few moments, then all was still.

"I tried to put all the things she loves into the calling-on," he said. "Painting and friendship and crows and whimsy, but it's not working. Wherever she's gone, it's further than I can reach."

"How did it happen anyway?" the professor asked. "All she did was touch him. Meran did the same and she wasn't taken away."

"Jilly's too open and trusting," Meran said. "She didn't think to guard herself from the man's spirit. When we fall away into death, most of us will grab hold of anything we can to stay our fall. That's what happened to her—he grabbed her and held on hard."

"He's dying?"

Meran glanced at the professor and nodded.

"I should never have brought him here," Lucius said.

"You couldn't have known."

"It's our fault," Zia said.

Maida nodded glumly. "Oh, we're the most miserably bad girls, we are."

"Let's worry about whose fault it was some other time," Meran said. "Right now I want to concentrate on where he could have taken her."

"I've never died," Lucius said, "so I can't say where a dying man would draw another's soul, but I've withdrawn from the world . . ."

"And?" Meran prompted him.

"I went into my own mind. I lived in my memories. I didn't *remember*. I lived in them."

"So if we knew who he was," Cerin said. "Then perhaps we could—"

"We don't need to know who he is," Meran broke in. "All we need to know is what he was thinking."

"Would the proverbial life flashing before one's eyes be relevant here?" the professor asked. "Because that could touch on anything."

"We need something more specific," Cerin said.

Meran nodded. "Such as . . . where the crow girls found him. Wouldn't he be thinking of his surroundings at some point?"

"It's still a one-way door," Cerin pointed out.

"But if we can open it even a crack," Lucius said.

Cerin smiled. "Then maybe we can pull them out before it closes on us again."

"We can do that," Maida said.

Zia nodded. "We're very good at opening things."

"Even better when there's sweets inside."

Zia rapped on the man's head with a knuckle.

"Hello, hello in there," she said. "Can you hear me?"

"Zia!" Lucius said.

"Well, how else am I supposed to get his attention?"

"Hold on," Meran said. "Perhaps we're going about this all wrong. Instead of concentrating on the door he is, we should be concentrating on the door Jilly is."

"Oh, good idea," Maida said.

The crow girls immediately turned their attention to Jilly. They leaned close, one on either side, and began whispering in her ears.

7

"So I guess this is sort of like a recording," Jilly said, "except instead of being on pause, we're in a tape loop."

Which was why the traffic noise she heard was so repetitive. Being part of his memory, it, too, was in a loop.

"You have such an interesting way of looking at things," the buffalo man said.

"No, humor me in this. We're in a loop of your memory, right? Well, what's to stop you from thinking of something else? Or concentrating and getting us past the loop."

"To what purpose?"

"To whatever comes next."

"We know what comes next," he said.

"No. You assume we do. The last thing you seem to remember is lying here in this alleyway. You must have passed out at that point, which is the loop we're in. Except, I showed up and you're conscious and we've been talking—none of this is memory. We're already somewhere else than your memory. So what's to stop you from taking us further?"

"I have no memory beyond the point where I closed my eyes."

But Jilly was on a roll.

"Of course not," she said. "So we'll have to use our imaginations."

"And imagine what?"

"Well, crows would be good for starters. The crow girls would have been flying above, and then they noticed you and . . ." She paused, cocking her head. "Listen. Can you hear that?"

At first he shook his head, but then his gaze lifted and the strip of sky above the alley went dark with crows. A cloud of them blocked the sun, circling just above the rooftops and filling the air with their raucous cries.

"Wow," Jilly said. "You've got a great imagination."

"This isn't my doing," he said.

They watched as two of the birds left the flock and came spiraling down on their black wings. Just before they reached the pavement, they changed into a pair of girls with spiky black hair and big grins.

"Hello, hello!" they cried.

"Hello, yourselves," Jilly said.

She couldn't help but grin back at them.

"We've come to take you home," one of them said.

"You can't say no."

"Everyone will think it's our fault if you don't come."

"And then we won't get any sweets."

"Not that we're doing this for sweets."

"No, we're just very kind-hearted girls, we are."

"Ask anyone."

"Except for Raven."

They were tugging on her hands now, each holding one of hers with two of their own.

"Don't dawdle," the one on her right said.

Jilly looked back at the buffalo man.

"Go on," he said.

She shook her head. "Don't be silly."

For some reason that made the crow girls giggle.

"There's no reason you can't come, too," she said. She turned to look at the crow girls. "There isn't, is there?"

"Well . . ." one of them said.

"I suppose not.

"The door's closed," the buffalo man told them. "I can feel it inside, shut tight."

"Your door's closed," one of the girls agreed.

"But hers is still open."

Still he hesitated. Jilly pulled away from the crow girls and walked over to him.

"Half the trick to living large," she said, "is the living part."

He let her take him by the hand and walk him back to where the crow girls waited. Holding hands, with one of the spiky-haired girls on either side of them, they walked toward the mouth of the alleyway. But before they could get halfway there . . .

*   *   *

Jilly blinked and opened her eyes to a ring of concerned faces.

"We did it, we did it, we did it!" the crow girls cried.

They jumped up from Jilly's side and danced around in a circle, banging into furniture, stepping on toes and generally raising more of a hullabaloo than would seem possible for two such small figures. It lasted only a moment before Lucius put a hand on each of their shoulders and held them firmly in place.

"And very clever you were, too," he said as they squirmed in his grip. "We're most grateful."

Jilly turned to look at the man lying next to her on the sofa.

"How are you feeling?" she asked.

His gaze made a slow survey of the room, taking in the Kelledys, the professor, Lucius and the wriggling crow girls.

"Confused," he said finally. "But in a good way."

The two of them sat up.

"So you'll stay?" Jilly asked. "You'll see it through this time?"

"You're giving me a choice?"

Jilly grinned. "Not likely."

8

Long after midnight, the Kelledys sat in their living room, looking out at the dark expanse of their lawn. The crows were still roosting in the oaks, quiet now except for the odd rustle of feathers, or a soft, querulous croak. Lucius and the crow girls had gone back down the street to the Rookery, but not before the two girls had happily consumed more cookies, chocolates and soda pop than seemed humanly possible. But then, they weren't human, they were corbæ. The professor and Jilly had returned to their respective homes as well, leaving only a preoccupied buffalo man who'd finally fallen asleep in one of the extra rooms upstairs.

"Only a few more days until Christmas," Cerin said.

"Mmm."

"And still no snow."

"Mmm."

"I'm thinking of adopting the crow girls."

Meran gave him a sharp look.

He smiled. "Just seeing if you were paying attention. What were you thinking of?"

"If there's a word for a thing because it happens, or if it happens because there's a word for it."

"I'm not sure I'm following you."

Meran shrugged. "Life, death. Good, bad. Kind, cruel. What was the world like before we had language?"

"Mercurial, I'd think. Like the crow girls. One thing would flow into another. Nothing would have really been separate from anything else because everything would have been made up of pieces of everything else."

"It's like that now."

Cerin nodded. "Except we don't think of it that way. We have the words to say this is one thing, this is another."

"So we've lost . . . what? A kind of harmony?"

"Perhaps. But we gained free will."

Meran sighed. "Why did we have to give up the one to gain the other?"

"I don't know for sure, but I'd guess it's because we need to be individuals. Without our differences, without our needing to communicate with one another, we'd lose our ability to create art, to love, to dream . . ."

"To hate. To destroy."

"But most of us strive for harmony. The fact that we can fall into the darkness, is what makes our choice to reach for the light such a precious thing."

Meran leaned her head on his shoulder.

"When did you become so wise?" she asked.

"When you chose me to be your companion on your journey into the light."

Second Chances

There was a time, long ago, when speaking was a ceremony. This was before written laws and books and all the other little boxes we've got to put words in now. Back then, everything had a voice. The land, people, animals. It was all tribes, and words were a tribe of their own, a ceremony we could share with each other, an allowance that cut across species, connecting crow and woman and cedar and stream. Because everything was connected in those days. Still is, I guess, but we don't see the pattern of it so clearly anymore. What we said had weight in those days because its effects could carry on for generations. We didn't speak about the world, we spoke the world into being.

Those times are gone now. But every once in a while something stirs that old tribe and some of those words wake up. And then, for a moment, anything can happen.

* * *

I found myself in the Harp one night at the tail end of the year. It was a music night—not a session; they'd set up a little stage in one corner of the bar and the Kelledys were playing, harp and flute, a few songs, a lot of stories. I'd planned to stop in for a pint and then go, but the tunes got my foot tapping and the stories held me to the barstool. There are people that need stories, that can't exist without them. I'm one of those people, always have been. Nose in a book, ear cocked for gossip, wouldn't go to bed without a story and that lasted for a lot longer for me than it does for most kids. I still read for an hour or so before I go to sleep.

I didn't recognize a lot of the tunes. They seemed to be mostly original, though in the tradition. But I picked out "Eliz Iza" not long after I got there, and later the flute player sang a haunting, wordless version of "Airde Cuan," the harp backing her up with rich, resonating chords. I remembered both airs from this album by Alan Stivell that I played to death in the seventies. I hadn't heard either of them, or the rest of the album for that matter, in years.

When the harper finished a story that he attributed to Seamus Ennis, about the origins of a piece called "The Gold Ring," and the pair launched into the actual tune, I turned to the bar and ordered another Caffrey's from the barman. A woman sat down beside me, but I barely noticed her. I had a sip of the beer, foam mustaching my upper lip, and returned my attention to the band.

"Joey?" she said. "Joey Straw?"

A closer look told me that I knew her but it still took me a moment to figure out from where. When I did, I couldn't believe that it had taken any time at all. The black-rimmed glasses were what threw me off. The last time I'd seen Annie Ledford she'd been wearing contacts. I decided I liked the glasses. Combined with her short blonde hair and black jeans, they gave her a funky look.

"How've you been, Annie?" I said. "You're looking great."

She could still blush like a schoolgirl. I remember how that used to drive her crazy. I guess it still did, because she bent her head for a moment like she was checking out our footwear. Her eyes were bright behind the glasses when she looked up at me again. I wondered if it was the beer, or loneliness, or if she really was that happy to see me. Time's a funny thing. Sometimes it exaggerates a memory; sometimes it just lets it fade away.

"I've been good," she said. "It's been forever, hasn't it? What have you been up to?"

Nothing I could be proud of, but I figured this wasn't show and tell. I didn't have to go into details.

"Nothing much," I told her. "I've been keeping a low profile. And you?"

Turned out she was a booking agent now. The reason she was here tonight was that she was the one who brought the Kelledys in for the weekend.

"Good choice," I said.

She smiled. "Like it was a hard sell. They always draw a good crowd."

Our conversation died then. I don't get out much, and when I do, I usually keep to myself. But I felt I owed her something. An explanation, if nothing else.

"Look," I said. "About the way I just walked out on you . . ."

"It's okay," she said. "It's not like I didn't hear about your brother."

Yeah, Nicky had been a piece of work all right. He'd still be serving a life sentence in a federal pen for all the things he'd done if he hadn't taken his own life in an NPD jail cell. He was finally arrested for killing a man in Fitzhenry Park, but that came after a lot of years on the run for the murder of his own family. I'll never forget getting the call that night, my father's choked voice as he told me what had happened.

"Everything changed that night," I said, surprised to hear the words coming out of my mouth. "It wasn't just finding out that Nicky was this monster, but the way everybody treated the rest of us. Like we were responsible. Like it was in our blood and we could snap any moment, just like he did. It broke my mother's heart and my father's spirit. My sister's still not talking to any of us. I don't know where she moved, I just know it was far."

"And you?" she asked.

I shrugged.

"I tried calling you," she said. "A lot."

"I went away. I had to. I stopped answering the phone after the first reporter called. Just packed up and left the city."

She didn't say anything for a long moment. On the stage, the harper was announcing the last piece for this set. I had some more of my Caffrey's. The room seemed awfully hot to me.

"I told myself you weren't running away from me," Annie said as the harp began to play a syncopated intro. "From us."

"I wasn't. In the end I realized I was just running away from myself."

"So you came back."

I nodded. "I got tired of drifting, doing piecework. But it hasn't been much better since I got back."

"Were you going to call me?"

I shook my head. "And say what? I figured you had a new life by now, a better one. The last thing you'd need was Nicky Straw's brother back in it again."

"So you're still running," she said.

I gave her a humorless smile. "Only this time I'm doing it standing still."

She gave me a sad nod. "I have to go to the ladies' room. Watch my seat for me, would you?"

"Sure."

"You'll still be here when I get back?"

"I'm not going anywhere," I said.

Though to tell you the truth, I didn't expect her to come back. What was there to come back for?

There was a deep ache in my chest as I watched her go. I guess I always knew that by returning to the city, this day would come. I just thought I'd be better prepared for it.

I was only half aware that the Kelledys had finished their set and some canned music was playing. Generic Irish. Fiddles and pipes, a guitar hammering out the rhythm. A woman sat down in Annie's seat. I started to say something, then realized it was the flute player. She caught me off guard with a warm smile. Up close, I was surprised to see that the green tints in her hair hadn't been put there by the stage lights.

"Are you a friend of Annie's?" she asked.

"We go back a while."

"I'm Meran," she said and offered me her hand.

"Joey Straw," I said as I shook.

Her handclasp took me off guard. Her hand was soft, but the grip showed steel.

"Annie's talked about you," she said.

My heart sank. I live for stories, but I don't like the idea of my life being one for others. Still, what can you do? I looked around for her husband, the harper, thinking he'd come by and our conversation could focus on safer ground. We could talk about their music, maybe. Even the weather. But he was sitting at a table near the stage, chatting with a couple who didn't seem to be old enough to be up this late, never mind ordering a beer. I remember feeling so mature at their age; now they looked like infants to me.

"It's not what you're thinking," Meran went on. "Annie's never blamed you. She talked about you because she missed you."

"I missed her, too," I said, turning back to look at her. "But it's old history now."

"Is it?"

"What do you mean?"

"What is it you're so afraid of?"

"That they were right. That what happened to Nicky could happen to me."

I didn't know why I was telling her this. I should have been saying, look, you seem like a nice lady, but this is really none of your business. But there was something about her that inspired confidences. That called them forth before you could even stop to think about what you were saying, what secrets you were revealing that were better left unspoken.

"Do you really believe that?" she asked.

"Hell, Nicky was a choirboy," I tell her. "What he did—it came out of nowhere. There was no history of, you know, hurting animals and stuff. He wasn't abused—at least not so's I ever knew. Anybody hurt my little brother, I'd have had a piece of him. So you tell me: What happened?"

"Let me tell you a story instead," she said.

That's when she told me about how words had their own tribe, back in some long ago. How when you spoke, you weren't just talking about the world, you were remaking it.

"I don't understand," I said. "Why are you telling me this?"

"Annie's a dear friend of ours. I'd like her to be happy."

"Don't worry. I'm not going to mess up her life again."

Meran shook her head. "I never thought you would."

"How can you say that? You don't even know me."

"The Joey she told me about would never hurt her."

"But I did."

"Yes. But you wouldn't hurt her again, would you?"

"Of course not, but . . ."

This conversation was making my head spin. I felt like I'd been walking forever with my shoes on the wrong feet and my coat on backwards.

"Annie's got her own life now," I said. "And what could I offer her anyway?"

"Truth. Trust. Love."

I felt a strange sense of disassociation. I wondered when Annie was coming back from the ladies' room, if she was coming back at all. But then I realized that time didn't seem to be moving the way it should. It was as though the inside of the pub had turned into a pocket world where everything was different from the world outside its doors, as though I was looking at everything from the corner of my eye. The air swayed. Every minute held the potential of an eternity.

"I can wake up that old tribe of words for you," she said. "Not for long, but for long enough. Tell me which ones you need."

I understood what she was saying, but it didn't make any sense. Things just don't work in the real world the way they do in a story. Strangers only offered magical assistance in fairy tales.

"Look—"

"Don't question it," she said. "You know it can happen."

The weird thing is, I believed her. I can't even begin to explain why. It really did feel like we were sideways to the world at that moment. That anything could happen.

"Magic words," I said. "Can they change the past?"

She shook her head. "They can only change the present."

"But everything we say or do changes the present."

She shook her head again. "Not like this. The words I can wake for you will bring about true transformation. Which will you choose?"

There was no contest. Until I'd seen Annie tonight I hadn't realized what it was that had really brought me back to the city.

"Trust enough for a second chance," I said.

"Done," Meran told me and she smiled.

I heard a rumbling deep underground, like distant thunder reverberating in the belly of the world. The vibration of it rose up, shivering the floor, rattling the glasses and liquor bottles behind the bar. Something swelled inside me, something too big and old and weighty to fit in my body, in my head, in my soul. Then it was gone, like a cat shaking water from its fur.

I looked around, but no one in the pub seemed to have noticed. Only the harper, Meran's husband. He lifted his head and slowly studied the room until his gaze reached us. Then he nodded and returned to his conversation.

"What . . . ?" I began.

"Here she comes," Meran said. She squeezed my elbow before she stepped away. "Now you have to do your part. Earn your second chance."

I turned to see Annie coming toward me and didn't worry about the explanation I'd thought I needed so desperately a moment ago. Everything seemed out of focus right then, except for her. I didn't know where I was going to begin. But I knew I had to try.

"What was Meran talking to you about?" she asked as she sat back down on her stool. "The pair of you looked positively conspiratorial."

"Second chances," I said.

Annie's eyes went bright behind her glasses again.

"I've got a lot to tell you," I said.

She studied me for a long moment, swallowed a couple of times. I knew what she was thinking. Once burned, twice shy. Who could blame her? I just prayed the magic words would do their stuff.

"I'm listening," she said.

* * *

It's funny the difference a month can make.

I managed to get a job at a garage a couple of days after that night. I've always been good with cars and my boss is helping me work out a schedule so that I can take the courses I need to get my mechanic's license.

Annie and I are taking it slow. We go on dates, we talk incessantly—on the phone if we're not together. We don't make promises, but we keep them all the same.

I didn't see Meran again until I went to a gallery opening with Annie at the end of January. It was a group show by some friends of hers. The Kelledys were there. Cerin was playing his harp in a corner of the gallery while Meran mingled with the other guests. I waited until I had the chance to talk to her on her own. She was studying a canvas that depicted a flood of wildflowers growing in a junkyard. It was only when you looked close that you saw these little people peeking out at you from among the flowers. They looked like they were made of nuts and twigs, held together with vines, but you could tell they were alive.

"Lovely, isn't?" Meran said.

I nodded. I liked the way it looked both realistic and like a painting, if you know what I mean. All the information was there, but you could still see the brush strokes. Art like this tells a real story; you just have to work out the details on your own.

"I want to thank you for helping me," I told her.

Meran turned to look at me and smiled.

"I didn't do anything you couldn't have done for yourself," she said. "Except maybe give you the courage to try. Everything else was already inside you, just waiting for the chance to come out." She waited a beat, then added, "But you're most welcome all the same."

I felt so disappointed, the way you do when you finally figure out there isn't a Santa Claus, an Easter Bunny, a Tooth Fairy.

"So . . . the words . . ." I said. "There was no magic in them?"

Of course there wasn't. How could there have been?

Meran kept smiling, but now there was an enigmatic look in her eyes.

"Oh, there's always magic," she said.

Forest of Stone

"I lived in a tree," he said. "Not in some little house, nestled up in its branches, but deep inside the trunk itself where the sap flows and old secrets cluster. It was a time, let me tell you, but long gone now. Then I was a king in a forest of green; now I live like a beggar in a forest of stone."

I let him talk. He always had some story or other to tell, and if he invariably came back to this one, I didn't mind. There was something in the telling of this particular story that woke a pleasant buzz in the back of my head, a sweet humming sound like a field full of insects on a summer's day. His quiet voice created a resonance that made me more aware of my own heartbeat and how it resounded against the drum of the world below my feet.

There was a melody playing against that rhythm, but I could never quite grasp it fully. Maybe we never do and that's why there's always a Mystery underlying the world.

"How long did you live there?" I asked when he fell silent, rheumy eyes gazing off into distant memories.

I tried to imagine him as he'd describe himself in the story: strong and tall, dressed all in green, chestnut hair flowing down his back, a great beard half hiding his face. Advisor to kings, a wizard in a tree. But all I could see in my mind's eye was the person who sat here with me on the steps of St. Paul's, an old broken man plagued with a continual cold, hawk's nose dripping, a cough wracking his chest. The only green was an echo of the forest, hidden in those watering eyes.

"How long?" he said. "Forever and a day. Until I befriended a little girl in need of a friend and she pulled me out of my tree with her love. I was free to go then, across the water to the Region of Summer Stars, and so I did. But it wasn't what I thought it would be. I found no peace there, no rest for my old soul." He coughed, gaze turning from the traffic passing on the street in front of us to meet my own. "Perhaps it was because I didn't die. Because I crossed over, upright and on my own two feet, taking my blood and bones with me."

Like the forest with its prison tree, this place of summer stars was always vague to me. He gave no details that I could hold on to. From his description, or rather lack of the same, it could be any place or every place.

I took it to mean a pagan heaven, like Tir na nOg, some after-world of the Gael, but that didn't tally except as metaphor. People, even a homeless man such as this with a mystic bent, didn't return from the dead. That was the providence of avatars and saviors and I greatly doubted he was either. But what he was, or once had been, I was unable to say.

"You should leave your bones behind when you go," he told me. "I learned that quickly enough. Safely buried, or better still, leave them as ashes, burned in a bone-fire. Otherwise this world calls to them and you can never be content. Your blood moves to the tides you left behind and there is ever a yearning for something other than twilight. You long for the sun, and the dark of a moonless night. You long for life."

"Why is it always twilight there?"

He shrugged. "Maybe it isn't. Maybe it was only twilight for me because the ribbons of my life there were still entwined with this world, this life."

"Do you still want to go back there?" I asked. "To return?"

"I don't know what I want or don't want. I only know I've been too long in this world, if only viewing it through the bark of a tree for most of my years. I miss something, but I don't know what. Perhaps my old life, before I let curiosity snare me with its woody embrace."

"What were you in your old life?"

He took so long to answer that I thought he hadn't heard me.

"Let me tell you a story of a king and his advisor," he said finally. He smiled, eyes clear for a moment. "It explains nothing, but it will pass the time."

"What if pigeons were really angels?" Jilly said.

Geordie looked down the wide sweep of steps that fronted St. Paul's Cathedral. The usual, unruly flock of pigeons were mooching for handouts from the tourists and passersby up and down their length. In the midst of the birds he could see the old homeless man that everybody called Woody, ragged coat sleeves flapping as he tossed handfuls of sunflower seeds he couldn't really afford to buy. For some reason the sight of the old man made Geordie think of Tanya. Maybe it was because of the stories Woody told, rambling accounts that mixed up well-known fables and fairy tales with pure make-believe. That was the world Tanya lived in, more months out of the year than Geordie cared to dwell on. Hollywood. A more contemporary Land of Make-Believe.

"Sometimes," Jilly went on, "when I hear the flutter of their feathers in the air, I forget that we don't have wings, too, and I just want to fly."

"I'm tired of long-distance romances," Geordie said.

Jilly sighed. "I know you are, Geordie, me lad. That's why I'm trying to cheer you up with pigeon angels." She waited a beat, then added, "You could always move to L.A. to be with her."

"And be what?"

"Yourself."

"And you could always get a job doing storyboards for an ad agency."

"It's an honorable position."

Geordie smiled. "Maybe. But it's not you."

"This is true."

"That's how it'd be for me out there. I'm all scruff and too poor to be considered eccentric. Could you imagine me going to a premiere or some awards show?"

"You clean up well," Jilly assured him.

He shook his head. "I'd only embarrass her. She wouldn't say anything, she might not even think it, but come on. Beauty and the beast is an old story. It doesn't play anymore."

Jilly put an arm around his shoulders and gave him a hug. "You're very broody today and it doesn't suit you at all. Leave the brooding to your brother. Writers are supposed to brood about things. Fiddlers don't. Remember jigs and reels? Happy things?"

Geordie sighed. "I know. I hate mopey people, and here I am, doing it all the same."

They sat quietly for a moment. Below them the pigeons kept rising in nervous clouds as some imagined danger startled them—a tourist coming too close, the sudden whoosh of a bus—before the flock settled once more.

Without looking at her, Geordie said, "Do you ever get the feeling that although you've never seen a thing, you still know it?"

"Like what?"

"You know, when someone's describing a place you've never been, and it's all familiar, not because you've ever been there, but because you know that one day you'll go there?"

Jilly gave him an odd look. "I suppose . . ."

"That's how I feel with Tanya sometimes—like I can already see the time when we won't be together anymore."

"That kind of thinking makes things happen," Jilly told him. "Whatever you think makes something happen."

"I suppose. So wouldn't it behoove us to think positively?"

Geordie had to smile. "Behoove?"

"It's a word."

"I know it is. I've just never heard it used in ordinary conversation before. Wait," he added, forestalling her next comment. "I know. Conversations should never be ordinary."

"That's not true. I like ordinary conversations. But I also like twisting, windy ones where we work out all the great mysteries of the world in whatever time we have and then sit back and have another cup of tea, knowing it's a job well done."

"I'd miss you if I moved to L.A."

Jilly nodded. "I'd miss you, too." She hesitated, before adding, "But maybe it's something you have to do."

"Perhaps it was only that you left something undone," I said the next time the old man and I talked. "That's why you came back."

"I'm not a ghost."

"Well, no. Of course not."

"And we all—the living and the dead—leave things undone. It seems to be part and parcel of human nature to put off today what we hope to do tomorrow."

"Well, then maybe you simply missed someone."

He considered that. "No. I don't think that. My lover betrayed me, my king had a sword sheathed in his chest, my father abandoned me to the forest. There was no one else."

"You sound bitter."

And had every right to, I suppose, if anything he was saying was true. Even if it was only true in a metaphorical sense.

"Do I?" he said, genuinely surprised. "I suppose I do. But I don't have reason to. Once you have lived as part of a forest you learn to forgo such things."

"What about the little girl? The one you befriended?"

"The girl?" He shook his head. "She is gone now as well. I think it was a long time ago that we were friends."

"People don't just stop being friends."

"Of course. I only meant I hadn't seen her for many years."

He was quiet for a moment, wiped his runny nose on a raggedy sleeve.

"But perhaps you're right," he finally said. "I remember telling a reluctant knight once that if certain things don't happen, the spirit never rests. Perhaps some piece of unfinished business waits for me here."

I waited to see if he had anything more to say, another story to tell, but he looked down at the pavement, silent.

"Do you want a pretzel?" I asked him. "I'm getting one."

He patted his pockets. "Yes, that would be nice, but I seem to be a little short of the required currency . . ."

"I can cover it."

He smiled, still not entirely back with me yet. "And perhaps something for our feathered friends . . ."

I went to get us coffee and pretzels from one of the food carts out by the curb. The vendor gave me a plastic bag with some stale hot dog buns in it when I asked if he had any day-old bread. I took it back with me.

"I think you should do the honors," he said when I started to hand him the bag.

I took a sip of my coffee, then set it aside and began to break up the buns, tossing the pieces to the pigeons.

"I think I'm supposed to die," he said as he watched the birds eat. "That's the business I've left unfinished."

I shot him a worried look.

"Oh, don't worry. I'm not feeling suicidal or anything."

"Well, that's a relief."

"But when I do die, would you make a fire of my bones, burn them down to ash and scatter them from here to there, dust to dust and all that?"

"You're saying you want to be cremated." I made a statement of it, tossed some more bits of bread to the pigeons. "I guess I could do that . . ." Though where I'd get the money to be able to afford a cremation for him was a whole other kind of mystery, secular, but no less puzzling.

He shook his head. "Not in some . . . factory. No, in an honest fire, wood and bones. With a friend like you to watch over the flames."

"They've got laws against the illegal disposing of bodies," I told him, smiling, making a joke of it.

"There won't be a body," he assured me. "Only bones."

"This isn't like one of your stories . . ."

"No, of course not." He put a hand on my arm. "You're throwing too hard. Do it like this."

He took a handful from me and tossed it with an oddly graceful motion, like it was a dance, but only his arm was moving. I watched the way the little pieces of bread seemed to sail out and among the birds in slow motion.

"Now you try it."

I did, but I couldn't capture his grace.

"That's better," he said.

I gave him a surprised look.

"It's because now you're paying attention," he said. "Doing it like you mean it. You'd be surprised how much satisfaction you can get from the simplest task if you impart it with meaning."

"She's lined up some work for me," Geordie said. "A recording gig for this guy who's making a film. Tanya played him a tape of some of my music and apparently it's just what he wants for a couple of scenes."

Jilly beamed proudly. "That's great."

"I guess."

"Can you bring your enthusiasm down a notch or two—you're blinding me with the glare of your happiness."

Geordie gave her a rueful smile. "I know. I should be happy."

"So what's the problem? That you didn't get the gig on your own?"

"Well, yes. I mean, no. It's just . . ."

"It was your music on the tape, right?"

"Sure."

"So . . . what?"

Geordie sighed. "I don't know. It's like everything's slipping out of control."

"You're in a relationship," Jilly told him. "That means there's give and take. Compromise. She can't make a living here, but maybe you can make one out there. It's not like you're being asked to be someone you're not. And since when did you start worrying about control?"

"I don't mean that I want to be in charge of everything. It's just . . . I'll be leaving everything and everyone behind."

"You're scared."

He nodded.

"That's okay," Jilly told him. "Big, life-changing things are always scary. But that doesn't mean they're bad."

"I know."

"So when did she tell you about this?"

"Last night."

Jilly poked him in the shoulder with a stiff finger. "And? So what did you say?"

"That I'd let her know."

"Oh, Geordie."

"No, it's okay. She understands. I'm calling her tomorrow morning."

"We won't stop being friends if you move," Jilly assured him. "We'll just have bigger phone bills."

I guess I never really expected him to die. Or at least not so soon.

Like most of the street people I ended up talking to, I never knew where he came from—really came from, that is. If I believed his stories . . . But I didn't. People called him Woody, but he answered to a half-dozen names. Robin Wood. Jack Green. Sammy King. Merle Hode. Some others that I've forgotten now. Woody was the one that stuck.

I was busking the line-ups in the theater district that night, always a good place to make a little money, when Bridie Grey gave me the message that Woody wanted to see me. She always reminded me of a gangly, wingless bird with her large eyes and twig-limbs. A recovered junkie, she still looked like she had a jones. Dark circles around her eyes like smeared kohl, spiky blonde hair with an inch of dark roots showing, hollow cheeks. Heroin chic. Some people never lost that look.

"He's waiting for you in the Tombs," she said, "up Flood Street, past MacNeil."

I was doing okay—pulling the popular tunes from the four strings of my fiddle: "St. Anne's Reel," "Greensleeves," "Old Joe Clark"—though not as good as when *Riverdance* was in town. Then any even vaguely Irish tune was guaranteed to fill my fiddle case with change.

"I won't be long," I told her.

"Whatever."

She took off before I could ask what Woody was doing in that no man's land of abandoned buildings and old factories. The Tombs is a rough part of town, full of bikers, junkies, runaways, just a lot of people with a chip on their shoulder. The older homeless guys didn't usually go too far in once the sun went down, not unless they traveled in a group, and Woody was a loner.

I tried to play another tune, but my concentration was off, so I packed up and left my spot to a waiting guitarist. I took the subway as far as Gracie Street, then walked over to Flood and up into the Tombs. I could feel a prickle between my shoulderblades as I left the lights of Gracie Street behind. I don't like the Tombs in the day; coming here at night feels like walking into an ambush. But I had this going for me: I've been on the street scene for a lot of years. Most people know me and leave me alone. Not because I'm so tough, but because I've come to fit into the scenery. Like background. I hoped that Woody was as lucky. Sometimes people get the idea that it's funny to douse a bum with gasoline and chase him with a match. Or beat him senseless, just because they can.

There's an empty lot at the corner of Flood and MacNeil—one of those places where the demolition started but never got further than knocking a few blocks of tenements down. It's been years now since the wrecking crews left, long enough for the rubble to be half-covered with weeds and scrub, some of which has actually succeeded in the struggle to grow into scraggly trees. I knew Woody didn't like being inside, so I started checking out the lot first, ignoring the abandoned buildings that were still standing on the other three corners. What I found gave me the serious creeps.

In about the middle of the lot, someone had piled up a heap of wood, an unlit bonfire of twigs and branches, scrap wood, old fixtures and other woodwork from some of the surrounding buildings. On top of it all was a bundle of clothes that I recognized as belonging to Woody and what looked for all the world like a human skull, artfully displayed on a pyramid of bones. I knew it couldn't be real, the skull, the bones, but it made my pulse quicken all the same.

"Okay," I said. "Very funny, Woody."

Because I remembered what he'd said. There wouldn't be a corpse when he died. Just the bones. I wondered where he'd found them.

Only then I noted the birds.

I don't know why I didn't notice them walking in. The trees were full of them, more pigeons than I'd ever seen together in one place, eight or nine times the huge flock that gathers daily on the steps in front of St. Paul's. They were all quiet, except for the odd restless rustle of their feathers as one or another shifted position. Once you've seen that Hitchcock movie, you can't help but get a little weirded out over big gatherings of birds like this.

The streetlights of Gracie Street seemed a hundred miles away. Like this was another world. It is another world.

I sat down on some brickwork that had been a part of a wall in some other life and laid my fiddle case down by my feet. I was seriously creeped. My night vision was good, so it was hard to ignore the unlit funeral pyre, the birds, the damned skull that seemed to be staring right back at me. I tried not to look at it.

I don't know how long I sat there, staring off into the dark. After a while I heard footsteps, someone scuffling their way across the rubble. In this place it could have been anybody. A junkie, a runaway, some psycho. I was hoping for Woody, to hear him laugh and tell me, "Gotcha." Instead it was Jilly who came wandering up to me, out of the dark. I had to shake my head.

"How'd you know I was here?"

Jilly shrugged. "I don't know. It's just . . ."

"This gift you have."

She gave me a smile. I don't know why I was surprised. Jilly and I seem to have this connection, always running into each other whenever one of us wants to see the other. We don't even have to think about it. It just happens. And she's fearless when it comes to walking around the city at night. It's not like she doesn't care what happens to her. More like she's made some pact with the darkness, the city, the danger. Or maybe the night itself looks out for her, an unexpected random act of kindness pulled out of its shadows like a magician's rabbit.

She sat down beside me on my memory of a wall and we looked at the bones for a while.

"Woody set this up," I said finally.

She nodded. "Joe told me."

Joe was Joseph Crazy Dog, a friend of hers who always makes me feel a little uneasy. It isn't anything he says or does, but something in his eyes. Or mostly in his eyes, because he can come out with the damnedest things, weird pronouncements that he lets drop like most people do comments about the weather. On the street everybody knows him as Bones because of this fortune-telling thing he does with a handful of small animal bones.

I sighed. More bones. There used to be an old woman who wandered the streets collecting animal bones that she tied up with wire and made into skeletons. With my luck, she'd be showing up here tonight as well.

Jilly tapped my knee with hers, a companionable bump.

"I didn't know Woody well," she said, "but I always liked him. It's too bad he had to go."

I shook my head. "He's not gone anywhere. This is just something he set up to get me going."

Jilly gave me an odd look.

"Whose bones do you think those are?" she asked.

"No way," I told her, starting to wonder if she was in on the joke. "If that's Woody, then who put all this together? The pyre, the bones."

"Geordie, me lad," she said. "We're talking about an enchanter. A magician. Didn't you listen to his stories?"

"Yeah, but . . ."

"You didn't believe."

"Well, no. I mean, Red tells me he's a werewolf. Am I supposed to believe that as well?"

She shrugged. "Depends. What's he like when there's a full moon?"

"Jilly . . ."

"I'm joking."

But I wasn't so sure. The things she accepts as matter-of-course would have most people knocking on the front door of the Zeb and asking for a padded room if they started seeing them as well.

"But not about Woody," she added.

I don't know why, but I believed her. I guess it's that I've known her too long. If this was a joke, she wouldn't be in on it, because it wasn't her style. She'd never go out of her way to make anybody feel bad, and if this really was Woody, bad didn't begin to describe the way it made me feel.

That's hard to explain, too, because we weren't as close as maybe I've made it out. I'd only known him for a few months, but I liked the guy. He had a certain dignity that most of us don't, and genuinely cared about, well, pretty much everything. Still, I only saw him once or twice a week, listened to his stories, bought him a meal or a sandwich when he looked like he needed it, which was all the time.

"Did you ever notice how many storytellers there are living on the streets?" I found myself saying to Jilly. "I wonder why that is."

"Everybody's got a story they need to tell," she said. "Stockbrokers, bankers, plumbers, housewives. The thing about street people is that often their stories are *all* they have."

I nodded, my gaze pulled back to the funeral pyre. I'd come all the way around to believing now, though I was no closer to understanding why there wasn't a corpse, only those bones. I only had Jilly's explanation and that was no explanation at all. But if I didn't know how we'd come to this place—Jilly, me, Woody's bones—I knew why. Woody wanted to get off the streets. He wanted back into that story he stepped out of all those years ago. The trouble was . . .

"I don't think I can do it," I said. "This is just too weird."

"You have to do it," Jilly said. "You made him a promise."

Like I promised Tanya things would work out, that I'd stand by her, except there she was and here I was, and it didn't look like we'd ever be together except for when she had a break from work and could get away to come back to visit me. I mean well, I really do, but I'm not so good at following through. It comes from a lack of trust, from having put up walls a long time ago, tall and thick and a lot stronger than the little memory of a brick wall we were sitting on. People didn't get in behind those walls so much as I looked over the stones at them.

Jilly was the only one who got all the way through, but that's because she's got her own walls. Everybody thinks she's this light-hearted piece of sunshine, and that's a part of who she is, no question, but it hides the shadows. Some people deal with their problems, others like Jilly and I, we simply put them away. Jilly uses her good humor and her art; I use my music. We've known each other for so long, been through so much together, that I guess our walls are made of the same stones by now. We're kind of standing there together, on the inside, looking out at the rest of the world.

"You can't break a promise," Jilly said.

Well, you can. But then you have to live with yourself after.

I felt the weight of her gaze on me and finally had to turn to look at her. She didn't say anything else, but she didn't have to. I nodded. Opening my fiddle case, I took out a pack of matches I keep to light the candles in my apartment. Some nights all I want is a flickering light, something that moves like music.

I was hoping the wood wouldn't take. That it'd be damp, or the pieces too big, or something. So that I would have tried, but not been able to follow through, because I still didn't want to do this thing. But when I stepped closer I saw that there were old newspapers, twisted into the wood. I lit a match and put the flame to one, moving on when the newspaper caught. It took me four matches to walk all the way around the pyre, to start the flames so that they rose up evenly on all sides, rushing up, the smaller wood crackling and popping as the fire reached for the pyramid of bones, the clothes underneath it, the skull on top.

A promise kept, I thought.

Woody seemed very close at that moment. I felt the echo of the heartbeat of the world drumming inside me, slowly, softly, like it did when he was telling me his stories. It was inside my walls. So was Woody. And so was somebody else, though maybe she didn't know it yet. It was long past time that I did more than simply tell her how much she meant to me.

As I watched the flames lick the bones, I knew I had other promises to keep.

Things burn in the Tombs and no one questions what or why. The streets are too choked with rubble and abandoned cars for the fire trucks to get in, and the truth is, nobody really cares. If you took a poll, you'd find most people would like to see the whole eyesore this place is burned to the ground, the buildings leveled, the night people driven out because there's no place for them to hide anymore.

So we wouldn't be disturbed.

We sat there while the fire burned, bones and wood, the smoke trailing up into the sky throughout the night, thin tendrils still visible against the sky as dawn pinked the distant horizon. I felt like I was in a kind of dream state, an effect that was heightened when all those pigeons that had come to see Woody off suddenly took to the air at the same time. Their wings were like thunder as they circled around the fire, once, twice, three times, then went spiraling straight up, following the last trails of smoke as they drifted apart, high in the dawn sky.

I remembered what Jilly had said about pigeons and angels and watched the cloud they made fade into the distance. When I turned around, Jilly was smiling.

"What are you thinking about?" I asked.

"Just how wonderful the world is."

"Of course."

"No, really. And you know what's the best thing about it? That it doesn't matter if we're here or not. It just goes on being this wonderful place. That's what people forget. It's not here for us. It's just here, and the gift we were given is that we're allowed to experience it."

"I wish I could see it the way you do, but I guess I'm too much of a cynic."

"Oh, don't say that. I can think of nothing sadder than cynicism."

"It's the way things are."

Jilly shook her head. "Only if you see them that way."

Woody would have agreed with her. Nobody invested everything she did with as much attention and meaning put into the smallest parts of it as Jilly did. Maybe she didn't open up her own secret self, but she was open to everybody and everything. She was there to hear them, to mark the movement and meaning of their lives and bear witness, no matter who or what or how strange things were.

That was her real gift, and her burden.

When the fire had died down completely, I gathered some ashes in a paper bag and we went to scatter them on the steps of St. Paul's.

My brother Christy drove me out to the airport in that old Dodge wagon of his, Jilly and his girlfriend Saskia coming along for the ride. They wanted to wait inside with me, but I knew that'd be too hard for all of us, so we said our good-byes outside. I got my seat at the ticket counter and went through security. All I brought with me was in a knapsack carry-on and my fiddle case. Everything else, what little I'd accumulated over the years, I'd put into storage in the basement of Christy and Saskia's apartment. I figured for a new life, I'd need new belongings, things that didn't carry too much old history in them.

Walls are hard to take down. I hoped that Tanya would have patience while I fumbled my way through the unfamiliar task.

I listened to Woody tell me stories all the way out on the flight to L.A. I'd swear he was sitting right there in the seat beside me, whispering in my ear, instead of in my memory. I promised him that I'd try my best to impart everything I did with meaning.

I'd start with Tanya.

Embracing the Mystery

I heard a dog speak once.

It was Christmas Eve, 1993. His name was Fritzie, a gangly, wirehaired, long-legged mutt that I inherited when my best friend Gina drowned herself. There's a legend that for one hour after midnight on Christmas Eve, animals were given voices so that they could praise the baby Jesus. But Fritzie wasn't praising anybody that night. Instead we talked about how much we missed Gina.

This isn't something I imagined, though I can understand your thinking so. Truth is, I'm the last person to believe anything improbable, even given such an experience. I don't care what anyone says. One miracle doesn't make fairy tales and that weird world you can only find in supermarket tabloids suddenly real, though you wouldn't know it from some of my friends.

But I'm getting ahead of myself.

While I heard a dog speak, it was only that one time. Fritzie never spoke to me again. Not all through that year, not the next

Christmas Eve when the bells struck midnight, nor on any Christmas Eve after that. Though it's funny. Right now he's looking at me as I write this—with that big, sad-eyed gaze dogs do so well—and it's like he knows I'm writing about him. Still, that's only my anthropomorphizing him.

It's not that I don't think he has feelings. I know he does. He just doesn't talk, except for that one time, and I don't know what that was. A miracle, I suppose. Or a dream that I want to have been real because right then, that night, I really needed to talk to someone who'd been as close to Gina as I'd been and there was no one else except for Fritzie.

I don't know.

What I do know is that animals don't talk. Hey-diddle-diddle, dishes and spoons can't run. Neither Elvis nor Kurt Cobain will be gigging again any time soon. Sorry.

"Okay," Jilly says, holding up a finger to get everyone's attention. "Question: If you were the eighth dwarf, what would your name be?"

"Lazy," Sophie says.

Wendy smiles. "As if. I'd be Willy," she adds to a general round of laughter.

"What, what?" she asks.

"You don't even have one," Sophie says. "Not unless you've been keeping the operation from us."

"Oh, please. I was referring to Shakespeare, as in poet, writer—you know, your general, all-purpose scribe."

"What about you, Sue?" Jilly asks.

"Tired," I say.

Jilly shakes her head. "Too close to Sleepy. Try again."

"What would yours be?" I ask instead.

"Oh, that's easy," Wendy puts in before Jilly can answer. "She'd be Silly."

Jilly attempts a stern expression while muttering, "Bloody poets," but she can't hold it.

"I think I'd have preferred Saucy," she says.

"Or Spacy," Sophie offers.

"Would it work the same for Spice Girls?" Wendy asks.

"Then I'd definitely want to be Saucy Spice," Jilly tells us.

We're sitting in the Yo-Man club, waiting for the band to come on stage, two artists, a poet and a city architect who spends more time in meetings than at her drawing board: Jilly and Sophie, Wendy, and me. They're the ones who draw inspiration out of thin air to make their art, but I think of them as the three muses, *my* three muses, because they remind me of the world I'm not a part of. They ground me, connect me to the art I can't seem to release from the end of my own pencils and brushes anymore.

Sometimes they're like fairy tale presences in my life, moving to a hickory-dickory-dock sound track, three blind mice that can see more clearly than I ever can. They're the wise women who live in those cottages deep in fairy woods with herbs drying from the rafters and dark-eyed birds perched in the corners. Three small, tangle-haired women with the knowledge of some otherworld in their eyes and enchantment in their fingers. It's all so real for them. Wendy collects fairy tales. Jilly believes in fairy tales. And Sophie . . . well, Sophie pretty much *is* a fairy tale.

Like I said, I don't really believe in fairy tales or the magical things that can happen in them, except for that one time, when Fritzie spoke. But I find myself thinking about Gina more and more these days, and now I really want to hear Fritzie's voice again. I want him to remind me of things I might have forgotten, because while I can't let go of Gina, I'm losing her all the same. I'm losing the details of who she was. I'm shedding them like snake skins until one day all I'm going to have left of her is the fact that she drowned herself.

Fritzie almost died after that Christmas Eve when he talked to me. It was as though, without Gina, there was no point in his living, and he just started to pine away. I brought him back. I don't know how, exactly. Lots of loving, I guess. But even now, five years later, he still carries an air of melancholy. I know he hasn't stopped missing her any more than I do. I know he needs to talk about her, too. And maybe he does, only I'm not able to hear him anymore.

"How long do dogs live?" I ask.

The question pops out of me during a lull in our conversation, out of the blue, with no connection to what's gone before. But that doesn't faze this group. They can jump from topic to topic, helter-skelter, as though all words are part of this one large ongoing conversation in which no subject is inappropriate.

"I think it would depend on the breed," Jilly says. "Holly would know."

Holly Rue has a used book store on the edge of town. Because of this Internet-based information storage program called the Wordwood that she helped to develop, all of her friends have taken to thinking of her almost as an oracle: If you have a question, Holly can find the answer. Anyone with a computer and a modem can access the Wordwood themselves, which is where Holly gets her answers, but most of this crowd don't own either. I've logged onto it a couple of times, but something about the site bothers me and I haven't pointed my web browser in its direction for a long time now.

"I think I heard somewhere," Wendy puts in, "that little ones live longer than big ones."

"Are you worried about Fritzie?" Sophie asks. "How old is he now?"

"I'm not sure. Ten or eleven, at least."

"Dogs can live a long time," Jilly assures me.

Wendy nods. "I've heard of them living until they're eighteen, or even older."

Except the clock's running out, I think. It's ticking for all of us, but it moves much faster for animals. I take a breath, put aside the practical, commonsensical Susan Ashworth these women know, and say what's really on my mind.

"I'd like to hear him talk again," I say.

This is the only group to whom I could come out with something like that and not have them laugh at me.

Jilly and Sophie exchange glances.

"You really need to ask Holly," Sophie says.

"Or visit the Wordwood yourself," Jilly says. "You're on-line, aren't you?"

I nod, unsure how to explain that something about that place spooks me. In the end I don't say anything at all.

But when I get home, I log on to my server, download my email, then activate the bookmark that will take me to the Wordwood. When the home page comes up, I sit there and look for a long time at the image of a deep, old English oak forest that probably doesn't even exist in Britain anymore. Finally I type my question in the little box provided.

How can you make a dog speak?

And hit return. My cursor turns into an hourglass and I wait for a few moments. The Wordwood works a bit like this search engine called Ask Jeeves, except instead of bringing up a page of links to other sites, it brings up links to various books and discussions that might exist on its own voluminous site. Or it asks you to clarify your question.

That's the thing that I find so eerie. No matter what the time of day or night, the Wordwood responds as though there's a person manning a keyboard, somewhere out there in its pixelated kingdom, and we're in chat mode. The words even appear on my screen as though they're being typed, the letters dropping neatly into the somewhat larger white box that has replaced the one that was first waiting for me when I arrived at the site.

>>When you say 'speak' are you referring to an actual, interactive conversation?<

I hesitate for a moment, then type in "Yes."

>>This might take a moment.<

I stare at the trees behind the box. They're like a video, rather than a static image—real smooth streaming, too. I swear I can see leaves moving and there's nothing jerky about their shivering movement. A sound like a breeze comes up out of my computer's speakers. I leave the site when I think I see a little figure moving in the shadows behind an enormous branch just beside the white reply box—a small shape, the size of a squirrel, or a monkey, but human. Wearing clothes.

I'm not stupid. I know it's not real. I know they can do pretty much anything with special effects these days, and the Internet's always been cutting edge. But it spooks me all the same. I can't shake the feeling that the image of that forest is a real-time video of some forest that only exists out there in whatever space it is that the World Wide Web occupies. Not the hard drives that house all those hundreds of thousands of Internet sites, but some other place that can't be measured, or weighed, or touched. A place that should be impossible to access, like the other music that lies in the silences between the notes we hear in a song. The invisible words that lie between the lines of a story or a poem.

Between, between . . .

That's where Jilly says all magic begins. In the hidden places that lie between things.

I turn off my computer and take Fritzie for a walk. That night I dream of Gina in a wood. An old oak wood like the one that was on my computer screen before I went to bed. She's no bigger than the size of my hand, sitting there on a branch, looking down at me, and she's about to tell me something very important but my alarm goes off and I wake up.

When I get off work that day, I go home and change, stick a few dog biscuits in my pocket, and take Fritzie for a walk. He seems a little confused because we're not out as long as we normally are, but he perks right up when I take him to the car instead of back inside. I wish it were that easy for me.

I wasn't joking when I said if I were the eighth dwarf I'd be called Tired. I'm forever tired these days, it doesn't matter how much sleep I get. There's always too much to do at the office, where downsizing only means that people keep getting laid off and their workload is divided up between those of us still left, like we weren't already overworked. It's impossible to get any sense of accomplishment because nothing ever seems to actually get completed.

Jilly keeps saying I should simply quit and go back to doing fine art like I did when we first met—"You were *so* good," she'd say. But even then, it was a hobby for me, not a vocation. She doesn't really understand that while I might have retained my motor skills as an artist—I still do some hands-on art at work, for all the endless meetings my department head insists upon—I don't seem to have the heart of an artist anymore. I can appreciate. But I can't create. At least not anything outside the realm of architectural drawings.

Fritzie doesn't have to think about those kinds of things.

"Do you know where we're going?" I ask him as I open the passenger door for him. "To visit Snippet."

He gives me a grin, tongue lolling. Maybe he recognizes the name of Holly's little Jack Russell, maybe it's just because we're together and going for a drive. Life's simple for a dog.

I don't really know Holly that well myself. She has a used book store up in the north end of the city. It's not an area where I normally go on my own, but I'm forever giving rides to Christy and Jilly and the others, so I guess we've become something more than acquaintances over the years. And Fritzie and Snippet took to each other straightaway. Often when I'm chauffeuring someone up to the store, I leave them with Holly and just take the dogs out for a ramble in the fields behind the store.

I'm not a book person the way Holly and Christy are. I'm just as happy reading whatever's new and in paperback as I am some rare old classic that hasn't been in print for thirty years. Though I do have to admit that I was quite taken with a Robert Nathan novel that Holly lent me once; so much so, in fact, that when I realized none of his books were still in print—and how could that even be, he was so amazing—I went and borrowed them from the library, one by one, until I'd read them all.

I'm thinking of Nathan's books as I pull into the small parking lot by Holly's store. Maybe I should ask her to recommend someone else to me. But first things first.

I let Fritzie out of the car. He runs to a nearby telephone pole to check his pee-mail and leave a new message of his own, then rejoins me at the front of the store. We can see Snippet in the window, muzzle pressed against the glass just under the modest store sign that reads:

HOLLY RUE—USED BOOKS

When Fritzie notices her, the two of them dance and try to touch noses through the window. I can see Holly inside, laughing at the pair of them, and I wave to her.

The store is its usual jumble. I have to admit that I find something just a little disconcerting about a retail establishment that offers up its goods in such a haphazard manner. It feels like you have to be part pack rat, part spelunker, just to make your way through it all. I give Snippet and Fritzie each one of the biscuits I stuck in my pocket earlier, then make my way by a circuitous route to where Holly's sitting.

She looks the way she always does, red hair held back from her face with bobby pins, hazel eyes bright and welcoming, the same fashion sense as Jilly: all baggy clothes on a small trim figure.

"This must be a first," Holly says. "I don't think I've ever seen you up here on your own."

I take a few books from a chair and put them on one of what seems like twenty cardboard boxes full of books that are clustered around Holly's desk like livestock at a feeder.

"It's possible I've gone all literary on my own, isn't it?" I say as I sit down.

"Eminently so," she assures me.

"But not true," I tell her. "I've just come to pick your brain instead."

Holly's eyebrows rise in a question. I have to gather my courage—this isn't Jilly or the others I'm talking to now.

"I was wondering," I say, talking quickly to get it all out before

I lose my nerve, "if you could check in the Wordwood to see if there's a way to make a dog talk."

"You mean bark?"

I shake my head. "No. I mean to really be able to communicate with them. Share a conversation."

Holly smiles.

"I'm serious," I say.

"I wasn't making fun of you," she tells me. "Or if I was, I was making fun of both of us, because I've already looked it up for myself."

It takes a moment for that to register.

"What did you find?" I finally ask.

Holly shrugs. "Nothing terribly useful. The most effective method seems to be to get the Welsh goddess Cerridwen to let you stir her cauldron and then sneak a few drops of the magical brew when she's not looking."

I just look at her.

"Well, apparently it worked for Taliesin," she says. "He was able to immediately understand the language of birds and animals after one taste."

"A Welsh goddess . . ."

"I know. You won't exactly find one setting up shop at the local mall . . . or even in the Market. One of my own favorite bits of animal lore comes from *The Book of Bright Secrets* by A. S. Ison. She says that if you look between a dog or cat's ears, you can see what they're seeing—not just what's in front of them, but those mysterious things that only they can see."

I know what she means. Fritzie can sometimes spend a half hour or longer simply staring at a corner of the room, like there's a window to a whole other world hidden there.

"And then there's Christy," Holly goes on. "In one of his books he talks about this idea that if you put your forehead against that of a cat or a dog and lock gazes with them, you can see what they've seen."

"Have you ever tried any of these things?" I find myself asking.

Holly smiles. "I haven't run into Cerridwen yet, but yes on both counts to the other two. All I got for my trouble was one very happy dog and a face full of licks."

"So they didn't work."

"They didn't work for me," Holly says. "Maybe I'm just not magical enough."

If you have to have magic to make them work, then I'm really out of luck.

"There was a whole bunch of other stuff in the Wordwood," Holly goes on, "none of which struck me as having any more practical application than the ones we've already talked about. But you could look them up. Are you on-line? I can give you the Word- wood's URL if you like."

"I've already got it bookmarked."

Holly waits for a long moment, then says, "But visiting the site makes you uncomfortable."

"How did you know that?"

She shrugs. "People either fall in love with it, or get spooked— though most of the ones who do get spooked would probably never admit that, even to themselves. They'll just convince themselves it's too boring to revisit."

"So there *is* something weird about it."

"There's something weird about everything," Holly says, sounding like Jilly.

"Do you believe in magic?" I have to ask.

"I think so. I believe in something. There's too much anecdotal evidence to discount the idea that there's more to the world than what we can see. I believe that there's *always* been more, but each generation categorizes it a little differently."

"How so?"

"I correspond with this fellow in Arizona named Richard Kunz," Holly says, "and he has a really interesting take on all of this. He thinks that the detonation of the first atom bomb forever changed the way that magic would appear in the world. That the spirits live in the wires now instead of the trees. They live and travel through phone and modem lines, take up residence in computers and appliances, and live on electricity and lord knows what else. How else do you explain the spooky ways computers act sometimes?"

"So the Wordwood . . . ?"

My question trails off because I'm not even sure what it is that I want to ask.

"We started the Wordwood simply as a digital storehouse of knowledge," Holly says. "An electronic library of all the world's books. But then we started noticing texts appearing in it that none of us had entered and its URL no longer led to a hard drive with a physical address. The spirits got into it and now it's something else again, something we can no longer control and can't explain." There's an odd look in her eyes when she adds, "And some of those spirits have even crossed back over into our world again."

"What do you mean?" I ask.

"Do you know Christy's girlfriend, Saskia?"

I nod.

"I think she was born in the Wordwood."

"But that . . . that's impossible."

Holly nods. "So's magic."

We sit for a while, Holly with Snippet on her lap, me with Fritzie's head on mine. I'm anthropomorphizing him again, but I'd swear he's been following our conversation. I think about Saskia Madding. I've only met her a few times, but there is something . . . well, luminous about her. Like a Madonna or one of the saints in a

Botticelli painting. She just glows. I would never have thought magic. Charisma, yes. But maybe that's a part of magic. A glamour . . .

"You know what I'd do?" Holly says.

I pull myself up out of my thoughts to look at her and shake my head.

"I'd make my own ritual," she says.

"What do you mean?"

She straightens a couple of books on her desk, before lifting her gaze up to meet mine.

"It's just what Christy and Jilly say," she tells me. "The magic's already there. Here. All around us. To tap into it you have to really be able to focus on it—it's like what mystics do when they meditate. It's all intent and concentration. That's the whole idea behind spells and rituals. They force you to focus completely on what you're doing."

"So they don't really work," I say.

Holly shakes her head. "No, they do. But not for the reason we think they do. They work because they make us concentrate so completely that the magic has to pay attention to us. It's like communion and singing hymns in church. People really do get closer to God because they're focusing on these rituals and no longer listening to that constant dialogue that goes on inside their heads."

"I wouldn't know how to make up a ritual," I tell her.

She smiles. "Me, neither. But it sounds good in theory, doesn't it?"

That night I give it a try, making it up as I go. Fritzie follows me from room to room as I gather up candles and herbs and whatever else I can think of and bring them all into the dining room. I turn off all the lights and sit in the dark for a few moments before I light the candles. I burn some piñon incense. I paint symbols on a clay platter from a mixture I've made up of red wine, spit and flower pollen. I have an old Tangerine Dream album playing at low volume on the stereo. I write the words, "I want to hear Fritzie talk," on a slip of rose-colored paper, then cut it up into tiny pieces and burn it on the platter with pinches of herbs. Anise. Thyme. Cilantro. Mint.

The odd thing is, the more I get into it, the more I feel it's actually going to work. I can feel something, like the charge in the air before a big storm.

Be patient, I tell myself. Focus. Believe.

I sit there for a long time, taking in the acrid smell of burning paper and dried herbs as it mixes with the piñon.

Then I have to laugh at myself.

"So what do you think, boy?" I ask Fritzie. "Is any of this making you feel talkative?"

He comes over and licks my hand.

"Yeah, I thought about as much."

I turn on the overhead and put everything away. I don't know why I thought it would work in the first place. It's weird the things we'll do for hope.

Before I go to bed, I check my e-mail. I delete the messages as I read them, reply to a couple. Then I find this one:

Date: Wed, 08 Jun 1999 17:55:42-0700
From: Webmaster@TheWordwood.com
To: SueAsh@cybercare.com
Subject: Your question
Why do you want to speak to your dog?
The Wordwood
http://www.thewordwood.com/

I stare at it, my cursor arrow hovering on the link to the site, but I don't click my mouse to take me there. After a long moment I remember to breathe. I close my e-mail reader and turn off the computer.

It's late and I should get to bed. Instead I go out and sit on the balcony, Fritzie lying at my feet. I stare out at the darkened city and have no idea what I'm thinking about. I just sit there, waiting for morning.

Remember when I said that Sophie is a fairy tale? It's this theory that Jilly has. She says Sophie has fairy blood, but Sophie only smiles when the topic comes up, so who knows what she really thinks. But Sophie does have these fascinating serial dreams that, if you were given to believing in parallel worlds and the like, would certainly lend credence to the theory. She has this whole other life, apparently, over there in her dream world, but the strange thing is that she says she's met people here, in what Christy calls the World As It Is, that know her from her dreams.

It's not a traditional fairy tale, but then, Jilly says, it's not supposed to be. And we're still in the middle of it, so it's hard to say how it will all turn out.

Do I believe it's true? Of course not. But when I've had a glass or two of wine, and Jilly's there pumping Sophie for the latest installment of her dream serial, and Sophie's describing these wonderful things, all so matter-of-factly, like how her boyfriend there is this guy named Jeck who can turn into a crow, or this wonderful shop where you can buy all the books and paintings that never got made in our world, somehow it all does make a certain kind of lopsided sense. And I realize that whether or not it's true isn't what's important; what's important it's that we have the story.

Because, getting back to Robert Nathan's books for a moment, there's this bit in *The Elixir* where he says that the difference between man and animals isn't that we have thumbs, but that we have fairy tales. Everything has a history, even the rocks and trees. But we have legends and dreams that weave into one another. We're part of them, and they're part of us. The trees have history, but they have no legends.

I think of it all as a metaphor for imagination, but I want it to be real. I want what we call Jinx, the reason that mechanical objects don't work properly around Sophie—her wristwatch running backwards, Christy's computer crashing when she tries to use it, her radio bringing in signals from Australia when it's tuned to a local frequency—to have a magical rather than a biochemical explanation.

So the next morning, as soon as the hour's decent, I take Fritzie out for his morning constitutional and follow a meandering path that leads us to the door of Sophie's building. Because what I need now is for one of my muses to lend me some of her imagination.

Sophie sits us out on the old sofa on her balcony for tea and biscuits. She seems a little amused when I tell her why we've come—not amused at me; more amused at the idea of her fairy blood, the way she always is, but not denying it either.

"I can't do anything here," she says after a long pause. "But maybe in Mabon you can find someone who can help you." She smiles. "Since it exists because of magic, somebody there should know how to make an enchantment work."

Mabon is the name of her dream city. Fritzie seems to pick up his ears when she mentions it.

"Can you take us there?" I ask, but then I think of how often Jilly's asked the same question.

Sophie shakes her head. "People seem to have to find their own way," she says. "I don't think it's a rule so much as just the way it works."

"Find my own way," I repeat.

"Have you ever tried lucid dreaming?" she asks.

"I wouldn't know where to start."

"You have to picture the place you want to be when you start to dream," she says.

I sigh. More of this focus/centering oneself business.

"But I've never been there before," I tell her.

How could I? The place doesn't exist except in Sophie's dreams.

But she smiles and gets up. When she returns from inside, she's carrying a small ink drawing of an old-fashioned storefront. The leaded windows are crammed full of books and above the door a sign reads:

MR. TRUEPENNY'S BOOK EMPORIUM AND GALLERY

"Try using this," she says as she gives it to me. "That's where it started for me."

When I get home I put the drawing beside my bed. I called in sick before I went out this morning, but I'm feeling too guilty to take the whole day off. There are so many projects on the go at the moment and if I'm not there it just means everybody else has to take up my slack and work that much harder. So I change into my office clothes, send this email:

Date: Wed, 09 Jun 1999 11:49:34-0400
From: SueAsh@cybercare.com
To: Webmaster@TheWordwood.com
Subject: Re: Your question
>Why do you want to speak to your dog?
Because he used to live with my best friend before she died and I want to talk to him about her.

And go to work.

*   *   *

There's no reply from the Wordwood when I return to the apartment that evening. Fritzie and I go for a long walk after supper. I do a little work on some files I brought home from the office, then try to watch some TV, but I can't concentrate. I keep thinking of the drawing that Sophie gave me, of lucid dreaming and the possibility that it might actually take me into Mabon—in the sense of my dreaming I'm there, of course. I have a bath to try to get rid of some of the day's tension, but it doesn't really help. When I finally go to bed, Fritzie curled up on the end where he usually sleeps, I can't stop thinking.

I lie awake for hours until finally I get up and check my email again. Still nothing from the Wordwood.

When I finally fall asleep, it's almost four in the morning and the next thing I know my alarm's going off. I drag myself out of bed, walk Fritzie, then hurry off to work. Getting home, I find this waiting for me:

Date: Wed, 10 Jun 1999 16:51:57-0400
From: Webmaster@TheWordwood.com
To: SueAsh@cybercare.com
Subject: Re: Your question
>I want to talk to him about her.
Perhaps he simply has nothing he wants to say.
The Wordwood.
http://www.thewordwood.com/

"Is that true?" I ask Fritzie.

It's not something I ever considered. That maybe he can talk; he just doesn't want to.

Fritzie cocks his head like a curious crow. He knows I'm asking

him something, but since I'm not using his primary vocabulary—
"Hungry," "Walk," "Get the ball"—he can't do anything except
wag his tail and look at me. So scratch that theory, Mr. Webmaster.

I try the lucid dreaming again that night, fixing the image from
Sophie's drawing firmly in my mind before I go to bed, but I'm so
tired that I drop off like I've been drugged. If I have any dreams, I
don't remember them.

I think maybe the intense focus everybody's telling me about isn't
the way to go with this. Maybe magic can only be approached from
the side. Maybe it wants you to slip up on it like an image will in the
corner of your eye.

I'm thinking this because I have no luck the next night either.
On the fourth, I don't even think about it. Fritzie and I stay up to
watch the news, then go to bed after Leno's monologue and the
next thing I know we're standing on a cobblestoned street looking
at the physical counterpart to the bookshop in Sophie's drawing.
By the light, it seems to be late afternoon. There are people around
us, window-shopping, or simply out walking. They're of all sorts—
from Bohemians to those dressed for the office—and of all nation-
alities. No one pays any attention to the fact that I simply popped
into existence here, though one little girl across the street gives me
a happy wave with her free hand, the other held fast in her
mother's.

I wave back, then study my surroundings a little more.

What surprises me the most isn't that it worked, that I've
dreamed my way into Sophie's city, or at least my own version of it,
but that Fritzie's here with me. He looks at me, grinning, tail slapping the cobblestones. I expect him to say something—after all,
we're in a dream now; we're in this magical city—but he only gives
me that "test the limits" look animals get, then gets up and casually

walks over to the nearest lamppost to give it a sniff, checking over his shoulder to see if I'm going to call him back.

As he lifts his leg, I turn away and study the signs on the other shops that line the street. Halfway down the block, on the other side of the street, I spy a sign that reads:

KERRY'S CAULDRON
HOPES MET, DREAMS FULFILLED

I remember the story Holly told me about the Welsh goddess and her magical cauldron. Kerry is close enough to Cerridwen, so far as I'm concerned. And anyway, this is my dream, isn't it? If I want there to be a shop here with a magical solution waiting for me in it, then why shouldn't it simply be here as needed?

I call Fritzie and he trots along at my side as I cross the street. The lack of motorized vehicles reminds me of the Market area back home, but I can hear traffic, cars and buses, one or two blocks away. A bell tinkles when I enter the shop and my eyes have to adjust to the dim lighting. It's like an old-fashioned apothecary inside and has a bewildering smell: herbal, but like a garden, too, and underneath it all, something wild. There are shelves and shelves of bottles holding all sorts of powders and dried herbs, each neatly identified with small, handwritten labels. Bunches of herbs hang from the ceiling behind the long wooden counter with its glass top and sides. I spy boxes of candles, mortar and pestles, sacks and little boxes of oddly-named teas, innumerable packages and pouches with labels in no language I can recognize.

A lace curtain behind the counter is pulled aside and a tall, dark-haired woman steps out from behind it. She looks a bit like a Gypsy—or at least my romanticized image of one: dark complexion, white blouse, flower-print skirt, long black hair spilling in loose tangles from under a red kerchief. Her gaze goes to Fritzie who's sniffing a barrel by the window with great interest.

"Oh, I'm sorry," I say. "I never thought to ask if he could come in. Come here, Fritzie," I add, hoping he doesn't decide to pee on the barrel.

She smiles. "True dreamers are always welcome here."

I don't know what to say to that. Does she mean me or Fritzie?

"How can I help you?" she adds.

That I can answer. It's why I'm here, after all.

"Hmm," is all she says once I've explained.

Then she lifts a lovely paisley scarf off what I realize is a notebook computer and starts it up.

"What are you doing?" I ask.

"I don't know that spell," she tells me, "so I need to look up the recipe in the Wordwood."

"You're kidding me, right?"

Bad enough a database is sending me e-mail. Why does it have to be in my dream as well?

She looks puzzled. "Why would you think that?"

"I don't want it here," I say.

"You don't—?"

I'm feeling like a petulant child, but I can't seem to stop myself.

"It's my dream," I tell her, "and I don't want that . . . that whatever it is in it with me."

She gives me a long look and then that smile returns. "This is your first visit to Mabon, isn't it?"

I nod.

"I thought so," she goes on. "Did you get here by accident, or did someone show you the way?"

"Someone showed me. But—"

"Well, the first thing you need to know is that you're not

dreaming. It's true that Mabon exists because Sophie Etoile first brought it into being, but it's taken on a life of its own since then."

"You know Sophie?"

"Do you know the founders of the country you come from?" She doesn't wait for my answer. "The point is, that Mabon and our life here in the city goes on, whether you're visiting us or not."

"But the Wordwood—how can you access it here?"

"How can we not? The site's stored in the computers that are housed in the basement of the university library."

I suppose, in some ways, that explains a lot, but I'm still not comfortable with the idea of the Wordwood being here as well. Before the woman can access its site, I tell her that I've changed my mind. I call to Fritzie and he follows me back out onto the street—somewhat reluctantly, I think, until his ears suddenly prick up. I turn to see what's caught his attention and can't believe who I see coming down the street toward us.

"I was just thinking of you," Gina says as she draws closer.

She looks the same as always, thin features, tall, rangy frame. She's dressed in jeans and a T-shirt, a black cotton jacket overtop, wearing those crazy red and yellow cowboy boots that she always loved. Her dark curls spill out from under a wide-brimmed hat. Bending down, she accepts Fritzie's wet kisses and lifts her face to me, smiling under the brim of her hat. I see the difference then. That haunted look I remember always being in her eyes those last few years isn't present.

"Are you a . . . ghost?" I ask.

She laughs. "Are you?"

"No, but I'm not . . ."

"Dead," she finishes for me when my voice trails off.

She sits down on the curb and Fritzie half crawls onto her lap, tail slapping the cobblestones. After a moment I sit down beside them.

"I guess it is confusing," Gina adds.

She turns to look at me, her eyes merry. I can't remember the last time I saw her genuinely happy. She was so sad, for so long.

"So . . . do you live here?" I ask her.

She has to think about that for a moment. "I think so. I think someone needed to see me so badly that they dreamed me into being here."

Me, I think. Only then I look at Fritzie, wriggling on her lap as she pats him. I remember what the woman in the store said when I asked if it was okay for him to be inside. Something about true dreamers always being welcome. I realize that I didn't bring Fritzie here with me; he brought me.

"Did Fritzie ever talk to you?" I ask her. There are a hundred things I want to ask her, but this is what comes out.

She smiles and shakes her head. "But he's a good listener. Aren't you, my brave little boy?"

"I don't understand any of this," I say.

"That's probably a step in the right direction," Gina tells me.

"What's that supposed to mean?"

"Well, you know how you like to make sure everything fits in its proper little box."

"I don't."

She ignores me because we both know it's true. "I think it's better to believe in what you don't know. What you don't know encompasses everything. Embrace it and you embrace the mystery of the world, of the whole universe. It brings you closer to the great spirit that made everything and to which everything returns when its time is done."

I guess being here in dreamland is why that actually seems to make sense.

"What's it like?" I ask her. "The place where we go when we die?"

She gives a slow shake of her head. "I don't really know. I think I'm there and here at the same time and the me that's here isn't privy to everything the me that's there knows."

"Fritzie brought you here," I say.

"I know."

After that we don't talk so much—or at least not about anything important. We go wandering through Sophie's dream city like children on a holiday, curious about everything, unconcerned with the world where things fit into a box and make sense. We're just being pals, the way we were before the world turned dark on Gina and I started figuring out what fit in which box and made sure it stayed that way.

When I finally wake up, I find that Fritzie has crawled up from the end of the bed to lie with his head beside me on the pillow. The first thing I see when I open my eyes is the wall of my bedroom, over the top of his head, looking between his ears. I remember Mabon and Gina, like being there with her really happened. The dream seems so vivid that I have trouble focusing on where I am. This world has the dreamlike quality, not simply at this moment, when I wake, but throughout the day.

I almost quit work that day, I hate being there so much, though of course I don't. I can't. I could never leave everybody hanging like that. But I find myself doodling during the morning meeting, and later on the phone, too. Sketches of what I remember of some of the places I saw in my dream. The funny café where we had lunch—all the umbrellas had the same red and yellow pattern as Gina's boots. This odd street we followed that dwindled until it was only the narrowest of footpaths squeezed between two buildings. Fritzie having a staring contest with a cat, the old tom lying in the display window of an antique shop between a stuffed rooster and a stack of old books. And Gina, of course. The way the wind caught her hair, the crinkle of her smile, the laughter in her eyes.

They're simple sketches, but they're good, too. I can tell. The lines have character as I put them down.

That evening our walk takes Fritzie and me to Jilly's studio where she and Wendy are sitting on the sofa, taking turns reading to each other from a new fairy tale picture book loosely based on *A Midsummer Night's Dream* that's going to be published in the fall. It's something Wendy's supposed to review for *In the City*, which is why they have this advance copy of it. Wendy's particularly chuffed since she and the book's illustrator share the same first name.

Fritzie immediately makes himself comfortable on the Murphy bed, which I don't think I've ever seen folded back into the wall. I pull a chair over by the sofa.

"I'm so jealous," Jilly says when I tell them my story and pull out my sketches.

I blink in surprise.

"Oh, not of these," she says, tapping the sketches with a paint-stained nail. "Which are wonderful. I told you that you still had it, didn't I just?"

"So you're jealous because . . . ?"

"That you got to go to Mabon. I've been wanting to go there for simply forever . . ."

Wendy nods in agreement.

"But we're glad you got to go," Jilly adds.

"And at least I've got a great new story for my tree," Wendy says.

Wendy has an oak tree that she secretly planted in Fitzhenry Park and feeds with stories. I told you they were like fairy tale people. Who else would accept my story at face value?

"What was it like seeing Gina again?" Jilly asks.

"Weird," I tell her. "It's hard to explain. Mostly it was like we were just taking up from before—as though her death had never come in between. But then every once in a while I'd get this sudden, sharp ache in my heart and I'd remember. But before it could really take root, Gina would sweep it away with something outrageous or sweet or simply thoughtful."

"You're going back, right?" Wendy says.

"I'm certainly going to try."

But whatever magic let me slip up on it sideways and take me away doesn't come back. At least not for me. But I know Fritzie's making regular trips to Mabon. I guess it's not hard for him, being a true dreamer.

I finally log back on to the Wordwood site and get it to drop down a list of links on how to make a dog speak. There are well over three hundred entries, from the cauldron business that Holly told me about to this really convoluted process that wakes up the diluted animal blood many of us are supposed to have running through our veins, none of them really practical, or workable. Most of them are the kind of thing that you have to slip up on from the side, which isn't very easy for a put-things-in-their-box person like me.

Holly doesn't really seem surprised when I tell her where the Wordwood's URL leads.

"But don't you think it's amazing?" I ask her.

She grins. "Of course it's amazing. But then everything about the Wordwood is pretty much unbelievable and amazing."

"Can a person be jaded by that sort of thing?"

"I suppose," she says. "But wouldn't that be sad?"

I nod in agreement.

* * *

I don't expect Sophie to be able to help me get back to Mabon, and she can't, though it's not from a lack of desire on her part.

"I'd love to have all my friends there," she says, "but I don't make the rules." Then she laughs. "I don't even know if there are rules. I mean, why do some people see ghosts and fairies, while other people don't? Or can't?"

"Maybe some people are just gifted," I say. "Or more observant."

She grins. "I suppose. Or maybe they're crazier."

But I know what I'll do if I do get back. I'll find a travel agent and see if I can pick up the Mabon version of a rail pass, something that'll let me travel back and forth at will, the way a rail pass lets you take any train you want. I mention this to whatever the entity is that talks to me from the Wordwood. We've struck up an e-mail correspondence. The reply I get reads:

Date: Tue, 29 Jun 1999 08:10:20-0400
From: Webmaster@TheWordwood.com
To: SueAsh@cybercare.com
Subject: Re: Rail passes and boxes
Why not? It seems worth a try. And boxes and magic aren't mutually exclusive. After all, look at me.
The Wordwood
http://www.thewordwood.com/

I suppose that's true. Anything can be categorized. But then I think of what Gina told me, about embracing one's ignorance of the universe, and I think maybe that's true as well. We can categorize what we know, put everything into its box as it fits. But we also have to leave our minds open to embrace the great mystery of the world—all those things we know nothing about. Because if we do that with an open and generous enough heart, we might find the mystery embracing us back.

I still miss Gina.

I heard a dog speak once.

I've been to the magical dream city of Mabon.

I'm drawing more and that's sharpening my observational skills, because when I pay attention to the detail I can see, it reminds me about all the other detail that I can't. At least not yet.

I think Robert Nathan was wrong about one thing. Trees and rocks *do* have their own fairy tales and legends. Everything does. The trouble is, we only ever understand our own. And so long as that's all we do, we're putting ourselves in a box that doesn't simply categorize what we know, but also shuts us away from all we don't.

Fritzie dreams well—I can tell by the way his tail beats against the comforter when he's sleeping. Maybe tonight I'll lie down beside him. We'll be like a couple of spoons and my dreaming eyes will see how the world looks when viewed from between his ears.

Masking Indian

It's the last thing I expect to find hanging on the wall of my apartment when I get home. I haven't seen that costume in ten years, not since I left New Orleans. Back then it was hooked up in a place of honor on another wall, the one in Lawrence Boudreaux's front room.

Larry died last year. I would've made it back for the funeral but I only heard about it afterward, when it was too late to go.

I drop my jacket and purse on the sofa now and slowly walk up to where that plumed extravaganza hangs. The colors are so bright they dull everything in my living room and I'm not exactly known for my good taste. The lime-green bust of Elvis sitting on top of my TV is perhaps the subtlest thing I own. What can I say? I like kitsch.

But this costume . . .

When I lift a hand to touch one of the plumes, the whole thing fades away before my fingers can make contact. It figures. I've been looking for years for a miracle to clear up the mess of my life, but when the impossible does come my way, this is what I get: a moment of special effects.

I stare at the wall where the costume was hanging. Thinking of it, of Chief Larry, wakes a flood of old memories that take me back to when I was a runaway, a little white girl looking for her black roots among the Black Indian tribes that rule the Mardi Gras.

"You'll like this," Wendy said. "Marley says she's got a ghost in her apartment."

Jilly looked up from her canvas to where Wendy sat on the Murphy bed at the other end of the studio, her blonde curls pressed up against the headboard, legs splayed out in front of her on the comforter.

"Who's Marley?" Jilly asked.

"The art director's new assistant at *In the City.* You met her at that party at Alan's a couple of weeks ago."

"I remember. She was the one with the bright red buzz cut and the pierced eyebrow, right?"

"That's her."

"But she's not exactly the happiest camper, is she?" Jilly went on. "I remember being struck by how she seemed so outgoing, but there was all this other stuff going on behind her eyes."

"Sounds like you're describing yourself," Wendy said.

Jilly laughed, but Wendy caught the momentary empathy that flickered in her friend's sparkling blue eyes.

"So what kind of ghost does she have?" Jilly asked.

Wendy had to grin. "The ghost of a Big Chief's Mardi Gras costume."

Jilly put down her brush and came over to the bed.

"A what?" she asked.

"You know, one of those huge feather and sparkle affairs they wear in the parades."

"Except it's the *ghost* of it?"

"Mm-hmm," Wendy said. "Except, how can an inanimate object even have a ghost? You'd think it'd have to be alive first . . . so that it could die and become a ghost, I mean."

Jilly shook her head. "Everything has spirit."

"Even a costume?"

"Maybe especially a costume. It's already made to be a secret, isn't it?"

"Or to hide one."

Jilly got a dreamy look in her eyes. "The ghost of costume. I love it. Do you think she'd let us see it?"

"I'll have to ask."

"A long time ago," the old black man says. "Back when we were slaves. The only ones who welcomed us here were the Indians. That's why we respect them like we do, why we call up their spirits with the drumming and parades."

He was brought up in one of those Black Indian tribes in New Orleans: a Flagboy, running information from the Spyboys to the Second Chiefs; a Wildman with the buffalo horns poking out of his headdress, scattering the crowds when they got too close to the chiefs and could maybe mess up the ornate costumes; finally a Big Chief, Chief Larry of the Wild Eagles, squaring off against the other chiefs, spasm band setting up a polyrhythmic racket at his back while he strutted his stuff.

I can't keep my gaze off the outfit where it's hooked up on the wall of his home—a spirit guide, he tells me. An altar and a personal shield, a reflection of his soul.

It boggles my mind. I can't imagine how much it cost to put that fantastic explosion of flash and thunder together. It's a masterpiece of dyed plumes, papier-mâché and broken glass, peacock and turkey feathers, glass beads, eggshells, sequins and fish scales, velvet and sparkles and lord knows what else. The headdress rises three feet above the top of his head when he puts it on and the whole costume has to weigh a hundred or so pounds, but he can carry it like it has no weight at all.

Tired as he was last night, he didn't let that stop him. He was up the whole night before, sewing and helping others in the tribe with their suits. He marched twenty or thirty miles through the city yesterday, carried his tribe through over a dozen confrontations with other tribes, drank straight vinegar to cut the cramps, but he was still so swollen when he got home last night that they had to cut him out of his suit.

Yeah, he's something, Chief Larry, but he's still got time to talk to a street kid like me.

"Thing is," he says, "people forget this wasn't always a show. Time was we governed the neighborhoods. We kept the music and spirit alive—hell, we were priest and police, all in one. Masking Indian was just a little piece of what the tribes were all about. We were like the spiritual churches then—we looked after the souls of our people."

"What happened?" I ask.

He shrugs. "Progress happened."

He says the word "progress" like it's an epithet. I guess for him it is.

I don't know why he ever took to me. Maybe he felt sorry for me. Maybe he just liked the idea of helping a little white runaway connect with the black blood that she got from her great-grandpa, blood so thin it doesn't show any more than the winter coat of a hare against a snowdrift. But he lets me hang around the Wild

Eagles' practices. I sit in the back and bang away on a cowbell, adding my own little clangs to the throbbing, primal rhythm of bass and snare drums, tambourines, congas, percussion sticks, pebble gourds, bucket drums and anything that can make a noise and fill out the beat.

The tempo just keeps building until everything seems like total pandemonium, but Chief Larry's actually exercising a strict spiritual and physical control over the proceedings. Comes a moment when everything feels transcendent, like we're plugging straight into the heart of some deep, old, primal magic. When we're one, all the Wild Eagles, everybody in that room.

It's better than crack, but just as addictive.

"Sometimes," he tells me, "people ought to just leave well enough alone. Everything's moving too fast these days. We're so busy, we can't see what's in front of our noses anymore. We don't need to know everything that's happening, every place in the world, every damn second of the day."

He pauses to look at me, to make sure he's got my attention.

"What we need," he goes on, "is to connect to what's around us and the spirit that moves through it. Our families, our neighbors, the neighborhood."

"The tribe," I say.

"Same difference."

Marley Butler was on the computer when Wendy arrived at the *In the City* offices the next morning. She was working on a collage to illustrate an article on the upcoming festivities organized by the Good Serpent Club at the end of Lent. Every year they put on a kind of a mini–Mardi Gras, more block party than parade. A half-dozen streets in Upper Foxville were closed off and people from all over the city gathered to listen to live bands, sample Cajun and other

Louisiana-style cooking, and march around in costumes and masks. The only gathering as colorful was in July when the Gay Pride Parade finished up a week of celebrations, but for that they closed off Williamson Street all the way from Kelly Street to the lake.

Marley was using scans from photos taken during previous years' Mardi Gras festivals, combining them in such a manner that the individual photos were still recognizable, but taken as a whole, they became a masked face.

"That's pretty cool," Wendy said, looking over Marley's shoulder.

"Thanks."

Wendy slid into a seat beside the computer desk, and popped the lid on her coffee.

"So . . . do you still have your ghost?" she asked and took a sip.

Marley gave her a wary look. "Why?"

"Well, I was telling Jilly about it last night and she was wondering if we could come over and see it."

"You're making fun of me."

Wendy shook her head. "No, really. I swear I'm not. We just like weird stuff."

"Weird stuff," Marley repeated, obviously dubious.

"Look, I've told you about Jilly—how she's really into this kind of thing."

Marley gave a slow nod. "And you?"

"I just like a good story."

"You're not telling me something," Marley said.

Wendy hesitated. How did she explain this without coming off as a complete flake?

But, "Okay," she said. "Fair's fair. See, I've got this tree that grows on stories. I raised it from an acorn and ever since it's been the tiniest thing, I've given it stories. It's huge now—way bigger than it could possibly be if it wasn't a magical tree—but I still give it new stories whenever I can."

Marley said nothing. Her gaze held Wendy's, but Wendy couldn't figure out what the other woman was thinking.

Wendy tried on a smile. "So now you can make fun of me," she added.

"You've got a tree that grows on stories," Marley finally said.

Wendy nodded. "A Tree of Tales."

"Where is it?"

"I transplanted it to Fitzhenry Park when it got too big for the pot I was keeping it in. You should see it. It's already huge."

"So do you find it cathartic, feeding it your stories?"

Wendy shrugged. "I guess. Depends on the story. Why do you ask?"

"Because I've got a story I'd like to tell it."

"I remember a time," Chief Larry tells me one day, "when things really meant something. Everything had a meaning. The difference now is, things only seem to have a meaning if we give it to them. But it shouldn't be that way. Is the crawdad any less of a crawdad if we're not there to acknowledge it?"

I like that he tells me this kind of stuff. Growing up, all I ever heard was, "Shut up. No one's talking to you."

"It's like a Zen thing, right?" I say.

I read about this once when I was hiding out in the public library from the truant officer. Let me tell you, that's the last place they'll come looking for you. I've learned about more stuff skipping school than I ever did in the classroom.

"You know," I add by way of explanation. "Does a tree falling in the forest make a sound if no one's there to hear it?"

" 'Course it makes a sound. That's the whole point of what I'm telling you."

"But what about quantum physics and this whole business about observable phenomena that scientists are studying now? They're saying that things like quarks only take on a discernible identity when they're being observed."

"I don't know quarks from farts," Larry says. "I just know the world doesn't need us to give it meaning. Just like nothing was put here for our use. If we're caretakers, it's only to leave things a little better than when we got here. Me, I think we're just one more animal, messier and more mean-spirited than most."

"It's not always here," Marley said as she unlocked the door of her apartment.

She's worried we're going to think she made it all up, Wendy thought, but Jilly was nodding beside her.

"That's the way these things work," Jilly said. "If they were predictable, they wouldn't be very mysterious, would they?"

Marley gave her a grateful look.

"It's funny," she said as she ushered them in. "I never once stopped to wonder if I was crazy. I just knew it was really there, even if it fades away whenever I try to touch it."

Her guests made no reply. Marley's hallway let straight into her living room and there, hooked up on the wall, was the costume, an extravaganza of reds and pinks so vibrant that it seemed to pulse. Jilly moved forward, Wendy trailing behind her, until they were both standing directly in front of it.

"Oh my," Jilly said.

Neither of them tried to touch it, though Wendy was sorely tempted.

"What's it doing here?" she said.

"Just being gorgeous," Jilly told her. "It doesn't have to be doing anything. That's what I like best about this sort of thing. It just is."

"No, I meant why would it appear here?"

"I used to know the guy who owned it," Marley told them. "It showed up about a week or so after I found out he'd died."

"Were you close to him?" Jilly asked.

Marley nodded. "Once upon a time. It was years ago, back in New Orleans."

"I'm sorry."

"Me, too. I should've gone back to see him, but I always thought, there'll be time. But there never is, is there?"

"Never as much as we'd like," Jilly said.

Marley said nothing for a long moment, gaze locked on the costume, then she blinked and turned to her guests.

"You guys want a beer or something?"

"Beer is always good," Jilly said.

"So did he ever wear it?" Wendy asked when they returned from the kitchen with their drinks.

Marley nodded. "You bet. He looked amazing in it. Some of the tribes, they saw those red and pink plumes coming towards them on Mardi Gras night, they'd just head down another street so they wouldn't lose a confrontation to Chief Larry and his Wild Eagles." She smiled at the blank looks on the faces of her guests. "Do you know anything about the Black Indian tribes down in New Orleans?"

When they shook their heads, she started to tell them. Not about how she ended up on the street, or the simple gift that Chief Larry had given her by treating her as a human being, but describing the tribes and their influence, how it all came together on Mardi Gras night in a pageant of wonder and noisy magic.

Just before they left, Marley walked up to the costume and

reached out a hand. Wendy gasped when it vanished. Innocuous as a ghostly costume might be, there was still something disquieting about the fact that it even existed in the first place. Turning, she saw that Jilly was only smiling, her sapphire blue eyes shining bright with pleasure.

This night after the Mardi Gras, Larry tells me it's his last year of leading the Wild Eagles.

"I'm getting too old to carry the weight," he tells me.

I wonder if he means the costume, or his responsibility as Big Chief. Probably both.

Like me, he's got no blood family. The difference is, his people died; they didn't turn their backs on him. Two sons were shipped home in coffins from Vietnam. His wife was killed in a car crash by a drunk driver. That left him with the Wild Eagles. Just like me now. My great-grandpa on my mother's side used to run with his dad, back in the old days. That's how come I ended up on his doorstep in the first place, wanting to know about that part of my family. I already knew too much about the Jordan side of the family tree.

"So what are you going to do?" I ask.

"I don't know," he tells me.

There's something different in his voice. Like all the strength has gone out of it.

"You'll still have the Wild Eagles," I say.

He nods. "But it won't be the same. I was the Big Chief. Now I'll just be another guy, banging a drum."

I don't want to say, that's more than I've got. I'm just a hanger-on.

But it sort of comes out anyway.

"But you're still part of the tribe," I say. "You don't have to be alone."

He nods again, but his gaze changes. I can tell he's no longer feeling sorry for himself. He's feeling sorry for me.

"That family of yours," he says. "They must've hurt you pretty bad. Other people, too, I'm guessing."

I shrug.

"But you never gave in to anybody, did you?"

Once, I think. But that was enough.

"No," I tell him. "I just ran away."

"Sometimes that's all you can do," he says.

I can only look at him. Bad as things were, I still feel kind of ashamed for running. In all the books I read, people stand up for themselves when things get bad. But I wasn't brave enough.

"Sometimes it's not just the smart thing to do," he adds. "Sometimes it's the brave thing, too."

It's like he's reading my mind.

"Doesn't seem so brave to me," I say.

He shakes his head. "You just don't know enough yet to make that kind of a pronouncement. Wait'll some time goes by."

"It's going to have to be a lot of time."

"Could be," he says. "If that's what it takes . . ."

Wendy felt a little awkward taking Marley to where she'd planted the Tree of Tales in Fitzhenry Park. The tree was a miracle, but you wouldn't know that from looking at it and she was afraid Marley wouldn't understand. She'd grown it from an acorn, nourished it through a winter, then transplanted the sapling here in the Silenus Gardens, that part of the park that was dedicated to the poet Joshua Stanhold. And it had grown . . . how it had grown. But while a botanist might be surprised to find such a large and healthy example of *Quercus robur*—the common oak of Europe—growing here among a handful of native oaks, most people wouldn't give it a second glance except to admire its lines.

As they approached the tree, walking along the concrete path and keeping out of the way of the in-line skaters and joggers who seemed to think they owned the park, Wendy could see a man sitting under it, talking, except he was alone there under the boughs.

She smiled. There was proof, though she didn't need it, that she wasn't alone in sharing her stories with the tree.

He got up as they arrived and gave them a friendly nod before walking away.

"*This* is it?" Marley said.

Wendy nodded.

Marley craned her neck, staring up into the sweeping canopy that spread above them.

"But this tree looks like it's . . ."

"I know," Wendy said. "A hundred years old."

Marley shook her head. "But if it grew so fast . . ." She looked to Wendy. "How could nobody have noticed?"

"People don't pay attention to things that are impossible," Wendy said. "At least that's what Jilly and Christy are always saying. That's why all these improbable things like a Tree of Tales—or the ghost of a costume—can exist with hardly anybody noticing. They don't *want* to see them."

"And we did?"

"I didn't think so in the beginning," Wendy said. "When John Windle—the crazy old guy who got me involved with taking care of the tree—first approached me, I didn't want to know about it for a minute."

"What changed your mind?"

Wendy shrugged. "I don't really know. Jilly was always telling me about these wonderful magical things that happened to her, but I thought they sounded more scary than exhilarating. But once I gave in and started taking care of the tree, I came to understand what she meant. Everything seemed bigger and more in focus. Everything seemed to have meaning—not necessarily meaning to me, but to itself. I guess what was most important was when I realized that. Everything's here for its own purpose, not for how it relates to me. I'm a part of it, but just that. A part."

"You remind me of Chief Larry," Marley said. "He used to tell me stuff like that."

Wendy smiled. "Of course, the intensity of what I felt didn't last. Which is probably just as well, since I've also got to live in the world that everyone else inhabits and it's kind of hard to interact with people when you're always looking to see if they've got an elf sitting on their shoulder or something."

Wendy shook her head as Marley's eyes widened.

"No," she added. "I don't see that kind of thing. That's more up Jilly's alley. But I do have this." She lifted her arms to encompass the oak boughs spreading above them. "And it's magic enough for me."

"And you really planted it?" Marley asked.

"Yup. Eight years or so ago, it was wintering in a pot on the windowsill of my kitchen."

"Wow."

"Mmm," Wendy said, a dreamy look in her eyes. "Whenever Jilly tells me some really improbable story, I come here and I'm reminded that the world is bigger and stranger and more wonderful than it sometimes seems to be. And I don't think I'm alone. Remember that guy who was sitting under the tree when we arrived?"

Marley nodded.

"I'll bet he was telling the tree a story. I find lots of people come to sit here and talk to it. Most of them probably don't even know why they do it, except it makes them feel good. But they're nourishing the tree all the same."

"I . . ." Marley began, but then her voice trailed off.

"I understand," Wendy told her. "You want to tell it your story, but you want to do it in private."

"I don't mean to be rude."

Wendy smiled. "You're not. Want me to wait for you by the memorial?"

"I might be a while."

"That's okay. I don't mind waiting." Wendy patted her shoulder bag. "I've got a book and, well, maybe you'll want some company when you're done."

Before Marley could protest, Wendy gave her a jaunty wave and headed back the way they'd come.

So here I am, talking to a tree. To tell you the truth, I don't feel any magic in it. Even with a ghost in my own apartment, Wendy's claims just seem like too much . . . I don't know. Wishful thinking. But I talk all the same. I tell my story. There's nothing particularly original about it, and what does that say about this world we live in? Too many kids grow up just like I did, unwanted, unloved, never knowing a kind word or even a kiss until, in my case, I hit puberty, started to get some curves on my skinny-ass frame, and the guy in the trailer park who used to baby-sit kids for whoever was stupid enough to trust the freak with their children "made me a woman," as he put it.

But that wasn't the worse of it. The worst was when I told my parents. I don't know why I did; I already knew they wouldn't care. But the old man goes ballistic. Starts screaming about my "goddamned nigger blood" and beats the crap out of both me and my mother. I'd have more sympathy for her, living with such a monster, but she wasn't ever that much better. That night she just spat on me and then hauled herself to her feet and staggered out of the kitchen to leave me lying there on the cracked linoleum.

I ran away that night.

I'd already known that my great-grandpa on my mother's side was black, or partly black, though you wouldn't know it from looking at me. I'm so fair-skinned that just thinking of going out into the sun gives me a burn. The funny thing is my old man's darker-skinned than I am—got some Seminole blood a few generations back, Creole, who knows what else. Mostly meanness.

Anyway, I decide to go find out about the ancestors on my mother's side. She's no saint herself, but I already know the Jordan side of the family is made up of these mean-spirited sonsabitches, so what have I got to lose? I knew the Butlers came from the city, so I head up to New Orleans and ask around about my great-grandpa Gilbert Butler, did anybody know him?, and that's how I finally run into Larry Boudreaux.

Life gets a little better. I'm still living on the street when I connect with the Wild Eagles, scraping by the best I can, but I find what I'm looking for. My great-grandpa was a good man; it turns out that the blood didn't turn bad until it came around to my mother and who knows how much marrying into the Jordan family had to do with that. But better still, I find a friend in Larry. I learn that there are people here in the world who'll treat me like a human being instead of just the family's ugly pet, or street trash.

But the thing is, it's still hard. No matter how far away I get from it, I still feel like the kid in the trailer park who had to run away. The kid who lived on the street like a feral cat, never quite trusting the hand held out to it. I can only go so far with people, only look over the wall I've got built up inside me, instead of coming around or letting them in. Maybe that kind of thing never goes away.

It did when I was with Larry, but once I moved, all the doubts came back again. I guess I could've gone back, but I had my pride. I wanted to make it on my own, prove how I could be a real success, before I went back. But now it's too late. Larry's dead and I know he's the only one who wouldn't have cared one way or the other, only that I was happy.

I tell the tree all of that and then I lie back on the grass and stare up into its boughs. I don't feel cleansed or relieved or like I've touched any kind of magic. Wendy's Tree of Tales is a piece of work all right, but there's more mystery in why the ghost of Larry's Mardi Gras costume likes to hang on the wall of my apartment.

But thinking of that costume gives me an idea.

Wendy wasn't much help as they worked on the costume in Marley's living room, trying to copy the ghost of Chief Larry's suit that was still hooked up on the wall, but Jilly threw herself into it with cheerful enthusiasm. Even when Marley and Wendy had to go to the office, Jilly left her own work unattended in her studio and spent long hours at Marley's apartment, pasting and gluing and stitching. But then, that was Jilly, always ready for an adventure, always ready to drop everything and lend a hand.

Still, Wendy helped out where she could, and if she was klutzy with the detail work, she was good at sorting beads and dying feathers and putting together meals. The other two would get so caught up in what they were doing that they wouldn't even have thought of eating if it hadn't been for her.

She also liked to see how Marley was loosening up, not just with Jilly, but at work, too. Mostly Marley kept to herself—it was only because of Wendy that they'd hung out, eaten lunches together, relaxed enough so that while Marley didn't talk about her past, she'd talk about other things. Like the ghost of a Mardi Gras suit hanging on her living room wall.

There wasn't much they had to go out and buy. Marley had a surprising amount of the raw materials they needed for the project, as though she'd been planning to make a costume like this for years. She pulled out boxes and tins and plastic bags filled with sequins and glass beads, fabric remnants, rhinestones, seashells, colored glass and the like.

"I'm just a pack rat," she explained with a shrug.

Jilly grinned. "With ever such conservative tastes."

They dyed bundles of ostrich, turkey and peacock feathers, made a frame for the headdress with wire and covered it with papier-mâché, constantly using the ghost costume for a reference. But while they started out copying, before too long their costume took on a life of its own.

"Which is the way it should be," Jilly said. "Don't you think?"

Marley nodded. "Larry wouldn't want a tribute—he'd want this suit to have a life of its own."

Not to mention an afterlife, Wendy thought, looking at the ghost hanging on the wall.

I leave New Orleans not long after Chief Larry steps down from his leadership of the Wild Eagles. By this time I've got a room in a boarding house and between a couple of part-time jobs, I've been taking night school to get my high school diploma. The diploma gets me into a one-year computer arts program at Butler University, so I make the move. I can't afford my own equipment, but the labs there are really impressive and as a student I can use them whenever I want. I'm in there a lot.

I don't know when I realized I wanted to be an artist. It's not like I grew up always drawing or anything. I guess it came from doing posters advertising gigs for groups that people I knew were in. It was something I liked and was actually good at. Eventually I discovered that I enjoyed collage work the most, which is what drew me to the computer studies. If you've got the material on your hard drive, you can manipulate and play with it forever. And with the quality of printers these days, and if you're using the right kind of inks and paper, every print you run off is archival quality.

But I never make more than one print of a piece.

That's something I learned from Chief Larry and the Wild Eagle practices. Anything really good is always different. Unique. You might start out aiming to copy something, but if it's got any heart, if it's got any real spirit, it'll be something else again when it's done.

It'll be its own thing.

Works for people, too.

It took them the better part of a week and a half to get the costume finished. Finally, Marley lifted it up on its hanger. She looked at Wendy and Jilly, then carried the suit over to the wall where the ghost of Chief Larry's hung. When she hung it up, the ghost didn't so much fade away as fade into the costume they'd made.

For a long moment, none of them spoke. A tingle ran up Wendy's spine and she saw Jilly wearing that contented smile of hers again, the one that always came when some piece of the big mystery underlying the world manifested itself for a moment.

"What are you going to do with it?" Wendy finally asked.

Marley grinned. "What do you think? I'm going to wear it to the Mardi Gras that the Good Serpent Club's putting on."

"Can we come?" Jilly asked. "We could bang the drums and stuff."

"You want to join the new tribe?"

"You bet."

Wendy nodded as well, though she wasn't sure how well she'd do, galivanting around on the street, dancing and banging a drum. She didn't have quite the abandon Jilly did for this sort of thing. "There are no public spectacles," Jilly liked to say. "There's only fun."

"What are you going to call your tribe?" Wendy asked.

Marley thought about that for a moment. "I don't know. Maybe the Unforgotten Ones."

"Keep in mind," Chief Larry says another time when we're talking about Mardi Gras costumes. "Masking Indian's not about hiding yourself. It's about revealing yourself. It's about remembering the ones who went before and the spirit that's in everything, and honoring both. Your suit's a shield against hurt, but it's also an altar of belief and faith and hope."

"I'll remember."

He smiles. "I know the world can be a hard and wicked place and sometimes it's all we can do not to want to just check out and leave it behind. But it's our job—people like you and me who care— to fight those wrongs best we can and offer up a hope of something better. Every time we do a good thing, the spirits smile and the world's that much better. I know it's no big deal. It's not going to change the whole world. But it's a start.

"See, the people watching and laughing and having themselves a party . . . it doesn't matter if they understand; it only matters that we do. Because masking Indian's not just a reminder of the good spirits that share the world with us, it's a celebration of them, of us, and how we can all get along if we just make an effort."

And thanks to Larry, and his ghostly costume, that's something I'm not likely to forget again.

Granny Weather

My friend Jilly and I have this ongoing argument. She says there's magic, right here in this world. With all you've experienced, she asks, how can you pretend otherwise? I'm not the only one who knows you have faerie blood, Sophie, or that the Moon is your mother.

But I tell her there's a big difference between this world and the once upon a time of my dreamlands. Anything can happen in a dream. What you bring back isn't magic, it's experience, and they're not the same thing at all.

It's the last thing I expect, a bogle sitting on the end of my bed, bringing the smell of stagnant water and rotting logs into my room. He's naked, like they usually are in the swamps where I've seen them before, and ugly as phlegm. Gangly limbs, fingers and toes each with an extra joint, and he's hairless, skin black and slick as motor oil. The eyes are too big for the triangular head, Halloween-slit eyes glowing just like there's a hot fire burning behind them. The nose lies flat against his face, like that of a pug dog, and the mouth has way too many pointed teeth in it.

I thought I was going to sleep. I guess maybe I am asleep and this time the dreamlands have taken me back into my own bedroom where this little nightmare is waiting for me. For some reason I don't feel as scared as I know I should be, though that doesn't stop me from checking out the shadows in the corners of my room to see how many little friends the bogle might have brought with him. He seems to be alone, so now I start looking for something to hit him with if he gets out of line.

"Sophie."

There's something in the sibilant tone of his voice that jumps my gaze back to him. Not innocence—these things wouldn't know innocence if it jumped up and bit them—but a sense that, whatever he's doing here, he doesn't mean me any harm. So I decide to hear him out, though I'm not saying I actually trust him. Quicks and haunts and bogles. You can't trust any of the little monsters.

"What's your name?" I ask.

I sit up, pulling the bedclothes along with me as I do. I'm wearing an oversize T-shirt as a nightie, but it doesn't feel like enough on its own. The hot coals of his gaze make me feel like I'm wearing nothing at all.

"You can call me Serth," he says after a moment's hesitation.

Not his name, I assume, but it's all I'm going to get so it'll have to do.

"So what do you want, Serth?"

"There's trouble in the fens," he tells me.

"What's that got to do with me?"

"You helped Granny Weather when we tried to drown the moon," he says.

I give a reluctant nod. It seems a long time ago, in another life.

"Now we need your help to stop her," he says.

I can't imagine a less likely scenario and tell him so.

His eyes blaze. "Even if I tell you that she's eating our children?"

And that would be bad, how? I think. Gross, certainly, but bad? Less bogle children means less bogle adults leading the unwary into the fens and drowning them.

I don't say anything, but he can read it in my face.

"Every time she eats one of us," he says, "a piece of the night goes away."

"And why is this my problem?"

"Without night, there's no day." He holds up a hand to stop me from interrupting. "Time will come to a halt."

"And?"

He glares at me. "Our world will dissolve. And once it does, the sickness will move on, spreading across the dreamlands. Eventually, even into your precious Mabon. And let me tell you, the more worlds that fall, the harder the sickness will be to defeat."

I shake my head. "Why are you coming to me? There are hundreds of you . . ." I bite my tongue before saying "little monsters." I pretend I had to clear my throat. "You people," I finish.

"You're the only one she trusts."

"And what makes that useful?" I ask.

"You can get close to her and slip a knife in between her ribs before she even suspects you mean her ill."

Somehow I doubt that, Granny Weather being who and what she is. But I've no interest in finding out anyhow.

"It's not going to happen," I tell him.

He nods. "We'll see what song you sing when the death she wakes comes creeping down Mabon's streets."

"Oh, please," I say. "This whole thing sounds like some stupid comic book."

He looks like one, too. Not the kind I grew up with—*Archie, Little Lulu*—but the kind they make nowadays where the heroes are dark and creepy and you can't tell them from the bad guys.

He glares at me. "You'll see," he says.

And then he's gone.

I'm not sure if I blinked, or woke up, but I'm alone in my room now and I appear to be awake. No bogles, though the smell of him seems to linger the way bad smells do.

I let the bedclothes fall and sit up straighter. I owe Granny Weather too much to ever think of betraying her, but I suppose I'll have to go talk to her now.

This is how it works.

I go to sleep and the next thing I know, I'm in the dreamlands. I'm still asleep, here in my apartment, my body stretched out in bed or curled up on the old sofa out on my balcony, but I'm somewhere else at the same time, transported to a place that feels just as physical and real. I've been doing it for years. It started out as daydreaming when I was a kid, then I forgot about it for the longest time until I got pulled into a dream that wouldn't let me go. After that . . . well, I don't know what made the difference, but now I go there every night, to Mabon, to the dreamlands.

Christy calls it serial dreaming, where every time you fall asleep you pick up where you left off in last night's dream, but it's more than that. What, exactly, I have no idea. I'm so used to it, I don't even think it's strange anymore. Even my friends accept it as a matter of course, which maybe tells you more about them than me.

It's funny, but Jilly, who's never even been here, has the best name for where I go. She calls it the cathedral world, because everything feels taller and bigger and brighter here. It's not that it is, only that it feels that way. It's like there's a singing inside you—in your chest, your head, your heart—and it fills you up like nothing else ever has. Only being in love comes close.

So anyway, Mabon's easy for me to reach—I kind of founded the city, though a lot of other people's dreams have built it up since—but the fairy-tale world where Granny Weather and the bogles live, that's a whole other thing. I've never gone there on my own. Granny Weather's the one who first brought me there, when she showed me how to defeat the bogles and rescue the moon.

Granny Weather. She's wizened and small, shoulders hunched over and everything about her seems dry as kindling: fingers, hair, limbs. You think she's so helpless until you look into her eyes. There you find all the mysteries of the world lying thick and dark and you realize she's much more than what she seems to be. Powerful and earthy. Formidable. The proverbial goodwife, living in her cottage, deep in an enchanted forest.

Could she be eating bogle babies? The thought brings the taste of bile to my throat. I can't imagine it. But I suppose anything's possible and if she really has taken on the role of the wicked witch in some bogle version of "Hansel and Gretel," then she must have a good reason for it. More likely, the bogle who came into my bedroom was lying. I'll only find out the truth by asking her.

At least I know a way to get to her cottage. My boyfriend Jeck originally came from that same fairy-tale world. Oh, I know what you're thinking. How pathetic can it be when your boyfriend only exists in the dreamlands. But it works for us. It's complicated, but it works.

*   *   *

"This is not a good idea," Jeck says. "The fens are dangerous."

We're slouched at an outdoor table in front of Johnny Brews, the coffee shop that's just down the block from the apartment we share in Mabon. Jeck's looking drop-dead gorgeous as usual, my handsome boyfriend that I can only be with in dreamland. His eyes are like no one else's I know, deep violet with long moody lashes, and his hair is as iridescent and black as a crow's wing. I reach out and brush the cowlick back from his brow.

"I know," I tell him. "And this whole business doesn't make much sense either. What makes them think I'd help them hurt Granny Weather? And that stupid story about her eating bogle babies . . ."

He gets a bit of a funny look, then.

"What?" I say. "What?"

"Maybe you don't know her as well as you think you do."

"I don't really know her at all. I only met her that one time."

He nods.

"You're not telling me she *does* eat bogle babies?"

"I just don't think it's a good idea to get involved," Jeck says.

"Except the bogle said it could affect things everywhere—in all the dreamlands."

Jeck sighs. "Bogles are also liars."

This was certainly true.

"And besides," he adds. "What does playing the hero ever get a person?"

"It got me you."

"Ah . . ."

And then he doesn't know what to say.

"So will you take me?" I ask. "Or at least show me the way?"

"That was never in question," he tells me.

                    ☙   ☙   ☙

The trick to magic is that it lies in between. In between what? It almost doesn't matter. It just has to be in between. Not blue or yellow, but green. Not sun or moon, but the light of dusk. Not river or land, but the bridge that spans the water.

So after we pay for our coffees, Jeck takes me by the hand and leads me into the alleyway that runs alongside of Johnny Brews—a narrow little lane with brick buildings rising tall on either side. A place between, you see. You can find them anywhere.

I don't notice exactly how he calls the traveling magic up, but one moment we're walking with cobblestones underfoot and the next there's damp dirt. The smell of the fens rises up around us and the city is gone. Still in the dreamlands, I know, but true dreaming's not as arbitrary as the regular kind. It takes intent and a strong will to readily move from one world to another.

Which is another way of saying, it takes magic.

We've arrived on higher ground in a grove of gnarled crack willows, boughs reaching up for the night stars, the fens around us. The grove lies about halfway between Granny Weather's cottage and the bogles' nest deep in the swamp, a lonely place. I turn to Jeck, but before I can speak, a heavy rope net drops from the boughs above and knocks us both to the ground. I can hear sibilant snickering as we try to untangle ourselves. The effort's wasted as our captors pull the net in tight, pinning us against each other, our limbs trapped between our bodies.

They're bogles, of course. Dozens of the ugly little monsters. I stare up at them from where we lie on the ground, wondering if my night visitor Serth is among them, but it's impossible to tell, they all look too much alike. Then it no longer matters. Three men, each of whom could be Jeck's twin brother, come stepping out from under the drooping boughs of the willows. I can't tell them apart, except that one of them has a small bone hanging from a thong around his neck.

The men look down at us with their dark gazes and I glance at Jeck, note the tight line of his lips. There's no love lost here, that's for sure.

"Bring them along," one of the men says.

The three of them move off. A half-dozen bogles hoist us up in the net and then, willy-nilly, we're following along behind.

I've got a hundred questions for Jeck, but now's not the time for any of them.

I never knew the bogles had actual habitations. I always pictured them living in the wet mud like newts or water snakes. And maybe most of them do, but this bunch has an old stone round tower that's half falling in on itself, perched up on a vague island of higher ground. Or maybe it belongs to Jeck's nasty kin.

See, he's related to the three men who look so much like him. They're crows, but they're also men—though nothing like the crows and ravens that Jilly likes to talk about.

"We're only blackbirds in that other world," Jeck told me once after he'd moved to Mabon. "The enchantment that lets us shift shape wasn't born in our bones and blood; it lies in the air of that otherworld. We breathe it in and we can change, but we're not even remotely related to the corbæ in your friend's stories."

That's true enough. There's nothing whimsical or charming about these brothers of his; they're just mean. I know, because I've met them before, when they were trying to drown the moon.

There's seven of them all told, including Jeck, but he's the youngest, which meant right from the start there were big things in store for him, this being a fairy-tale world and he being the seventh son and all. But he wasn't having any part of it—chucked it all and came to live in Mabon instead. Maybe that's why his brothers hate him. But while I don't really know why they've got it in for him—Jeck doesn't talk much about his family—it's not hard to figure out why they don't like me. I'm the one who rescued the moon from the watery grave that they and the bogles had prepared for her.

Even half fallen down, the tower looms above us, old stone, water-stained and overhung with vines and moss. At another time, I'd love to be here. I love old places like this. Unlike Jilly, who can call up an unfeigned interest in pretty much any place, I'm drawn primarily to these sorts of structures, buildings steeped in history. Doesn't have to be big, important bits of history; just the sense that hundreds of lives have touched a place down through the years.

The bogles take us down into the tower's basement—which is less than pleasant with its slimy stones and damp, cold air—and dump us unceremoniously on the floor. The place reeks of wet straw and old urine and my skin crawls at the thought of lying here in a bogles' toilet. It takes us a few minutes to work free from the snarls of the net, but by then this huge warped wooden door has closed us in and we hear a crossbar drop into place on the other side. A barred window set high in the wall lets in a little light, but it's not particularly comforting and the bars are too narrow for even a bird-shaped Jeck to slip through. Once we finally get the net off, we have a chance to look around a little more and realize we're not alone.

Granny Weather sits there in a corner of the room, shaking her head at the bedraggled pair we make.

"How did they trap you?" she asks. "I didn't think they'd be able to bring you back into our world against your will."

"Actually," I tell her, tugging a hand through my hair to remove bits of straw, "we found our own way."

"Whatever for?"

"They thought I might kill you for them."

It pops out of my mouth before I even realize it's going to, but Granny Weather only laughs.

"And what made you decide not to?" she asks. "You *did* decide not to, I assume."

She still looks amused, but a sudden dark light in her eyes makes me nod quickly. I tell her about Serth's unwelcome visit.

"The best lies hold a breath of the truth," she says when I'm done.

"You mean you *are* eating their babies?"

"Hardly. But an infant bogle is still an innocent, born to the dark or not, and the death of any innocent diminishes the world."

"So who is eating their babies?" I ask.

She shakes her head in exasperation. "No one. They would have told you anything to bring you across."

"I don't buy that," I say. "I can't think of a lamer reason to get me here. I've never hurt anybody in my life. Why would I start with you?"

"But it was enough to make you feel you needed to speak to me," she says.

"That's true."

"What they really wanted was for that one to bring you," she adds, pointing her chin at Jeck.

There's not much love lost between them either, though it's more on her side than Jeck's. She's never trusted him and doesn't think I should, but I don't judge anybody by their family.

He gives her a steady look. "I grew up on stories of you," is all he says.

"Yes, yes. The wicked witch in the wood. How original."

He shrugs. "If I shouldn't believe those stories, why can't you trust me?"

"Because . . ." Her voice trails off. "Because of habit," she says finally. "You're right. I can be as guilty of misjudgment as any."

"Well, I hate to break up this Hallmark moment," I say, "but don't you think we should be thinking about a way to get out of here? And what do they want with us anyway?"

"Not us," Granny Weather says and points to Jeck again. "But him. The heart of a seventh son—particularly one such as Jeck, who is the seventh son of a seventh son—is a potent ingredient for any number of spells. My guess is they plan to grind it up and feed it to the crack willow by Coffin Rock, to give it mobility and make it their brother." She shook her head. "Imagine that evil old spirit given a blackbird's wings and set loose upon the world. Bogles would be the least of our worries."

I don't even want to think about how they'll get the heart to grind it up in the first place.

I look at Jeck. "They'd do that?" I ask. "They'd cut out your heart?"

He shrugs. "We're related by blood," he says. "Not temperament. They've always had large ambitions and need a powerful ally to achieve them. When they failed to give the old willow the light-blood of a drowned moon, they would have had to look elsewhere for a gift." He placed the palm of his hand against his chest. "I can see how giving it my heart would amuse them."

I turn back to Granny Weather. "But why are we here?"

"I, because I could stop them," she says. "If they hadn't caught me off-guard and separated me from my cronebone, we wouldn't even be having this conversation. The fens would be choked with the bodies of dead bogles and blackbird brothers." She gives me a wicked grin. "I never could abide either of them."

I was wondering how she came to be stuck here in the bogles' toilet with us.

"And you're here," she adds, "because their brother would never have returned if it hadn't been for you."

She said something along those lines a few moments ago, but it didn't really register the way it does now.

"Is this true?" I ask Jeck. "You're only here because of me?"

I get another shrug in response and feel just awful. It never even occurred to me that I was putting him in danger.

"At least escaping isn't a problem for you," Granny Weather says. "All you have to do is wake up."

I hadn't thought of that. I suppose I could have done it the moment the net dropped onto us.

I shake my head. "I'm not leaving either of you behind."

"But you must," she says. And then she tells me why.

I wake up in my bedroom and nothing feels right. It's not hard to figure out why. I'm safe, escaped from the dreamlands, while my boyfriend's lying in a bogle toilet with Granny Weather, waiting for his brothers to cut out his heart.

Then I realize that we never discussed how I'll get back to the fairy-tale world once I've collected the things that Granny Weather told me I needed to bring. And how am I even supposed to bring all that stuff over with me? When I enter the dreamlands, most of the time I can choose what I'm wearing, but I can't bring objects with me. I've tried, but unless I can imagine it in my pocket, it doesn't cross over with me. Knapsacks and purses don't work either, and this stuff Granny Weather wants me to get sure won't fit in a pocket.

So I've already screwed up, I think, until I realize that I can at least gather the objects in Mabon. That'll bring me part of the way, already into the dreamlands. And if I can't find a way over to the fairy-tale world on my own, I might be able to find someone else who can show me.

I go back to my bed and lie down again. It's already getting light outside my window and I can hear the morning traffic starting up, along with a chorus of rowdy birdsong, but I've gotten good at dropping off to sleep whenever I need to.

I wake up in Jeck's and my apartment in Mabon, already

dressed for business: jeans, long-sleeved jersey, canvas jacket, sturdy walking shoes. The only concession to practicality is my digital wristwatch. I can't wear them outside of the dreamlands because when they don't stop entirely working, they tend to simply flash a random time. It's like my real-world curse, what Jilly calls Jinx because she thinks everything should have a name. Ordinary wrist-watches run backwards and all sorts of mechanical and electrical things don't work properly when I'm around. I can still remember the look on Christy's face when I tried to use his computer and crashed the hard drive just by switching it on.

I don't waste time in the apartment. Its emptiness simply drives home the fact that for every moment I'm here, Jeck's that much closer to having his heart cut out of his chest.

My first stop is the Catholic church down the street. I'm not Catholic, and I'm not even sure how much I believe in God, but when I follow Granny Weather's instructions and steal one of the votive candles—sneaking it out of the church while it's still lit, and don't think that's easy until you've tried it—the nape of my neck prickles and I know I'm waiting for lightning to strike me down dead. But it doesn't happen. Maybe the candle I bought and left in the stolen one's place evened things out in the eyes of the angels. Maybe nobody up there was paying attention.

Once outside, I blow the candle out and stow it in the pocket of my jacket, sucking at my finger where the hot wax gave me a bit of a burn.

From there I go to Kerry's Cauldron, an herb and witchery shop just down the street from Mr. Truepenny's. Kerry herself is at the counter. She's a tall, dark-haired woman, given to wearing Gypsy outfits—the romantic kind you see in movies: low-cut white blouse, flower-print skirt, hair pushed up under a red kerchief. I've met her before, but I've never been inside her shop. It's got a wonderful smell, earthy and herby, with a touch of something feral, like a mix of deep forest loam and wild roses. Everywhere I look there are shelves of small bottles with handwritten labels, the dark glass hiding mysterious powders, dried herbs and other less identifiable things.

Kerry and I exchange pleasantries, then she asks me what I need.

"Do you, um, carry mouse hair?" I ask.

She nods. "Do you want a full pelt, a whole dried mouse, or just the loose hairs?"

I didn't expect there to be choices.

"Just the hair," I say. "I only need enough to roll into a small ball to put inside a loaf of bread."

She nods again. "Of course. You're making gifting bread."

"I guess I am."

"That's a very old recipe for favors. You don't hear much about them anymore, but I suppose that's because they don't work for everyone."

"They don't?"

My heart sinks.

Kerry shakes her head. "Not unless you're an adept or have faerie blood. So you'll be okay."

Jilly started this whole business about me having faerie blood and she's never even been to Mabon, but everybody here seems to think the same thing. I've given up arguing about it.

"Have you considered what good memory you'll offer up to the spirit of the loaf when you bake it?" she asks. "It's always good to think about that kind of thing in advance so that you don't get all rushed at the end and give away something you'll regret later."

Granny Weather had said something about keeping pleasant memories in my head while I was baking the bread, a different one for each loaf, but she didn't say why.

"What do you mean give away?" I ask.

"You don't get it back," she says. "Didn't you know that?"

I shake my head. "You really know all about this kind of thing, don't you?"

"Well, it *is* my business."

Duh.

"Don't mind me," I tell her. "I left my brain in my other jacket."

She smiles. "Do you need anything else?"

I name the other item on my list, kernels of dried Indian corn, and she saves me the trip to the feed store by pulling a jar of them up from under the glass-topped display counter that stands between us. While she's packaging my order, I ask her if she knows Granny Weather.

"I'm afraid not. She sounds like an old goodwife. They all had names like that in the old days—to keep their true names private. Nowadays we just use our own, since the old naming magics have pretty much fallen by the wayside."

"So when you say goodwife," I ask, "you mean she's okay."

She turns from the table where she's measuring out my mouse hairs to give me a blank look.

"I mean, she wouldn't be a bad person," I say.

"No," Kerry tells me. "I mean like how we refer to the little people as the good neighbors as a sign of respect so that we don't get on their bad side." She pauses a moment, then adds, "Are you baking this for Granny Weather?"

I nod.

"Well, make sure you follow her instructions exactly," she says. "You don't want to annoy a goodwife."

I remember Granny Weather's bloodthirsty comment on what she'd do to the bogles and Jeck's brothers, and find myself wishing I'd let well enough alone when the bogle first showed up in my bedroom. I should have listened to Jeck. Because if I screw this up . . .

"But I'm sure you'll do fine," Kerry says as she deposits two small paper bags on the counter. "After all, you—"

"Have faerie blood," I say, finishing it for her.

She smiles. "Exactly."

I wish I was as confident.

I pay for my purchases. "One last question," I say before I leave. "Do you have any tips on traveling between the dreamlands?"

"Be very clear about where it is you want to go," she says, "or you could end up anywhere."

That wasn't quite what I was hoping for.

"I was thinking more *how* to do it," I tell her.

She turns away and rummages in one of the drawers that line the wall beside her worktable. When she returns to the front counter, she places a piece of twine with a knot in it on the glass.

"Find a place in between," she says. "Do you know what I mean by that?"

I nod.

"Once you're there, keep your destination clearly in mind and untie the knot. I'm afraid it's only a one-way traveling knot. Return ones are very hard to find and much more expensive."

"That's okay," I tell her as I pay for it. "I've got somebody there to bring me back."

If we survive. If I don't screw up Granny Weather's preparations. If, if, if. I hate fairy-tale dreams.

Once I have the first loaf ready to go in the oven, I find myself stalling. What memory do I want to lose? None, of course. The better question would be, which one am I willing to lose?

I know now that it's got to be a good one. Something of significance—to me at least—or it wouldn't be a sacrifice. That's the trouble with this sort of magic, you always have to pay for it and what you pay is never something normal like putting down a few dollars and change in a store.

I stare out the kitchen window. It looks out over the backyard and from my second-floor vantage I can see almost all the way down the block, a narrow quilt of backyards. A big orange cat is crying outside of Mrs. Rowling's back door, trying to scrounge a meal. Mr. Potter is weeding his garden again—like a weed would dare make an appearance among his flowers and vegetables.

Sighing, I look back at the little piece of paper on the table in front of me. I write down on it:

The first time I sold a painting.

Then I get up and put the loaf in the oven. I think about that day, how amazing it was. I got a hundred dollars and I felt like a millionaire. Not so much because of the money, I suppose, as that it validated this crazy idea of making my living as an artist.

I start to feel a little nauseous and I sniff at the air, figuring it's the ball of mouse hair, hidden away inside the dough, but all I can smell is baking bread. The queasiness won't go away until finally the timer on the stove goes off. I pull the baking pan out and all I've got is a black lump of a burnt loaf to show for my efforts.

I check the time in case I somehow lost track, but only an hour has passed—not nearly enough time to reduce the loaf to this. And how come I didn't even smell it burning?

Not a powerful enough memory, I decide.

After another trip to Kerry's Cauldron for more mouse hair, I try it again.

Think of something good, I tell myself. Jeck's life is at stake here.

Jeck.

I hesitate for a long moment, then write down on the paper:

The first time Jeck and I made love.

I hate this.

But then it gets worse. Where the first time I felt a little queasy, this time a stomach cramp knocks me off my chair. One moment I'm reveling in the memory of that day in the barn, the smell of the hay, that first touch, our breath mingling, the amazing intimacy I'm finding in this handsome stranger that Jeck is at the time, and the next I'm lying curled up on the floor in a fetal position ready to die, alternately burning and freezing from hot and cold flashes. In moments I'm drenched in sweat, my pulse drumming so fast I feel like my heart's going to pop out of my chest.

I feel like I'm going to faint, but that would be too easy, I guess. Instead I spend an eternity wracked with pain. When the cramps finally fade enough so that I can sit up, it's to find that it's only been ten minutes or so. I get to my feet on wobbly legs, wait for the spinning to subside, then stagger into the living room where I collapse on the couch. Drifting in and out of a daze, I almost don't hear the timer when it goes off.

The loaf is perfect and smells like heaven, never mind that there's a ball of wadded up mouse hair in the middle of it. I set it down on the counter to cool, then look at the paper I'd written my memory prompter on. I guess I was expecting to come up blank when I read the line, but the memory's still there. It just has no life left in it. All I have in my head is the plain fact of the first time Jeck and I made love, no more detailed than what I'd written down.

Well, this sucked. And I still have two more loaves to go. But then I think of Jeck and Granny Weather and put the next loaf in the oven, the one with a ball of wax from the votive candle in it.

The memory I lose this time is of that mad night that Jilly and I bonded after I met her in the hallway of one of Butler U's lecture halls, becoming more sisters than friends. And the cramps take me down again. If anything, they're worse than the first attack.

It takes me a long time before I can summon up the courage to put the final loaf in, the one with dried corn kernels in the center. I lose the last time I saw my dad alive. I didn't even mean to, it just popped into my head and then the cramps came and it was too late to get it back.

I end up lying on the floor of the kitchen for the full hour it takes the loaf to bake. I'm so weak when the timer goes off that I can barely get up to take the bread out of the oven. The only thing that gets me on my feet is the thought of having to go through this another time.

I have to sit for a couple of hours before I can do anything else. I drink some tea and nibble on soda crackers to settle my stomach, then finally pack away the loaves, what's left of the candle and some matches in a knapsack. I sling the knapsack over my shoulder and stand in the doorway between the kitchen and the living room, which is about as between as I have the energy to do. There I undo the traveling knot, careful to keep my destination clear in my mind.

I expect some new bout of cramps or sickness, but all that happens is that I end up in the middle of the herb garden that lies on the other side of the path separating the fens from Granny Weather's cottage. It's dusk, the sun just setting.

"There's spiders in that garden," she told me before I left the bogles' tower, "and their webs will keep you safe from the likes of little nightmares. Make your way there to work the spell."

Luckily, I'm not afraid of spiders.

I stay in the middle of the cobwebby garden and put the knapsack on the dirt at my feet.

Work the spell.

I'm less than happy with this whole witchy business of Granny Weather's, but there's no turning back now. If I don't go on, Jeck will die and everything I've already been through today will have been for nothing. It's not like he can wake up and be safe back home. Though sometimes I wonder about the people I meet here in the dreamlands. Do they really originate here, or are they asleep and dreaming someplace else themselves? If Jeck is, he has no memory of it, but I know I can't take that as gospel or anything. Lots of people don't know they're dreaming when they are.

I take out the candle and light it. It takes me a moment to remember which loaf goes first. The mouse hair one. I take it out of the knapsack and hold it up in both hands, facing west.

"Come," I say, repeating the words that Granny Weather told me to use. "You of the wind. I have a gift for you."

I say it three times, always facing west, but the last time, I kneel in the dirt. I don't know what to expect, who or what will come. Maybe nothing. Maybe I already screwed up. Didn't bake the loaf right. Used too many mouse hairs. Or not enough. Didn't say the words right.

Then I hear it, the slow flap of wings. It comes from the west, borne on the last rays of the setting sun, an enormous owl. When it lands on the ground in front of me, I place the loaf by its talons.

"Is this gift freely given?" a voice says.

I'm not sure if I actually hear the owl speak, or if its words are simply forming in my mind. I look at the loaf and I think of what I had to go through to bake it. It wasn't without cost to make, I think, but I suppose it is being freely given, so I nod.

The owl eats the bread far more quickly than I would have thought possible.

"I would return your kind gift with a favor," it says, those big round eyes settling their gaze on me.

I clear my throat. "Um. Granny Weather would like to get her cronebone back."

I have no idea what this is, and Granny Weather wasn't particularly forthcoming when I asked, but the owl seems to know exactly what I'm talking about.

"It shall be done."

And then he's gone, those enormous wings lifting it up into the air and away, deep into the fens. I listen to the fading whisper of them for a long moment before bringing out the second loaf, the one with the wax ball in it.

This one calls up a cloud of moths, thick as mist. Moths don't eat bread so far as I know, but this is the fairy-tale world, so I suppose anything's possible. The loaf certainly disappears quickly enough. I don't ask them for a favor. Granny Weather told me to simply tell them where their murderers are.

"Moths are spirits of the uneasy dead," she told me when I asked about that. "The ones that will come to you will be the ghosts of all of those that the bogles have led astray and drowned in the fens."

When they fly off in the same direction as the owl, I bring out the last loaf. I wonder what the corn kernels will call up. Mouse for the owl. Candle for the moths. That makes sense. Maybe this'll bring me chickens, I think. I realize I'm getting a little hysterical when that idea sets off a spate of giggling.

I catch my breath and go through the summoning for the third time.

By this point, I'm pretty much used to the unusual, but what shows up is right out of Looney Tunes. There's a little outbuilding that stands in behind Granny Weather's cottage. I don't know what she uses it for. To keep her wood dry, maybe for storage. I didn't realize it was a pet.

For that's what comes in response to the third summoning, an animated hut, its wooden walls creaking and cracking as the hut shifts back and forth, walking on hen's legs like in the story of Baba Yaga.

"Is this gift freely given?" it asks, like the others did, its high, cartoon voice ringing inside my head.

All I can do is nod.

It stands there, its windows looking like eyes, gaze locked on me. Finally I get up from where I'm kneeling and toss the loaf in through its open door. There's a weird chewing sound, then a small burp. I don't know whether to laugh or run.

"I would return your kind gift with a favor," it tells me.

The voice kills me. The chicken legs are bad enough, but the voice makes me feel like any minute the herbs and vegetables around me are going to pull out of the ground and start up some song and dance routine.

"Granny Weather would like her skycloak," I manage to reply.

"It hangs inside the door of her cottage."

Again there's this long pause. Then I realize that I'm supposed to go fetch the cloak. It's the only piece of clothing hanging there and seems to weigh next to nothing when I take it off the hook. I feel like I'm walking on air as I return to the herb garden, holding the cloak against my chest.

The hut's back on the ground now, like it's just a normal outbuilding. I guess the chicken legs are folded under it, out of sight. I approach its door cautiously and start to toss the cloak inside, but the cartoon voice stops me.

"The cloak should not touch the ground," the hut tells me. "Better that you carry it."

No way, I think. I'm not getting inside that thing. I can still remember the chewing sound after I tossed the loaf of bread in.

"Why do you hesitate?" it asks.

"I have this thing about stepping inside a stranger's mouth," I say.

Cartoon laughter rings in my head. The hut gives a kind of shrug. There's a creak in the wood. A cedar shingle falls off the roof.

"Then Granny Weather will have to do without her skycloak," it says. "She won't be pleased."

I think about what Kerry said about getting on the wrong side of a goodwife's temper, and sigh. Gingerly I step over the threshold. There's nothing inside. Plain wooden boards on the floor, no furnishings except for a ratty old club chair that looks like it was rescued from a dump, lopsided, the stuffing coming out of the sides.

"Sit," the hut tells me.

I don't think so.

But then the hut lurches onto its chicken legs and I go sliding across the room. I only just keep my balance and make it to the chair where I sit with the cloak bundled up on my lap. The chair doesn't move as the hut heads into the fens with a staggering walk, but it feels like my stomach does.

Oddly, I don't get sick.

Well, I tell myself. At least I don't have to find my own way back to the bogles' tower.

There seems to be a heavy mist around the tower as we approach. It's not until we're really close that I see it's not mist but a huge cloud of the white moths. Bogles are running everywhere in a panic, batting at the things with their weird extra-jointed fingers. There's already a carpet of downed moths on the wet ground, but there are so many in the air that it doesn't seem to make much difference. The moths swarm over the bogles, covering every inch of their black, oily skin, suffocating the nasty little buggers. The bogles' only defense is to submerge into the fen water, but as soon as they come up for air, the moths are waiting for them, flying into their pug noses and mouths.

Poetic justice, I guess, considering that the moths are the ghosts of the drowned victims of the bogles.

Jeck's brothers are out in the middle of this strange mêlée, but the moths don't seem interested in them. The brothers are trying to help the bogles, but they're not having much luck. Then one of them gives a cry. I look, just in time to see the owl drop out of the sky and tear something from around his neck. The owl rises up again, chased by six blackbirds. From its talons dangles what looks like a necklace. A little bone on a leather thong. I remember seeing it before, when they first captured us. Now I realize it must be Granny Weather's cronebone.

The blackbirds are quick, but they're like gnats compared to the owl. It bulls through them, scattering birds in a cloud of black feathers, dropping to a small window in the tower that's just above ground level. The owl slips the necklace through the bars, then flies away to a perch on a nearby tree, its job done, I guess. The black-birds hover for a long moment. Then, screaming, they take flight.

No sooner do they go, than the tower cracks in two like a walnut, the great sides crashing down into the fens to send up tidal waves of stagnant water in which bob dead and drowning bogles. I see Jeck and Granny Weather, standing in the wreckage, unharmed. Granny Weather has her arms raised above her head, her eyes glittering with an inner fire.

The hut lurches forward until it's standing above the cracked ruin of the tower. Granny Weather's fiery gaze locks with my own.

"Give me the cloak," she says.

I toss it down.

She whips it over her shoulders and a great wind comes shrieking out of nowhere, lifting her into the sky. Seconds later, she's gone, in pursuit of the blackbirds.

I don't wait for the hut to kneel on its chicken legs. I jump down from the doorway. I look back up at my weird mount for a moment and tell it thanks before I run over to Jeck. Holding him, I offer up thanks to the moths and owl as well for the fact that he's still alive. Jeck gives me an odd look. I guess even in this fairy-tale world people don't really talk to walking huts and animals all that much.

By the time we've finished hugging, I realize that the hut's gone. I turn to see that it's almost out of sight, lurching its way back across the fens to Granny Weather's cottage. There are dead bogles everywhere, scattered on the little island and amidst the ruins of the tower, tangled up in the reeds, floating in the water. I look at their faces, wondering if Serth is among them. The white moths are dispersing; the owl's already gone. There's just us and the dead and it's all so horribly depressing.

"Let's go home," I say.

Jeck shakes his head. "Not just yet. We need to see how it ends."

I look at the carnage around us, but I realize he doesn't mean this. He means his brothers. Or maybe what's going to happen to us.

So we start slogging our way back to Granny Weather's cottage.

"What exactly is a cronebone?" I ask him as we push our way through the sedge and weeds. I've already figured out what a sky-cloak is from how Granny Weather took off into the air once she had it.

He nods. "Among the old goodwives, it was a way to keep their power safe from those who meant them ill. They would cut off a finger or a toe and invest the bone with their magic."

"That's too gross."

"It gets worse," he adds. "The younger they were when they did it, the more powerful the bone became. The story is that Granny Weather was three years old when she cut off her own toe to make hers."

"She did it to herself?"

"They have to do it themselves. But imagine being that young and knowing so clearly what you wanted. And being willing to do such a thing to gain it." He looks at me and picks something out of my hair. A twig. An errant leaf. "That's why you have to be so careful in your dealings with her. She is utterly focused and does nothing unless she can benefit from it."

"But she helped me rescue the moon," I say.

"Yes, but she requires the moon's light for some of her magics." He glances my way again, but his gaze slides away from mine. "I'm just saying to be careful around her and think before you speak."

"What's *that* supposed to mean?"

He gets a pained look and only shakes his head. I get the awful premonition that something really bad is going to happen.

That's another thing I hate about the fairy-tale world. Everything's oblique and anything important can only be approached in riddles. So now I know something's going to happen when we see Granny Weather again, but Jeck can't tell me what, because it's something I have to deal with without coaching or we'll have already lost.

The only thing I can know for sure is that it'll be dangerous.

Granny Weather's waiting for us by her cottage. She's disheveled and there's a wild light in her eyes. Hanging from her belt are six dead blackbirds. I glance at Jeck, but although he seems tense, I don't think it has anything to do with the fate of his brothers.

Think before I speak, he told me. I also know about the old reporter's trick, how if you keep silent the other person will feel obliged to fill that silence with something, but I have a couple of questions that are nagging at me.

"Why did the candle have to be stolen?" I ask.

Granny weather shrugs. "Unlike the Christ man himself, the churches aren't as free with his magics."

"So the magic had to be stolen?"

She nods. I wonder what she'd think if she knew that I replaced the candle I stole with a new one that I'd paid for. It didn't seem to hurt the magic.

"And the last time I was here," I go on. "Why did you need me to rescue the moon? It seems to me you could have just done it yourself."

"The moon can be a fickle mistress," Granny Weather says. "It needed someone of her own bloodline to pull her free."

So we're back to faerie blood and Jilly's assertion that the moon was really my mother, straying into the waking world long enough to give birth to me before the fairy-tale world called her back again. I remember the face of the moon woman, sleeping there under the fen water. She had my face. But I still don't buy it. Maybe things like that can happen in the dreamlands, but not in the waking world.

"Still, we're not here to talk of old business," Granny Weather says. "I am in your debt for your rescuing of me today, and I always pay my debts. What would you ask of me?"

I feel Jeck stiffen at my side, but I don't need a warning here. I've already been through this the last time, when his brothers promised me anything in exchange for letting the moon drown. The one thing you don't do in the fairy-tale world is serve yourself. There's some moral code underlying the structure of the world, just like there is in fairy tales, and a sure way to get yourself in trouble here is to be greedy.

"Think of it as a gift," I tell her. "Freely given."

There's a long moment of silence.

Granny Weather smiles and I can't tell if she's hiding her annoyance, or if it's that I've managed to earn her respect.

"Don't come back till the next time," she says.

No sooner does she speak the last word, than we're back in our apartment in Mabon once more. The only reminder of where we've been is the stink of the fens that rises from our clothes.

I look at Jeck. "So what just happened?"

"You put yourself on equal terms with her," he said. "Because you asked for nothing in return, she's now duty-bound to leave you and anyone under your protection untouched by her magics."

"And if we hadn't?"

"We'd be hanging from her belt along with my brothers."

"So it was a good thing."

"A very good thing," he says with a smile

I take his hand. "Come on," I tell him. "We need a long, hot shower."

Jilly loves these stories about the dreamlands. We're sitting on the old sofa out on my balcony, sharing a bottle of wine while I tell her this latest one. The window's open behind us and the nouveau flamenco playing on the stereo inside is drifting out to us. Because Jilly is here, the old mangy stray tom who lives in the alley below has actually come up onto the balcony by way of the fire escape and is letting Jilly pat him. I've been feeding him for months, but though he eats the kibbles I put out for him, we don't actually have a relationship beyond that. But then I'm not Jilly. Strays naturally gravitate to her.

"You're so lucky," she says. "Having these adventures and all."

I don't know if lucky is quite the right word. I wouldn't want to lose Mabon, but my times in the other dreamlands are never comfortable. Even though I can come back any time, simply by waking up, I don't usually remember that when I'm there. The dangers feel too real and I'm always changed when I get back. The experiences linger and become part of who I am, and that's a little disconcerting to say the least when you consider where they've taken place.

"I don't feel lucky," I tell her.

"The loaves," she says, her voice filled with sympathy.

I nod. It's not as though I've simply forgotten something. The absence of those memories are like dark holes that have been bored into my heart and they won't go away. Instead, the more time that passes since I lost them, the more I feel their absence. It's as though the rest of my memories are pulling away from these dark holes, magnifying their presence.

"I try to forget what I've gone and lost," I say, "but that just seems to make me focus on them more. It's like a heartache that gets worse instead of better."

"Then don't," Jilly says. "Don't try to forget them," she adds at my confused look. "They were taken away by magic, right? So use your own magic to deal with the loss."

"How many times do I have to tell you? I don't have faerie blood. There's no magic in me."

She only smiles. "I meant your art."

And then I understand. The art of creating something out of nothing is an act of magic. It's not only something born out of joy and love, but also out of our hurts and sorrows. And while it may not be a cure for the emotions that can assail us, it does allow us to step past the barrage of helpless sensation into other, less numbing, perspectives where it's possible to find a breathing space, and perhaps even some emotional balance.

So I get up and go into my studio, right then and there, leaving Jilly out on the balcony with the cat.

For a long moment I stand in the doorway, taking in the scent of turps and paint, then I step through, soft-soled shoes scuffing on the hardwood floor. I don't even think about what I'm doing as I squeeze paint onto my palette, put a new canvas on my easel, grab a handful of brushes. I start to lay in a loose, unformed background and I get a picture in my head of what I'm painting, a combination of my lost memories, the three of them tangled and interwoven like vines among the thorns and red berries of a hawthorn hedge.

Already, with every stroke of the brush, I can feel my anxieties lose some of their immediacy. The dark holes are still there, but I'm no longer so panicked that I think they're going to swallow me whole.

Jilly's right. It is magic, set free from the dreamlands by our imagination. Any act of creation is, from the fine arts to building a mudpie or a cat's cradle.

And if that's faerie blood, then we've all got its potential somewhere inside us, just waiting for us to call it up. Don't ever let anyone tell you different.

The Witching Hour

For the longest time I had no idea why I killed Michael Hill.

I had nothing against him. Didn't know his history, for sure. Didn't know he was reaching for a sawed-off shotgun under the counter when I shot him.

It started out plain and simple, the way complicated things usually do. A gas bar out on Highway 14, north of the city, late at night, going on three A.M. Forget midnight. That's the real witching hour. Mine anyway. The highway was empty, like it usually is; a long gray ribbon that starts down by the lake as a city street then heads off into the hills until it finally trickles out into a dirt road. I've been up and down its length a thousand times that time of night. Until the commuters start showing up around six, you can count the headlights you pass on one hand. Come the witching hour, pretty much all the drunks are home in bed, sleeping it off, or piled up in a ditch somewhere.

That night I stopped for gas, filled the tank with a stolen credit card, then went inside, like I wanted to buy some smokes. Hands in the pockets of my jacket. The clerk behind the counter was in his late teens, no more than a kid, really.

His eyes went big when I pulled out the .38. He handed over the money like I told him and I stuffed it in the inside pocket of my jacket. Halfway out the door, I had this brief flash of vertigo. I guess that's what made me turn. He was starting to bend down below the counter and I lifted my .38. I fired once. The bullet lifted him off his feet and smashed him back against the candy and cigarette display that covered the wall behind him. He went down in a spray of blood, chocolate bars, chip bags and cigarette packages.

I stood there in the doorway, half deaf from the gunshot, watching him twitch. Watching until he was still.

There was no surveillance camera. Nobody out on the highway to note my stolen car, this crap Buick with a set of plates lifted from somebody else's vehicle. The kid was dead—I didn't need a coroner to tell me that—and nothing could help him now.

But I walked back across the room anyway. Laying the gun on the glass counter, I picked up the phone. I dialed 911, told the dispatcher what had gone down, then I went out and sat on a chair by the pumps and waited for the sirens to reach me.

It was only at the trial that it all came out. How he had the sawed-off under the counter and was going for it. How he had all these souvenirs in his duffel bag. How DNA linked him to at least a half-dozen unsolved murders.

The court-appointed lawyer played it up big and I came out smelling pretty good for a two-bit hustler looking to face the chair. They ended up calling it manslaughter. I didn't walk, but the ten years I pulled felt like a cakewalk when you size it up against the death penalty.

Only the whole time this was going on, I still know what I did.

I'd no idea about the gun under the counter, or all this other freak business the kid was into. I just turned and shot him and, the way I see it, I don't deserve clemency.

But I don't say anything.

I tried once, just to my lawyer, this fresh-faced kid not much older than the one I shot. Earnest. Bright. Wants to do the right thing.

He held up his hand when I started to speak, didn't want to hear anymore. Didn't put me on the stand—he didn't have to. When he plea-bargained murder one down to manslaughter, the only formality left was the sentencing.

I read in the papers how the kin of the victims—the ones Hill did in—were calling me a hero. Story got so twisted around, I might have come to believe it myself, but I know what I did. So did his sister. I saw her sitting there in the courtroom, studying me, something dark and unreadable in her eyes. She was like one of those old places you can stumble upon in the piney wood hills. You step into a meadow, or underneath one of those touch-the-sky pines, and the hair stands up at the nape of your neck. A chill crawls across your skin, even though it's high summer. You're not scared, but you know you've touched something bigger than you. Strayed into a piece of some old, dark mystery that was here long before we crawled up out of the mud and took to standing around on our hind legs.

She's just a slip of a girl, but she was like those places all the same, like something big and impossible you can't explain. Don't ask how I knew, I just did.

So when she shows up in my cell, one night around that old witching hour of mine, I don't even ask how she got here. I feel myself fall into her eyes and that's when I have this memory that I've seen her before, not just in the courtroom, but someplace else. I just can't remember when or where. It's like she's been inside me, walking around in my head.

She stands there watching as I make a rope of my sheets, tie it around my neck. I put my chair on my cot and get the other end knotted up around the bars of my window. Taking hold of the bars, I push the chair and cot away with my feet. Then I let myself go. It's not a long drop, but it's enough to do the job.

I expect the darkness. Welcome it when it comes.

What I don't expect is to open my eyes again.

We're in the hills above the prison, standing under the pines looking down on the exercise yards and the stone walls, topped with barbed wire. There's a thin cover of snow on the ground, but no footprints leading to where we're standing. I guess we've been standing here a time, but I don't remember how we left the prison. I don't remember walking here.

All I remember is the snap of my neck and the hot embrace of the darkness back in my cell.

I turn to look at Michael Hill's sister.

There's not a whole lot of family resemblance, at least not between her and the picture of Hill they kept running in the paper. I can't really remember his face from the filling station, either. Just the thundering echo of the gunshot. The blood and all those candy bars and cigarette packages tumbling down on his twitching body.

She's short and dark-haired. Got a face like a child's—big head, large eyes, the small nose and mouth set close to her chin—but a body like a woman. Not like some showgirl, but mature. It makes for an unsettling contrast, like she's not quite one thing or the other.

"I don't know your name," I find myself saying.

"But you know who I am."

I nod. "Michael Hill's sister."

"According to the papers." Before I can say anything, she adds, "But then they've got their own take on things, don't they? They thought you were a hero."

"I'm no hero."

"Oh, hell. I know that. But I'm thinking you might still be useful."

"Who are you?" I ask. "How did you . . ."

The prison cell seems like a long time ago. When I let myself fall . . .

"How did we get here?"

Her smile makes me uncomfortable. "And what do I want with you?" she says.

"That, too, I guess."

It's around then I realize I'm dreaming. What else could it be?

"You're not dreaming," she says, like she can read my mind. "You're dead."

"But—?"

"Shh," she says. "You're talking too much."

She lifts her hand and everything goes black again.

The next time I open my eyes we're sitting in a junked Chevy out in front of some brick tenements. I figure we're down in the city now. Upper Foxville, maybe. Or the Rosses. I don't have a watch, but I know it's that time again. Three A.M. I can always feel the witching hour when it comes.

"You don't know why you killed him, do you?" she says.

I shake my head. "Not really."

"I do."

I wait for her to explain. For a long time she doesn't say anything and we just sit there, staring out the cracked windshield. I haven't seen a car go by since we got here, but I can hear a distant siren through the broken window on my side of the car.

"I made you do it," she says finally.

I give her a blank look.

"It's complicated," she tells me. "I'm one of the girls he killed."

"Wait a minute. I thought you were his sister. That's what the papers said."

She shrugs. "People see what they want to see. You notice nobody tried to interview me?"

I hadn't thought about that, but now it did seem odd.

"So what's your name?" I ask.

"Judy," she says. "Judy Moore."

"And you're telling me . . . what? That you're a ghost?"

"I don't know what I am. I'm just something that carried on. I wasn't the first girl they killed, but I think maybe I died the hardest. Maybe that's why I'm still here while the others got to go on."

"What do you mean 'they'? No one said anything about his having any partners."

"Partner," she says. "As in singular. Her name's Susan Green."

"He had a woman helping him?"

"Why's that so hard to believe? You think we're all victims?"

"No. I just . . ."

She shakes her head. "She's counting on guys like you. If she ever gets caught, you know? She'll be all sweet-faced and 'who me?' and no one's going to think she could hurt a flea."

I let that sink in and have to admit she's probably right. Show a bit of cleavage, flash us some leg, and most of us will stop using our brains.

"Hill was the one who got to play with us," she goes on, "and he cleaned up the messes when they were done. But Green was the one who collected us for him. She's the one that did all the cutting."

The simple way she tells it is all the more chilling for her voice being so matter-of-fact.

"I'm sorry," I say.

"Why? You didn't do anything."

"Yeah, but no one deserves to die like that."

"Stop it," she says. "I might start to think you have a heart."

She starts to lift her hand, but I remember what happened the last time she did that. Everything went black.

I catch her hand. Her gaze locks onto mine and for a long time I'm fighting the dark mystery I see in her eyes. Finally she lets her hand drop.

"You said you made me kill him," I say. "But I've never seen you before."

"Are you sure?"

I shake my head slowly.

"I was one of the first they killed," she tells me, "so I've been around awhile. I've had time to think. To find things out. People can see us, but not all the time, and not necessarily when we want them to. I didn't plan to be seen in the courtroom. That just happened."

"Why were you there?"

"I wanted to see what happened to you."

The way she says it I hear an intellectual curiosity, nothing to make me think she cared. No surprises there.

"Mostly we just drift through life," she goes on. "Seeing people, but not seen. And we can't touch them. So I guess we are like ghosts, or phantoms of some kind. But if we can find someone who's empty enough, we can borrow them for a time. To get things done."

"What do you mean by 'empty'?"

She shrugs. "Like you. You don't care about yourself or anybody else. Nobody cares about you."

I could have protested, but what would be the point? Because she's right. My whole life has pretty much been going through the motions, running on empty, though it wasn't always like that. I can remember when I cared about things. That stopped around the time I was four or five.

My parents weren't at my sentencing, but I didn't expect them. I thought maybe my brothers might show, but the only person there for me was my lawyer, and that was because the court had appointed him. I know he didn't like me. I didn't hold it against him. I don't much like myself.

"So you borrowed me to kill Michael Hill?" I say, still trying to get around the idea.

She nods.

"And now you're going to do the same for this Green woman."

"I would," she says. "But I can't. You only get the one shot at riding somebody, and I used it up on you. I would've had you kill her too, but you went and got yourself put in prison."

"So you . . . what?"

I flash back on my cell. Twisting the sheets, making the rope out of them. Letting go of the bars.

"So you had me kill myself?" I say.

"Oh, don't look at me like that," she tells me. "We don't even know each other and you're acting like I betrayed you or something."

I shake my head. "But maybe you betrayed your humanity."

"Get with the program. I'm not human. I'm dead. And so are you."

"And the point of me being dead?" I ask. "I'm guessing you didn't just want some company."

"I can't ride anybody else."

"Yeah, you already told me that."

She doesn't say anything. Just looks at me with those mystery eyes.

I give my head another shake when I get it.

"Oh no," I tell her. "I'm not killing anybody else for you."

"Even though she deserves it? Even though they'll probably never catch her and she'll just find somebody else to play her sick little games with her? Do you want the blood of more innocent victims on your hands?"

"They won't be on my hands."

"Yes they will. And the only way you can stop it from going on is to pick somebody for you to ride. Borrow their body and get the job done."

This just keeps getting worse. It's bad enough what she did to me, but now she expects me to do the same to somebody else?

"I'm not a killer," I tell her.

"You didn't fight me when I had you shoot Hill."

"No. But I took responsibility for it."

She gives me this anguished look.

"Don't do this," she says. "Don't have redeeming qualities."

She doesn't say any more, but I know what she means. She can deal with using a loser, but not with having used somebody who might one day have pulled himself out of the empty life he was living in.

So I relent, at least as much as I can.

"Don't worry," I tell her. "I was going nowhere. You probably did me a favor. But I'm not doing this to someone else."

"You won't be able to travel on," she says. "You know, wherever it is we go when we're not held back here in ghost limbo."

"You're holding me back," I say. I don't make a question of it.

She nods. "I have to. But do this for me and I'll let you go on."

I look away, out the windshield. We've been talking for hours and daybreak is pinking the eastern horizon. You can just see the faint blush of dawn lightening the sky above the roofs of the tenements.

"I can't," I tell her.

She lifts her hand. I guess she's got some kind of control over me that puts me in idle mode when she doesn't want to talk or argue with me. Or when I won't do what she wants.

This time I don't try to stop her. I let the darkness wash over me.

When I open my eyes again we're in a club. Drums and bass are thundering from the sound system, colored lights are strobing. There's a thick knot of dancers out on the floor, abandoning themselves to the music. Judy and I are sitting on a balcony of sorts, off to one side, watching it all through a haze of smoke.

"That's her," she tells me.

Loud as the music is, I have no trouble hearing her. Maybe we're locked in our own little limbo world because of this connection she made between us.

"The blonde in the black dress," Judy adds.

I look to where she's pointing and get my first look at Susan Green.

Simply put, Green is stunning. Face of an angel, the body of a devil, as the old songs used to say. She's wearing some tight little black dress that accentuates her curves, heels so high I can't see how she dances in them. Her hair falls in a perfect waterfall over her shoulders. She's the kind of woman who'd never look twice at a guy like me, not unless she's slumming and wants to bring back a story to her friends of this encounter she had with some bad boy street tough.

Judy sighs. "You see what I was saying? You can't imagine her being what I say she is, can you?"

Actually, I can. I've met women like Green before and their casual cruelty doesn't surprise me anymore. So it's not an impossible stretch to the more serious cruelties that have been attributed to her in particular.

Susan Green hasn't won me over. But there's another trust issue that's bothering me.

"I can imagine anything," I tell her. "But why should I trust you? Look what you did to me."

She starts to raise her hand.

"Don't," I tell her.

But she was only brushing her hair back from her face this time.

"I don't know how to prove it to you," she says.

"Look," I say. "Instead of putting me on hold or whatever it is you do to me when you lift your hand, leave me alone for awhile. Let me think on this."

"So you'll do it?"

Something bad happened to her. I don't doubt that. Something woke this fierce urge for vengeance in her and it wasn't anything she chose. But it's not my fault either.

"I didn't say that," I tell her. "But I need some time on my own to work this through. If I'm supposed to trust you . . ."

She gives a slow nod. "Then I should reciprocate."

"Something like that."

She gives me another nod.

"Okay," she says. "Do what you need to do. But don't wait too long." She looks back to where Green's stepping it out on the dance floor and my own gaze follows hers. "She's not going to stop just because Hill got himself shot."

I give her a slow nod. I find myself going back to what she said about how she chose me.

"Tell me something," I say. "Back at that gas bar . . ."

"You were in the right place at the right time," she says before I can finish. "You had a gun in your hand. I didn't look too hard to see if there was any hope left in you. I didn't stop to see if you could ever be more. I saw the emptiness and just jumped into you as you were going out the door."

Our gazes lock and this time the dark mystery in her eyes doesn't reach out and grab me.

"And then later," she goes on. "In your cell. It's like I told you before. I only had the one chance and I used it up on you. I can't ride anybody else. Believe me, I tried. But I couldn't wait another ten years or whatever for you to get out of prison again either, so I . . . I . . ."

Her words trail off and I can't speak either. There's an anguish in her that words could never ease. Bad enough she died so hard. Now she's done this.

"I'm sorry," she finally manages to tell me.

"I know."

"But if I could take it back . . ." She swallows hard, looks away. "I don't know if I would."

I stand up. It's not in me to forgive her, but I can't really blame her either. If our circumstances were reversed, I might have done the same thing myself. Figured out the problem and acted on it like she did? Probably not. My heart's hard, not mean. But in the heat of the moment, when this guy's leaving the gas bar with a gun in his hand, and the freak's just standing there, not a damn care in the world . . .

I really don't know.

Hell, you look at it another way, she probably saved my life. Hill was going for that shotgun, after all.

Except then she came into my cell and took my life anyway.

"I have to go," I tell her.

She nods her head, won't look at me.

But she lets me go. This time the shadows don't swallow me and

I get to walk away under my own steam. I leave her in the club, staring at Susan Green, and head out into the night.

I don't look back.

You know how ghosts are said to haunt a certain place, like where they died or something? Well, it isn't true. Or at least it wasn't true for me. That singularity of purpose they're supposed to have wasn't mine either.

When I left the club, I meant to just go out and think about things. Walk around for a while and clear my head. But once I started walking, I didn't stop. I just went on, wandering, day after day, out of the city, out of the country, across the world. And I didn't think about anything at all. I forgot who I was, how I'd died, this business with Hill and Green. Everything.

It's a few years before I'm back in North America, standing at a newsstand in Newford. I'm not here because of any decision on my part. It's just where my wandering brought me today.

There's an article on the front page of *The Daily Journal* about a missing girl. It's not until I start to read it, that it all comes back to me. Judy Moore and what she'd done to me. The kid I'd killed in the gas bar, and his partner who'd gotten away clean because nobody knew what she'd done except for a pair of ghosts.

I start walking again, but this time I'm concentrating on the things that happened to me before I died, and all those things that Judy told me about. For some reason I don't hold her to blame for any of it, not least of which for what she did to me. Don't ask me why. I guess it's like she said: My life was just never that important to me. I'm wondering about how I got to a place like that when I feel a tug in my chest, where my heart'd be if I was still alive.

I look up to see that I'm in Lower Crowsea. The tug draws my attention to a second floor window and I let myself float up to it, drifting through the glass panes. I don't recognize the room, or the pretty blonde woman talking on the phone. But looking through a door, I recognize the man in what appears to be a study. There are books everywhere. He's at a big desk, bent over some paperwork. Writing, I realize.

It's my brother Christy, the middle kid in my family. I can't remember the last time I've seen him, but he looks to be doing good. Better than I ever did, anyway. He's got a nice place, a girlfriend. A life.

I listen to the scratch of his pen on the paper for a long time.

"Christy," I say.

He looks up with a start, but his gaze goes right through me. I've long since discovered that it's like Judy said. People can see us, but not all the time, and not necessarily when we want them to. Though if he could see me, what would I say to him? I'm glad you didn't screw up as badly as I did. I'm glad those books of yours were able to steer you in a different direction from the one I took.

Would he even know what I was talking about? Maybe. But would he care?

After a while, he goes back to his writing, but he looks up once or twice before I leave, as though he senses my presence.

That could have been my life, I think. There was a time I was the one in the family with all the words, when Christy used to run out in the woods, pretending he was different kinds of animals. I even won some awards, back before I dropped out of school. I don't know what happened. I guess it started when Christy took up writing, too, and the teachers all started fussing over him. Our parents sure didn't, not for any of us. We were both getting into our fair share of trouble by then, me more than Christy, and I guess one delinquent writing prodigy was all the teachers felt they could save. And I didn't care anymore, anyway. Somewhere along the line the words just weren't easing the pain for me and I found other ways to push it out of my head. Getting drunk, making out, hanging at the pool hall, racing cars out on the backroads. Cheap thrills, maybe, but they did the job. For a while, anyway.

I look over Christy, let my gaze run across the books on the shelves behind him. There's almost a whole shelf with his byline on the spines. I guess our teachers made the right choice. I've never been able to stick to anything.

I notice a photo of Geordie, then, propped up at the end of another shelf. He's our younger brother, the one who used our old man's cast-off fiddle for his escape from that strange circus of a family we were born into. I'm wondering where he is when I hear the woman laughing into the phone in the other room.

"Oh, come *on*, Geordie," she says. "Even you can't believe Tanya did that on purpose."

A moment's silence while she listens. Then another small laugh.

"Well," she says. "That'll just teach you not to show up at some fancy do in jeans and a T-shirt, won't it?"

I let myself drift down into the floor, through somebody else's apartment, the rooms all deserted, then walk through the wall and out onto the street. I look up at the window again, still feeling the tug.

That's what it's like to have a real life, I think. And I'm happy for them. That Christy and Geordie were able to pull themselves out of the past, brush off the crap that was still clinging to them, and move on.

I guess I just wasn't strong enough.

Or willing to trust. To make the friends that can help pull you through when your family isn't there for you.

I go on a little tour then.

Being a ghost has this much going for it: You can get from here to wherever pretty much just by thinking about it. You walk around only out of habit. Or because you're hanging onto the idea of being alive, I guess.

First stop's that rundown clapboard house in back of Jackson Pond where we grew up. I half expect to see the old man's pickup parked on the front lawn, Ma hanging out the washing, but the place is all boarded up and falling in on itself, and they're long gone anyway. He died of a heart attack when I was in prison. Stepped out of that pickup, the way I heard it, grabbed his chest and just keeled over dead. Ma moved to live with her sister in a Florida trailer park and got hit by a drunk driver not a week after she got there.

I don't know what that means. Or if it even means anything.

I go by the prison next, the last place I lived. Nobody's missing me there. Just before Judy helped me die I'd spent three days in the hole, pulled solitary for mixing it up with one of the Nazi skinheads in the exercise yard. The Aryan Brotherhood didn't like the fact that I wouldn't join them—in prison, everything's got sides. If you're not on this one, you're automatically on the other. I didn't bother to explain that I didn't like the militant blacks any more than the skinheads—hate doesn't need a skin color to be ugly. I just beat the crap out of the guy, trying to smash that swastika tattoo on his forehead clean through to the other side of his head. It's simpler that way.

I visit a few other haunts—juke joints and flophouses where I've spent some time when I wasn't in some jail or other. I don't recognize anybody. I end up at my own grave and look down at the cheap granite maker lying flat on the ground. It's got my name, Paddy Riddell, a couple of dates, and that's it. Pretty much sums up my life, I guess. I did my time.

The last place I go is the Lower Crowsea branch of the public library. A con I knew on the inside once told me it's got the best research facilities of any of the city's libraries. He used it to plan robberies, escape routes, things like that.

I can't physically touch anything, but when I stare at one of the computers long enough, it comes on and eventually accesses the information I'm looking for. I read through the reports of Judy's death. First she was just missing. Then they found the body. It wasn't until the fourth girl died that they started to link them together, realized what they were dealing with. I read through it all, right up to where I came into the picture. When I get to the article about the new missing girl, I can't read any more.

I lean my head on my folded arms, the light from the screen washing over me.

After a while, I get up and go walking again. This time I'm checking out the bums and winos, roaming through the Tombs, going into the squats that people have made in all those abandoned warehouses and tenements. I find every kind of loser. The lost, the hopeless, the walking dead.

Judy's right. We can't let it continue. Susan Green has to be stopped. The missing girl has to be found before she winds up dead like us. If she's not already dead.

Only how do you choose somebody empty enough that it wouldn't matter if you borrowed their body to kill a freak? How do you know that they couldn't be redeemed, if they just got the right break?

And there'll be two of them now. Green and whoever she's found herself for a partner.

I still don't know what I'm going to do when I find them, but I go looking for them all the same.

By the time I find the girl, it's too late.

It's closing in on three A.M., my own personal witching hour, and Green and her new freak friend have already had their fun. They're cleaning themselves up in another room. This time they picked one of the old abandoned buildings on the edge of the

Tombs—far enough away from anybody who cares that no one would have investigated the girl's screams, if they'd even heard them. Green and her friend must have brought her here after I made my own sweep through the area earlier. From the gas cans standing by the door, I figure they're planning to torch the place once they're ready to leave.

I guess I shouldn't be surprised to find Judy sitting in the room with the dead girl. She looks up when I come in, all the hurt and pain in the world gathered in her eyes.

"Look at her," Judy says.

I don't want to. Not again. One look was enough.

"We could've stopped this," she adds.

She's being kind. What she really means is I could have stopped it.

I drift back into the other room where Green and her partner are giggling as they clean themselves off. They're both in their underwear, sloshing water over each other. Their clothes never got near the blood. They'd left them piled neatly by the door near the gas cans.

No, I think. They don't deserve to live. They don't have one redeeming quality between the pair of them . . .

I have one of those moments then, when everything shrinks down to a pinpoint of sharp focus. And I know what to do.

I don't know why it never occurred to either Judy or me before. We didn't need to find anybody else. All the losers we needed were right here in the room with me.

I step into the guy. Judy explained it to me, but hearing it's one thing, doing it is another. Nothing could have prepared me for the sensation of getting into his skin. His body folds around me like wet, oily phlegm, hot and yielding, and I want to get out of there so bad it hurts. I never felt Judy when she rode me, but this guy fights my presence. There was never much subtlety about me when I was alive and I guess it carried over now that I'm dead. I bear down hard, backing him into a corner of his head where all he can do is watch.

"Jesus," Green says, giving me/her partner a weird look. "What's the matter with you?"

"Nothing," I tell her. I don't recognize the voice coming out of the mouth I'm using.

"Well, then why're you looking so weird?"

I don't want to talk, so I hit her. I hate the way it feels. Like I've become my old man.

She goes down, scrabbling across the floor to get away from me. But I'm quicker. I land on her back and hold her down with the weight of my borrowed body. When she tries to buck me off, I grab her hair and whack her head against the floor, stunning her. It gives me enough time to rip the arms off her freak friend's shirt and tie her up, legs and arms.

Judy comes into the room as I'm emptying the first of the gas cans over Green, over the floor, splashing it on the wall. For a moment she doesn't get it, but then she sees something in the guy's eyes—a piece of me, I guess, and she nods.

I throw the empty can into a corner, open another. This one I start to pour over myself.

"The girl," Judy says.

I give her a blank look.

"Don't let her body burn with them," she tells me.

I go into the other room. This time I've got a body. I retch at what they did to her. Tears blind my eyes as I pick her up as gently as I can and carry her outside. Then I go back inside.

I find the lighter in the guy's pants.

"Say good-bye," I tell him as I set us on fire.

*   *   *

I haven't seen Judy since that night.

While I'm hoping she was finally able to travel on to wherever it is we get to go when our lives in this world are done, I doubt it played out that way. We had good reasons for killing them, I guess, but the way we did it isn't the sort of thing that wins you any kind of eternal peace.

Hell, right now I'd settle for oblivion.

I pray for it.

Judy said she'd let me go when Green was dead, and I'm sure she did, loosed that hold she had on me and set me free. But I can't travel on. There doesn't seem to be a place for me to go on to. I think we're locked into what we've done now—real ghosts, just like in the stories. She's probably haunting the place where she died. As for me, I can't seem to leave this place.

I don't move. I don't really think except to replay that night in my head.

I sit on the stoop of an abandoned tenement in the Tombs . . .

Staring across the street at the charred rubble of the building I burned down.

Listening to the screams of Green and her partner ring in my head.

Waiting for oblivion to finally come.

But like Judy said. If I had to do it over, even if I knew it meant damning myself like this, I'd probably do the same thing again.

Pixel Pixies

Only when Mistress Holly had retired to her apartment above the store would Dick Bobbins peep out from behind the furnace where he'd spent the day dreaming and drowsing and reading the books he borrowed from the shelves upstairs. He would carefully check the basement for unexpected visitors and listen for a telltale floorboard to creak from above. Only when he was very very sure that the mistress, and especially her little dog, had both, indeed, gone upstairs, would he creep all the way out of his hidden hobhole.

Every night, he followed the same routine.

Standing on the cement floor, he brushed the sleeves of his drab little jacket and combed his curly brown hair with his fingers. Rubbing his palms briskly together, he plucked last night's borrowed book from his hidey-hole and made his way up the steep basement steps to the store. Standing only two feet high, this might have been an arduous process all on its own, but he was quick and agile, as a hob should be, and in no time at all he'd be standing in among the books, considering where to begin the night's work.

There was dusting and sweeping to do, books to be put away. Lovely books. It didn't matter to Dick if they were serious leather-bound tomes or paperbacks with garish covers. He loved them all, for they were filled with words, and words were magic to this hob. Wise and clever humans had used some marvelous spell to imbue each book with every kind of story and character you could imagine, and many you couldn't. If you knew the key to unlock the words, you could experience them all.

Sometimes Dick would remember a time when he hadn't been able to read. All he could do then was riffle the pages and try to smell the stories out of them. But now, oh now, he was a magician, too, for he could unearth the hidden enchantment in the books anytime he wanted to. They were his nourishment and his joy, weren't they just.

So first he worked, earning his keep. Then he would choose a new book from those that had come into the store while he was in his hobhole, drowsing away the day. Sitting on top of one of the bookcases, he'd read until it got light outside and it was time to return to his hiding place behind the furnace, the book under his arm in case he woke early and wanted to finish the story while he waited for the mistress to go to bed once more.

I hate computers.

Not when they do what they're supposed to. Not even when I'm the one who's made some stupid mistake, like deleting a file I didn't intend to, or exiting one without saving it. I've still got a few of those old war-horse programs on my machine that don't pop up a reminder asking if I want to save the file I was working on.

No, it's when they seem to have a mind of their own. The keyboard freezing for no apparent reason. Getting an error message that you're out of disk space when you know you've got at least a couple of gigs free. Passwords becoming temporarily, and certainly arbitrarily, obsolete. Those and a hundred other, usually minor, but always annoying, irritations.

Sometimes it's enough to make you want to pick up the nearest component of the machine and fling it against the wall.

For all the effort they save, the little tasks that they automate and their wonderful storage capacity, at times like this—when everything's going as wrong as it can go—their benefits can't come close to outweighing their annoyances.

My present situation was partly my own fault. I'd been updating my inventory all afternoon and before saving the file and backing it up, I'd decided to go on the Internet to check some of my competitors' prices. The used book business, which is what I'm in, has probably the most arbitrary pricing in the world. Though I suppose that can be expanded to include any business specializing in collectibles.

I logged on without any trouble and went merrily browsing through listings on the various book search pages, making notes on the particularly interesting items, a few of which I actually had in stock. It wasn't until I tried to exit my browser that the trouble started. My browser wouldn't close and I couldn't switch to another window. Nor could I log off the Internet.

Deciding it had something to do with the page I was on—I know that doesn't make much sense, but I make no pretence to being more than vaguely competent when it comes to knowing how the software actually interfaces with the hardware—I called up the drop-down menu of "My Favorites" and clicked on my own home page. What I got was a fan shrine to pro wrestling star Steve Austin.

I tried again and ended up at a commercial software site.

The third time I was taken to the site of someone named Cindy

Margolis—the most downloaded woman on the Internet, according to the *Guinness Book of World Records*. Not on this computer, my dear.

I made another attempt to get off-line, then tried to access my home page again. Each time I found myself in some new outlandish and unrelated site.

Finally I tried one of the links on the last page I'd reached. It was supposed to bring me to Netscape's home page. Instead I found myself on the web site of a real estate company in Santa Fe, looking at a cluster of pictures of the vaguely Spanish-styled houses that they were selling.

I sighed, tried to break my Internet connection for what felt like the hundredth time, but the "Connect To" window still wouldn't come up.

I could have rebooted, of course. That would have gotten me off-line. But it would also mean that I'd lose the whole afternoon's work because, being the stupid woman I was, I hadn't had the foresight to save the stupid file before I went gadding about on the stupid Internet.

"Oh, you stupid machine," I muttered.

From the front window display where she was napping, I heard Snippet, my Jack Russell terrier, stir. I turned to reassure her that, no, she was still my perfect little dog. When I swiveled my chair to face the computer again, I realized that there was a woman standing on the other side of the counter.

I'd seen her come into the store earlier, but I'd lost track of everything in my one-sided battle of wits with the computer—it having the wits, of course. She was a very striking woman, her dark brown hair falling in Pre-Raphaelite curls that were streaked with green, her eyes both warm and distant, like an odd mix of a perfect summer's day and the mystery you can feel swell up inside you when you look up into the stars on a crisp, clear autumn night. There was something familiar about her, but I couldn't quite place it. She wasn't one of my regulars.

She gave me a sympathetic smile.

"I suppose it was only a matter of time before they got into the computers," she said.

I blinked. "What?"

"Try putting your sweater on inside out."

My face had to be registering the confusion I was feeling, but she simply continued to smile.

"I know it sounds silly," she said, "but humor me. Give it a try."

Anyone in retail knows, you get all kinds. And the secondhand market gets more than its fair share, trust me on that. If there's a loopy person anywhere within a hundred blocks of my store, you can bet they'll eventually find their way inside. The woman standing on the other side of my counter looked harmless enough, if somewhat exotic, but you just never know anymore, do you?

"What have you got to lose?" she asked.

I was about to lose an afternoon's work as things stood, so what was a little pride on top of that?

I stood up and took my sweater off, turned it inside out, and put it back on again.

"Now give it a try," the woman said.

I called up the "Connected to" window and this time it came up. When I put the cursor on the "Disconnect" button and clicked, I was logged off. I quickly shut down my browser and saved the file I'd been working on all afternoon.

"You're a lifesaver," I told the woman. "How did you know that would work?" I paused, thought about what I'd just said, what had just happened. "*Why* would that work?"

"I've had some experience with pixies and their like," she said.

"Pixies," I repeated. "You think there are pixies in my computer?"

"Hopefully not. If you're lucky, they're still on the Internet and didn't follow you home."

I gave her a curious look. "You're serious, aren't you?"

"At times," she said, smiling again. "And this is one of them."

I thought about one of my friends, an electronic pen pal in Arizona, who has this theory that the first atom bomb detonation forever changed the way that magic would appear in the world. According to him, the spirits live in the wires now instead of the trees. They travel through phone and modem lines, take up residence in computers and appliances where they live on electricity and lord knows what else.

It looked like Richard wasn't alone in his theories, not that I pooh-poohed them myself. I'm part of a collective that originated this electronic database called the Wordwood. After it took on a life of its own, I pretty much keep an open mind about things that most people would consider preposterous.

"I'd like to buy this," the woman went on.

She held up a trade paperback copy of *The Beggars' Shore* by Zak Mucha.

"Good choice," I said.

It never surprises me how many truly excellent books end up in the secondary market. Not that I'm complaining—it's what keeps me in business.

"Please take it as thanks for your advice," I added.

"You're sure?"

I looked down at my computer where my afternoon's work was now safely saved in its file.

"Oh, yes," I told her.

"Thank you," she said. Reaching into her pocket, she took out a business card and gave it to me. "Call me if you ever need any other advice along the same lines."

The business card simply said "The Kelledys" in a large script. Under it were the names "Meran and Cerin" and a phone number. Now I knew why, earlier, she'd seemed familiar. It had just been seeing her here in the store, out of context, that had thrown me.

"I love your music," I told her. "I've seen you and your husband play several times."

She gave me another of those kind smiles of hers.

"You can probably turn your sweater around again now," she said as she left.

Snippet and I watched her walk by the window. I took off my sweater and put it back on properly.

"Time for your walk," I told Snippet. "But first let me back up this file to a Zip disk."

That night, after the mistress and her little dog had gone upstairs, Dick Bobbins crept out of his hobhole and made his nightly journey up to the store. He replaced the copy of *The Woods Colt* that he'd been reading, putting it neatly back on the fiction shelf under "W" for Williamson, fetched the duster, and started his work. He finished the "History" and "Local Interest" sections, dusting and straightening the books, and was climbing up onto the "Poetry" shelves near the back of the store when he paused, hearing something from the front of the store.

Reflected in the front window, he could see the glow of the computer's monitor and realized that the machine had turned on by itself. That couldn't be good. A faint giggle spilled out of the computer's speakers, quickly followed by a chorus of other voices, tittering and snickering. That was even less good.

A male face appeared on the screen, looking for all the world as though it could see out of the machine. Behind him other faces appeared, a whole gaggle of little men in green clothes, good-naturedly pushing and shoving each other, whispering and giggling. They were red-haired like the mistress, but there the resemblance ended. Where she was pretty, they were ugly, with short faces, turned-up noses, squinting eyes and pointed ears.

This wasn't good at all, Dick thought, recognizing the pixies for what they were. Everybody knew how you spelled "trouble." It was P-I-X-Y.

And then they started to clamber out of the screen, which shouldn't have been possible at all, but Dick was a hob and he understood that just because something shouldn't be able to happen, didn't mean it couldn't. Or wouldn't.

"Oh, this is bad," he said mournfully. "Bad bad bad."

He gave a quick look up to the ceiling. He had to warn the mistress. But it was already too late. Between one thought and the next, a dozen or more pixies had climbed out of the computer onto her desk, not the one of them taller than his own waist. They began riffling through her papers, using her pens and ruler as swords to poke at each other. Two of them started a pushing match that resulted in a small stack of books falling off the side of the desk. They landed with a bang on the floor.

The sound was so loud that Dick was sure the mistress would come down to investigate, she and her fierce little dog. The pixies all stood like little statues until first one, then another, started to giggle again. When they began to all shove at a bigger stack of books, Dick couldn't wait any longer.

Quick as a monkey, he scurried down to the floor.

"Stop!" he shouted as he ran to the front of the store.

And, "Here, you!"

And, "Don't!"

The pixies turned at the sound of his voice and Dick skidded to a stop.

"Oh, oh," he said.

The little men were still giggling and elbowing each other, but there was a wicked light in their eyes now, and they were all looking at him with those dark, considering gazes. Poor Dick realized that he hadn't thought any of this through in the least bit properly, for now that he had their attention, he had no idea what to do with it. They might only be a third his size, individually, but there were at least twenty of them and everybody knew just how mean a pixy could be, did he set his mind to it.

"Well, will you look at that," one of the pixies said. "It's a little hobberdy man." He looked at his companions. "What shall we do with him?"

"Smash him!"

"Whack him!"

"Find a puddle and drown him!"

Dick turned and fled, back the way he'd come. The pixies streamed from the top of Mistress Holly's desk, laughing wickedly and shouting threats as they chased him. Up the Poetry shelves Dick went, all the way to the very top. When he looked back down, he saw that the pixies weren't following the route he'd taken.

He allowed himself a moment's relief. Perhaps he was safe. Perhaps they couldn't climb. Perhaps they were afraid of heights.

Or, he realized with dismay, perhaps they meant to bring the whole bookcase crashing down, and him with it.

For the little men had gathered at the bottom of the bookcase and were putting their shoulders to its base. They might be small, but they were strong, and soon the tall stand of shelves was tottering unsteadily, swaying back and forth. A loose book fell out. Then another.

"No, no! You mustn't!" Dick cried down to them.

But he was too late.

With cries of "Hooray!" from the little men below, the book-case came tumbling down, spraying books all around it. It smashed into its neighbor, bringing that stand of shelves down as well. By the time Dick hit the floor, hundreds of books were scattered all over the carpet and he was sitting on top of a tall, unsteady mountain of poetry, clutching his head, awaiting the worst.

The pixies came clambering up its slopes, the wicked lights in their eyes shining fierce and bright. He was, Dick realized, about to become an ex-hob. Except then he heard the door to Mistress Holly's apartment open at the top of the back stairs.

Rescued, he thought. And not a moment too soon. She would chase them off.

All the little men froze and Dick looked for a place to hide from the mistress's gaze.

But the pixies seemed unconcerned. Another soft round of gig-gles arose from them as, one by one, they transformed into soft, glit-tering lights no bigger than the mouth of a shot glass. The lights rose up from the floor where they'd been standing and went sailing toward the front of the store. When the mistress appeared at the foot of the stairs, her dog at her heels, she didn't even look at the fallen bookshelves. She saw only the lights, her eyes widening with happy delight.

Oh, no, Dick thought. They're pixy-leading her.

The little dog began to growl and bark and tug at the hem of her long flannel nightgown, but she paid no attention to it. Smiling a dreamy smile, she lifted her arms above her head like a ballerina and began to follow the dancing lights to the front of the store. Dick watched as pixy magic made the door pop open and a gust of chilly air burst in. Goose bumps popped up on the mistress's forearms but she never seemed to notice the cold. Her gaze was locked on the lights as they swooped, around and around in a gallitrap circle, then went shimmering out onto the street beyond. In moments she would follow them, out into the night and who knew what terrible danger.

Her little dog let go of her hem and ran ahead, barking at the lights. But it was no use. The pixies weren't frightened and the mistress wasn't roused.

It was up to him, Dick realized.

He ran up behind her and grabbed her ankle, bracing himself. Like the pixies, he was much stronger than his size might give him to appear. He held firm as the mistress tried to raise her foot. She lost her balance and down she went, down and down, toppling like some enormous tree. Dick jumped back, hands to his mouth, appalled at what he'd had to do. She banged her shoulder against a display at the front of the store, sending yet another mass of books cascading onto the floor.

Landing heavily on her arms, she stayed bent over for a long time before she finally looked up. She shook her head as though to clear it. The pixy lights had returned to the store, buzzing angrily about, but it was no use. The spell had been broken. One by one, they zoomed out of the store, down the street and were quickly lost from sight. The mistress's little dog ran back out onto the sidewalk and continued to bark at them, long after they were gone.

"Please let me be dreaming . . ." the mistress said.

Dick stooped quickly out of sight as she looked about at the sudden ruin of the store. He peeked at her from his hiding place, watched her rub at her face, then slowly stand up and massage her shoulder where it had hit the display. She called the dog back in, but stood in the doorway herself for a long time, staring out at the street, before she finally shut and locked the door behind her.

Oh, it was all such a horrible, terrible, awful mess.

"I'm sorry, I'm sorry, I'm sorry," Dick murmured, his voice barely a whisper, tears blurring his eyes.

The mistress couldn't hear him. She gave the store another survey, then shook her head.

"Come on, Snippet," she said to the dog. "We're going back to bed. Because this is just a dream."

She picked her way through the fallen books and shelves as she spoke.

"And when we wake up tomorrow everything will be back to normal."

But it wouldn't be. Dick knew. This was more of a mess than even the most industrious of hobs could clear up in just one night. But he did what he could until the morning came, one eye on the task at hand, the other on the windows in case the horrible pixies decided to return. Though what he'd do if they did, probably only the moon knew, and she wasn't telling.

Did you ever wake up from the weirdest, most unpleasant dream, only to find that it wasn't a dream at all?

When I came down to the store that morning, I literally had to lean against the wall at the foot of the stairs and catch my breath. I felt all faint and woozy. Snippet walked daintily ahead of me, sniffing the fallen books and whining softly.

An earthquake, I told myself. That's what it had been. I must have woken up right after the main shock, come down half asleep and seen the mess, and just gone right back to bed again, thinking I was dreaming.

Except there'd been those dancing lights. Like a dozen or more Tinkerbells. Or fireflies. Calling me to follow, follow, follow, out into the night, until I'd tripped and fallen . . .

I shook my head slowly, trying to clear it. My shoulder was still sore and I massaged it as I took in the damage.

Actually, the mess wasn't as bad as it had looked at first. Many of the books appeared to have toppled from the shelves and landed in relatively alphabetical order.

Snippet whined again, but this time it was her "I really have to go" whine, so I grabbed her leash and a plastic bag from behind the desk and out we went for her morning constitutional.

It was brisk outside, but warm for early December, and there still wasn't any snow. At first glance, the damage from the quake appeared to be fairly marginal, considering it had managed to topple a couple of the bookcases in my store. The worst I could see were that all garbage canisters on the block had been overturned, the wind picking up the paper litter and carrying it in eddying pools up and down the street. Other than that, everything seemed pretty much normal. At least it did until I stopped into Café Joe's down the street to get my morning latté.

Joe Lapegna had originally operated a sandwich bar at the same location, but with the coming of Starbucks to town, he'd quickly seen which way the wind was blowing and renovated his place into a café. He'd done a good job with the décor. His café was every bit as contemporary and urban as any of the other high-end coffee bars in the city, the only real difference being that, instead of young college kids with rings through their noses, you got Joe serving the lattés and espressos. Joe with his broad shoulders and meaty, tattooed forearms, a fat caterpillar of a black mustache perched on his upper lip.

Before I could mention the quake, Joe started to tell me how he'd opened up this morning to find every porcelain mug in the store broken. None of the other breakables, not the plates or coffee makers. Nothing else was even out of place.

"What a weird quake it was," I said.

"Quake?" Joe said. "What quake?"

I waved a hand at the broken china he was sweeping up.

"This was vandals," he said. "Some little bastards broke in and had themselves a laugh."

So I told him about the bookcases in my shop, but he only shook his head.

"You hear anything about a quake on the radio?" he asked.

"I wasn't listening to it."

"I was. There was nothing. And what kind of a quake only breaks mugs and knocks over a couple of bookcases?"

Now that I thought of it, it was odd that there hadn't been any other disruption in my own store. If those bookcases had come down, why hadn't the front window display? I'd noticed a few books had fallen off my desk, but that was about it.

"It's so weird," I repeated.

Joe shook his head. "Nothing weird about it. Just some punks out having their idea of fun."

By the time I got back to my own store, I didn't know what to think. Snippet and I stopped in at a few other places along the strip and while everyone had damage to report, none of it was what could be put down to a quake. In the bakery, all the pies had been thrown against the front windows. In the hardware store, each and every electrical bulb was smashed—though they looked as though they'd simply exploded. All the rolls of paper towels and toilet paper from the grocery store had been tossed up into the trees behind their shipping and receiving bays, turning the bare-branched oaks and elms into bizarre mummylike versions of themselves. And on it went.

The police arrived not long after I returned to the store. I felt like such a fool when one of the detectives came by to interview me. Yes, I'd heard the crash and come down to investigate. No, I hadn't seen anything.

I couldn't bring myself to mention the dancing lights.

No, I hadn't thought to phone it in.

"I thought I was dreaming," I told him. "I was half asleep when I came downstairs and didn't think it had really happened. It wasn't until I came back down in the morning . . ."

The detective was of the opinion that it had been gang-related, kids out on the prowl, egging each other on until it had gotten out of control.

I thought about it when he left and knew he had to be right. The damage we'd sustained was all on the level of pranks—mean-spirited, to be sure, but pranks nonetheless. I didn't like the idea of our little area being the sudden target of vandals, but there really wasn't any other logical explanation. At least none occurred to me until I stepped back into the store and glanced at my computer. That's when I remembered Meran Kelledy, how she'd gotten me to turn my sweater inside out and the odd things she'd been saying about pixies on the Web.

If you're lucky, they're still on the Internet and didn't follow you home.

Of course that wasn't even remotely logical. But it made me think. After all, if the Wordwood database could take on a life of its own, who was to say that pixies on the Internet was any more improbable? As my friend Richard likes to point out, everyone has odd problems with their computers that could as easily be attributed to mischievous spirits as to software glitches. At least they could be if your mind was inclined to think along those lines, and mine certainly was.

I stood for a long moment, staring at the screen of my computer. I don't know exactly at what point I realized that the machine was on. I'd turned it off last night before Snippet and I went up to the apartment. And I hadn't stopped to turn it on this morning before we'd gone out. So either I was getting monumentally forgetful, or I'd turned it on while sleepwalking last night, or . . .

I glanced over at Snippet, who was once again sniffing everything as though she'd never been in the store before. Or as if someone or something interesting and strange *had*.

"This is silly," I said.

But I dug out Meran's card and called the number on it all the same, staring at the computer screen as I did. I just hoped nobody had been tinkering with my files.

Bookstore hobs are a relatively recent phenomenon, dating back only a couple of hundred years. Dick knew hobs back home in the old country who'd lived in the same household for three times that length of time. He'd been a farm hob himself, once, living on a Devon steading for two hundred and twelve years until a new family moved in and began to take his services for granted. When one year they actually dared to complain about how poorly the harvest had been put away, he'd thrown every bit of it down into a nearby ravine and set off to find new habitation.

A cousin who lived in a shop had suggested to Dick that he try the same, but there were fewer commercial establishments in those days and they all had their own hob by the time he went looking, first up into Somerset, then back down through Devon, finally moving west to Cornwall. In the end, he made his home in a small cubbyhole of a bookstore he found in Penzance. He lived there for years until the place went out of business, the owner setting sail for North America with plans to open another shop in the new land once he arrived.

Dick had followed, taking up residence in the new store when it was established. That was where he'd taught himself to read.

But he soon discovered that stores didn't have the longevity of a farm. They opened and closed up business seemingly on nothing

more than a whim, which made it a hard life for a hob, always looking for a new place to live. By the latter part of this century, he had
moved twelve times in the space of five years before finally settling
into the place he now called home, the bookstore of his present mistress with its simple sign out front:

HOLLY RUE—USED BOOKS

He'd discovered that a quality used book store was always the
best. Libraries were good, too, but they were usually home to displaced gargoyles and the ghosts of writers and had no room for a
hob as well. He'd tried new book stores, but the smaller ones
couldn't keep him busy enough and the large ones were too bright,
their hours of business too long. And he loved the wide and eclectic
range of old and new books to be explored in a shop such as Mistress Holly's, titles that wandered far from the beaten path, or wor-
thy books no longer in print, but nonetheless inspired. The stories
he found in them sustained him in a way that nothing else could, for
they fed the heart and the spirit.

But this morning, sitting behind the furnace, he only felt old and
tired. There'd been no time to read at all last night, and he hadn't
thought to bring a book down with him when he finally had to leave
the store.

"I hate pixies," he said, his voice soft and lonely in the darkness.
"I really really do."

Faerie and pixies had never gotten along, especially not since the
last pitched battle between them in the old country when the faeries
had been driven back across the River Parrett, leaving everything
west of the Parrett as pixyland. For years, hobs such as Dick had
lived a clandestine existence in their little steadings, avoiding the
attention of pixies whenever they could.

Dick hadn't needed last night's experience to tell him why.

After a while he heard the mistress and her dog leave the store so he crept out from behind the furnace to stand guard in case the pixies returned while the pair of them were gone. Though what he would do if the pixies did come back, he still had no idea. He was an absolute failure when it came to protecting anything, that had been made all too clear last night.

Luckily the question never arose. Mistress Holly and the dog returned and he slipped back behind the furnace, morosely clutching his knees and rocking back and forth, waiting for the night to come. He could hear life go on upstairs. Someone came by to help the mistress right the fallen bookcases. Customers arrived and left with much discussion of the vandalism on the street. Most of the time he could hear only the mistress, replacing the books on their shelves.

"I should be doing that," Dick said. "That's my job."

But he was only an incompetent hob, concealed in his hidey-hole, of no use to anyone until they all went to bed and he could go about his business. And even then, any ruffian could come along and bully him and what could he do to stop them?

Dick's mood went from bad to worse, from sad to sadder still. It might have lasted all the day, growing unhappier with each passing hour, except at midmorning he suddenly sat up, ears and nose quivering. A presence had come into the store above. A piece of an old mystery, walking about as plain as could be.

He realized that he'd sensed it yesterday as well, while he was dozing. Then he'd put it down to the dream he was wandering in, forgetting all about it when he woke. But today, wide awake, he couldn't ignore it. There was an oak king's daughter upstairs, an old and powerful spirit walking far from her woods. He began to shiver. Important faerie such as she wouldn't be out and about unless the need was great. His shiver deepened. Perhaps she'd come to reprimand him for the job so poorly done. She might turn him into a stick or a mouse.

Oh, this was very bad. First pixies, now this.

Whatever was he going to do? How ever could he even begin to explain that he'd meant to chase the pixies away, truly he had, but he simply wasn't big enough, nor strong enough. Perhaps not even brave enough.

He rocked back and forth, harder now, his face burrowed against his knees.

After I'd made my call to Meran, Samuel, who works at the deli down the street, came by and helped me stand the bookcases upright once more. The deli hadn't been spared a visit from the vandals either. He told me that they'd taken all the sausages out of the freezer and used them to spell out rude words on the floor.

"Remember when all we had to worry about was some graffiti on the walls outside?" he asked when he was leaving.

I was still replacing books on the shelves when Meran arrived. She looked around the store while I expanded on what I'd told her over the phone. Her brow furrowed thoughtfully and I was wondering if she was going to tell me to put my sweater on backwards again.

"You must have a hob in here," she said.

"A what?"

It was the last thing I expected her to say.

"A hobgoblin," she said. "A brownie. A little faerie man who dusts and tidies and keeps things neat."

"I just thought it didn't get all that dirty," I said, realizing as I spoke how ridiculous that sounded.

Because, when I thought about it, a helpful brownie living in the store explained a lot. While I certainly ran the vacuum cleaner over the carpets every other morning or so, and dusted when I could, the place never seemed to need much cleaning. My apartment upstairs required more and it didn't get a fraction of the traffic.

And it wasn't just the cleaning. The store, for all its clutter, was organized, though half the time I didn't know how. But I always seemed to be able to lay my hand on whatever I needed to find without having to root about too much. Books often got put away without my remembering I'd done it. Others mysteriously vanished, then reappeared a day or so later, properly filed in their appropriate section—even if they had originally disappeared from the top of my desk. I rarely needed to alphabetize my sections while my colleagues in other stores were constantly complaining of the mess their customers left behind.

"But aren't you supposed to leave cakes and cream out for them?" I found myself asking.

"You never leave a specific gift," Meran said. "Not unless you want him to leave. It's better to simply 'forget' a cake or a sweet treat on one of the shelves when you leave for the night."

"I haven't even done that. What could he be living on?"

Meran smiled as she looked around the store. "Maybe the books nourish him. Stranger things have been known to happen in Faerie."

"Faerie," I repeated slowly.

Bad enough I'd helped create a database on the Internet that had taken on a life of its own. Now my store was in Faerie. Or at least straddling the border, I supposed. Maybe the one had come about because of the other.

"Your hob will know what happened here last night," Meran said.

"But how would we even go about asking him?"

It seemed a logical question, since I'd never known I had one living with me in the first place. But Meran only smiled.

"Oh, I can usually get their attention," she told me.

She called out something in a foreign language, a handful of words that rang with great strength and appeared to linger and echo longer than they should. The poor little man who came sidling up from the basement in response looked absolutely terrified. He was all curly hair and raggedy clothes with a broad face that, I assumed from the laugh lines, normally didn't look so miserable. He was carrying a battered little leather carpetbag and held a brown cloth cap in his hand. He couldn't have been more than two feet tall.

All I could do was stare at him, though I did have the foresight to pick up Snippet before she could lunge in his direction. I could feel the growl rumbling in her chest more than hear it. I think she was as surprised as me to find that he'd been living in our basement all this time.

Meran sat on her haunches, bringing her head down to the general level of the hob's. To put him at ease, I supposed, so I did the same myself. The little man didn't appear to lose any of his nervousness. I could see his knees knocking against each other, his cheek twitching.

"B-begging your pardon, your ladyship," he said to Meran. His gaze slid to me and I gave him a quick smile. He blinked, swallowed hard, and returned his attention to my companion. "Dick Bobbins," he added, giving a quick nod of his head. "At your service, as it were. I'll just be on my way, then, no harm done."

"Why are you so frightened of me?" Meran asked.

He looked at the floor. "Well, you're a king's daughter, aren't you just, and I'm only me."

A king's daughter? I thought.

Meran smiled. "We're all only who we are, no one of more importance than the other."

"Easy for you to say," he began. Then his eyes grew wide and he put a hand to his mouth. "Oh, that was a bad thing to say to such a great and wise lady such as yourself."

Meran glanced at me. "They think we're like movie stars," she explained. "Just because we were born in a court instead of a hob-hole."

I was getting a bit of a case of the celebrity nerves myself. Court? King's daughter? Who exactly *was* this woman?

"But you know," she went on, returning her attention to the little man, "my father's court was only a glade, our palace no more than a tree."

He nodded quickly, giving her a thin smile that never reached his eyes.

"Well, wonderful to meet you," he said. "Must be on my way now."

He picked up his carpetbag and started to sidle toward the other aisle that wasn't blocked by what he must see as two great big hulking women and a dog.

"But we need your help," Meran told him.

Whereupon he burst into tears.

The mothering instinct that makes me such a sap for Snippet kicked into gear and I wanted to hold him in my arms and comfort him. But I had Snippet to consider, straining in my grip, the growl in her chest quite audible now. And I wasn't sure how the little man would have taken my sympathies. After all, he might be child-sized, but for all his tears, he was obviously an adult, not a child. And if the stories were anything to go by, he was probably older than me— by a few hundred years.

Meran had no such compunction. She slipped up to him and put her arms around him, cradling his face against the crook of her shoulder.

It took a while before we coaxed the story out of him. I locked the front door and we went upstairs to my kitchen where I made tea for us all. Sitting at the table, raised up to the proper height by a stack of books, Dick told us about the pixies coming out of the computer screen, how they'd knocked down the bookcases and finally disappeared into the night. The small mug I'd given him looked enormous in his hands. He fell silent when he was done and stared glumly down at the steam rising from his tea.

"But none of what they did was your fault," I told him.

"Kind of you to say," he managed. He had to stop and sniff, wipe his nose on his sleeve. "But if I'd b-been braver—"

"They *would* have drowned you in a puddle," Meran said. "And I think you were brave, shouting at them the way you did and then rescuing your mistress from being pixy-led."

I remembered those dancing lights and shivered. I knew those stories as well. There weren't any swamps or marshes to be led into around here, but there were eighteen-wheelers out on the highway only a few blocks away. Entranced as I'd been, the pixies could easily have walked me right out in front of any one of them. I was lucky to have only a sore shoulder.

"Do you . . . really think so?" he asked, sitting up a little straighter.

We both nodded.

Snippet was lying under my chair, her curiosity having been satisfied that Dick was only one more visitor and therefore out-of-bounds in terms of biting and barking at. There'd been a nervous moment while she'd sniffed at his trembling hand and he'd looked as though he was ready to scurry up one of the bookcases, but they quickly made their peace. Now Snippet was only bored and had fallen asleep.

"Well," Meran said. "It's time we put our heads together and considered how we can put our unwanted visitors back where they came from and keep them there."

"Back onto the Internet?" I asked. "Do you really think we should?"

"Well, we could try to kill them . . ."

I shook my head. That seemed too extreme. I started to protest, only to see that she'd been teasing me.

"We could take a thousand of them out of the web," Meran said, "and still not have them all. Once tricksy folk like pixies have their foot in a place, you can't ever be completely rid of them." She smiled. "But if we can get them to go back in, there are measures we can take to stop them from troubling you again."

"And what about everybody else on-line?" I asked.

Meran shrugged. "They'll have to take their chances—just like they do when they go for a walk in the woods. The little people are everywhere."

I glanced across my kitchen table to where the hob was sitting and thought, no kidding.

"The trick, if you'll pardon my speaking out of turn," Dick said, "is to play on their curiosity."

Meran gave him an encouraging smile. "We want your help," she said. "Go on."

The little man sat up straighter still and put his shoulders back.

"We could use a book that's never been read," he said. "We could put it in the middle of the road, in front of the store. That would certainly make me curious."

"An excellent idea," Meran told him.

"And then we could use the old spell of bell, book and candle. The churchmen stole that one from us."

Even I'd heard of it. Bell, book and candle had once been another way of saying excommunication in the Catholic church. After pronouncing the sentence, the officiating cleric would close his book, extinguish the candle, and toll the bell as if for someone who had died. The book symbolized the book of life, the candle a man's soul, removed from the sight of God as the candle had been from the sight of men.

But I didn't get the unread book bit.

"Do you mean a brand new book?" I asked. "A particular copy that nobody might have opened yet, or one that's so bad that no one's actually made their way all the way through it?"

"Though someone would have had to," Dick said, "for it to have been published in the first place. I meant the way books were made in the old days, with the pages still sealed. You had to cut them apart as you read them."

"Oh, I remember those," Meran said.

Like she was there. I took another look at her and sighed. Maybe she had been.

"Do you have any like that?" she asked.

"Yes," I said slowly, unable to hide my reluctance.

I didn't particularly like the idea of putting a collector's item like that out in the middle of the road.

But in the end, that's what we did.

The only book I had that passed Dick's inspection was *The Trembling of the Veil* by William Butler Yeats, number seventy-one of a thousand-copy edition privately printed by T. Werner Laurie, Ltd. in 1922. All the pages were still sealed at the top. It was currently listing on the Internet in the $450 to $500 range and I kept it safely stowed away in the glass-doored bookcase that held my first editions.

The other two items were easier to deal with. I had a lovely brass bell that my friend Tatiana had given me for Christmas last year and a whole box of fat white candles just because I liked to burn them. But it broke my heart to go out onto the street around two A.M., and place the Yeats on the pavement.

We left the front door to the store ajar, the computer on. I wasn't entirely sure how we were supposed to lure the pixies back into the store and then onto the Internet once more, but Meran took a flute out of her bag and fit the wooden pieces of it together. She spoke of a calling-on music and Dick nodded sagely, so I simply went along with their better experience. Mind you, I also wasn't all that sure that my Yeats would actually draw the pixies back in the first place, but what did I know?

We all hid in the alleyway running between my store and the futon shop, except for Snippet, who was locked up in my apartment. She hadn't been very pleased by that. After an hour of crouching in the cold in the alley, I wasn't feeling very pleased myself. What if the pixies didn't come? What if they did, but they approached from the fields behind the store and came traipsing up this very alleyway?

By three-thirty we all had a terrible chill. Looking up at my apartment, I could see Snippet lying in the window of the dining room, looking down at us. She didn't appear to have forgiven me yet and I would happily have changed places with her.

"Maybe we should just—"

I didn't get to finish with "call it a night." Meran put a finger to her lips and hugged the wall. I looked past her to the street.

At first I didn't see anything. There was just my Yeats, lying there on the pavement, waiting for a car to come and run over it. But then I saw the little man, not even half the size of Dick, come creeping up from the sewer grating. He was followed by two more. Another pair came down the brick wall of the temporary office help building across the street. Small dancing lights that I remembered too clearly from last night dipped and wove their way from the other end of the block, descending to the pavement and becoming more of the little men when they drew near to the book. One of them poked at it with his foot and I had visions of them tearing it apart.

Meran glanced at Dick and he nodded, mouthing the words, "That's the lot of them."

She nodded back and took her flute out from under her coat where she'd been keeping it warm.

At this point I wasn't really thinking of how the calling music would work. I'm sure my mouth hung agape as I stared at the pixies. I felt light-headed, a big grin tugging at my lips. Yes, they were pranksters, and mean-spirited ones at that. But they were also magical. The way they'd changed from little lights to little men . . . I'd never seen anything like it before. The hob who lived in my bookstore was magical, too, of course, but somehow it wasn't the same thing. He was already familiar, so down-to-earth. Sitting around during the afternoon and evening while we waited, I'd had a delightful time talking books with him, as though he were an old friend. I'd completely forgotten that he was a little magic man himself.

The pixies were truly puzzled by the book. I suppose it would be odd from any perspective, a book that old, never once having been opened or read. It defeated the whole purpose of why it had been made.

I'm not sure when Meran began to play her flute. The soft breathy sound of it seemed to come from nowhere and everywhere, all at once, a resonant wave of slow, stately notes, one falling after the other, rolling into a melody that was at once hauntingly strange and heartachingly familiar.

The pixies lifted their heads at the sound. I wasn't sure what I'd expected, but when they began to dance, I almost clapped my hands. They were so funny. Their bodies kept perfect time to the music, but their little eyes glared at Meran as she stepped out of the alley and Pied-Pipered them into the store.

Dick fetched the Yeats and then he and I followed after, arriving in time to see the music make the little men dance up onto my chair, onto the desk, until they began to vanish, one by one, into the screen of my monitor, a fat candle sitting on top of it, its flame flickering with their movement. Dick opened the book and I took the bell out of my pocket.

Meran brought the flute down from her lips.

"Now," she said.

Dick slapped the book closed, she leaned forward and blew out the candle while I began to chime the bell, the clear brass notes ringing in the silence left behind by the flute. We saw a horde of little faces staring out at us from the screen, eyes glaring. One of the little men actually popped back through, but Dick caught him by the leg and tossed him back into the screen.

Meran laid her flute down on the desk and brought out a garland she'd made earlier of rowan twigs, green leaves and red berry sprigs still attached in places. When she laid it on top of the monitor, we heard the modem dial up my Internet service. When the connection was made, the little men vanished from the screen. The last turned his bum toward us and let out a loud fart before he, too, was gone.

The three of us couldn't help it. We all broke up.

"That went rather well," Meran said when we finally caught our breath. "My husband Cerin is usually the one to handle this sort of thing, but it's nice to know I haven't forgotten how to deal with such rascals myself. And it's probably best he didn't come along this evening. He can seem rather fierce and I don't doubt poor Dick here would have thought him far too menacing."

I looked around the store.

"Where *is* Dick?" I asked.

But the little man was gone. I couldn't believe it. Surely he hadn't just up and left us like in the stories.

"Hobs and brownies," Meran said when I asked, her voice gentle, "they tend to take their leave rather abruptly when the tale is done."

"I thought you had to leave them a suit of clothes or something."

Meran shrugged. "Sometimes simply being identified is enough to make them go."

"Why does it have to be like that?"

"I'm not really sure. I suppose it's a rule or something, or a geas—a thing that has to happen. Or perhaps it's no more than a simple habit they've handed down from one generation to the next."

"But I *loved* the idea of him living here," I said. "I thought it would be so much fun. With all the work he's been doing, I'd have been happy to make him a partner."

Meran smiled. "Faerie and commerce don't usually go hand in hand."

"But you and your husband play music for money."

Her smile grew wider, her eyes enigmatic, but also amused.

"What makes you think we're faerie?" she asked.

"Well, you . . . that is . . ."

"I'll tell you a secret," she said, relenting. "We're something else again, but what exactly that might be, even we have no idea anymore. Mostly we're the same as you. Where we differ is that Cerin and I always live with half a foot in the otherworld that you've only visited these past few days."

"And only the borders of it, I'm sure."

She shrugged. "Faerie is everywhere. It just *seems* closer at certain times, in certain places."

She began to take her flute apart and stow the wooden pieces away in the instrument's carrying case.

"Your hob will be fine," she said. "The kindly ones such as he always find a good household to live in."

"I hope so," I said. "But all the same, I was really looking forward to getting to know him better."

Dick Bobbins got an odd feeling listening to the two of them talk, his mistress and the oak king's daughter. Neither was quite what he'd expected. Mistress Holly was far kinder and not at all the brusque, rather self-centered human that figured in so many old hob fireside tales. And her ladyship . . . well, who would have thought that one of the highborn would treat a simple hob as though they stood on equal footing? It was all very unexpected.

But it was time for him to go. He could feel it in his blood and in his bones.

He waited while they said their good-byes. Waited while Mistress Holly took the dog out for a last quick pee before the pair of them retired to their apartment. Then he had the store completely to himself, with no chance of unexpected company. He fetched his little leather carpetbag from his hobhole behind the furnace and came back upstairs to say good-bye to the books, to the store, to his home.

Finally all there was left to do was to spell the door open, step outside and go. He hesitated on the welcoming carpet, thinking of what Mistress Holly had asked, what her ladyship had answered. Was the leaving song that ran in his blood and rumbled in his bones truly a geas, or only habit? How was a poor hob to know? If it was a rule, then who had made it and what would happen if he broke it?

He took a step away from the door, back into the store and paused, waiting for he didn't know what. Some force to propel him out the door. A flash of light to burn down from the sky and strike him where he stood. Instead all he felt was the heaviness in his heart and the funny tingling warmth he'd known when he'd heard the mistress say how she'd been looking forward to getting to know him. That she wanted him to be a partner in her store. Him. Dick Bobbins, of all things.

He looked at the stairs leading up to her apartment.

Just as an experiment, he made his way over to them, then up the risers, one by one, until he stood at her door.

Oh, did he dare, did he dare?

He took a deep breath and squared his shoulders. Then, setting down his carpetbag, he twisted his cloth cap in his hands for a long moment before he finally lifted an arm and rapped a knuckle against the wood panel of Mistress Holly's door.

Trading Hearts at the Half Kaffe Café

CHERISH EACH DAY
Single male, professional, 30ish, wants more out of life. Likes the outdoors, animals. Seeking single female with similar attributes and aspirations. Ad# 6592

The problem is expectations.

We all buy so heavily into how we hope things will turn out, how society and our friends say it should be, that by the time we actually have a date, we're locked into those particular hopes and expectations and miss everything that could be. We end up stumbling our way through the forest, never seeing all the unexpected and wonderful possibilities and potentials because we're looking for the idea of a tree, instead of appreciating the actual trees in front of us.

At least that's the way it seems to me.

Mona

"You already tried that dress on," Sue told me.

"With these shoes?"

Sue nodded. "As well as the red boots."

"And?"

"It's not a first date dress," Sue said. "Unless you wear it with the green boots and that black jacket with the braided cuffs. And you don't take the jacket off."

"Too much cleavage?"

"It's not a matter of cleavage, so much as the cleavage combined with those little spaghetti straps. You're just so *there*. And it's pretty short."

I checked my reflection. She was right, of course. I looked a bit like a tart, and not in a good way. At least Sue had managed to tame my usually unruly hair so that it looked as though it had an actual style instead of the head topped with blonde spikes I normally saw looking back at me from the mirror.

"But the boots would definitely punk it up a little," Sue said. "You know, so it's not quite so 'come hither.' "

"This is hopeless," I said. "How late is it?"

Sue smiled. "Twenty minutes to showtime."

"Oh god. And I haven't even started on my makeup."

"With that dress and those heels, he won't be looking at your makeup."

"Wonderful."

I don't know how I'd gotten talked into this in the first place. Two years without a steady boyfriend, I guess, though by that criteria it should *still* have been Sue agonizing over what to wear and me lending the moral support. She's been much longer without a steady. Mind you, after Pete moved out, the longest relationship I'd been in was with this grotty little troll of a dwarf, and you had to lose points for that. Not that Nacky Wilde had been boyfriend material, but he *had* moved in on me for a few weeks.

"I think you should wear your lucky dress," Sue said.

"I met Pete in that dress."

"True. But only the ending was bad. You had a lot of good times together, too."

"I suppose . . ."

Sue grinned at me. "Eighteen minutes and counting."

"Will you stop with the Cape Canaveral bit already?"

Lyle

"Just don't do the teeth thing and you'll be all right," Tyrone said.

"Teeth thing? What teeth thing?"

"You know, how when you get nervous, your teeth start to protrude like your muzzle's pushing out and you're about to shift your skin. It's not so pretty."

"Thanks for adding to the tension," I told him. "Now I've got that to worry about as well."

I stepped closer to the mirror and ran a finger across my teeth. Were they already pushing out?

"I don't even know why you're going through all of this," Tyrone said.

"I want to meet someone normal."

"You mean not like us."

"I mean someone who isn't as jaded as we are. Someone with a conventional life span for whom each day is important. And I know I'm not going to meet her when the clans gather, or in some bar."

Tyrone shook his head. "I still think it's like dating barnyard animals. Or getting a pet."

"Whatever made you so bitter?"

But Tyrone only grinned. "Just remember what Mama said. Don't eat a girl on the first date."

Mona

"Now don't forget," Sue said. "Build yourself up a little."

"You mean lie."

"Of course not. Well, not a lot. And it might help if you don't seem quite so bohemian right off the bat."

"Pete liked it."

Sue nodded. "And see where that got you. The bohemian artist type has this mysterious allure, especially to straight guys, but it wears off. So you have to show you have the corporate chops as well."

I had to laugh.

"I'm being serious here," Sue said.

"So who am I supposed to be?" I asked.

Sue started to tick the items off on her fingers. "Okay. To start with, you can't go wrong just getting him to talk about himself. You know, act sort of shy and listen a lot."

"I *am* shy."

"When it does come to what you do, don't bring up the fact that you write and draw a comic book for a living. Make it more like art's a hobby. Focus on the fact that you're involved in the publishing field—editing, proofing, book design. Everybody says they like bold and mysterious women, but the truth is, most of them like them from a distance. They like to dream about them. Actually having them sitting at a table with them is way too scary."

Sue had been reading a book on dating called *The Rules* recently, and she was full of all sorts of advice on how to make a relationship work. Maybe that was how they did it in the fifties, but it all seemed so demeaning to me entering the twenty-first century. I thought we'd come further than that.

"In other words, lie," I repeated and turned back to the mirror to finish applying my mascara.

I couldn't remember the last time I'd worn any. On some other date gone awry, I supposed, then I mentally corrected myself. I should be more positive.

"Think of it as bending the truth," Sue said. "It's not like you're going to be pretending forever. It's just a little bit of manipulation for that all-important first impression. Once he realizes he likes you, he won't mind when it turns out you're this little boho comic book gal."

"Your uptown roots are showing," I told her.

"You know what I mean."

Unfortunately, I did. Everybody wanted to seem normal and to meet somebody normal, so first dates became these rather strained, staged affairs with both of you hoping that none of your little hang-ups and oddities were hanging out like an errant shirttail or a drooping slip.

"Ready?" Sue asked.

"No."

"Well, it's time to go anyway."

Lyle

"So what are you going to tell her you do for a living?" Tyrone asked as we walked to the café. "The old hunter/gatherer line?"

"Which worked real well in Cro-Magnon times."

"Hey, some things never change."

"Like you."

Tyrone shrugged. "What can I say? If it works, don't fix it."

We stopped in front of the Half Kaffe. It was five minutes to.

"I'm of half a mind to sit in a corner," Tyrone said. "Just to see how things work out."

"You got the half a mind part right."

Tyrone shook his head with mock sadness. "Sometimes I find it hard to believe we came from the same litter," he said, then grinned.

When he reached over to straighten my tie, I gave him a little push to move him on his way.

"Give 'em hell," he told me. "Girl doesn't like you, she's not worth knowing."

"So now you've got a high opinion of me."

"Hey, you may be feeble-minded, but you're still my brother. That makes you prime."

I had to return that smile of his. Tyrone was just so . . . Tyrone. Always the wolf.

He headed off down the block before I could give him another shove. I checked my teeth in the reflection of the window—still normal—then opened the door and went inside.

Mona

We were ten minutes late pulling up in front of the Half Kaffe.

"This is good," Sue said as I opened my door. "It doesn't make you look too eager."

"Another one of the 'Rules'?"

"Probably."

"Only probably?"

"Well, it's not like I've memorized them or done that well with them myself. You're the one with the date tonight."

I cut her some slack. If push came to shove, I knew she wouldn't take any grief from anyone, no matter what the rule book said.

I got out of the car. "Thanks for the ride, Sue."

"Remember," she said, holding up her phone. Folded up, it wasn't much bigger than a compact. "If things get uncomfortable or just plain weird, I'm only a cell phone call away."

"I'll remember."

I closed the door before she could give me more advice. I'd already decided I was just going to be myself—a dolled-up version of myself, mind you, but it actually felt kind of fun being all dressed up. I just wasn't going to pretend to be someone I wasn't.

Easy to promise to myself on the ride over, listening to Sue, but then my date had to be gorgeous, didn't he? I spotted him as soon as I opened the door, pausing in the threshold.

("I'll be holding a single rose," he'd told me.

("That is *so* romantic," Sue had said.)

Even with him sitting down, I knew he was tall. He had this shock of blue-black hair, brushed back from his forehead, and skin the color of espresso. He was wearing a suit that reminded me of the sky just as the dusk is fading and the single red rose lay on the table in front of him. He looked up when I came in—if it had been me, I'd have looked up every time the door opened, too—and I could have gone swimming in those dark, dark eyes of his.

I took a steadying breath. Walking over to his table, I held out my hand.

"You must be Lyle," I said. "I'm Mona."

Lyle

She was cute as a button.

("Here's my prediction," Tyrone had said. "She'll be three hundred pounds on a five-foot frame. Or ugly as sin. Hell, maybe both."

("I don't care how much she weighs or what she looks like," I told him. "Just so long as she's got a good heart."

(Tyrone smiled. "You're so pathetic," he said.)

And naturally I made a mess of trying to stand up, shake her hand and give her the rose, all at the same time. My chair fell down behind me. The sound of it startled me and I almost pulled her off her feet, but we managed to get it all straightened without anybody getting hurt.

I wanted to check my teeth, and forced myself not to run my tongue over them.

We were here for the obligatory before-dinner drink, having mutually decided earlier on a café rather than a bar, with the unspoken assumption that if things didn't go well here, we could call the dinner off, no hard feelings. After asking what she wanted, I went and got us each a latté.

"Look," she said when I got back. "I know this isn't the way it's supposed to go, first date and everything, but I decided that I'm not going to pretend to be more or different than I am. So here goes.

"I write and draw a comic book for a living. I usually have ink stains on my fingers and you're more likely to see me in overalls, or jeans and a T-shirt. I know I told you I like the outdoors like you said you did in your ad, but I've never spent a night outside of a city. I've never had a regular job either, I don't like being anybody's pet boho girlfriend, and I'm way more shy than this is making me sound."

She was blushing as she spoke and looked a little breathless.

"Oh boy," she said. "That was really endearing, wasn't it?"

It actually was, but I didn't think she wanted to hear that. Searching for something to match her candor, I surprised myself as much as her.

"I'm sort of a werewolf myself," I told her.

"A werewolf," she repeated.

I nodded. "But only sort of. Not like in the movies with the full moon and hair sprouting all over my body. I'm just . . . they used to call us skinwalkers."

"Who did?"

I shrugged. "The first people to live here. Like the Kickaha, up on the rez. We're descended from what they call the animal people—the ones that were here when the world was made."

"Immortal wolves," she said.

I was surprised that she was taking this all so calmly. Surprised to be even talking about it in the first place, because it's never a good idea. Maybe Tyrone was right. We weren't supposed to mingle. But it was too late now and I felt I at least owed her a little more explanation.

"Not just wolves, but all kinds of animals," I said. "And we're not immortal. Only the first ones were and there aren't so many of them left anymore."

"And you can all take the shapes of animals."

I shook my head. "Usually it's only the ones who were born in their animal shape. The human genes are so strong that the change is easier. Those born human have some animal tributes, but most of them aren't skinwalkers."

"So if you bite me, I won't become a wolf."

"I don't know where those stories come from," I started, then sighed. "No, that's not true. I do know. These days most of us just like to fit in, live a bit in your world, a bit in the animal world. But it wasn't always like that. There have always been those among us who considered everyone else in the world their private prey. Humans and animals."

"Most of you?"

I sighed again. "There are still some that like to hunt."

Mona

You're probably wondering why I was listening to all of this without much surprise. But you see, that grotty little dwarf I told you about earlier—the one that moved in on me—did I mention he also had the habit of just disappearing, poof, like magic? One moment you're talking to him, the next you're standing in a seemingly empty room. The disembodied voice was the hardest to get used to. He'd sit around and tell me all kinds of stories like this. You experience something like that on a regular basis and you end up with more tolerance for weirdness.

Not that I actually believed Lyle here was a werewolf. But the fact that he was talking about it actually made him kind of interesting, though I could see it getting old after a while.

"So," I said. "What do you do when you're not dating human girls and running around as a wolf?"

"Do?"

"You know, to make a living. Or were you born wealthy as well as immortal."

"I'm not immortal."

"So what do you do?"

"I'm . . . an investment counselor."

"Hence the nice suit."

He started to nod, then sighed. When he looked down at his latté, I studied his jaw. It seemed to protrude a little more than I remembered, though I knew that was just my own imagination feeding on all his talk about clans of animals that walk around looking like people.

He lifted his head. "How come you're so calm about all of this?"

I shrugged. "I don't know. I like the way it all fits together, I suppose. You've obviously really thought it all through."

"Or I'm good at remembering the history of the clans."

"That, too. But the question that comes to my mind is, why tell me all of this?"

"I'm still asking myself that," he said. "I guess it came from your saying we should be honest with each other. It feels good to be able to talk about it to someone outside the clans."

He paused, those dark eyes studying me more closely. Oh, why couldn't he have just been a normal guy? Why did he have to be either a loony, or some weird faerie creature?

"You don't believe me," he said.

"Well . . ."

"I didn't ask for proof when you were telling me about your comic books."

I couldn't believe this.

"It's hardly the same thing. Besides—"

I got up and fetched one of the freebie copies of *In the City* from their display bin by the door. Flipping almost to the back of the tabloid-sized newspaper, I laid open the page with my weekly strip, "Spunky Grrl," on the table in front of him. This was the one where my heroine, the great and brave Spunky Grrl, was answering a personal ad. Write from your life, they always say. I guess that meant that next week's strip would have Spunky sitting in a café with a wolf dressed up as a man.

"It's not so hard to prove," I said, pointing at the byline.

"Just because you have the same name—"

"Oh, please." I called over to the bar where the owner was reading one of those glossy British music magazines he likes so much. "Who am I, Jonathan?"

He looked up and gave the pair of us a once-over with that perpetually cool and slightly amused look he'd perfected once the café had become a success and he was no longer run ragged trying to keep up with everything.

"Mona Morgan," he said. "Who still owes me that page of original art from 'My Life as a Bird' that featured the Half Kaffe."

"It's coming," I said and turned back to my date. "There. You see? Now it's your turn. Make your hand change into a paw or something."

Lyle

She was irrepressible and refreshing, but she was also driving me a little crazy and I could feel my teeth pressing up against my lips.

"Maybe some other time," I said.

She smiled. "Right. Never turn into a wolf on the first date."

"Something like that," I replied, remembering Tyrone's advice earlier in the evening. I wondered what she'd make of that, but decided not to find out. Instead I looked down at her comic strip.

It was one of those underground ones, not clean like a regular newspaper strip but with lots of scratchy lines and odd perspectives.

There wasn't a joke either, just this wild-looking girl answering a personal ad. I looked up at my date.

"So I'm research?" I asked.

She shrugged. "Everything that happens to me ends up in one strip or another."

I pointed at the character in the strip. "And is this you?"

"Kind of an alter ego."

I could see myself appearing in an upcoming installment, turning into a wolf in the middle of the date. The idea bothered me. I mean, think about it. If you were a skinwalker, would you want the whole world to know it?

I lifted my gaze from the strip. This smart-looking woman bore no resemblance to her scruffy pen-and-ink alter ego.

"So who cleaned you up?" I asked.

I know the idea of showing up in her strip was troubling me, but that was still no excuse for what I'd just said. I regretted the words as soon as they spilled out of my mouth.

The hurt in her eyes was quickly replaced with anger. "A *human* being," she said and stood up.

I started to stand as well. "Look, I'm sorry—" I began but I was already talking to her back.

"You owe me for the lattés!" the barman called as I went to follow her.

I paid him and hurried outside, but she was already gone. Slowly I went back inside and stood at our table. I looked at the rose and the open paper. After a moment, I folded up the paper and went back outside. I left the rose there on the table.

I could've tracked her—the scent was still strong—but I went home instead to the apartment Tyrone and I were sharing. He wasn't back yet from wherever he'd gone tonight, which was just as well. I wasn't looking forward to telling him about how the evening had gone. Changing from my suit to jeans and a jersey, I sat down on the sofa and opened my copy of *In the City* to Mona's strip. I was still staring at the scruffy little blonde cartoon girl when the phone rang.

Mona

As soon as I got outside, I made a quick beeline down the alley that runs alongside the café, my boots clomping on the pavement. I didn't slow down until I got to the next street and had turned onto it. I didn't bother looking for a phone booth. I knew Sue would pick me up, but I needed some downtime first and it wasn't that long a walk back home. Misery's supposed to love company, but the way I was feeling it was still too immediate to share. For now, I needed to be alone.

I suppose I kind of deserved what he'd said—I had been acting all punky and pushing at him. But after a while the animal people business had started to wear thin, feeling more like an excuse not to have a real conversation with me rather than fun. And then he'd been just plain mean.

Sue was going to love my report on tonight's fiasco. Not.

I'm normally pretty good about walking about on my own at night—not fearless like my friend Jilly, but I'm usually only going from my local subway stop or walking down well-frequented streets. Tonight, though . . .

The streets in this neighborhood were quiet, and it was still relatively early, barely nine, but I couldn't shake the uneasy feeling that someone was following me. You know that prickle you can get at the nape of your neck—some leftover survival instinct from when we'd just climbed down the from the trees, I guess. A monkey buzz.

I kept looking back the way I'd come—expecting to see Mr.

Wolf Man skulking about a block or so behind me—but there was never anybody there. It wasn't until I was on my own block and almost home that I saw the dog. Some kind of big husky, it seemed, from the glance I got before it slipped behind a parked car. Except its tail didn't go up in that trademark curl.

I kept walking toward my door, backward, so that I could look down the street. The dog stuck its head out twice, ducking back when it saw me watching. The second time I bolted for my apartment, charged up the steps and onto the porch. I had my keys out, but I was so rattled, it took me a few moments to get the proper one in the lock. It didn't help that I spent more time staring down the street than at what I was doing. But I finally got the key in, unlocked the door, and was inside, closing and locking the door quickly behind me.

I leaned against the wall to catch my breath, positioned so that my gaze could go down the street. I didn't see the dog. But I did see a man, standing there in the general area of where the dog had been. He was looking down the street in my direction and I ducked back from the window. It was too far away to make out his features, but I could guess who he was.

This was what I'd been afraid of when I'd first seen the dog: that it wasn't a dog. That it was a wolf. That Mr. Wolf Man really *could* become a wolf and now he'd turned into Stalker Freak Man.

I was thinking in capitals like my superhero character Rocket Grrl always did when she was confronting evildoers like Can't Commit Man. Except I wasn't likely to go out and fight the good fight like she always was. I was more the hide-under-the-bed kind of person.

But I was kind of mad now.

I watched until the man turned away, then hurried up the stairs to my apartment. Once I was inside, I made sure the deadbolt was engaged. Ditto the lock on the window that led out onto the fire escape. I peered down at the street from behind the safety of the curtains in my living room, but saw no one out there.

I changed and paced around the apartment for a while before I finally went into the kitchen and punched in Mr. Wolf Man's phone number. I lit into him the minute he answered.

"Maybe you think it's a big joke, following me home like that, but I didn't appreciate it."

"But I—" he started.

"And maybe you can turn into a wolf or a dog or whatever, or maybe you just have one trained to follow people, but I think it's horrible either way, and I just want you to know that we have an anti-stalking law in this city, and if I ever see you hanging around again, I'm going to phone the police."

Then I hung up.

I was hoping I'd feel better, but I just felt horrible instead. The thing is, I'd found myself sort of liking him before he got all rude and then did the stalking bit.

I guess I should have called Sue at this point, but it was still too freshly depressing to talk about. Instead I made myself some toast and tea, then went and sat in the living room, peeking through the curtains every couple of minutes to make sure there was no one out there. It was a miserable way to spend an evening that had held the potential of being so much more.

Lyle

I hung up the phone feeling totally confused. What had she been talking about? But by the time Tyrone got home, I thought I had a clue.

"Did you follow her home?" I asked.

He just looked confused. "Follow who home?"

"My date."

"Why would I do that?"

"Because we got into a fight and you're always stepping in to protect me or set people straight when you think they've treated me badly."

I could see that look come into his eyes—confirming my feelings, I thought, until he spoke.

"Your date went bad?" he asked.

"It went horribly—but you already know that."

Tyrone sighed. "I was nowhere near the café, or wherever you guys went after."

"We didn't have time to go anywhere after," I said, and then I told him about how the evening had gone.

"Let's see if I've got this straight," Tyrone said. "She tells you she likes to dress casually and draws comics for a living, so you tell her you're a skinwalker."

"We were sharing intimacies."

"Sounds more like lunacies on your part. What were you thinking?"

I sighed. "I don't know. I liked her. I liked the fact that she didn't want to start off with any B.S."

Tyrone shook his head. "Well, it's done now, I guess. With any luck she'll just think you're a little weird and leave it at that." He paused and fixed with me with a considering look. "Tell me you didn't shift in front of her."

"No. But from this phone call . . ."

"Right. The phone call. I forgot. You don't think you put that idea into her head?"

"She sounded a little scared as well as pissed off. But if it wasn't you and it wasn't me, I guess her imagination must have been working overtime."

Tyrone shrugged. "Maybe. Except . . . did you touch her at all?"

"Not really. We just shook hands and I grabbed her shoulders when I stumbled and lost my balance."

"So your scent was on her."

I nodded. "I suppose."

I saw where he was going. We don't actually go out marking territory anymore—at least most of us don't. But if another wolf had caught my scent on her it might intrigue him enough to follow her. And if he was one of the old school, he might think it fun to do a little more than that.

"I've got to go to her place and check it out," I said.

"And you'll find it how?" Tyrone asked.

He was right. I didn't even know her phone number.

"That we can deal with," Tyrone said.

I'd forgotten what we can do with phones these days. Tyrone had gotten all the bells and whistles for ours and in moments he'd called up the digits of the last incoming call on the liquid crystal display.

"It still doesn't tell us where she lives," I said. "And I doubt she'd appreciate a call from me right now. If ever."

"I can handle that as well," Tyrone told me and he went over to the computer.

I hadn't lied to Mona. I did deal with investments—on-line. I was on the computer for a few hours every day, but I wasn't the hacker Tyrone was. I watched as he hacked into the telephone company's billing database. Within minutes, he had an address match for the phone number. He wrote it down on a scrap of paper and stood up.

"This is my mess," I told him. "So I'll clean it up."

"You're sure?"

When I nodded, he handed me the address.

"Don't kill anybody unless you have to," he said. "But if you do, do it clean."

I wasn't sure if he meant Mona or her stalker and I didn't want to ask.

Mona

After I finished my toast and tea, I decided to go to bed. I wasn't really tired, but maybe I'd get lucky and fall asleep and when I woke up, it would be a whole new day. And it would sure beat sitting around feeling miserable tonight.

I washed up my dishes, then took one last look out the window. And froze. There wasn't one dog out there, but a half-dozen, lounging on the sidewalk across the street like they hadn't a care in the world. And they weren't dogs. I've seen enough nature specials on PBS to know a wolf when I see one.

As I started to let the curtain drop, all their heads lifted and turned in my direction. One got to its feet and began to trot across the street, pausing halfway to look down the block. Its companions turned their gazes in that direction as well and I followed suit.

He was dressed more casually now—jeans and a windbreaker—but I had no trouble recognizing him. My date. Mr. Stalker Man. Oh, where was Rocket Grrl when you needed her?

I knew what I should be doing. Finding something to use as a weapon in case they got in. Dialing 911 for sure. Instead, all I could do was slide down to my knees by the window and stare down at the street.

Lyle

It was worse than I'd thought. A pack of cousins had gathered outside the address I had for Mona. From the smell in the air, I knew they were out for fun. The trouble is, skinwalker fun invariably results in somebody getting hurt. We're the reason true wolves get such a bad rap. Whenever we're around, trouble follows.

The alpha male rose up into a man shape at my approach. His pack formed a half-circle at his back, a couple more of them taking human shape. I could tell from the dark humor in their eyes that I'd just raised the ante on their night of fun. I realized I shouldn't have turned down Tyrone's offer to help, but it was too late now. I had to brave it out on my own.

"Thanks for the show of force," I said with way more confidence than I was feeling, "but I don't really need any help to see my girlfriend."

"She's not your girlfriend," the alpha male said.

"Sure, she is."

"Bullshit. That little chickadee's so scared you can smell her fear a block away."

"Well, you're not exactly helping matters," I told him.

He gave me a toothy grin, dark humor flicking in his eyes.

"I was walking by the café when she dumped you," he said.

I shrugged. "We had a little tiff, no big deal. That's why I'm here now—to make it up with her."

He shook his head. "She's as scared of you as she is of us. But tell you what, back off and you can have whatever's left over."

Some of us fit in as we can, some of us live a footloose life. Then there are the ones like these that went feral in the long ago and just stayed that way. Some are lone wolves, the others run in packs.

Mostly they haunt the big cities now because in places this large, who's going to notice the odd missing person? People disappear every day.

"Time was," I said, "when we respected each other's territories. When we put someone under our protection, they stayed that way."

It was a long shot, but I had this going for me: We're a prideful people. And honor's a big thing between us. It has to be, or we'd have wiped each other out a long time ago.

He didn't like it. I don't know if I spoke to his honor, or whether it was because he couldn't place my clan affiliation and didn't know how big a pack he'd be calling down upon himself if he cut me down and went ahead and had his fun.

"You're saying she's your girlfriend?" he asked.

I nodded.

"Okay. Let's go up and ask her. If she lets you in, we'll back off. But if she doesn't . . ."

He let me fill in the blank for myself.

"No problem," I said.

Not like I had a choice in the matter. This was a win-win situation for him. If she let me in, he could back off without losing face. And if she didn't, no one in the clans would take my side because it would just look like I was homing in on their claim.

He stepped back and I walked toward Mona's building. The pack fell in behind me, all of them in human shape now. I glanced up and caught a glimpse of Mona's terrified face in the window. I tried to look as harmless as possible.

Trust me, I told her, willing the thought up to her. It's your life that's hanging in the balance here.

But she only looked more scared.

Then we were on the stairs and I couldn't see her anymore.

"Don't even think about trying to warn her," the alpha male

said from behind me. "She's got to accept you without a word from you or all bets are off."

The door to the front hall was locked when I tried it. The alpha male reached past me and grabbed the knob, giving it a sharp twist. I heard the lock break, then the door swung open and we were moving inside.

Did I mention that we're stronger than we look?

Mona

I was still trying to adjust to the fact that the wolves really had turned into people, when my stalker led them into the apartment building. He looked up at me just before they reached the stairs, his face all pretend sweetness and light, but it didn't fool me. I knew they were going to tear me to pieces.

Get up, get up, I told myself. Call the police. Sneak out onto the fire escape and run for it.

But all I could do was sit on the floor with my back to the window and stare at my front door, listening to their footsteps as they came up the stairs. When they stopped outside my door, I held my breath. Somebody knocked and I just about jumped out of my skin. This uncontrollable urge to laugh rose up in me. Here they were, planning to kill me, yet they were just knocking politely on the door. I was hysterical.

"We can smell you in there."

That wasn't Lyle, but one of his friends.

I shivered and pressed up against the wall behind me.

"Come see us through the peephole," the voice went on. "Your boyfriend wants to know if you'll let him in. Or are you still too mad at him?"

I didn't want to move, but I slowly got to my feet.

"If you don't come soon, we'll huff and we'll puff, just see if we won't."

I stood swaying in the middle of my living room, hugging myself. Wishing so desperately that I'd never left the apartment this evening.

"Or maybe," the mocking voice went on, "we'll go chew off the faces of the nice couple living below you. They do smell good."

I was moving again, shuffling forward, away from the phone, toward the door. It was too late to call for help anyway. Nobody was going to get here in time. If they didn't just smash through my door, maybe they really would go kill the Andersons who had the downstairs apartment. And this wasn't their fault. I was the one stupid enough to go out on a blind date with a werewolf.

"That's it," the voice told me. "I can hear you coming. Show us what a good hostess you are. What a forgiving girlfriend."

I was close enough now to hear the chorus of sniggers and giggles that echoed on after the voice had finished. When I reached the door, I rose slowly up on my tiptoes and looked through the peephole.

They were all out there in the hall, my stalker and his pack of werewolf friends.

God, I thought, looking at Lyle, trying to read his face, to understand why he was doing this. How could I ever have thought that I liked him?

Lyle

I knew it was over now. There was no way Mona was going to open the door—not if she had an ounce of sense in her—but at least I'd gotten the pack into a confined space. I couldn't take them all down, but maybe I could manage a few.

I could smell Mona the same as the pack did—smell her fear. She was numbed by it. But maybe once I set on the pack, it'd snap her out of her paralysis long enough to flee out onto the fire escape I'd noticed running up the side of the building. Or perhaps the noise would be enough for the neighbors to call the police. If they could get here before the pack battered down the door, there was still a chance she could survive.

She was on the other side of the door now. Looking out of the peephole. I tried to compose myself, to give her a look that she might read as hope. To convey that I meant her no harm.

But then the alpha male gave me a shove. Without thinking, I snarled at him, face partially shifting, jaws snapping. He darted back, laughter triumphant in his eyes, and I knew what he'd done. He'd shown Mona that I was no different from them. Just another skinwalker. Another inhuman creature, hungry for her blood.

"All you have to do is answer a couple of questions," the alpha male said, facing the door. "Do you forgive your boyfriend? Will you invite him in?"

There was a long silence.

"Why . . . why are you doing this?" Mona finally said, her voice muffled by the door. But we all had a wolf's hearing.

"Tut, tut," the alpha male said. "You're not playing by the rules. You're not supposed to ask a question, only answer ours."

I knew she was still looking from the peephole.

"I'm sorry, Mona," I said. "For everything."

The alpha male turned on me with a snarl. I drew him aside before he could speak, my back to the door.

"Come on," I told him, my voice pitched low. "You know we had a quarrel. How's this supposed to be fair with you scaring the crap out of her and here I haven't even apologized to her? I mean, take a vote on it or something."

He turned to his companions. I could see they didn't like it, but my argument made sense.

"Fine," he said. "You've made your apology."

He turned to the door and let his face go animal.

"Well?" he snarled. "What's your answer, little chickadee? Your boyfriend says he's sorry so can he come in and play now?"

Mona

I almost died when Lyle's face did its half-transformation. The wolfish features disappeared as fast as they had appeared. He turned to me with those beautiful dark eyes of his, and I couldn't see the same meanness and hunger in them that were in the eyes of the others. And I was looking for it, believe me. Then, while I was still caught in his gaze, he went and apologized to me, like none of this was his doing. Like he was sorry for everything, the same as I was. Not just for what he'd said to me in the café, but because we'd liked each other and then we'd let it all fell apart before we ever gave it a chance to be more.

Call me naïve, or maybe even stupider still, but I believed that apology of his was genuine. It was something he needed to say, or that I needed to hear. Maybe both.

I was so caught up in the thought of that, that I didn't even start when the other guy did his half-wolf face thing and began snarling at me. Instead, I flashed on something Lyle had said to me earlier in the evening, back at the café.

These days most of us just like to fit in, he'd told me. Live a bit in your world, a bit in the animal world. But it wasn't always like that. There have always been those among us who considered everyone else in the world their private prey.

Most of you? I'd asked.

I remember him sighing, almost like he was ashamed, when he'd shaken his head and added, But there are still some that like to hunt.

Like this guy with his animal face and snarl, with his pack of wolfish friends.

But I was done being afraid. I was Rocket Grrl, or at least I was trying to be. I concentrated on this question the wolf-faced leader of the pack kept asking, focusing exactly on what it was he was asking, and why. It felt like a fairy tale moment and I flashed on "Beauty and the Beast," the prince turned into a frog, the nasty little dwarf who'd moved in on me until an act of kindness set him free. All those stories pivoted around the right thing being said.

That doesn't happen in real life, the rational part of my mind told me.

I knew that. Not usually. But sometimes it did, didn't it?

Lyle

"Time's up, chickadee," the alpha male said.

I got myself ready. First I'd try to knock as many of them down the stairs as I could, then I'd shift to wolf shape and give them a taste of what it felt like being hurt. I knew I didn't have a chance against all of them, but I'd still be able to kill a few before they took me down. I'd start with the alpha male.

Except before I could leap, I heard the deadbolt disengage. The door swung open, and then she was standing there, small and blonde and human-frail, but with more backbone than all of this sorry pack of skinwalkers put together, me included. We all took a step back. Mona cleared her throat.

"So . . . so what you're asking," she said, "is do I forgive Lyle?"

The alpha male straightened his shoulders. "That's it," he said. "Part one of a two-parter."

She didn't even look at him, her gaze going over his shoulder to me.

"I think we were both to blame," she said. "So of course I do. Do you forgive me?"

I couldn't believe what I was hearing. I wasn't even worrying about the pack at that moment. I was just so mesmerized with how brave she was. I think the pack was, too.

"Well?" she asked.

All I could do was nod my head.

"Then you can come in," she said. "But not your friends."

"They're not my friends," I told her.

The alpha male growled with frustration until one of the pack touched his arm.

"That's it," the pack member said. "It's over."

The alpha male shook off the hand, but he turned away and the pack trooped down the stairs. When I heard the front door close, I let out a breath I hadn't been aware I was holding.

"You were amazing," I told Mona.

She gave me a small smile. "I guess I have my moments."

"I'll say. I don't know how you knew to do it, but you gave them exactly the right answer."

"I wasn't doing it for them," she told me. "I was doing it for us."

I shook my head again. "It's been a weird night, but I'm glad I got to meet you all the same."

I started for the stairs.

"Where are you going?" she asked. "They could be waiting out there for you."

I turned back to look at her. "They won't. It's an honor thing.

Maybe if I run into them some other time there'll be trouble, but there won't be any more tonight."

"We never finished our date," she said.

"You still want to go out somewhere with me?"

She shook her head. "But we could have a drink in here and talk awhile."

I waited a heartbeat, but when she stepped aside and ushered me inside, I didn't hesitate any longer.

"I was so scared," she said as she closed the door behind us.

"Me, too."

"Really?"

"There were six of them," I said. "They could have torn me apart at any time."

"Why didn't they?"

"I told them you were my girlfriend—that we'd just had a fight in the café. That way, in their eyes, I had a claim on you. The honor thing again. If you were under my protection, they couldn't hurt you."

"So that's what you meant about my giving them the exact right answer."

I nodded.

"And if I hadn't?" she asked.

"Let's not go there," I said. But I knew she could see the answer in my eyes.

"You'd do that even after what I said to you on the phone?"

"You had every right to feel the way you did."

"Are you for real?"

"I hope so." I thought about all she'd experienced tonight. "So are you going to put this in one of your strips?"

She laughed. "Maybe. But who'd believe it?"

Mona

It's funny how things work. When I was leaving the café earlier, I could have happily given him a good bang on the ear. Later, when I thought he was stalking me, I was ready to have him put in jail. When the pack was outside my window and he joined them, I was so terrified I couldn't move or think straight.

And now I'm thinking of asking him to stay the night.

Making a Noise in This World

I'm driving up from the city when I spot a flock of crows near the chained gates of the old gravel pit that sits on the left side of the highway, about halfway to the rez. It's that time of the morning when the night's mostly a memory, but the sun's still blinking the sleep from its eyes as it gets ready to shine us into another day.

Me, I'm on my way to bed. I'm wearing gloves and have a take-out coffee in my free hand, a cigarette burning between the tobacco-stained gloved fingers of the one holding the wheel. A plastic bag full of aerosol paint cans, half of them empty, rattles on the floor on the passenger's side every time I hit a bump. Behind me I've left freight cars painted with thunderbirds and buffalo heads and whatever other icons I could think up tonight to tell the world that the Indians have counted another coup, hi-ya-ya-ya. I draw the line at dream-catchers, though I suppose some people might mistake my spider webs for them.

My favorite tonight has become sort of a personal trademark: a big crow, its wings spread wide like the traditional thunderbird and running the whole length of the boxcar, but it's got that crow beak you can't mistake and a sly, kind of laughing look in its eyes. Tonight I painted that bird fire engine red with black markings. On its belly I made the old Kickaha sign for *Bín-ji-gú-sân*, the sacred medicine bag: a snake, with luck lines radiating from its head and back.

I've been doing that crow ever since I woke one morning from a dream where I was painting graffiti on a 747 at the airport, smiling because this time my bird was really going to fly. I opened my eyes to hear the crows outside my window, squawking and gossiping, and there were three black feathers on the pillow beside me.

Out on the highway now, I ease up on the gas and try to see what's got these birds up so early.

Crows are sacred on the rez—at least with the Aunts and the other elders. Most of my generation's just happy to make it through the day, never mind getting mystical about it. But I've always liked them. Crows and coyotes. Like the Aunts say, they're the smart ones. They never had anything for the white men to take away and they sure do hold their own against them. Shoot them, poison them, do your best. You manage to kill one and a couple more'll show up to take its place. If we'd been as wily, we'd never have lost our lands.

It's a cold morning. My hands are still stinging from when I was painting those boxcars, all night long. Though some of that time was spent hiding from the railroad rent-a-cops and warming up outside the freight yard where some hobo skins had them a fire burning in a big metal drum. Half the time the paints just clogged up in the cans. If I'd been in the wind, I doubt they'd have worked at all.

The colors I use are blacks and reds, greens and yellows, oranges and purples. No blues—the sky's already got them. Maybe some of the Aunts' spirit talk's worn off on me, because when I'm train-painting, I don't want to insult the Grandfather Thunders. Blue's their color, at least among my people.

My tag's "Crow." I was born James Raven, but Aunt Nancy says I've got too much crow in me. No respect for anything, just like my black-winged brothers. And then there's those feathers I found on my pillow that morning. Maybe that's why I pull over. Because in my head, we're kin. Same clan, anyway.

There's times later when maybe I wished I hadn't. I'm still weighing that on a day-to-day basis. But my life's sure on the road to nowhere I could've planned because of that impulse.

The birds don't leave when I get out of the car, leaving my coffee on the dash. I take a last drag on my cigarette and flick the butt into the snow. Jesus, but it's cold. A *lot* colder here than it was in the freight yards. There I had the cars blocking the wind most of the time. Out here, it comes roaring at me from about as far north as the cold can come. It must be twenty, thirty below out here, factoring in the wind chill.

I start to walk toward where the birds have gathered and I go a little colder still, but this time it's inside, like there's frost on my heart.

They've found themselves a man. A dead skin, just lying here in the snow. I don't know what killed him, but I can make an educated guess considering all he's wearing is a thin, unzipped windbreaker over a T-shirt and chinos. Running shoes on his feet, no socks.

He must've frozen to death.

The crows don't fly off when I approach, which makes me think maybe the dead man's kin, too. That they weren't here to eat him, but to see him on his way, like in the old stories. I crouch down beside him, snow crunching under my knee. I can see now he's been in a fight. I take off my paint-stained gloves and reach for his throat, looking for a pulse, but not expecting to find one. He twitches at my touch. I almost fall over backwards when those frosted eyelashes suddenly crack open and he's looking right at me.

He has pale blue eyes—unusual for a skin. They study me for a moment. I see an alcohol haze just on the other side of their calm, lucid gaze. What strikes me at that moment is that I don't see any pain.

Words creep out of his mouth. "Who . . . who was it that said, 'It is a good day to die'?"

"I don't know," I find myself answering. "Some famous chief, I guess. Sitting Bull, maybe." Then I realize what I'm doing, having a conversation with a dying man. "We've got to get you to a hospital."

"It's bullshit," he says.

I think he's going to lose his hands. They're blue with the cold. I can't see his feet, but in those thin running shoes, they can't be in much better condition.

"No, you'll be okay," I lie. "The doctors'll have you fixed up in no time."

But he's not talking about the hospital.

"It's never a good day to die," he tells me. "You tell Turk that for me."

My pulse quickens at the name. Everybody on the rez knows Tom McGurk. He's a detective with the NPD that's got this constant hard-on for Indians. He goes out of his way to break our heads, bust the skin hookers, roust the hobo bloods. On the rez they even say he's killed him a few skins, took their scalps like some old Indian hunter, but I know that's bullshit. Something like that, it would've made the papers. Not because it was skins dying, but for the gory details of the story.

"He did this to you?" I ask. "Turk did this?"

Now it doesn't seem so odd, finding this drunk brave dying here in the snow. Cops like to beat on us, and I've heard about this before, how they grab some skin, usually drunk, beat the crap out of him, then drive him twenty miles or so out of town and dump him. Let him walk back to the city if he's up for some more punishment.

But on a night like this . . .

The dying man tries to grab my arm, but his frozen fingers don't work anymore. It's like all he's got is this lump on the end of his arm, hard as a branch, banging against me. It brings a sour taste up my throat.

"My name," he says, "is John Walking Elk. My father was an Oglala Sioux from the Pine Ridge rez and my mother was a Kickaha from just up the road. Don't let me be forgotten."

"I . . . I won't."

"Be a warrior for me."

I figure he wants his revenge on Turk, the one he can't take for himself, and I find myself nodding. Me, who's never won a fight in his life. By the time I realize we have different definitions for the word "warrior," my life's completely changed.

I remember the look on my mom's face the first time I got arrested for vandalism. She didn't know whether to be happy or mad. See, she never had to worry about me drinking or doing drugs. And while she knew that train-painting was against the law, she understood that I saw it as bringing Beauty into the world.

"At least you're not a drunk like your father's brother was," she finally said.

Uncle Frank was an alcoholic who died in the city, choking on his own puke after an all-night bender. We've no idea what ever happened to my father, Frank's brother. One day we woke up and he was gone, vanished like the promises in all those treaties the chiefs signed.

"But why can't you paint on canvases like other artists do?" she wanted to know.

I don't know where to begin to explain.

Part of it's got to do with the transitory nature of painting freight cars. Nobody can stand there and criticize it the way you can a painting hanging in a gallery or a museum, or even a mural on the side of some building. By the time you realize you're looking at a painting on the side of a boxcar, the locomotive's already pulled that car out of your sight and farther on down the line. All you're left with is the memory of it; what you saw, and what you have to fill in from your own imagination.

Part of it's got to do with the act itself. Sneaking into the freight yards, taking the chance on getting beat up or arrested by the rent-a-cops, having to work so fast. But if you pull it off, you've put a piece of Beauty back into the world, a piece of art that'll go traveling right across the continent. Most artists are lucky to get a show in one gallery. But train-painters . . . our work's being shown from New York City to L.A. and every place in between.

And I guess part of it's got to do with the self-image you get to carry around inside you. You're an outlaw, like the chiefs of old, making a stand against the big white machine that just rolls across the country, knocking down anything that gets in its way.

So it fills something in my life, but even with the train-painting, I've always felt like there was something missing, and I don't mean my father. Though train-painting's the only time I feel complete, it's still like I'm doing the right thing, but for the wrong reason. Too much me, not enough everything else that's in the world.

I'm holding John Walking Elk in my arms when he dies. I'm about to pick him up when this rattle goes through his chest and his head sags away from me, hanging at an unnatural angle. I feel something in that moment, like a breath touching the inside of my skin, passing through me. That's when I know for sure he's gone.

I sit there until the cold starts to work its way through my coat, then I get a firmer grip on the dead man and stagger back to my car with him. I don't take him back to the city, report his death to the same authorities that killed him. Instead, I gather my courage and take him to Jack Whiteduck.

I don't know how much I really buy into the mysteries. I mean, I like the idea of them, the way you hear about them in the old stories. Honoring the Creator and the Grandfather Thunders, taking care of this world we've all found ourselves living in, thinking crows can be kin, being respectful to the spirits, that kind of thing. But it's usually an intellectual appreciation, not something I feel in my gut. Like I said, train-painting's about the only time it's real for me. Finding Beauty, creating Beauty, painting her face on the side of a freight car.

But with Jack Whiteduck it's different. He makes you believe. Makes you see with the heart instead of the eye. Everybody feels that way about him, though if you ask most people, they'll just say he makes them nervous. The corporate braves who run the casino, the kids sniffing glue and gasoline under the highway bridge and making fun of the elders, the drunks hitting the bars off the rez . . . press them hard enough and even they'll admit, yeah, something about the old man puts a hole in their party that all the good times run out of.

He makes you remember, though what you're remembering is hard to put into words. Just that things could be different, I guess. That once our lives were different, and they could be that way again, if we give the old ways a chance. White people, they think of us as either the noble savage, or the drunk in the gutter, puking on their shoes. They'll come to the powwows, take their pictures and buy some souvenirs, sample the frybread, maybe try to dance. They'll walk by us in the city, not able to meet our gaze, either because they're scared we'll try to rob them, or hurt them, or they just don't want to accept our misery, don't want to allow that it exists in the same perfect world they live in.

We're one or the other to them, and they don't see a whole lot of range in between. Trouble is, a lot of us see ourselves the same way. Whiteduck doesn't let you. As a people, we were never perfect—nobody is—but there's something about him that tells us we don't have to be losers either.

Whiteduck's not the oldest of the elders on the rez, but he's the one everybody goes to when they've got a problem nobody else can solve.

So I drive out to his cabin, up past Pineback Road, drive in as far as I can, then I get out and walk the rest of the way, carrying John Walking Elk's body in my arms, following the narrow path that leads through the drifts to Whiteduck's cabin. I don't know where I get the strength.

There's a glow spilling out of the windows—a flickering light of some kind. Oil lamp, I'm guessing, or a candle. Whiteduck doesn't have electricity. Doesn't have a phone or running water either. The door opens before I reach it and Whiteduck stands silhouetted against the yellow light like he's expecting me. I feel a pinprick of nervousness settle in between my shoulder blades as I keep walking forward, boots crunching in the snow.

He's not as tall as I remember, but when I think about it, that's always been the case, the few times I've seen him. I guess I build him up in my mind. He's got the broad Kickaha face, but there's no fat on his body. Pushing close to seventy now, his features are a roadmap of brown wrinkles, surrounding a pair of eyes that are darker than the wings of the crows that pulled me into this in the first place.

"Heard you were coming," he says.

I guess my face reflects my confusion.

"I saw the dead man's spirit pass by on the morning wind," he explains, "and the manitou told me you were bringing his body to me. You did the right thing. After what the whites did to him, they've got no more business with this poor dead skin."

He steps aside to let me go in and I angle the body so I can get it through the door. Whiteduck indicates that I should lay it out on his bed.

There's not much to the place. A potbellied cast-iron stove with a fire burning in it. A wooden table with a couple of chairs, all of them handmade from cedar. A kind of counter running along one wall with a sink in it and a pail underneath to catch the run-off. A chest under the counter that holds his food, I'm guessing, since his clothes are hanging from pegs on the wall above his bed. Bunches of herbs are drying over the counter, tied together with thin strips of leather. In the far corner is a pile of furs, mostly beaver.

The oil lamp's sitting on the table, but moment by moment, it becomes less necessary as the sun keeps rising outside.

"*Mico 'mis,*" I begin, giving him the honorific, but I don't know where to go with my words past it.

"That's good," he says. "Too many boys your age don't have respect for their elders."

I'd take offense at the designation of "boy"—I'll be twenty-one in the spring—but compared to him, I guess that's what I am.

"What will you do with the body?" I ask.

"That's not a body," he tells me. "It's a man, got pushed off the wheel before his time. I'm going to make sure his spirit knows where it needs to go next."

"But . . . what will you do with what he's left behind?"

"Maybe a better question would be, what will you do with yourself?"

I remember John Walking Elk's dying words. *Be a warrior for me.*

"I'm going to set things right," I say.

Whiteduck looks at me and all that nervousness that's been hiding somewhere just between my shoulder blades comes flooding through me. I get the feeling he can read my every thought and feeling. I get the feeling he can see the whole of my life laid out, what's been and what's to come, and that he's going to tell me how to live it right. But he only nods.

"There's some things we need to learn for ourselves," he says finally. "But you think on this, James Raven. There's more than one way to be a warrior. You can, and should, fight for the people, but being a warrior also means a way of living. It's something you forge in your heart to make the spirit strong and it doesn't mean you have to go out and kill anything, even when it's vermin that you feel need exterminating. Everything we do comes back to us—goes for whites the same as skins."

I was wrong. He does have advice.

"You're saying I should just let this slide?" I ask. "That Turk gets away with killing another one of us?"

"I'm saying, do what your heart tells you you must do, *no'cicen*. Listen to it, not to some old man living by himself in a cabin in the woods."

"But—"

"Now go," he says, firm but not unfriendly. "We both have tasks ahead of us."

* * *

I leave there feeling confused. Like I said, I'm not a fighter. Whenever I have gotten into a fight, I got my ass kicked. But there's something just not right about letting Turk get away with this. Finding the dying man has lodged a hot coal of anger in my head, put a shiver of ice through my heart.

I figure what I need now is a gun, and I know where to get it.

"I don't know," Jackson says. "I'm not really in the business of selling weapons. What do you want a gun for anyway?"

That Jackson Red Dog has never been in prison is an ongoing mystery on the rez. It's an open secret that he has variously been, and by all accounts still is, a bootlegger, a drug dealer, a fence, a smuggler, and pretty much anything else against the law that's on this side of murder and mayhem. "I draw the line at killing people," he's said. "There's no percentage in it. Today's enemy could be tomorrow's customer."

He's in his fifties now, a dark-skinned Indian with a graying ponytail, standing about six-two with a linebacker's build and hands so big he can hold a cantaloupe the way you or I might hold an apple. He lives on the southern edge of the rez and works out of the back of that general store on the highway, just inside the boundaries of the rez, where he can comfortably do business with our people and anybody willing to drive up from the city.

"I figure it's something I need," I tell him. "You got any that can't be traced?"

He laughs. "You watch too much TV, kid."

"I'm serious," I say. "I've got the money. Cash."

I'd cleaned out my savings account before driving over to the store. I found Jackson in the back as usual, holding court in a smoky room filled with skins his age and older, sitting around a potbellied stove, none of them saying much. This is his office, though come spring, it moves out onto the front porch. When I said I needed to talk to him, he took me outside and lit a cigarette, offered me one.

"How much money?" Jackson asks.

"How much is the gun?" I reply.

I'm not stupid. I tell him what I've got in my pocket—basically enough to cover next month's rent and a couple of cases of beer—and that's what he'll be charging me. He looks me over, then gives me a slow nod.

"Maybe I could put you in touch with a guy that can get you a gun," he says.

Which I translate as, "We can do business."

"Just tell me," he adds. "Who're you planning to kill?"

"Nobody you'd know."

"I know everybody."

All things considered, that's probably true.

"Nobody you'd care about," I tell him.

"That's good enough for me."

There's laughter in his eyes, like he knows more than he's letting on, but I can't figure out what it is.

The gun's heavy in my pocket as I leave the store and drive south to the city. I don't know any more about handguns than I do fighting, but Jackson offers me some advice as he counts my money.

"You ever shoot one of these before?" he asks.

I shake my head.

"What you've got there's a .38 Smith and Wesson. It's got a kick and, to tell you the truth, the barrel's been cut down some and it's had a ramp foresight added. Whoever did the work wasn't exactly a gunsmith. The sight's off, so even if you were some fancy shot, you'd have trouble with it. Best thing you can do is notch a few crosses on the tips of your bullets and aim for the body. Bullet goes in and makes a tiny hole, comes back out again and takes away half the guy's back."

I feel a little sick, listening to him, but then I think of John Walking Elk dying in the snow, of Turk sitting in his precinct, laughing it off. I wonder how many others he's left to die the way he did Walking Elk. I get to thinking about some of the other drunks I've heard of that were supposed to have died of exposure, nobody quite sure what they were doing out in the middle of nowhere, or how they got there.

"You planning to come out of this alive?" Jackson asks when I'm leaving.

"It's not essential."

He gives me another of those slow nods of his. "That'll make it easier. You got the time, tell Turk it's been a long time coming."

That stops me in the doorway.

"How'd you know it was Turk?" I ask.

He laughs. "Christ, kid. This is the rez. Everybody here knows your business before you do. What, did you think you were excused?"

I think about that on the drive down to the city, how gossip travels from one end of the rez to the other. It's like my paintings, traveling across the country. I don't plan where they go, how they go, they just go. It's not something you can control.

I'm not worried about anybody up here knowing what I'm planning. I can't think of a single skin who would save Turk's life if they came upon him dying, even if all they had to do was toss him a nickel. I'm just hoping my mom doesn't hear about it too soon. I'd like to explain to her why I'm doing this, but I'm not entirely sure myself, and I know if I go to her before I do it, she'll talk me out of it. And if that doesn't work, she'll sit on me until the impulse goes away.

* * *

There are crows lined up on the power lines and leafing the trees for miles down the road. Dozens of them, more than I've ever seen. I know their roost is up around Pineback Road, near Whiteduck's cabin. A rez inside the rez. But they're safe there. Nobody on the rez takes pot shots at our black-feathered cousins.

When I come up on the entrance to the gravel pit, I see the crows are still there as well. I stand on the brakes and the car goes slewing toward the ditch. I only just manage to keep it on the road. Then I sit there looking in my rearview mirror. I see a man standing there among the crows, John Walking Elk, leaning on the gate at the entrance and big as life.

I back up until I'm abreast the gates and look out the passenger window at him. He smiles and gives me a wave. He's still wearing that thin windbreaker, the T-shirt and chinos, the running shoes without socks. The big difference is, he's not dead. He's not even dying.

I light a cigarette with shaking hands and look at him for a long moment before I finally open my door. I walk around the car, the wind knifing through my jacket, but Walking Elk's not even shivering. The weight of the gun in my pocket makes me feel like I'm walking at an angle, tilted over on one side.

"Don't worry," he says when I get near. "You're not losing it. I'm still dead."

And seeing a walking, talking dead man isn't losing it?

"Only why'd you have to go leave me with that shaman?" he adds.

My throat's as dry and thick as it was when I did my first two vision quests. I haven't done the other two yet. Train-painting distracted me from them.

"I . . . I thought it was the right thing to do," I manage after a long moment.

"I suppose. But he's shaking his rattle and burning smudge sticks, singing the death songs that'll see me on my way. Makes it hard not to go."

I'm feeling a little confused. "And that's a bad thing because . . . ?"

He shrugs. "I'm kind of enjoying this chance to walk around one last time."

I think I understand. Nobody knows what's waiting for us when we die. It's fine to be all stoic and talk about wheels turning and everything, but if it was me, I don't think I'd be in any hurry to go either.

"So you're going to shoot Turk, are you?" the dead man says.

"What, is it written on my forehead or something?"

Walking Elk laughs. "You know the rez . . ."

"Everybody knows everybody else's business."

He nods. "You think it's bad on the rez, you should try the spiritworld."

"No thanks."

"You try and kill Turk," he says, "you might be finding out firsthand, whether you want to or not." He gives a slow shake of his head. "I've got to give it to you, though. I don't think I'd have the balls to see it through."

"I don't know that I do either," I admit. "It just seems like a thing I've got to do."

"Won't bring me back," Walking Elk says. "Once the shaman finishes his ceremony, I'll be out of here."

"It's not just for you," I tell him. "It's for the others he might kill."

The dead man only shakes his head at that. "You think it starts and stops with Tom McGurk? Hell, this happens anyplace you got a cold climate and white cops. They just get tired of dealing with us. I had a cousin who died the same way up in Saskatchewan, another in Colorado. And when they haven't got the winter to do their job for them, they find other ways."

"That's why they've got to be held accountable," I say.

"You got some special sight that'll tell you which cop's decent and which isn't?"

I know there are good cops. Hell, Chief Morningstar's brother is a detective with the NPD. But we only ever seem to get to deal with the ones that have a hard-on for us.

I shake my head. "But I know Turk hasn't got any redeeming qualities."

He sighs. "Wish I could have one of those cigarettes of yours."

I shake one out of the pack and light it for him, surprised that he can hold it, that he can suck in the smoke and blow it out again, just like a living man. I wonder if this is like offering tobacco to the manitou.

"How come you're trying to talk me out of this?" I ask him. "You're the one who told me to be a warrior for you."

He blows out another lungful of smoke. "You think killing's what makes a warrior?"

"Now you sound like Whiteduck."

He laughs. "I've been compared to a lot of things, but never a shaman."

"So what is it you want from me?" I ask. "Why'd you ask me to be a warrior for you?"

"You look like a good kid," he says. "I didn't want to see you turn out like me. I want you to be a good man, somebody to make your parents proud. Make yourself proud."

I've no idea what would make my father proud. But my mom,

all she wants is for me to get a decent job and stay out of trouble. I can't seem to manage the first and here I am, walking straight into the second. But he's annoying me all the same. Funny how fast you can go from feeling awed to being fed up.

"You don't think I have any pride?" I ask.

"I don't know the first damn thing about you," he says, "except you were decent enough to stop for a dying man."

He takes a last drag and drops his butt in the snow. Studies something behind me, over my shoulder, but I don't turn. He's got a look I recognize—his gaze is turned inward.

"See, someone told me that once," he goes on, his gaze coming back to me, "except I didn't listen. I worked hard, figured I'd earned the right to play hard, too. Trouble is I played too hard. Lost my job. Lost my family. Lost my pride. It's funny how quick you can lose everything and never see it coming."

I think about my uncle Frank, but I don't say anything.

"I guess it was my grandma told me," the dead man says, "how there's no use in bringing hurt into the world. We do that well enough on our own. You meet someone, you try to give them a little life instead. Let them take something positive away from whatever time they spend with you. Makes the world a better place in the short and the long haul."

I nod. "Putting Beauty in the world."

"That's a warrior's way, too. Stand up for what's right. Ya-ha-hey. Make a noise. I can remember powwow dancing, there'd be so many of us out there, following the drumbeat and the singing, you'd swear you could feel the ground tremble and shake underfoot. But these last few years, I've been too drunk to dance and the only noise I make is when I'm puking."

I know what he means about the powwows, that feeling you can't get anywhere else except maybe a sweat and that's a more con-

templative kind of a thing. In a powwow it's all rhythm and dancing, everybody individual, but we're all part of something bigger
than us at the same time. There's nothing like it in the world.

"Yeah," the dead man says. "We used to be a proud people for
good reason. We can still be a proud people, but sometimes our reasons aren't so good anymore. Sometimes it's not for how we stand
tall and honor the ancestors and the spirits with grace and beauty.
Sometimes it's for how we beat the enemy at their own game."

"You're starting to sound pretty old school for a drunk," I tell
him.

He shakes his head. "I'm just repeating things I was told when I
was growing up. Things I didn't feel were important enough to pay
attention to."

"I pay attention," I say. "At least I try to."

He gives me a considering look. "I'm not saying it's right or
wrong, but what part of what you were taught has to do with that
gun in your pocket?"

"The part about standing up for ourselves. The part about
defending our people."

"I suppose."

"I hear what you're saying," I tell him. "But I still have to go
down to the city."

He gives me a nod.

"Sure you do," he says. "Why would you listen to a dead drunk
like me?" He chuckles. "And I mean dead in the strictest sense of
the word." He pushes away from the gates. "Time I was going.
Whiteduck's doing a hell of a job with his singing. I can feel the pull
of that someplace else getting stronger and stronger."

I don't know what to say. Good luck? Good-bye?

"Spare another of those smokes?" he asks.

"Sure."

I shake another one free and light it for him. He pats my cheek. The touch of his hand is still cold, but there's movement in all the fingers. It's not like the block of ice that tried to grab my sleeve this morning.

"You're a good kid," he says.

And then he fades away.

I stand there for a long time, looking at the gate, at the crows, feeling the wind on my face, bitter and cold. Then I walk back to my car.

Before I first started train-painting, I thought graffiti was just vandalism, a crime that might include a little creativity, but a crime nonetheless. Then one day I was driving back to the rez and I had to wait at a crossing for a freight train to go by. It was the one near Brendon Road, where the tracks go uphill and the freights tend to slow down because of the incline.

So I'm sitting there, bored, a little impatient more than anything else, and suddenly I see all this art going by. Huge murals painted on the sides of the boxcars and all I can do is stare, thinking, where's all that coming from? Who did these amazing paintings?

And then just like that, there's this collision of the synchronicity at seeing those painted cars and this feeling I've had of wanting to do something different with the iconology I grew up with on the rez—you know, like the bead patterns my mom sews on her pow-wow dresses. I turn my car back around and drive for the freight yards, stopping off at a hardware store along the way.

I felt a kinship to whoever it was that was painting those boxcars, a complete understanding of what they'd done and why they'd done it. And I wanted to send them a message back. I wanted to tell them, I've seen your work and here's my side of the conversation.

That was the day Crow was born and my first thunderbird joined that ongoing hobo gallery that the freights take from city to city, across the country.

It's a long ride down to the city. I leave the crows behind, but the winter comes with me, wind blowing snow down the highway behind my car, howling like the cries of dying buffalo. It's full night by the time I'm in the downtown core. It's so cold, there's nobody out, not even the hookers. I drive until I reach the precinct house where Turk works and park across the street from it. And then I sit there, my hand in my pocket, fingers wrapped around the handle of the gun.

Comes to me, I can't kill a man, not even a man like Turk. Maybe if he was standing right in front of me and we were fighting. Maybe if he was threatening my mom. Maybe I could do it in the heat of the moment. But not like this, waiting to ambush him like in some Hollywood western.

But I know I've got to do something.

My gaze travels from the precinct house to the stores alongside the street where I'm parked. I don't even hesitate. I reach in the back for a plastic bag full of unused spray cans and I get out of the car to meet that cold wind head on.

I don't know how long I've got so I work even faster than usual. It's not a boxcar, but the paint goes on the bricks and glass as easy as it does on wooden slats. It doesn't even clog up in the nozzle—maybe the Grandfather Thunders are giving me a helping hand. I do the crow first, thunderbird style, a yellow one to make the black and red words stand out when I write them along the spread of its wings.

TOM MCGURK KILLS INDIANS.

I add a roughly-rendered brave with the daubed clay of a ghost-dancer masking his features. He's lying face-up to the sky, power lines flowing up out of his head as his spirit leaves his body, a row of crosses behind him—not Christian crosses, but ours, the ones that stand for the four quarters of the world.

HE HAULS THEM OUT OF TOWN, I write in big sloppy letters, AND LEAVES THEM TO DIE IN THE COLD.

I'm starting a monster, a cannibal windigo all white fur and blood, raging in the middle of a winter storm, when a couple of cops stop their squad car abreast of where I parked my own. They're on their way back to the precinct, I guess, ending their shift and look what they've found. I keep spraying the paint, my fingers frozen into a locked position from the cold.

"Okay, Tonto," one of them says. "Drop the can and assume the position."

I couldn't drop the can if I wanted to. I can barely move my fingers. So I keep spraying on the paint until one of them gives me a sucker punch in the kidneys, knocks me down, kicks me as I'm falling. I lose the spray can and it goes rattling across the sidewalk. I lose the gun, too, which I forgot I was carrying.

There's a long moment of silence as we're all three staring at that gun lying there on the pavement.

They really work me over then.

So as I sit here in county, waiting for my trial, I think back on all of this and find I'm not sorry that I didn't try to shoot Turk. I'm not sorry that I got busted in the middle of vandalizing a building right across the street from the precinct house, either. But I do regret not getting rid of the gun first.

The charges against me are vandalism, possession of an unlicensed weapon, carrying a concealed weapon, and resisting arrest. I'll be doing some time, heading up to the pen, but I won't be alone in there. Like Leonard Peltier says on that song he does with Robbie Robertson, "It's the fastest growing rez in the country," and he should know, they've kept him locked up long enough.

But something good came out of all of this. The police didn't have time to get rid of my graffiti before the press showed up. I guess it was a slow news day because pictures of those paintings showed up on the front page of all three of the daily papers, and made the news on every channel. You might think, what's good about that? It's like prime evidence against me. But I'm not denying I painted those images and words, and the good thing is, people started coming forward, talking about how the same thing had happened to them. Cops would pick them up when the bars closed and would dump them, ten, twenty miles out of town. They identified Turk and a half-dozen others by name.

So I'm sitting in county, and I don't know where Turk is, but he's been suspended without pay while the investigation goes on, and it looks like they've got to deal with this fair and square because everybody's on their case now, right across the city—whites, blacks, skins, everybody. They're all watching what the authorities do, writing editorials, writing letters to the editor, holding protest demonstrations.

This isn't going away.

So if I've got to do some jail time, I'm thinking the sacrifice is worth it.

My cousin Tommy drives my mom down from the rez on a regular basis to visit me. The first time she comes, she stands there looking at me and I don't know what she's thinking, but I wait for the blast I'm sure's coming my way. But all she says is, "Couldn't you have stuck with the boxcars?" Then she holds me a long while, tells me I'm stupid, but how she's so proud of me. Go figure.

Some of the Creek aunts have connections in the city and they found me a good lawyer, so I'm not stuck with some public defender. I like him. His name's Marty Caine and I can tell he doesn't care what color my skin is. He tells me that what I did was "morally correct, if legally indefensible, but we'll do our damnedest to get you out of this anyway." But nobody's fooled. We all know that whatever happens to the cops, they're still going to make a lesson with me. When it comes to skins, they always do.

I see Walking Elk one more time before the trial. I'm lying on my bunk, staring up at the ceiling, thinking how, when I get out, I'm going on those last two vision quests. I need to be centered. I need to talk to the Creator and find out what my place is in the world, who I'm supposed to be so that my being here in this world makes a difference to what happens to the people in my life, to the ground I walk on and the spirits that share this world with us.

I hear a rustle of cloth and turn my head to see John Walking Elk sitting on the other bunk. He's still wearing the clothes he died in. I assume he's still dead. This time he's got the smokes and he offers me one.

I swing my feet to the floor and take the cigarette, let him light it for me.

"How come you're still here?" I ask.

He shrugs. "Maybe I'm not," he says. "Maybe Whiteduck sent my spirit on and you're just dreaming."

I smile. "You'd think if I was going to dream, I'd dream myself out of this place."

"You'd think."

We smoke our cigarettes for a while.

"I'm in all the papers," Walking Elk says after a while. "And that's your doing. They wrote about how Whiteduck sent my body down to the city, how the cops drove me up there and dumped me in the snow. Family I didn't even know I had anymore came to the funeral. From the rez, from Pine Ridge, hell, from places I never even heard of before."

I wasn't there, but I heard about it. Skins came from all over the country to show their solidarity. Mom told me that the Warriors' Society up on the rez organized it.

"Yeah, I heard it was some turnout," I say. "Made the cover of *Time* and everything."

Walking Elk nods. "You came through for me," he says. "On both counts."

I know what he's talking about. I can hear his voice against the northern winds that were blowing that day without even trying.

Don't let me be forgotten.

Be a warrior for me.

But I don't know what to say.

"Even counted some coup for yourself," he adds.

"Wasn't about that," I tell him.

"I know. I just wanted to thank you. I had to come by to tell you that. I lived a lot of years, just looking for something in the bottom of a bottle. There was nothing else left for me. Didn't think anybody'd ever look at me like I was a man again. But you did. And those people that came to the funeral? They were remembering me as a man, too, not just some drunk who got himself killed by a cop."

He stands up. I'm curious. Is he going to walk away through the wall, or just fade away like he did before?

"Any plans for when you get out?" he asks.

I think about that for a moment.

"I was thinking of going back to painting boxcars," I say. "You see where painting buildings got me."

"There's worse places to be," he tells me. "You could be dead."

I don't know if I blinked, or woke up, but the next thing I know, he's gone and I'm alone in my cell. But I hear an echo of laughter and I've still got the last of that cigarette he gave me smoldering in my hand.

"Ya-ha-hey," I say softly and butt it out in the ashtray.

Then I stretch out on the bed again and contemplate the ceiling some more.

I think maybe I was dead, or half dead, anyway, before I found John Walking Elk dying in the snow. I was going through the motions of life, instead of really living, and there's no excuse for that. It's not something I'll let happen to me again.

Freak

1

"Do you understand the charges as they've been read to you?"

"Yes sir, I do."

"How do you plead?"

"Guilty, your honor."

2

"Get your head outta them comic books," Daddy'd say. "They're gonna rot your brain."

And I guess they did.

Or something happened to me that don't have any kind of an explanation that makes a lick of sense 'cause there's a mess inside the bones of my head that's been giving me a world of grief pretty much ever since I can remember.

I hear voices, see. Sometimes they're only pictures, or a mix of the two, but mostly it's them voices. Words. People talking. The voices show up inside my head with no never you mind from me and I can't shut 'em out.

They come to me about the same time I learned how playing with my pee-stick could be a whole lot of fun. I never knew it was good for anything but peeing until I woke up one night with it grown all big in my hand and I never felt anything near as good as when out comes this big gush of white, creamy pee. I felt bad after—like I was doing something dirty—but I couldn't seem to stop.

But when I finally did, the voices didn't.

For the longest time, I thought I was imagining them. I didn't have me a whole lot of friends, living out by the junkyard like we did, so it makes sense how maybe I'd get me an imaginary friend. But they was just voices. They didn't talk to me; they talked at me. Sometimes them voices used words I couldn't tell what they meant—they'd be too big or in some foreign language. And sometimes the pictures that come to me were of things that I'd never seen before—hell, stuff that I couldn't even start to imagine on my own—and sometimes they were of things I didn't *want* to imagine. People doing things to each other. Mean, terrible things.

I figured maybe the voices were punishment for all that playing I done with my pee-stick. You know, instead of growing hair on my palms, I got all this noise in my head.

But because they wasn't telling me nothing personal—they wasn't talking *to* me, I mean, like telling me I'd been bad or something—I come to realize that maybe I got something broke in my head. It was just something that happened, no accounting for it.

Like I'd become a kind of radio, tuned to a station only I could hear, and these voices was just coming to me outta the air.

I can't remember when I finally worked out that they was other people thinking, but that's what they are, sure enough.

Funny thing about 'em is how they come with a smell. Like, take Blind Henry, lives on the street, same as me. His thinking's like the tobacco juice usta build up in the spit pot in Daddy's office. It was my job to dump it. I'd take it out to that cinderblock building at the back of the junkyard where we been dumping all manner of things. Oil and dirty gas, yeah, but other stuff, too. You'd go into that building and your eyes'd start to sting something fierce and the taste of puke'd rise up in your throat.

I remember the first time I saw the pirates come—I knew they was pirates because they had the Jolly Roger on the side of the barrels they brought in that big truck of theirs and they come late at night, secret-like. I looked hard but I never saw no one with a peg leg or a parrot, still they had the skull and crossbones, so I knew 'em for what they was. That first night I snuck outta the trailer and followed Daddy and them pirates to the cinderblock building and stared in at 'em through the window. But they wasn't hiding any treasure. Them barrels with the Jolly Roger on 'em only had some kind of watery goo that Daddy dumped into the pit.

Anywise, I was telling you how every voice's got its own smell. Daddy's was sweaty leather, like that old belt of his he used to whup me whenever he got in a mood. Mama's was like fruit, rotting on the ground. Kinda sweet, but not right.

The best voice is Jenny Winston's. It smells just like she looks, fresh and kind, like apple blossoms and lilacs when the scent of them comes to you from a few backyards over. Not too strong, but you can't mistake it.

I learned pretty damn quick to hide the fact I could hear what a body was thinking. People don't like it. It don't make no never mind that I can't stop from hearing it. They just assume you're a-doing it on purpose.

But I'd give anything to make it stop.

I can't never make 'em go away completely, I guess, not unless I went to live on some desert island where there was nobody else to do any thinking, but how would I live in a place like that? I can't do much for myself 'cept look for handouts as it is.

But I can tune 'em down some by listening to music. I don't know why it works, it just does. That's why I always had me spare batteries for this little transistor radio of mine—I'd make sure I got batteries afore I saw to getting me enough to eat.

It's hard in here without that radio. The voices that fill my head are cold and mean and hurting.

But better 'n the radio was live music.

Sometimes, afore they put me in here, I'd go in back of the Rhatigan, that little jazz club over on Palm Street. I'd sit in the alley by the back door and listen to the house bands play. It was best in the summer when they got the door propped open and them cool, moody sounds come floating out—they don't just take the voices away; that music makes me feel good, even when the band's playing a sad song, or the blues.

3

"Bernie—can I call you Bernie?"

"Sure. That's my name."

"You know I'm here to help you."

"Sure."

"The court may have appointed me to represent you, but that doesn't mean I don't care about winning this case."

"Sure."

"I think we need to send you in for psychiatric evaluation."

"I'm not crazy."

"Bernie, copping an insanity plea is the only chance we're going to have to save you from long-term incarceration or worse."

"I'm not crazy."

"This state still has a death penalty."

"I know that."

"If we don't do something, Bernie, you could end up on death row."

"Maybe that's the best place for something like me."

4

Daddy died first of the cancer. It just started growing in him one day and afore you'd know it, it was spread all through him. He was in a lot of pain by the time it finally took him, which made him real hard to be around. My head was filled with the screaming of his thoughts the whole time. That was an ugly time.

Mama died not long after—cancer took her, too—but she went quietly. Like a long, drawn-out whimper.

Cousin Henry took possession of the junkyard and become my guardian until I turned sixteen. Then he sent me packing with hard words and meaner thoughts.

That's how I come to be living on the street this past couple of years. I tried to find work, but nobody wants something as ugly as me to look at, day after day.

See, I never had no chance at a normal life. It's not my hearing the voices—I learned pretty damn quick to keep that to my ownself. It's that I look like a freak. Got no meat on my bones, but I got a head big and round as a damn pumpkin, and my skin's all splotchy with big red marks like I got me freckles on steroids. It made the kids laugh afore I dropped out of school, but now people just stare, then look away, like I turn their stomach or something.

I always had that big head and I never did grow into it. There's times I wish it was even bigger so that I could get a steady gig in a sideshow or something. People'd still make fun of me, but it wouldn't be the same, would it? It'd be like my job. I'd be getting paid for being a freak.

In them comic books I used to read, I'd've been a hero, what with being able to read people's minds and all. I woulda got myself some fancy clothes and a mask and I'd go out and save people's lives 'n' stuff. It wouldn't matter if I looked like a freak 'cause I'd be part of some gang of superheroes, saving the world 'n' stuff and people'd admire us and like us, even me. In the comic books, a freak like me can still live a good life. Hell, sometimes they even get them a girl.

But I don't live in no comic book and the only time I tried to be a hero is what put me in here.

I ain't saying I didn't mean to do what I done. Hell, I'd do it again if the situation come 'round same as it done before.

How it happened was I was panhandling outside the gates of Fitzhenry Park. It's mostly women give me money. I guess, ugly as I am, they still want to mama me. Or maybe they're mamas themselves, thanking God their own kids didn't turn out like me and they drop a couple of bills in my cap like they would an offering of thanks in church.

I don't ask. I just keep my head down and say thank you ma'am, earphones in my ears and the music from my radio keeping me from hearing too much of what anybody's thinking.

The day it all went down, Jenny Winston comes by like she often does. She's one of Angel's people, them sorta social workers who help street people 'cause they care, not 'cause it's some job.

Jenny's good on the inside and out. I should know. She's the prettiest woman I ever saw, but anybody can see that. But I hear her thinking and there's not a bad thought in her head. She can look at me and all she sees is a person, not some freak with an oversize head.

This day she gives me a sandwich and a little carton of milk, asks me if I need anything, so I take the 'phones outta my ears to answer her properly. That's when I hear the thinking of the guy standing behind her.

The look of me turns his stomach, but that's no big surprise. It's what he's thinking 'bout Jenny that makes my blood run cold.

Lotsa people think bad things. The difference between bad people and good is that good people don't act on 'em. If you didn't know better, you might get confused as to which a fella might be, but I've got so's I can tell the difference.

And I can see in his head, he's done this afore. Courted a pretty gal and then done away with her. He's got him a whole set of graves, laid out in a nice little row, way back up in the mountains.

How come he never got caught? You'd think somebody'd have figured out he's got all these girlfriends disappearing on him. But there he is, standing behind Jenny, not a care in the world, just kinda daydreaming of the day he's gonna do her in, too, so I guess he's got something working for him.

There's folks like that. There's folks get away with pretty much anything. It's like common sense just turns its head away from them, don't ask me why. And the more I listen to him, the more I see he's a sly one. Not many folks know how serious him and the gal's getting. Usually he pretends he's getting a divorce so they can't let on how it is between 'em until the paperwork's done. So this gal, she's got herself a true love, they're gonna get married and all, but she can't tell anyone just yet.

I see all that in his head. It's something he thinks 'bout all the time—these are the things that make him feel good.

And this time he's gonna do it to my Jenny.

I don't mean I ever thought she'd be interested in the likes of me. Hell, I'm just an ugly freak; I ain't stupid. But she's been kind to me. She's kind to everyone. She's not like some of the others who work with Angel to help us street people. Most of the others come up offa the streets and it's their chance to give something back. But Jenny wasn't like that. She's helping 'cause she's got her too big a heart. She wasn't hurt as a kid. She didn't live on the streets. The thing is, she just can't stand by when others are in need. It's as simple as that.

So she's ripe for the plucking of a man like the one standing behind her now, accompanying her on their rounds afore they go to dinner, pretending to care so much for her. She don't see through him 'cause she can't read what's inside another's head like I can. 'Cause she only sees the good in people. While he, oh he's a-glorying in what's to come.

How come somebody as good as her attracts that kind of person?

I don't know. Same reason that people like my parents are allowed to have them kids, I guess. There's no sense to it, not unless we were really bad people in some other life and this is payback time. But I don't buy that. Life's just the way it is. Kids get born into families that don't even want 'em, never you mind love 'em. And good always attracts evil. The strong feed on the weak. Guess if there's any rule to living, that's what it is, and it's up to each of us to put what charity and kindness we can muster back into the world.

So I get up off my feet and I walk over to him. I reach under my coat to where I got me a sheath hanging under my armpit and pull out that old Randall knife I stole from my Daddy's office afore Cousin Henry sent me packing. It's got an edge sharp enough to shave with, which I've done a time or two. I don't say a word. I just whip the blade across his throat and cut him deep.

People mistake me. They think 'cause I'm so skinny, got this big head, that I can't move fast. But it ain't like that at all.

It's over and done afore anybody can make a move. Then he's falling, blood spurting outta his neck. Jenny's screaming—oh what she thinks of me hurts something fierce. There's other people on the sidewalk screaming and rushing around.

I try to tell Jenny what he was thinking, how I can read what's in people's heads, but she won't listen. She can't hear me. And I realize it don't make a whole lot of difference anywise.

I just drop the knife on the pavement and stand there, watching the real freak die while I wait for the cops to come and take me away.

5

"Do you have any last words?"

I look through the plate glass window to where the witnesses are sitting, staring back at me, all strapped down and waiting to die. There's a lot of dark thoughts coming my way, but I can pick out Jenny's real easy. I just follow the scent of apple blossoms and lilacs. She's sad, but there's a hardness in her, too. She's looking at me, thinking there's the man who killed the fella I loved. He deserves to die for what he done. But she's not easy about this business of a death penalty. It feels too much like revenge to her. And though there's a part of her wants revenge, she knows it's not right. Trouble is, she's not strong enough to stand up and say it's wrong neither.

Do I have any last words?

I could tell back what Jenny's thinking right now so that she'd know I was telling the truth. I could go right into her head and pull the thoughts out, word for word. But then she'd have to live with her part in putting to death the man who up and saved her and I can't let that happen.

She's safe now. That's all that matters.

"Yes sir," I say. "I ain't sorry for what I done. Best you give me that injection now."

And they do.

Big City Littles

The Fates seem to take a perverse pleasure out of complicating our lives. I'm not sure why. We do such a good job of it all on our own that their divine interference only seems to be overkill.

It's not that we deliberately set out to screw things up. We'd all like to be healthy and happy, not to mention independently wealthy—or at least able to make our living doing something we care about, something we can take pride in. But even when we know better, we invariably make a mess of everything, in both our private and our public lives.

Take my sister. She knows that boyfriends are only an option, not an answer, but that's never stopped her from bouncing from one sorry relationship to another, barely stopping to catch her breath between one bad boy and the next. Though I should talk. It's all well and fine to be comfortable in your own skin, to make a life for yourself if there's no one on the scene to share it with you. But too often I still feel like the original spinster, doomed to end her days forever alone in some garret.

I guess for all the strides we've made with the women's movement, there are some things we can still only accept on an intellectual level. We never really believe them in our hearts.

The little man sitting on Sheri Piper's pillow when she opened her eyes was a good candidate for the last thing she would have expected to have woken up to this morning. He wasn't really much bigger than the length from the tip of her middle finger to the heel of her palm, a small hamster-sized man, dressed in raggedy clothes with the look of a bird about him. His eyes were wideset, his nose had a definite hook to it, his body was plump, but his limbs were thin as twigs. His hair was an unruly tangle of short brown curls and he wore a pair of rectangular, wire-framed eyeglasses not much different than those Sheri wore for anything but close work.

She tried to guess his age. Older than herself, certainly. In his mid-forties, she decided. Unless tiny people aged in something equivalent to dog years.

If this were happening to one of the characters in the children's books she wrote and illustrated, now would be the time for astonishment and wonder, perhaps even a mild touch of alarm, since after all, tiny though he was, he was still a strange man and she *had* woken up to find him in her bedroom. Instead, she felt oddly calm.

"I don't suppose I could be dreaming," she said.

The little man started the way a pedestrian might when an unexpected bus suddenly roars by the corner where they're standing. Jumping up, he lost his balance and would have gone sliding down the long slope of her pillow if she hadn't slipped a hand out from under the bedclothes and caught him.

He squeaked when she picked him up, but she meant him no

harm and only deposited him carefully on her night table. Backing away until he was up against the lamp, his tiny gaze darted from side to side as though searching for escape, which seemed odd considering how, only moments ago, he'd been creeping around on her pillow mere inches from her face.

Laying her head back down, she studied him. He weighed no more than a mouse, but he was definitely real. He had substance the way dreams didn't. Unless she hadn't woken up yet and was still dreaming, which was a more likely explanation.

"Don't talk so loud!" he cried as she opened her mouth to speak again.

His voice was high-pitched and sounded like the whine of a bug in her ear.

"What are you?" she whispered.

He appeared to be recovering from his earlier nervousness. Brushing something from the sleeve of his jacket, he said, "I'm not a what. I'm a who."

"Who then?"

He stood up straighter. "My name is Jenky Wood, at your service, and I come to you as an emissary."

"From where? Lilliput?"

Tiny eyes blinked in confusion. "No, from my people. The Kaldewen Tribe."

"Who live . . . where? In my sock drawer? Behind the baseboards?"

Why couldn't this have happened *after* her first coffee of the morning when at least her brain would be slightly functional.

He gave her a troubled look. "You're not like we expected."

"What were you expecting?"

"Someone . . . kinder."

Sheri sighed. "I'm sorry. I'm not a morning person."

"That's apparent."

"Mind you, I do feel justified in being a little cranky. After all, you're the one who's come barging into my bedroom."

"I didn't barge. I crept in under the door, ever so quietly."

"Okay, snuck into my bedroom then—which, by the way, doesn't give you points on any gentlemanly scale that I know of."

"It seemed the best time to get your attention without being accidentally stepped on, or swatted like a bug."

Sheri stopped herself from telling him that implying that her apartment might be overrun with bugs his size also wasn't particularly endearing.

"Would it be too much to ask *what* you're doing in my bedroom?" she asked. "Not to mention in my bed."

"I might as well ask what you're doing in bed."

"Now who's being cranky?"

"The sun rose hours ago."

"Yes, and I was writing until three o'clock this morning so I think I'm entitled to sleep in." She paused to frown at him. "Not that it's any of your business. And," she added as he began to reply, "you haven't answered my question."

"It's about your book," he said. *"The Traveling Littles."*

As soon as he said the title, she wondered how she could have missed the connection. Jenky Woods, at her service, looked exactly like she'd painted the Littles in her book. Except . . .

"Littles aren't real," she said, knowing how dumb *that* sounded with an all too obvious example standing on her night table.

"But . . . you . . . you told our history . . ."

"I told a story," Sheri said, feeling sorry for the little man now. "One that was told to me when I was a girl."

"So you can't help us?"

"It depends," she said, "on what you need my help for."

But she already knew. She didn't have to go into her office to take down a copy of the book from her brag shelf. She might have written and illustrated it almost twenty years ago. She might not have recognized the little man for what he was until he'd told her himself. But she remembered the story.

It had been her first book and its modest, not to mention continuing, success was what had persuaded her to try to make a living at writing and drawing children's books. She'd just never considered that the story might be true, never mind what she'd said in the pages of the book.

The Traveling Littles

There are many sorts of little people—tiny folk, no bigger than a minute. And I don't just mean fairies and brownies, or even pennymen and their like. There are the Lilliputians that Gulliver met on his travels. Mary Norton's Borrowers. The Smalls of William Dunthorn's Cornwall. All sorts. But today I want to tell you about the Traveling Littles who live like Gypsies, spending their lives always on the move.

This is how I heard the story when I was a small girl. My grandpa told it to me, just like this, so I know it's true.

The Littles were once birds. They had wings and flew high above the trees and hills to gather their food. When the leaves began to turn yellow and red and frost was in the air, they flew to warmer countries, for they weren't toads to burrow in the mud, or bears to hibernate away the cold months, or crows who don't allow the weather to tell them where to live or when to move.

The Littles liked to travel. They liked the wind in their wings and to look out on a new horizon every morning. So they were always leaving one region for another, traveling more to the south in the winter, coming back north when the lilacs and honeysuckle bloom. No matter how far they traveled, they always returned to these very hills where the sprucey-pine grow tall and the grass can seem blue in a certain light, because even traveling people need a place they can call home.

But one year when the Littles returned, they could find nothing to eat. They flew in every direction looking for food. They flew for days with a gnawing hunger in their bellies.

Finally they came upon a field of ripe grain—the seeds so fat and sweet, they'd never seen the like, before or since. They swooped down in a chorusing flock and gorged in that field until they were too heavy to fly away again. So they had to stay the night on the ground, sleeping among the grain-straw and grass.

You'd think they would have learned their lesson, but in the morning, instead of flying away, they decided to eat a little more and rest in that field of grain for one more night.

Every morning they decided the same thing, to eat a little more and sleep another night, until they got to be so heavy that they couldn't fly anymore. They could only hop, and not quickly either.

Then the trees began to turn yellow and red again. Frost was on the ground and the winter winds came blowing. The toad burrowed in his mud. The bear returned to his den. The crows watched from the bare-limbed trees and laughed.

Because the Littles couldn't fly away. They couldn't fly at all. They were too fat.

The grain-straw was getting dry. The tall grass browned, grew thin and died. After watching the mice and squirrels store away their own harvests, the Littles began to shake the grain from the blades of grass and gather it in heaps with their wings, storing it in hidey-holes and hollow logs. The downy feathers of their wings became all gluey, sticking to each other. Their wings took the shape of arms and hands and even if they could manage to lose weight, they were no longer able to fly at all now for they'd become people—tiny people, six inches tall.

That winter they had to dig holes in the sides of the mountains and along the shores of the rivers, making places to live.

And it's been like that ever since.

In the years to follow, they've come to live among us, sharing our bounty the way mice do, only they are so secret we never see them at all. And they still travel, from town to town, from borough to borough, from city block to the next one over, and then the next one over from that. That's why we call them the Traveling Littles.

But the Traveling Littles are still birds, even if their arms are no longer wings. They can never see a tall building or a mountain without wanting to get to the top. But they can't fly anymore. They have to walk up there, just like you or me.

Still the old folks, those who know this story and told it to me, say that one day the Traveling Littles will get their wings back. They will be birds again.

Only no one knows when.

"You want to know how to become a bird again," she said.

Jenky Wood nodded. "We thought you would know. Yula Gry came across a copy of your book in a child's library last year and told us about it at our year's end celebration. Palko John—"

"Who are these people?"

"Yula is the sister of my brother's cousin Sammy, and Palko John is our Big Man. He's the chief of our clan, but he's also the big chief of all the tribe. He decided that we should look for you. When we found out where you lived, I was sent to talk to you."

"Why were you chosen?"

He had the decency to blush.

"Because they all say I'm too good-natured to offend anyone, or take offense."

Sheri stifled a laugh. "Well," she said. "I'm usually much less cranky when I've been awake for a little longer and have had at least one cup of coffee. Speaking of which, I need one now. I also have to have a pee."

At that he went beet-red.

"What, you people don't? Never mind," she added. "That was just more crankiness. Can I pick you up?"

When he gave her a nervous nod, she lowered her hand so that he could step onto her palm, keeping her thumb upright so he'd have something to hang on to. She took him into the kitchen, deposited him on the table, plugged in the kettle, then went back down the hall to the washroom.

Ten minutes later she was sitting at the table with a coffee in front of her. Jenky sat on a paperback book, holding the thimbleful of coffee she'd given him. She broke off a little piece of a bran cookie and offered it to him before dipping the rest into her coffee.

"So why would you want to become birds again, anyway?" she asked.

"Look at the size of us. Can you imagine how hard it is for us to get around while still keeping our secret?"

"Point taken."

Neither spoke while they ate their cookies. Sheri sipped at her coffee.

"Did your grandfather really tell you our story?" Jenky asked after a moment.

Sheri nodded.

"Could you bring me to him?"

"He passed away a couple of years ago."

"I'm sorry."

Silence fell again between them.

"Look," Sheri said after a moment. "I don't know any more than what you read in my book, but I could look into it for you."

"Really?"

"No, I'm actually way too busy. Joke," she added as his face fell. "It was a joke."

"Palko John said we could offer you a reward for your help."

"What sort of reward?"

"Anything you want."

"Like a magic wish?" Sheri asked, intrigued.

He nodded. "We only have the one left."

"Why don't you use it to make yourselves birds again?"

"They only work for other people."

"Figures. There's always a catch, isn't there? But I don't want your wish."

He went all glum again. "So you won't help us?"

"Didn't I already say I would? I just don't like the idea of magic wishes. There's something creepy about them. I think we should earn what we get, not have it handed to us on a little silver platter."

That earned her a warm smile.

"I think we definitely chose the right person to help us," he said.

"Well, don't start celebrating yet," Sheri told him. "It's not like I have any idea how to go about it. But like I said, I will look into it."

"I've decided to give up men," Sheri told Holly Rue later that day.

She'd arrived early at Holly's store for the afternoon book club meeting that the used book shop hosted on the last Wednesday of every month. The book they'd be discussing today was Alice Hoffman's *The River King*, which Sheri had adored. Since she had to wait for the others to get here to talk about it, she kept herself busy talking with Holly and fussing with Snippet, Holly's Jack Russell terrier, much to the dog's delight.

"I thought you'd already done that," Holly said.

"I did. But this time I really mean it."

"Have a bad date?"

"It's not so much having a bad date as, A, not wanting to see him again after said date, but he does and keeps calling; or B, wanting to see him again because it seemed we were getting along so well, but he doesn't call. I'm worn out from it all."

"You could call him," Holly said.

"I could. Would you?"

Holly sighed. "Not to ask him out."

"I thought women's lib was supposed to have sorted all of this out by now."

"I think it's not only society that's supposed to change, but us, too. *We* have to think differently."

"So why don't we?"

Holly shook her head. "Same reason they don't call, I guess. Give me a hob over a man any day."

Sheri cocked her head and studied Holly for a long moment.

"What?" Holly said. "Did I grow an extra nose?"

"No, I'm just thinking about hobs. I wanted to talk to you about them."

Holly's gaze went to an empty chair near the beginning of the store's furthest aisle, then came back to Sheri's.

"What about them?" she asked.

There was now something guarded in the bookseller's features, but Sheri plunged on anyway.

"Were you serious about having one living in your store?" she asked.

"Um . . . serious as in, is it true?"

A few months ago they'd been out celebrating the nomination of one of Sheri's books for a local writing award—she hadn't won. That was when Holly had mentioned this hob, laughed it off when Sheri had asked for more details, and then changed the subject.

"Because the thing is," Sheri said. "I could use some advice about little people right about now."

"You've got a hob living in your apartment?"

"No, I've got a Little—though he's only visiting."

"But Littles aren't—"

"Real," Sheri finished for her. "Any more than hobs. We both know that. Yet there he is, waiting for me in my apartment all the same. I've set him up on a bookshelf with a ladder so that he can get up and down, and got some of my old Barbie furniture out of my storage space in the basement."

"You kept your Barbie stuff?"

"And it's a good thing I did, seeing how useful it's proven to be today. Jenky—that's his name, Jenky Wood—likes the size, though he's not particularly enamoured with the colors."

"You're serious?"

"So it seems," Sheri told her. "Apparently he thinks I can find out how they can all become birds again."

"Like in your story."

Sheri nodded. "Though I haven't got the first clue."

"Well, I—"

But just then the front door opened and Kathryn Whelan, one of the other members of their book club, came in.

"I think I know someone who can help you," Holly said, before turning to smile at the new arrival.

Snippet lifted her head from Sheri's lap with interest—hoping for another biscuit like the one Sheri had given her earlier, no doubt.

"Someone tall, dark and handsome—not to mention single?" Sheri asked after they'd exchanged hellos with Kathryn.

"Not exactly."

"Who's tall, dark and handsome?" Kathryn asked.

"The man of my dreams," Sheri told her.

Kathryn smiled. "Aren't they all?"

* * *

Sheri was helping Jenky rearrange the Barbie furniture on the bookshelf she'd cleared for his use when the doorbell rang.

"That'll be her," she said, suddenly nervous.

"Should I hide?" Jenky asked.

"Well, that would kind of defeat the whole purpose of this, wouldn't it?"

"I suppose. It's just that letting myself be seen goes so against everything I've ever been told. My whole life has been a constant concentration of secrets and staying hidden."

"Buck up," Sheri told him. "If all goes well, you might be a bird again and it won't matter who sees you."

"I'd rather be both," he said as she went to get the door.

She paused, hand on the knob. "Really?"

"Given a choice, wouldn't you want to be able to go back and forth between bird and Little?"

She gave a slow nod. "I suppose I would."

She turned back to open the door and everything just kind of melted away in her head. Jenky's problem, the conversation they'd just had, the day of the week.

"Oh my," Sheri said.

The words came out unbidden, for standing there in the hallway was the idealization of a character she'd been struggling with for weeks. The new picture book hadn't exactly stalled, but she kept having to write around this one character because she couldn't quite get her clear in her head. She'd filled pages in her sketchbook with drawings, particularly frustrated because while she knew what the character was supposed to look like, she was unable to get just the right image of her down on paper. Or perhaps a better way to put it was that she didn't so much know what the woman should look like, she just knew when it was wrong.

But now here the perfect subject was, standing in the hallway. Where were her watercolors and some paper? Or just a pencil and the back of an envelope. Hell, she'd settle for a camera.

Though really, none of that would be necessary. Now that she'd seen her, it would be impossible for Sheri to forget her.

It wasn't that the woman was particularly exotic, though there were those striking green streaks that ran through her nut-brown hair. She wasn't dressed regally either, though her simple white blouse and long flower-print skirt nevertheless left an impression of royal vestments. It wasn't even that she was so beautiful—there were any number of beautiful women in the world.

No, there was an air about her, a quality both mysterious and simple that had been escaping Sheri for weeks when she was doing her character sketches. But she had it now. She'd begin with a light golden wash, creating a nimbus of light behind the figure's head, and then—

"I hope that's a pleased 'oh my,' " the woman said.

Her voice brought Sheri back into the present moment.

"What? Oh, yes. It was. I mean I was just . . ."

The woman offered her hand. "My name's Meran Kelledy. Holly did tell you I was coming by, didn't she?"

Her voice was soft and melodic with an underlying touch of gentle humor.

"I'm sorry," Sheri said as she shook Meran's hand. "I can't believe I've left you standing out there in the hall." She stood aside. "Please come in. It's just that you caught me by surprise. See, you look exactly like the forest queen I need for this book I'm working on at the moment and . . ." She laughed. "I'm babbling, aren't I?"

"What sort of forest is she the queen of?"

"An oak forest."

Meran smiled. "Well, that's all right, then."

With that enigmatic comment, she came into the apartment. Sheri watched her for one drawn out moment longer, then shut the door to join Meran and Jenky in the living room.

"I should also tell you that there's a wish up for grabs," Sheri said after she and Jenky had taken turns telling their story.

The two women were sitting at the kitchen table, Jenky on the table in a pink plastic chair. They all had tea—Jenky in his thimble since he didn't like the plastic Barbie dishware, the women in regular porcelain mugs.

"For the one who helps the Littles with this, I mean," Sheri added.

Meran shook her head. "I have no need for wishes."

Of course she wouldn't.

Meran was probably the calmest woman that Sheri had ever met. Neither meeting the Little nor the story the two of them had told seemed to surprise her. She'd simply given Jenky a polite hello, then sat and nodded while they talked, occasionally asking a question to clarify one point or another.

What world does she live in? Sheri had found herself thinking.

A magical one, no doubt. Like the forest in Sheri's latest picture book.

"You can have it," Meran said.

But Sheri shook her head right back. "I don't believe in something for nothing."

"Good for you."

What an odd response. But Sheri didn't take the time to dwell on it.

"So can you help us turn them back into birds again?" she asked.

"Unfortunately, no. Odd as it came to be, the Littles have evolved into what they now are and that kind of thing can't be turned back. It's like making the first fish who came onto land return to the sea. Or forcing the monkeys to go back up into the trees once more instead of becoming men and women. Evolution doesn't work that way. It moves forward, not back."

"But magic . . ."

"Operates from what appears to be a different law of physics, I'll admit, but that's only because it's misunderstood. If you have the right vocabulary, it can make perfect sense."

Sheri sighed. "So we're back where we started."

"No, because the clock doesn't turn backwards."

"I don't understand."

Sheri might have felt dumb, but Jenky looked as confused as she was feeling and he was a piece of magic himself, so she decided not to worry about it.

"What's to stop the Littles from continuing to evolve?" Meran asked. "Into, say, beings that can change from bird to Little at will, the way Jenky here has said he'd like to."

"Well, for one thing, we don't know how."

"Now there I can help you. Or at least I can set the scene so that you can help him."

"I'm still not following you."

"There's an old tribe of words," Meran explained. "Not the kind we use today, but the ones that go back to the before, when a word spoken created a moment in which anything can happen."

"The before?" Sheri asked.

"It's just another way to say the first days of the world," Jenky told her. "Our storytellers still tell the stories of those days, of Raven and Cody and the crow girls and all."

"It was a time of Story," Meran said. "Though of course every age has its stories, just as every person does. But these were the stories that shaped the world and part of that shaping had to do with this old tribe of words."

"A tribe of words," Sheri repeated, feeling way out of her depth here.

Meran nodded. "I can wake one of those words for you," she said. "Not for a long time, but for long enough."

"So you'll just say one of these words and everything'll be the way we want it to be?"

"Hardly," Meran said with a smile. "I can only wake one of that old tribe. You will need to say the words. It's a form of communal magic, which is mostly the kind I know. One person wakes it, another gives it focus."

"But I wouldn't know what to say. Maybe Jenky should do it."

"No, this works better when a human speaks the words."

That gave Sheri pause, the way Meran said the word "human." It was the way humans spoke of other species. She wanted to ask Meran what she was, but she supposed now wasn't the time. And it would probably be impolite.

"So what words do I say?" she asked instead.

"You'll know when the time is right."

"But . . ."

Meran gave her another of her smiles. "Don't worry so much."

"Okay."

Sheri looked from the magical woman sitting across the table from her to the even more magical little man sitting on a Barbie kitchen chair between them. Jenky watched her expectantly. Meran said nothing, did nothing. There was an odd, unfocused look to her gaze, but otherwise she seemed to merely be waiting, managing to do so without conveying the vaguest sense of pressure.

But there was pressure all the same—self-imposed on Sheri's part, but no less urgent for that.

What if she didn't say the right thing? How much was she supposed to say? How was she supposed to know when the time was right?

It was all so nebulous.

"So when do we start?" Sheri asked.

Meran's gaze came into focus and found Sheri's.

"Breathe," she said. "Slowly. Try to still the conversations that rise up in your head and don't concentrate on anything until you feel a change. You'll know it when you feel it."

Then she slowly closed her eyes.

Sheri copied her, closing her own eyes. Breathing deeply and slowly, she tried to feel this change. Something, anything. Maybe a difference in the air. Some sense that they were sideways from the world as she knew it, inhabiting a pocket of the world where magic could happen.

If magic *was* real, that was.

If it . . .

She wasn't sure where it originated, the sudden impression of assurance that came whispering through her, calm and sure and secret. She felt like she was at the center of some enormous wheel and that all the possibilities of what might be were radiating out from her like a hundred thousand filigreed spokes. It was like floating, like coming apart and reconnecting with everything. But it was also like being utterly focused as well. She could look at all those threads arcing away from her and easily find and hold the one that was needed in her mind.

"Hope," she said.

"Is that word for them or for you?"

As soon as Meran asked the question, Sheri saw how it could go. She realized that under the connection she felt to this wheel of possibilities, she'd continued to harbor her own need, continued to reach for that elusive partner every single person looked for, whether they admit it or not. He could be called to her with Meran's old tribal word. The right partner, the perfect partner. All she had to do was say, "for me."

Because magic was real, she knew that now. At least this magic was real. It could bring him to her.

But then she opened her eyes. Her gaze went to Jenky, watching her with expectant eyes and held breath.

Promises made. Promises broken.

What good were promises if you didn't keep them? How could you respect yourself, never mind expect anyone else to respect you, if you could break them so easily? What would the perfect man think of her when he learned how she'd brought him to her?

Not to mention what she'd said barely ten minutes ago, how it wasn't right to have something for nothing.

But that was before she'd realized it could really be made to happen.

That was before all the lonely nights were washed away with the promise of just the right man coming into her life.

"No," she said. "I meant faith. Belief. That bird and Little can be one again, the shape they wear being their own choice."

Meran smiled.

"Done," she said.

Sheri felt a rumbling underfoot, like a subway car running just under the basement of her apartment building. But there was no subway within blocks of her place. The tea mugs rattled on the table and Jenky gripped the seat of his chair. Something swelled inside her, deep and old, too big for her to hold inside.

And then it was gone.

Sheri blinked and looked at Meran.

Was that it? she wanted to ask. What happened? Did it work?

But before she could speak, there was a blur of motion in the middle of the kitchen table. Jenky leapt up, knocking his little chair down. He lifted his arms and they seemed to shrink back into his body at the same time as his fingers grew long, long, longer. Feathers burst from them in a sudden cloud. His birdish features became a bird's head in truth, and then the whole of the little man was gone and a gray and brown bird rose up from the tabletop, flapping its wings. It circled once, twice, three times around the room, then landed on the table again, the transformation reversing itself until Jenky was standing there.

He looked up at her, grinning from ear to ear.

Sheri smiled back at him.

"I guess it worked," she said.

A couple of days later, Sheri looked up from her drawing table, distracted by the tap-tap-tapping on her windowpane. A little gray and brown bird looked in at her, its head cocked to one side.

"Jenky?" she said.

The bird tapped at the glass again so she stepped around her table and opened the window. The bird immediately flew in and landed on the top of her drawing table where it became a little raggedy man. Sheri wasn't even startled anymore.

"Hello, hello!" Jenky cried.

"Hello, yourself. You're looking awfully pleased with yourself."

"Everyone's so happy. They all wanted to come by and say thank you and hello, but Palko John said that would be indecorous so it's just me."

"Well, I'm glad to see you, too."

Jenky looked like he wanted to dance around where he was standing, but he made himself stand straight and tall.

"I'm supposed to ask you if you've decided on your wish," he said.

"I already told you—I don't want a wish."

"But you helped us, and that was our promise to you."

Sheri shook her head. "I still don't want it. You should keep it for yourselves."

"And I already told you. We can't use it for ourselves."

Sheri shrugged. "Then find someone who really needs it. A person whose only home is an alleyway. A child fending off unwelcome attention. Someone who's dying, or hurt, or lonely, or sad. You Littles must go all over the city. Surely you can find someone who needs a wish."

"That's your true and final answer?"

"Now you sound like a game show host," she told him.

He wagged a finger at her. "It's too late in the day to be cranky. Even you have to have been up for hours now."

"You still don't get my jokes, do you?"

"No," he said. "But I'll learn."

"Anyway, that's my true and final answer."

"Then I'll find such a person and give them your wish."

With that he became a bird once more. He did a quick circle around her head, followed by a whole series of complicated loops and swirls that took him from one end of the room to the other, showing off.

"Come back and visit!" Sheri called as he headed for the window.

The bird twittered, then it darted out the window and was gone.

"So what's the deal with Meran?" Sheri asked Holly the next time she came by the bookstore. "Where do you know her from?"

"I had a . . . pixie incident that she helped me out with last year."

"A pixie incident."

Holly nodded. "The store was overrun with them. They came off the Internet like a virus and were causing havoc up and down the street until she helped us get them back into the Net."

"Us being you and your hob?"

Just as she had the last time the subject of the hob came up, Holly's gaze went to an empty chair near the beginning of the store's furthest aisle, only this time there was a little man sitting there, brown-faced and curly-haired. He gave Sheri a shy smile and lifted a hand in greeting.

"Oh-kay," Sheri said.

She could have sworn there was no one sitting there a moment ago and his sudden appearance made the whole world feel a little off-kilter. She'd only *just* gotten used to little men who could turn into birds.

"Sheri, this is Dick Bobbins," Holly said. "Dick, this is Sheri Piper."

"I like your books," the hob said.

His compliment gave Sheri perhaps the oddest feeling that she'd had so far in all of this affair, that a fairy tale being should like *her* fairy tale books.

"Um, thank you," she managed.

"He didn't appear out of nowhere," Holly assured her, undoubtedly in response to the look on Sheri's face. "Hobs have this ability to be so still that we don't notice them unless they want us to."

"I knew that."

Holly grinned. "Sure you did."

"Okay, I didn't. But it makes sense in a magical nothing-really-makes-sense sort of a way. Kind of like birds turning into Littles, and vice versa."

"So was Meran able to help you?"

The hob leaned forward in his chair, obviously as interested as Holly was.

Sheri nodded and told them about how it had gone.

"I understand why you didn't let Meran's magic bring you the right guy," Holly said when she was done. "I mean, after all. You *were* calling it up for the Littles. What I don't understand is, why didn't you use the wish they offered you?"

"Because it's something for nothing. It's like putting a love spell on someone. Isn't it better to get to know someone at a natural pace, work out the pushes and pulls of the relationship to make it stronger, instead of having it all handed to you on a platter?"

"I suppose. But what if you never meet the right guy?"

"That's the risk I have to take."

So here I am, still waiting like an idiot on the man of my dreams.

I don't know which bugs me more: that he hasn't shown up yet, or that I'm still waiting.

But I got to do a good turn and my picture book is done. Meran loved the paintings I did of her as the forest queen. Her husband even bought one of the originals once I'd gotten the color transparencies made.

What else? I've got a new friend who's a hob and at least once a week Jenky Wood flies up to my windowsill in the shape of a bird, tapping on my windowpane until I let him in. I've got my Barbie furniture permanently set up for him on a shelf in my studio, though I have repainted it in more subdued colors.

So what am I saying?

I don't know. That we all have ups and downs, I guess, whether we bring them on ourselves, or they come courtesy of the Fates. The trick seems to be to roll with them. Learn something from the hard times, appreciate the good.

I didn't really need fairy encounters to teach me that, but I wouldn't trade the experience of them for anything. Not even for that elusive, perfect man.

Sign Here

1

"**You'll never guess who came over** last night."

"You're right. I won't."

"Come on. You could at least try."

"Why do you want me to work for this? Just tell me already."

"It was Brenda."

"Bullshit."

"I'm serious."

"I thought she dumped you."

"No way. *I* dumped her. Nobody ever dumps me."

"Whatever. So what did she want?"

"Cheap sex."

"Now it really is bullshit."

"I'm kidding. She wants us to get back together."

"What did you say?"

"What do you mean?"

"Are you getting back together? Maybe you dumped her, but you're always talking about her."

"She was a great kisser."

"But?"

"No buts. I just don't know. I didn't say yes or no."

"So what did you do?"

"Nothing. We just talked."

"About getting back together."

"No. More about what we've been doing, old times, stuff like that. We must've been up until almost three."

"And then you had sex."

"No. Then she kissed me good night and went home."

"Still a good kisser?"

"She was always the best. We're supposed to get together again tonight."

"So it's semi-serious."

"I don't know what it is."

"You know what I did last night?"

"Jumped your own bones?"

"Oh, very funny. No, I met this guy in the Crossroads Bar and he showed me this trick. Look at this."

"How'd you do that?"

"I figure it's mostly a mental thing."

"What, like, you only hypnotized me into seeing it?"

"No, the flame's real. Good trick, isn't it? Be a great way to pick up a girl in a bar—just light her cigarette with a snap of your fingers."

"How'd you do it really?"

"It's this way of, I don't know. Seeing things differently. Like, you can actually see the molecules of the air and you just kind of convince them to be something other than what they are. Apparently, when you get good at it, you can do it with anything, and not just a tiny flame like this. But air to fire's supposed to be one of the easier ones so that's why he started me out with it."

"And he just showed it to you, out of the blue."

"Pretty much. He said he's been looking for someone to teach all this stuff he knows to and I looked like the right kind of guy. He said I was 'receptive.'"

"More like gullible."

"Hey, this is real."

"Let me—ow!"

"I told you."

"So what's he get out of it?"

"Nothing, really."

"Come on. He's got to want something."

"Well, he had me sign this piece of paper . . ."

"Jesus, what did you sign away?"

"My soul."

"Get real."

"That's all it said. He gets it when I die."

"This is too weird."

"Don't go all Catholic on me. I don't believe in souls and neither do you. Hell, when was the last time you were in a church?"

"Yeah, but think about it. That was based on limited knowledge."

"What are you talking about?"

"Well, souls are kind of like magic, right? And this trick the guy showed you is like magic."

"So."

"So if one kind of magic can be real, maybe other kinds can, too. Maybe we do have souls."

"You think?"

"Well, I'm leaning more to the affirmative right now."

"I've screwed myself, haven't I?"

"I guess it depends. What did he look like?"

"I don't know. Kind of normal."

"No horns—no tail?"

"Oh, for Christ's sake."

"You're the one he taught to make a flame by snapping your fingers."

"That's real."

"I know it's real. I saw it."

"I guess he looked kind of like Elvis, circa the Vegas years, only older."

"Elvis."

"Not exactly like him. More like Harvey Keitel sort of playing him in that movie we rented a while ago."

"*Finding Graceland?*"

"Yeah, that's the one."

"And you just up and traded him your soul to be able to light smokes for women in bars without using matches or a lighter."

"I don't own a lighter."

"I know you don't. I'm making a point here."

"I don't get it."

"The point is, how stupid can you be?"

"Hey, he's going to teach me other stuff. I'm going to be his protégé."

"Until you die and he gets your soul."

"Something like that. If I even have a soul."

"The more I think about it, the more I'm betting we do. I mean, why else would the guy ask you to sign it over to him? But the difference between you and me is, I still own mine."

"I am so screwed."

"Maybe, maybe not. We're smart guys. Maybe we can figure a way out of this. Hell, maybe we can even come out ahead."

"I'd settle on having my soul back."

"It's not gone yet."

"You know what I mean."

"Let me think on this."

2

"So did you ask him how to live forever?"

"Yeah. He said, if I can't figure it out for myself, then I don't deserve to know. But he showed me another good trick. All I have to do is concentrate, sort of like you do with the air molecules, except this is with molecules of time."

"I don't get it."

"It lets you predict the future."

"Get out of here."

"No, really. But it's a bitch. I can only look ten seconds or so ahead and it gives me a headache that makes a hangover feel good. But it's like the other thing, he said. The more I practice, the easier it'll get and the further ahead I can see."

"So you could predict lotteries and horse races and all kinds of crap."

"I guess."

"Did you get a name from this guy?"

"He said I could call him Mr. Parker."

"Meaning, it's not really his name. That's just all he'll give you."

"I guess."

"Well, I've figured out the living forever bit."

"Bullshit."

"No, he was right. It's pretty simple, really. Here. Look at these."

"What are these?"

"Souls."

"How'd you get them?"

"Well, I figured I'd try buying them. So I went into Your Second Home and kept offering the losers drinking in there five bucks if they'd sign over their soul to me. You'd be surprised at how many people who swear they don't believe in God will balk at signing over their soul, but I got a few takers."

"Yeah, well, I wish I'd been smart enough not to sign away mine."

"Doesn't matter now. You've got these."

"I don't get how it works."

"I don't either. Not yet. But there's got to be a reason your Mr. Parker wanted your soul, and I figure this has to be it. You must be able to use the souls you acquire to prolong your own life. And if you don't die, then he doesn't get yours."

"I don't know."

"Just take them. Ask him if you can trade for yours. Only don't offer them all at once."

"I won't."

3

"So how'd it go?"

"He didn't want them. He says there's varying grades of souls. The ones you got are only worth a year or so because the people that signed them over don't really care about their lives anymore."

"He could tell that just by looking at pieces of paper?"

"Apparently. He says you need higher quality ones to buy you a decent amount of time."

"But we're on the right track."

"I suppose. But it doesn't feel right."

"What doesn't?"

"Trading people's souls like this."

"Hey, they didn't have to sign them away."

"But they didn't know."

"So what are you saying? I should give them back?"

"I don't know. It's just . . . after signing away my own I can feel for them."

"I was just trying to help."

"I know. And I appreciate it."

"So what did he teach you today?"

"Nothing new. He just showed me some meditation techniques to make it easier for me to narrow my focus. You know, so that when I practice, it's more productive."

"Figures. He's already got you hooked."

"It's not what you're thinking. Maybe he conned me with the soul business, but the rest of what he's showing me's on the level. Here, look how hot I can make this flame."

"Jesus, it's like a tiny blowtorch."

"Cool, huh?"

"Sure, if you ever want to weld anything really, really small, I guess."

4

"Mr. Parker?"

"Yes?"

"My name's Robert Chaplin."

"Oh, yes. Peter's friend. The one who's trying to help him break his deal with the devil."

"*Are* you the devil?"

"The devil is rather a recent conceit. I'm much older than that."

"Which doesn't really answer my question."

"It's not really relevant. Was that all you wanted to know?"

"No. I . . . this stuff you're teaching Peter. Is it all just going to be parlor tricks?"

"What I've taught him, and will teach him, are hardly tricks. They are lessons that will help him to understand the underpinnings of the world. The more proficiency he gains, both in understanding the makings of the world and in manipulating them, the closer he will come to achieving the potential I see inside him."

"Unless he dies first."

"Everyone dies, Mr. Chaplin. Everything has an expiry date."

"Except for you."

"Even me. I'm long-lived, not immortal."

"So why Peter?"

"He has a bright fire in his soul. He has so much potential."

"But what's that to you?"

"I like to help people."

"By stealing their souls."

"That isn't how I'd phrase it."

"Then how would you phrase it?"

"I'm bound to help others. It's . . . part of the bargain I made."

"Of course. You had to make a bargain, too. Who'd you sell your soul to?"

"What exactly is it that you want from me, Mr. Chaplin?"

"Can you teach me?"

"Teach you what?"

"Everything."

"That depends. What can you give me in return?"

"I guess I've only got one thing you want."

"If you're referring to your soul, I'm afraid not. Even knowing you have it, does not make you value it any more than you did before you gained that knowledge."

"And Peter did? Valued his soul, I mean?"

"He did, indeed."

"He didn't believe any more than I did."

"I assume that's simply what he led you to believe. Your friend has hidden depths that it appears he never shared with you."

"Whatever. So I'm out of the loop."

"Not necessarily. Offer me the soul of someone who values what they have and perhaps we can do business."

"And once it's accepted, the contract can't be broken?"

"Not so long as both parties adhere to its conditions."

5

"I've got this weird idea, Brenda."

"What's that?"

"Well, things didn't work out so well before, did they? Between us, I mean."

"I don't blame you. Neither of us was pulling our weight. It takes two to make a relationship work."

"I know that. But I was just thinking . . . if we're really going to try to make it work this time, maybe we should, I don't know, put it all down in writing. Make it official."

"You want to get married?"

"Not this minute or anything, but that's certainly something to work toward. For now I was thinking more of a kind of contract— something to show that we're taking all of this seriously."

"A contract."

"Yeah. We each write down what we're putting into this and what we expect from the other person. We keep it simple."

"How do you think that will change things?"

"I don't know. It'll be a commitment in black and white. Something we can reread if we start to get frustrated or antsy. To remind us of how we really feel so that we don't say or do anything stupid."

"Like writing our own wedding vows."

"Sort of. Except this would be more our relationship vows."

"You're right, it is weird."

"Yeah, I thought it was. Too weird, right?"

"No. I actually like the fact that you're taking the time to think about this sort of thing."

6

"This is really nice."

"Thanks. But I can see I got a little long-winded, now that I'm reading yours."

"It's not about the length, Brenda. It's about what we mean."

"But you were able to put it so succinctly. 'If you give me your soul, I will always honor, cherish and respect you.' That's beautiful."

"Thanks."

"Only why do you say 'soul' instead of 'heart'?"

"I don't know. Heart didn't seem to encompass everything that we should be giving to each other."

"You know, I never saw this side of you before."

"I've had a lot of time to reflect since we broke up. Is it something you can sign? I can certainly sign yours."

"Hand me the pen."

7

"So? What do you think, Mr. Parker?"

"She has an extraordinary spirit. Strong and true and full of grace."

"You can tell that just by holding the paper up to your face and smelling it?"

"Hardly. But her essence permeates the paper. I was simply admiring its potency."

"That good, huh? Well, she always was a looker and she kisses like you wouldn't believe—though I guess you wouldn't be into that kind of thing."

"Let's just say I'm selective. I certainly appreciate your bringing her to my attention."

"Well, I know the best way for you to show that appreciation."

"I'm sure you do, Mr. Chaplin."

"So, do we have a deal? Her soul for what you can teach me?"

"I think an agreement can be made."

"Great. So where do we start? With the little flame business, or can we cut right to the living forever trick?"

"Patience, please. You haven't simply dialed an 800 number."

"Hey, I delivered. I expect you to do the same."

"And so I will. But first I need you to go home and reflect on your place in the world—where you are now and where you would wish to be in, oh, let's say start with five years from now."

"What for?"

"Then when you return to me we will have a better understanding of how to begin your education."

"That's not how it worked with Peter. You just started right in on showing him stuff."

"Indeed I did. But each of us is different, and so the paths we need to take to reach the same goal can also be very different. Peter doesn't jump into a new thing, so the best way to begin with him was by doing just that. You, on the other hand, are already an impetuous individual. So for you, we need to balance that higher energy with elements of a quieter meditative process. It all has to do with balance."

"So I just think about who I am, what I want?"

"Indeed."

"Okay. I guess I can live with that. Only tell me this. It's not all going to be this mumbo jumbo, right? You're going to show me something practical, too."

"I believe, Mr. Chaplin, that you will find that I can be the most practical of men."

8

"I can't believe you did that, man."

"Did what?"

"Tried to trade off Brenda's soul to Mr. Parker."

"Oh, please. What the hell was she doing with it?"

"You just don't get it, do you?"

"What's to get?"

"It's not about taking people's souls and using them to live longer yourself. It's about giving. It's only by helping other souls reach their full potential that your own lifetime is extended."

"Is that what Parker told you?"

"He didn't have to. I've been working on those meditative exercises he gave me and damned if I'm not starting to see connections between everything. There's not a thing we say or do that doesn't have repercussions. The smallest kindness can blossom into an age of renaissance while one cruel deed can bring down an empire."

"Jesus, did he see you coming or what."

"Yeah, I think he did. But not the way you think. I'm honored that he felt I already had such potential."

"And what about his not taking the souls of all those losers I offered him because they'd only give him a year or so more of life?"

"It's because they require too much work, Robert. There are so many people in the world that it's better to work with those that have the higher potential because if you can win them over, then they'll start doing the work, too."

"Work, work—what the hell are you talking about?"

"An enlightened world where everyone takes care of each other and the planet they live on."

"Right. That's why he was so happy when I traded him Brenda's soul."

"You didn't trade her soul. It wasn't yours to trade."

"Bullshit. I handed it over to him, signed and delivered."

"You're missing the point. If you don't keep up your side of the bargain, then the contract is void."

"I haven't had time to keep up my side."

"You had time enough to try to trade her soul."

"Then why was he so happy to get it?"

"He wasn't happy about that. He was happy because she's such an advanced soul. Waking her up to her full potential will take a fraction of the time it would normally take with others."

"Like you?"

"Sure, like me. I'm not ashamed to say I've got a ways to go. But at least I'm on the road."

"And I'm not?"

"I don't know what you are, Robert. I guess I never did. You're a hell of a lot darker than I could ever have guessed. I mean, what do you even care about, besides yourself?"

"Wait a minute here. If Parker's helping people, why does he need them to sign over his soul to them?"

"It's just to make a connection. A powerful connection. Yeah, it's sort of freaky when you realize that you really do have a soul and you've just signed it away. But the more you work at what he gives you, the quicker you come to understand that he couldn't possibly keep it. If he did, he wouldn't advance any more. He wouldn't be able to help other people anymore."

"This is such a load of crap."

"Let me tell you about this thing I found, Robert. It's a void. You know, a place where none of your senses can come into play because there's nothing there for them to sense."

"Am I supposed to be listening to this?"

"There's a place like that inside each one of us. I think it's where we go when we need to mend, like when you go into a coma."

"And your point is?"

"I think you need to go there. Not just because you're hurting yourself, but because you're hurting others."

"Hey, keep back."

"I'm not going to hit you. I'm just going to touch you—here."

"Where . . . what the hell did you do? I can't see anything . . ."

"Mr. Parker says that sight goes first, hearing last."

"I'm going to kill you, you—"

"You're not going to do anything. You're not going anywhere."

"Christ, I can't feel anything. Don't do this to me, Peter."

". . ."

"Peter."

". . ."

"Come on. Quit screwing around."

". . ."

"I'm not a bad guy."

". . ."

"Peter?"

". . ."

"Oh, Jesus. Anybody . . . ?"

Seven Wild Sisters

"It's a long lane that never has no turns."
—Arie Carpenter

Spirits in the Woods

There's those that call it ginseng, but 'round here we just call it 'sang. Don't know which is right. All I know for sure is that bees and 'sang don't mix, leastways not in these hills.

Their rivalry's got something to do with sweetness and light and wildflower pollen set against dark rooty things that live deep in the forest dirt. That's why bee spirits'll lead the 'sang poachers to those hidden 'sang beds. It's an unkindness you'd expect more from the Mean Fairy—you know, the way he shows up at parties after the work's all done. He's happy as all get out, flirting around and drinking and playing music, but then he can just turn no account mean, especially when he has a woman alone.

What's that?

'Course there's spirits in the hills. How could there not be? You think we're alone in this world? We have us a very peopled woods, girl, and I've seen all kinds in my time, big and small.

The Father of Cats haunts these hills. Most times he's this big old panther, sleek and black, but the Kickaha say he can look like a handsome, black-haired man, the fancy takes him. I only ever saw him as a panther. Seeing yourself a panther is unusual enough, though I suppose it's something anybody who spends enough time in these woods can eventually claim. But I heard him talk.

Don't you smile, girl. I don't tell lies.

Then there's the Green Boy—you want to watch out for him. He lives in the branches of trees and he's got him this great big smile because he's everybody's friend, that's a certain fact. He loves company, loves to joke and tell stories, but one day with him is like a year for everybody else you left behind.

See, some places, you've got to be careful on how the time passes. There's caves 'round these parts that can take you right out of this world and into another, but the days go by slower there, like they did for Rip van Winkle. I met an artist once, he was gone twenty years in this world, but only a few days had passed for him on the other side.

What happened? He went back. That's another caution you need to heed. Places like that can take a powerful hold of you, make you feel like everything in your life is empty because you're not breathing magic.

There's wonders, no question, but there's danger, too, and that's not the only one. You listen to what I'm telling you.

Old Bubba's been seen more than once in these parts, but you stay wide clear of him. I know there's some have said they got the better of that old devil man, but if you bargain with him, I believe you'll carry a piece of his darkness inside you way into forever, doesn't matter that you got the best of him.

And you meet a blacksmith in these woods, you stay clear of him, too, I don't care how honey-sweet his voice is or what nice things he might be telling you. He's just waiting for pretty girls like you. He takes them back into the fairy mound and once you're there, no one's ever going to see you again.

I suppose the one I know best is the Apple Tree Man, lives in the oldest tree of the orchard. Do you know that old song?

Jimmy had a penny,
he put it in a can;
he give it to the night
and the Apple Tree Man
Singing, pour me a cider,
like I never had me one.
Pour me a cider,
give everybody some.

I've known him since I was younger than you, but he hasn't changed much in all those years. He's still the same wrinkled, gnarly old fellow he was the first time I met him. The time is right, maybe I'll introduce the two of you.

Fairies? Oh, I've seen them, all right. Not every day, but I know they're out there. First time, I was just a little girl. They were these little foxfire lights, dancing out there in the field like flickerbugs. It wasn't any snakebit fever that let me see them, though I did have the venom in me from a bite I got earlier in the day. I could have died, lit a shuck right out of this world and there's me, no more than twelve years old, but the Apple Tree Man drew the poison right out of me with a madstone soaked in milk. Him and the Father of Cats, they saved my life, though only the Father of Cats wanted payment, so I owe him a favor. If I can't pay it when he comes asking, then one of my descendants has to. Trouble is, I never had any children. I'm the last of this line of Kindreds, so far as I know.

Anywise, instead of dying, I got me a big piece of magic that night. It was hard to hang onto for a time, but I know no matter what else I experience in this world, scraps and pieces of that magic'll be with me forever. I don't question that.

You get on in years and it can be hard for a body to tell a difference between things that happened and things you thought might have happened, but I know better. There's a veil, thin as a funeral shroud, that divides this world from some other. You do it right and you can walk on either side of it. The world you find on one side or the other, the people you meet, they're all real.

I reckon it's been seventy years, maybe longer, since the Father of Cats came out of the forest and made me beholden to him. I'm getting on in years now. I'm not saying my time is come, but it's getting there. Year by year. And I guess I'd just like to see him again. Pay my debt before it's time for me to move on.

2

Sarah Jane Dillard didn't think the old woman was crazy, though most everybody else did. Folks liked her well enough—they'd pass the time with her when she came into town and all—but what else could you think about a woman in her eighties, living alone on a mountaintop, an hour's walk in from the county road?

It wasn't like she was a granny woman who needed her solitude. She had her herbs and simples, and she'd be the first to lend a hand, somebody needed help, but she wasn't known in these parts for cures and midwifery like the Welch women were. She was just an old woman, kept herself to herself. Not unfriendly, but not looking to step into social circles any time soon either.

"What does she *do* up there, all on her own?" someone or other would ask from time to time.

They might not know, but Sarah Jane did.

Aunt Lillian lived the same now as she had since she was a child. She had no phone, no electricity, no running water. The only food she bought was what she couldn't grow herself, or gather from the woods around her.

So most of her time was taken up with the basic tasks of eking out a living from her land and the forest. It took a lot of hours in a day to see after her gardens, the cow and chickens, the orchard and hives. To go into the woods in season to gather greens and herbs, nuts and berries and 'sang. There was water needed to be carried in from the springhouse, a woodbox to be filled, and any number of other day-to-day chores that needed doing.

It wasn't so much a question of what she did, as there hardly being the time in a day to get it all done.

"But don't you find it hard?" Sarah Jane had asked her once. "Keeping up with it all?"

Aunt Lillian smiled. "Hard's being confined to a sick bed like some my age are," she said. "Hard's not having your health and being able to look after yourself. What I do . . . it's just living, girl."

"But you could buy your food instead of having to work so hard at growing it."

"Sure, I could. But I'd have to have me the money to do that. And to get the money, well, I'd have to work just as hard at something else, except it wouldn't necessarily be as pleasing to my soul."

"You find weeding a garden pleasing?"

"You should try it, girl. You might be surprised."

*   *   *

The trail to Aunt Lillian's house started in the pasture beside the Welchs' farm, then took a winding route up into the hills, traveling alongside the creek as it flowed down the length of the hollow.

In spring, the creek grew swollen, the water tumbling over stone staircases, overflowing pools and running quickly along the narrows, until it finally reached the pasture where it dove under the county road before continuing on its way. By fall, the creek was reduced to a trickle, though it never dried up completely. There were always a few deep pools even in the hottest months of the summer, home to fish, spring peepers and deep-throated bullfrogs, and perfect for a cool dip on a sweltering day.

Tall, sprucey-pine grew on either side of the trail, sharing the steep slopes of the hollow with yellow birch, oak and beech. Under them was a thick shrub layer of rhododendrons and mountain laurel. Higher up, tuliptrees and more sprucey-pine rose on either side with a thick understory of redbud, magnolia and dogwood. Even with her yellow hound Root at her side, Sarah Jane had seen deer, fox, hares, raccoons and possum, not to mention the endless chorus of birds and squirrels scolding all intruders from the safety of the trees—when they weren't occupied with their own business, that is.

The walk through these woods, with the conversation of the creek as constant company, was something Sarah Jane quickly grew to love. It didn't matter if she was just ambling along with Root, or pulling Aunt Lillian's cart—fetching the supplies that were dropped off for Aunt Lillian at the Welchs' farm, or bringing them back to her old house up in the hills.

Sarah Jane's own family lived next door to the Welchs on what everybody still called the old Shaffer farm. Though they'd been living there for the better part of ten years now, and her grandparents for five years before that, she'd become resigned to knowing that it would probably never be called the Dillard farm.

They'd moved here from Hazard after her father died—she, her mother and her six sisters—to live with Granny Burrell, her maternal grandmother. The Burrells had bought the farm from the Shaffers a few years before Sarah Jane's family arrived and hadn't had any more luck losing the Shaffer name than they did. When Granny Burrell died, she left the farm to Sarah Jane's mother and now it was home to their little clan of red-haired, independent-thinking women.

"If you weren't so bullish," Granny Burrell would say, "you'd have better luck getting another father for those wayward girls of yours."

"Maybe they don't want another father," Sherry Dillard would tell her mother. "And I sure plan to be choosy about the next man I have in my life. I'd just as soon have none, than get me one that won't match up to my Jimmy."

"You're going to ruin your life."

"Least it's my life," their mother would say, an unspoken reference to her brother Ulysses, who'd so badly mismanaged the investment company he'd opened that its failure left a trail of bankruptcies from one end of the county to the other.

But if their mother had a mind of her own, her daughters gave a whole new meaning to independent thinking.

Adie, named after their paternal grandmother Ada, was the eldest at nineteen. From the time she could walk, she'd always been in one kind of trouble or another, from sassing the teachers in grade school to eloping at sixteen with Johnny Garland, the two of them hightailing it out of the county on Johnny's motorcycle. She came back seven months later, unrepentant, but done with boyfriends for the time being. Her celibacy had lasted about a month, but so far she hadn't taken off again.

The twins, Laurel and Bess, were born the year after her. They were also mad about boys, but their first love was music—making it, dancing to it, anything there might be that had to do with it. They both sang, making those sweet harmonies that only sisters can. Laurel played the fiddle, Bess the banjo, and the two could be found at any barn dance or hooley within a few miles radius of the farm, kicking up their heels on the dance floor with an ever-rotating cast of partners, or playing their instruments on the stage, keeping up with the best of them. When they were home, just the two of them, they'd amuse themselves arranging pop music from the seventies and eighties into old-timey and bluegrass settings.

Sarah Jane was born two years after the twins. She was the middle child, double-named because this time her mother meant to be ready if she had another set of twins. They'd be Sarah or Jane if they were girls, Robert or William if they were boys. When she got just the one girl, she couldn't decide which of the two girl's names to pick, so she used them both.

As the middle child, Sarah Jane bridged her sisters not only in years but also in temperament. Like her older sisters, she loved to dance and run a little wild. But she also loved reading and drawing and could sit quietly with her younger sister Elsie for hours, watching the light change on the underwater stones as the creek streamed above them, or contemplating the possibility that what the crows rasped and cawed at each other might actually be some ancient hidden language that people had forgotten.

Elsie was different from her sisters in other ways. While the Dillard women before her had grown early into their women's bodies, at fifteen she still had a boyish figure. She was lean and wiry, the quietest of the girls, more so since they'd moved here. Now she spent all her time in the surrounding woods and hills, stalking anything and everything, from bugs and birds to fox and deer.

Their mother jokingly referred to Elsie as her feral daughter and that wasn't far off the mark. Elsie was always happiest out in the woods, day or night and no matter what the season. She could run as fast as a deer, but she could be almost preternaturally still, too.

Sarah Jane had never known anyone who could sit so quietly for so long. "I'm just watching the grass grow," Elsie would say when she was found in a meadow, gazing off across the wildflowers and weeds.

And finally there were Ruth and Grace, also twins. Thirteen now, they'd belied the Biblical ring of their names from the moment they came home from the hospital, working like a tag team as they insured that if they couldn't get a full night's sleep for their first two years in the world, then no one else in the household would either. No sooner would one drop off, than the other would start in crying, and there would be two fussing infants to be dealt with once more.

The older they grew, the more of a handful they became. They could never simply do a thing without first knowing the how and why of its needing to be done, and that knowing had to be explained, in great and painstaking detail. But it was better to take the time to explain else they could take a thing apart, just to see how it worked, and it might never get put back together again.

They grew up to be practical jokers, though never mean-spirited ones. And stubborn? A mule was a pushover compared to trying to shift them once they had their minds set on a thing.

Sarah Jane had known for years that some old woman lived at the end of the trail that began in the Welchs' pasture. She'd even seen her a few times, if only from a distance, which suited Sarah Jane just fine. Adie and the older twins were forever scaring the younger girls, telling them that if they weren't good, the old witch woman who lived in the hills would come and get them. She'd take them away and no one would ever see them again. She had this oven, see, big enough to hold a child trussed up like a roasting chicken . . .

For ages Sarah Jane and her younger sisters had lived in fear of her. But one summer, three years ago, when Sarah Jane was thirteen and Elsie was twelve, they dared each other to follow the trail to see where the old woman lived.

They took Root with them.

That yellow, short-haired hound of Sarah Jane's was a couple of years old at the time and full of beans, forever digging in the garden or wherever else he thought he might find a bone or a rabbit burrow, though Mama swore that he didn't need an excuse. Root was just a dog that was happy digging.

"It's your own fault," she'd tell Sarah Jane. "Giving him such a name."

How she got that dog was a whole other story, in and of itself.

She was lying abed one night the fall before, watching the shadow branches of the beech tree outside her window slowly make their way across the ceiling of her room, cast by the moon as it made its own journey across the night sky. She hadn't been able to sleep, but she didn't know why. Her head was filled with everything and nothing—a fairly common occurrence, really.

She heard the dog start to cry an hour or so after midnight—a distant whining that occasionally broke into louder barking. At first she thought that one of the neighbors had gotten a new pet and had either left it home alone, or put it out on a chain for its first night out. There was that desperation in its voice that dogs do so well and sometimes made her believe the theory that they live entirely in the present with no recollection of the past, no hopes for the future. This dog had been put out and so far as it could see, that was where it had to be for the rest of its life.

But as she lay there, alternately dozing and waking up when the cries got louder, she got to thinking about what if the dog was really in trouble. It might have broken loose from somewhere and gotten its chain wrapped around a tree or something. It had happened before and not so far from here. She'd overheard George Welch telling her mother about finding the bones of a dog one spring, how it had still been wearing a collar, its lead entangled in the roots of a tree.

"That was a hard death," she remembered him saying. "I wouldn't wish it on anyone, man or critter."

Sighing, she threw back the comforter and sat up. The floor was icy on her bare feet as she padded across the room to where she'd left her clothes on a chair. Elsie began to stir as Sarah Jane was getting dressed.

"Whatcha . . . doing . . . ?" Elsie asked, her voice thick with sleep.

"Nothing," Sarah Jane told her. "I'm just going to get a little air."

"But . . . it's the middle of the night . . ." Elsie murmured.

Like she herself hadn't been out and about in the woods in the middle of the night a hundred times before, looking for owls and bats and who knew what.

"Go to sleep," Sarah Jane said.

She thought Elsie might protest—after all, this was a midnight excursion into her beloved woods—but she'd already fallen back to sleep before Sarah Jane finished dressing and left the room.

Downstairs she put some biscuits in her pocket, got a length of rope from the shed, and went out into the fall night with a lantern that she didn't bother to light. The moonlight was enough. Once she'd closed the door behind her, she stood quietly for a long moment and tilted her face up to the sky, drinking in the stars, the dark, the wind.

Then she heard the dog again.

It took her a moment to decide where the sound was coming from—it was always tricky with a wind—then she started across the back fields and into the woods, going right up the mountain.

It didn't take her long to find the dog, trapped as it was. He had a rope around his neck, the loose end of which had gotten caught in some old barbed wire. By the time she reached him, he was so entangled that his head was pressed right against the old fence post. A barb from the wire was pricking him just above his eye and there was blood on his fur.

She approached quietly, speaking in a low and comforting voice. When she was close enough, she put out her hand so that he could smell her. She wasn't exactly nervous, but you never could tell. When he gave her hand a little lick, she gave up all pretense at caution.

He lay still while she worked the rope loose, wishing she'd brought a knife. Before she had him completely free, she made a noose with the rope she'd brought and slipped it over his neck. When she got the last of the old rope untangled, the dog stood up on trembling legs and leaned against her. He looked up at her, his eyes big in the moonlight.

"Now who do you belong to?" she asked ruffling the short hair between his ears.

He bumped his head against her. She smiled and brought him home, taking him right up into her room. After the night he'd had, she couldn't bear the idea of tying him up outside or locking him in a shed. He lay down on the floor beside her bed. As soon as she got under the covers, he was up on the bed with her, stretched out along her side.

Mama was going to kill her, she remembered thinking before she fell asleep with her hand on his chest.

When she woke, he was lying on the floor, and that was how Mama found them. She always felt that he'd done that on purpose, just to get on Mama's good side. And it had worked, once Sarah Jane told her story.

"You can keep him till we find who he belongs to," Mama said.

"Maybe we never will," Elsie said, her face hopeful.

All her sisters had immediately fallen in love with him.

"A dog that good-natured has to have someone who loves him," Mama replied.

"He does," Sarah Jane said. "He has us."

"You know what I mean."

Sarah Jane nodded.

But no one knew whose he was. No one came to claim him. And by the time the snows came, he and Sarah Jane were inseparable. He couldn't come to school with her, but wherever else she went, he was usually somewhere nearby. And best of all, he made Mama feel safer about when she or Elsie went wandering in the woods like they were doing now.

So with Root ranging ahead of them on the trail, or crashing through the underbrush on one side or the other, the two girls followed the well-worn path into the hills, walking arm in arm.

Sarah Jane felt brave enough with the company. But then Root took off and halfway to the old woman's cabin Elsie got intrigued by a hornet nest and insisted on studying it for a time. Sarah Jane was scared of bees and hornets, ever since a classmate of hers got stung to death last summer. It was an allergic reaction, she'd heard at the funeral, but she couldn't shake the thought that it could happen to anybody—like getting bit by a snake. So the last thing she wanted to do was stand around looking at that great big papery gray nest hanging from the branch of a small laurel. And that was the thing—how could such a slender branch support such a big nest anyway? There was just something not right about it.

"Come on, Elsie," she said. "What happened to our adventure?"

"I need to see this," Elsie said.

Her voice was distracted and Sarah Jane could tell that she was already in what Adie called full Indian scout mode. When she got like this, you could set off a firecracker under her feet and she wouldn't notice.

"You go on ahead," Elsie added.

Go on by herself?

Sarah Jane looked up the trail. The sun was breaking through the trees in cathedraling beams and it was pretty as all get out, but looks could be deceiving. Especially when you knew the trail ended at a witch's house. Except she didn't have to actually talk to the witch, she reminded herself. She could just go close enough to have a look at her house and then come back. That wouldn't be so hard. And it sure beat staring at that gray paper wasp's nest, waiting to get stung.

So on she went, but more slowly now, because nothing felt quite the same anymore. It might only be her imagination, but the shafts of sunlight didn't seem to penetrate the canopy as brightly as they had before and the woods felt darker. The sound of the squirrels as they rustled through the leaves was magnified so that she thought she heard much larger shapes moving about, just out of sight. Bears. Panthers. Wolves.

Her heart beat far too quickly.

Stop it, she thought. You're just scaring yourself.

She looked back and saw Elsie scrunched up in the small space between a bush and a hemlock, happily contemplating the wasp's nest, oblivious to any danger, either from wasps or whatever else might be in the woods, hungry to have itself a bite of a teenaged girl.

I'm not scared of these woods, she thought, trying to convince herself that she actually believed it. There was nothing here that was going to hurt her so long as she kept out of its way, and that included witches. She could go and spy on her just like Elsie was spying on those wasps. It was a time to be cautious, yes. But not scared.

So she squared her shoulders and set off again, whistling for Root. She wasn't ready to admit it just then, having already convinced herself that she could be brave all on her own, but she felt a great sense of relief when the dog came bounding down the hillside and skidded to a stop beside her. He mooshed his head against her leg, tongue lolling, gaze turned up to her face and plainly asking, "Where are my pats?"

"Yes, yes," she told him as she ruffled his short fur with both her hands. "You're my good boy."

Dog at her heel, she proceeded along the path, giving Root a soft call back every time he looked to go off exploring. And that was how she finally crept up on Aunt Lillian's homestead, back in the hills.

Aunt Lillian wasn't doing any sort of witchy things when Sarah Jane finally left the path and crept through the bushes to spy on her. Not unless tending garden had some witchy significance that Sarah Jane didn't know anything about. In fact, nothing about the old woman's homestead seemed to have anything to do with the grisly business of being a witch—or at least Sarah Jane's imagining of what a witch would be like and where she'd live.

There was no aura of evil and dread. No children's bones dangling from the trees. No strange and noxious liquids bubbling in cauldrons—unless those were hidden in the house. No capering goblins or familiars or other unholy consorts.

With a warning hand on Root's head to keep him quiet, she settled down in the bushes and studied the old woman's homestead. Closest to her was the garden where Aunt Lillian was weeding her vegetables, using a hoe that was no different from the one Sarah Jane used on their own garden back home. To the right, rising up the slope, was an apple orchard and several beehives. A clapboard house with a tin roof, corn crib and front porch stood on the far side of the garden, surrounded by a gaggle of hangers-on: a wood pile, a chicken house, a smoking shed, a springhouse, and various storage sheds. On the far side of the house and a little to the left, she could make out the roof of a small barn and what looked to be a cornfield, the young stalks no more than a foot high at the moment. The woods pressed close on the far side of the barn and along the edges of the orchard.

It all looked so normal. Just as the old woman did, hoeing her garden.

Sarah Jane was so caught up on trying to find some hidden, shadowy meaning to Aunt Lillian's work, that when the old woman suddenly started to speak, she thought her heart would simply stop in her chest. The old woman didn't look directly at her, but it soon became obvious that she knew Sarah Jane was there.

"Now the way I see it," Aunt Lillian said, "is there are only two reasons a body would hide in the bushes to spy on someone. Either they mean them harm, or they're too shy to say hello hello and spend their time skulking around in the bushes instead. I wonder which you are, girl."

Sarah Jane held herself stiller than she ever had before, her fingers tightening their pressure on Root's head until he began to squirm a little. But it was no use. The old woman knew she was there as surely as Sarah Jane's mother could spot a lie. She wasn't even looking in Sarah Jane's direction, but it was plain as plain could be who she was talking to.

" 'Course I'm hoping you're just shy," Aunt Lillian went on, "as I wouldn't be minding me someone to talk to every once in a while. I'm not saying I get lonely, living up here on my ownsome the way I do, but everybody enjoys a spot of company—maybe a lending hand with a strong young back to put behind it."

She didn't sound so awful, Sarah Jane thought. She didn't sound like her older sisters' stories at all.

Swallowing her fear, Sarah Jane slowly rose from the bushes. She and the old woman looked at each other for a long moment, the woman patient, Sarah Jane not sure what she should say or do. Root broke the silence. Freed of Sarah Jane's hand, he bounded out of the bushes.

"Shoo!" Aunt Lillian said. "Get out of my greens, you big lug!"

To Sarah Jane's surprise, Root stopped dead in his tracks and carefully backed out of the garden.

"How'd you do that?" she asked. "It takes me forever just to get his attention long enough to make him stop digging or whatever."

The answer came to her even while she was speaking: magic. The old lady was a witch woman. Of course she could make an animal do what she wanted it to.

She wished she'd never asked the question, but Aunt Lillian only smiled.

"He has to know you mean business," she said. "That's all. Dog's like a man. He doesn't think you're serious, he'll just carry right on with whatever mischief he's getting himself into." She cocked her head and winked. " 'Course you've still got a few years to go before you need to be worrying about men."

"I know all about men."

"Do you now?"

"Sure. I've got three older sisters. Adie says they only ever want one thing."

"What's that?"

"Sex."

Aunt Lillian nodded. "I suppose most of them do. You want some lemonade, girl?"

"Sure. My name's Sarah Jane."

"I'm guessing you'll be one of the Dillard girls—the ones living on the old Shaffer farm."

Sarah Jane shook her head. "No, it's the Dillard farm," she tried.

Aunt Lillian smiled again. "I'm Lily Kindred, but everybody calls me Aunt Lillian."

"Why do they do that?"

"Same reason some folks ask a lot of questions, I guess, and that's a different reason for each person. Now how about that lemonade?"

Sarah Jane followed the old woman back to her house. She sat on the steps of the porch with Root while Aunt Lillian went inside. Though the house itself was shaded by a beech tree on one side and a pair of old oaks on the other, there were no trees growing on the side where she was sitting. She had a fine view of the meadows that ran down the slope to the creek and watched a handful of crows playing in the air, dive-bombing each other like planes in an old war movie, until Aunt Lillian returned with a glass pitcher of lemonade. Ice clinked against the sides as she poured them each a tall glass.

"The ice house needs replenishing," Aunt Lillian said as she down beside Sarah Jane. "Reckon it's time to take a walk into town and make me a few orders."

"You really live out here all alone?"

"I do now. Used to live with my aunt, but she passed away some time ago, God rest her soul."

"Without running water or TV or anything?"

"Without anything? Girl, I've got the whole of the Lord's creation right at my front door."

"You know what I mean."

Aunt Lillian nodded. "I'm happy out here. It's where I've lived the most of my life. It's not so easy now as it was when I was younger, but I get help. Folks in town will help pack my goods up the trail and there's a fella lives deeper in the woods comes by from time to time to help me with the heavy work."

Sarah Jane couldn't imagine it.

"And what about you, girl?" Aunt Lillian said. "What brings you so far from home?"

Sarah Jane sighed.

"I guess you just forgot," she said. "My name's Sarah Jane."

She hoped she didn't sound impolite, but the way the woman kept referring to her as "girl" felt too much like someone talking about their dog or a cat.

"I didn't forget," Aunt Lillian said. "I may be a lot of things, but forgetful isn't one of them. I just don't like to be using a body's name too often. You never know who or what might be listening in."

That's when she first began to tell Sarah Jane her stories about the Apple Tree Man and the other magical creatures that peopled these hills.

3

So while Aunt Lillian wasn't really Sarah Jane's aunt, she as much became the one that Sarah Jane didn't have. After that first meeting, Sarah Jane was a regular visitor to the Kindred homestead, sometimes with one or more of her sisters in tow, but usually it was just Root and her. The old woman was happy for the company and Mama didn't seem to mind Sarah Jane neglecting some of her chores at home because she worked twice as hard for Aunt Lillian.

"She's being a good neighbor," Mama said one time when Laurel complained that, as far as she was concerned, the rest of them were doing far too many of what were supposed to be Sarah Jane's chores. "We should all be so lucky to have someone help us out when we get to Lillian Kindred's age."

But chores didn't seem like work around Aunt Lillian. There

was so much to learn—things that Sarah Jane had never even realized a curiosity about before, because there was so much about her life that she'd always taken for granted.

You wanted milk or eggs or butter? She'd always gone to the supermarket. But with Aunt Lillian you had to milk the cow, churn the butter, chase down the secret nests of the hens to find their eggs.

In the Dillard household you simply put something in the fridge to keep it cold. Aunt Lillian had an ice house that was as easy to use in the winter, but come summer you had to haul in the ice from where it was dropped off for her at the Welch farm, chipping pieces off to make ice cubes for their tea.

You didn't turn on the stove to cook. Before you could put on a single pot, you chopped wood, laid a fire in the big cast iron stove in the kitchen, started it up and waited for the heat to build.

Honey came fresh from a comb rather than a jar, though that was something Sarah Jane let Aunt Lillian harvest on her own. "You don't have to worry about my bees," Aunt Lillian assured a skeptical Sarah Jane. "I gift the spirits connected to them, so they don't sting me. It's the wild ones you need to be careful of."

Soap started with making lye by pouring water over the fireplace ashes in the ash hopper, the resulting liquid caught in an old kettle. When there was enough lye for a run of soap, it was brought to a boil, dipping a chicken feather into the solution from time to time to see if it was ready. When the lye took the fuzz off the stem of the feather, it was strong enough to make soap. At that point Aunt Lillian added fat that the Welchs had saved for her from when they killed their hogs. The lye would eventually eat the fat and become a thick, brown soap.

Aunt Lillian didn't take vitamins. Instead she made a tonic with a recipe that included ratsbane, bark from the yellow poplar, red dogwood and wild cherry, the roots of burdock, yellow dock and sarsaparilla. She boiled it all in water until the result was thick and black, then bottled it with enough whiskey added to keep it from spoiling. It tasted terrible, but Aunt Lillian took a tablespoon every day and she was never sick.

And on and on it went. Every new revelation gave Sarah Jane a deeper appreciation for all the necessities that she'd simply taken for granted before this. And then there was the satisfaction of knowing that they had this bounty from work they'd done themselves.

Food was where it really stood out in Sarah Jane's mind. Everything tasted so much better. The ice cream they made in summer was thick and creamy, bursting with flavor. Biscuits, breads, fried pies. Stews, soups, salads. Everything.

"That's because you're making it from the ground up," Aunt Lillian told her. "You know every moment of that plant's life, from when you put the seed in the dirt to its sitting on the table in front of you. It's like eating with family instead of strangers."

Sarah Jane couldn't explain to her sisters why it seemed like such a better way to live. She couldn't even remember how she'd once been as incredulous as they were now that someone could ignore a hundred years of progress that had made the simple business of living so much easier. All she could say was that she liked to do things Aunt Lillian's way. She finally understood what the term "an honest day's work" meant because after an afternoon tending to the animals and working in the garden, she just felt "righteously tired," as Aunt Lillian would put it. She would return home with a spring in her step, never mind the long day she'd put in.

And then there were the stories.

The stories.

Sarah Jane loved them all. It didn't matter if it was the simple history of some herb they were out looking for in the woods, the offhand explanation of why a strip of white cloth tied to a stake kept deer out of the garden, or the strange and tangled stories that centered around the magical neighbors that Aunt Lillian assured her lived in the woods all about them. It got so Sarah Jane *expected* to see fairies, or the Father of Cats, or *some* magical thing or other every time she made the trip through the woods, to and from Aunt Lillian's homestead.

But she never did. Not even the Apple Tree Man.

"He's a shy old fellow," Aunt Lillian explained one day when they were sitting on the porch, shucking peas. "I left biscuits under his tree every morning for more years than I can remember before he finally stepped out of the bark one day to talk to me."

"Does he still visit you?"

The old woman shook her head. "Not so much these past few years. Time was if I didn't talk to him every day, I'd at least see him crossing the meadow at dusk and we'd smile and wave to each other. But he's a funny old fellow. Gets all these notions in his head."

"Like what?" Sarah Jane wanted to know.

She was always full of questions when it came to Aunt Lillian's magical neighbors. The more she heard about them, the more she needed to know.

Aunt Lillian shrugged. "Oh, you know. 'Trouble's brewing' is a favorite of his, like there isn't always some sort of feud going on with the fairy folk. They can be as cantankerous as old Bill Widgins at the post office, ready to take offense at the slightest provocation."

"So do they fight each other?"

"You mean like with sticks and little swords and the like?"

Sarah Jane nodded.

"I suppose they might, but I've never seen it. From what I can tell, mostly they play tricks on each other. I guess the longest running feud in these hills is the one between the 'sangmen and the bee fairies. The Apple Tree Man has a song about how it all started, but

I can never remember the words. I do recall the melody, though. It's a lot like the one folks use for 'Shady Grove' these days."

"So who are the good guys?" Sarah Jane asked. "The 'sang fairies or the bee fairies?"

Aunt Lillian laughed. "There's no real good or bad when it comes to fairies, girl. Not the way we think of it. They just are, and their disagreements can be pretty much incomprehensible to the likes of you and me. The only thing I do know for sure is not to get mixed up in the middle of it. That's the one sure road to trouble."

"I wouldn't," Sarah Jane assured her.

Easy to say, sitting on the porch the way they were, shaded from the afternoon sun, sharing a pleasant task with a friend. But quite another matter, alone in the dark in the midnight woods, when the one sure thing it seemed was to choose a side or die.

Away

Sarah Jane

I was never much good in school, I don't know why. Grammar, math, geography, none of it meant all that much to me. I liked English for the stories, but I didn't take to all the rules about language. I liked history, too—more stories, only these were true—but I couldn't seem to care about what order they went in. Memorizing dates and names and such sure didn't seem to make them any better or worse than they already were.

I was sixteen and didn't know what I was ever going to do with my life. Laurel and Bess were eighteen now and they had their music. At fifteen, Elsie had her nature studies and art. The younger twins were only thirteen and not of an age where it mattered much yet. That left only Adie, at nineteen, and me, with our futures unaccounted for. I suppose you could say that Adie'd already taken on the role of the black sheep, though she hadn't done anything particularly colorful in months.

"I don't know what's going to come of you," Mama would say when I brought home another report card and none of it good.

I didn't either. Leastways, not until I met Aunt Lillian and you already know how that came about. But once I understood how there was another way a body could live than the one that seemed to lie afore me, well, I took to it like a kitten chasing a butterfly.

I guess my story really starts that year I was seventeen, the third year I went harvesting 'sang for Aunt Lillian, and maybe I should have started there. Miss Cook, my English composition teacher, says that's the way to do it. You start when the story's already underway and fit in whatever background you find yourself needing as you go along.

But I don't think that way. I like to know the long history of a thing, not just where and what it might be now, and since this is my story, I suppose I can tell it any way I like. It's not like Miss Cook's going to mark me on it.

The beginning of September is the start of 'sang season, running through to the first frost. 'Sang's one of the few things Aunt Lillian takes out of the ground that she didn't put in herself, and it's pretty much the only thing she takes to market. Most anything she needs she can grow or collect in the hills around her home, but she needs a little cash for the few items she can't, and that's where the 'sang comes in.

She never takes much, just enough for her own needs and for the few extra dollars she spends in town. I asked her about that the first time we went harvesting, me trailing after her like the big-footed, clumsy town girl I still was, her walking with the grace and quiet of a cat, though she was five times my age. And she seemed tireless, too. Like her old bones didn't know the meaning of being old.

I learned to walk like her. I learned pretty much everything I know from her.

"It doesn't pay to be greedy," she told me. "Truth is, I feel a little bad as it is, taking more than I need to pay my bills, but if I wasn't selling 'sang, I'd still be selling something, and the 'sang and me, we've come to an agreement about all of this."

I was kind of surprised when she let me go on my own that morning. It was the first time I can remember that she'd begged off on a ramble. She didn't come right out and say she was feeling too old—"Got a mess of chores to do this morning. You go on ahead, girl."—but I knew that's what it was and my heart near broke. Still I didn't say anything. Aunt Lillian was like us Dillard girls. She had her own mind about things and once it was made up, there was no shifting it. So I wasn't going to argue and say she wasn't too old. But I couldn't help remembering something Mama said earlier in the summer.

"It makes you wonder," she said as we were sitting down to breakfast. "What's she going to do when she can't make it on her own anymore?"

"She's got me," I said.

"I know, sweetheart. But you've got a life to live, too. There's going to come a point when Lily Kindred's going to need full-time care and I hate to think of her in a state-run nursing home."

"She'd die first."

Mama didn't say anything. She just nodded, standing at the stove, her back to me. I didn't say anything about how I was planning to move up to Aunt Lillian's and live there full-time once I was finished with school.

Anyway, I went out on my own that morning, leaving Root with Aunt Lillian. I love that dog but all he's got to do is see me digging and he'd be right in there, helping me out, and two shakes of a stick later the whole patch'd be dug up, and that's not the way to do it.

I had a knapsack on my back and a walking stick in hand and I made good time through the woods, heading for the north slopes where the 'sang grows best under a thick canopy of poplar and beech, maple, dogwood and oak. The ground's stony here and drains well, home to a whole mess of plants, each of them useful or just pretty. I smiled, thinking about that.

"That's got no use except to be pretty," Aunt Lillian told me once when I asked about some flower we came upon during one of our rambles. Then she grinned. "Though I guess pretty's got its own use, seeing how it makes us feel so good just to look on it."

In season, these slopes are home to all the 'sang's companion plants. Blue cohosh, baneberry and maidenhair fern. Jack-in-the-pulpit, yellow ladyslippers and trilliums. Bloodroot, false Solomon's Seal and what some call the "little brother of the 'sang": goldenseal. You find them and if the conditions are right, you could find yourself some 'sang.

Now there's a right and a wrong way to harvest 'sang.

The wrong way's to go in and just start in digging up plants with no never you mind. Stripping the area, or harvesting the first plants. You do any of that, it rankles the spirits and when you come back you won't find nothing growing but memories.

The right way's complicated, but it ensures that the spirits understand your respect for them and the patch'll keep growing. You've got to come with humility in your heart and offer up prayers before you even start in considering to dig.

I remember thinking it was funny the first time I saw Aunt Lillian doing it, this old woman making her offerings of words and smoke and tobacco to invisible presences that I wasn't entirely convinced were even there. But then she had me do it with her, the two of us saying the words, waving our smudgesticks, laying our tobacco offerings on the ground as we went through it all, once for each of the four directions, and I'll be damned if I didn't feel something.

I can't explain exactly what. A stir in the air. A warm feeling in my chest. The sure knowing that we weren't alone in that old patch, that there *were* invisible presences all around us who accepted our offerings and in return, would allow us to take some of the bounty of this place.

I looked at Aunt Lillian with big wide eyes and she just grinned.

"Start in a-digging, girl," she said. "We've got our permission. Only mind you don't take a plant until it's at least six years old."

"How can you tell?"

You ever see 'sang, growing in the wild? Ginseng, I guess some folks calls it. It doesn't grow much above a foot, a foot and a half in these hills, and has a stiff stalk holding up a pair of leaves, each leaf divided in five like the fingers on your hand and looking a bit like those you'd find on a chestnut. The little cluster of yellow-green flowers turns to red berries that drop off around the end of August. It takes a couple of years to come up from seed, slow-growing and long-lived if left alone. The roots are what gets used for medicine, but there's some that use the leaves for tea.

"See these prongs?" Aunt Lillian asked me. "Where the leaves are growing?"

I nodded.

"You only want to dig these here, with four or five prongs. They stay at a two-prong for at least two or three years, then grow into a three-prong and finally a four, if they stand long enough. We don't want to take them too young. The roots won't be that big, you see? But if we leave them stand, we can harvest them in a year or two.

This is an old patch that the poachers haven't found, so the ones we're going to take could be anywhere from six or seven years old to twenty-five."

"Where did you learn all of this?" I asked.

"Some I got from Aunt Em," she told me. "But most of this I learned from John Creek. That's his grandson Oliver I told you about before, camps up in the woods behind my place in the summer and comes down from time to time to lend me a hand with the heavy work when it's needed." She shook her head and smiled. "He was a busy man, John was. Had him sixteen daughters, plus another from his wife's first marriage."

I remember thinking then that I couldn't imagine sharing a bathroom with that many sisters, and nothing's changed since.

After harvesting, Aunt Lillian carefully washed those "green" roots and air-dried them under a shaded lean-to by the barn that she kept just for that purpose. It took maybe a month for them to dry. If you tried to heat them or dry them in the sun, they lost their potency. Once the roots were dried, Aunt Lillian boxed them up and took them into town to sell, though she always kept a few for her own tinctures and medicines.

When I got to the patch, I set down my walking stick and took off my knapsack. First thing I did was have me a long swallow of water, then I pulled out the things I'd need before I could start digging. It wasn't much. Smudgestick and matches. Dried tobacco leaves, rolled up and tied with red thread.

I was a little nervous, this being the first time I'd done this on my own, but by the time I was facing the last compass point, I was feeling, not so much confidence, but at peace. Everything seemed real quiet in the woods around me and I could sense a pressure in the air, pushing at me. Not like a wind, more like the air was leaning against me on all sides.

I laid down the last of the tobacco and picked up the smudgestick. Waving it slowly back and forth in front of me, I spoke through the smoke, talking to the spirits, honoring them the way Aunt Lillian taught me.

When I was done, I stuck the end of the smudgestick back into the ground and sat on my heels, drinking in the sensation that the prayers had left with me, this comforting feeling of being a part of something bigger than myself. I was still me, but whatever haunted this 'sang patch was letting me feel part of it as well.

Finally I reached over to my knapsack to get out the little wooden trowel I'd brought.

And froze.

I hadn't given much consideration to the little pile of sticks and moss and leaves that I'd set my knapsack down beside. But it was gone now and in its place was the strangest little creature I'd ever seen. It was a little man, I guess, if you can imagine a man that small, with roots for arms and legs, and mossy hair, skin brown as the dirt and wrinkled like cedar bark. He was maybe a foot long, dressed in some kind of mottled green and brown shirt that looked like it was made of leaves and belted at the waist. His head was heart-shaped, his features all sharp edges and angles.

He made a little moan and I started, suddenly aware that I hadn't been breathing. His eyes fluttered open, then closed again, huge saucer-shaped eyes as dark as blackberries.

It was obvious that there was something wrong with him and it wasn't hard to see what. He looked like he'd lost an argument with a porcupine as there were hundreds of little quills sticking out of his skin. I leaned closer to look at them and realized they were arrows. Tiny arrows.

I looked quickly around, expecting at any minute to be ambushed myself by a horde of little creatures with bows and arrows, but the 'sang patch was still. The little rootman and I had it to ourselves.

His eyes fluttered open again. This time they stayed open and I didn't flinch back.

"Are . . . are you okay?" I asked. Stupid question. Of course he wasn't okay. "Is there anything I can do to help you?"

"Arrows," he said.

His voice was husky and lower in timbre than I was expecting from a man the size of a small raccoon.

"Lots of them," I agreed.

"Need . . . out . . ."

I gave a slow nod. I could do that.

"Is it going to hurt you?" I asked.

"Not . . . as much as dying . . . from their venom . . ."

Great. Tiny *poisoned* arrows.

I pulled my knapsack over to me and took out the little pair of pliers I kept in it for when Root got himself a mouthful of porcupine quills. I hesitated for a moment, my hand hovering over a nearby twig, waiting for it to turn into a snake or who knows what. But it didn't, so I picked it up and held it near his mouth.

"Bite on this," I told him. "It'll help with the pain."

He made no response except to open his mouth. I swallowed quickly as I caught a glimpse of wicked looking teeth. When I put the stick in his mouth, I heard the wood crunch as he bit down on it.

I moved closer and put two fingers on either side of one of the tiny arrows, grasped its shaft with the pliers and pulled. He grunted and I heard the wood crunch again. I held the arrow up for a closer look. At least it wasn't barbed, but the tiny heads were still going to hurt as I pulled them out.

He passed out again by the time I'd gotten a dozen or so out. I felt horrible for him, but at least it let me work more quickly. I didn't have to wince in sympathy every time I pulled one out and saw the pain it caused him.

I counted the arrows as I got each one out and dropped them in a little pile on the ground by my knee. There were a hundred and thirty-seven in total.

Sitting back on my ankles, I reached forward and brushed some of the mossy hair from the little man's brow.

"What can I do now?" I asked him. "Is there someplace I can take you?"

There was no response. He was still alive—I could tell that much by the faint rise and fall of his chest—but that was it.

I didn't know what to do.

I assumed he had friends or family nearby, but though I called out for a while, no one answered. I soaked a bit of my sleeve with water from my drinking bottle and washed his brow.

I knew I couldn't just leave him here.

"Hello! Hello!" I tried one last time.

Finally I made an envelope from a folded-up piece of paper torn from the journal Elsie was trying to get me to keep and carefully scooped the arrows into it, using a twig and the little wooden trowel I'd brought along to dig up the 'sang roots. I put it and everything else in my knapsack and slipped my arms into the straps. Then, leaning my walking stick up against a beech where I'd be able to easily find it when I came back to actually harvest some 'sang, I carefully picked up the little man and started back to Aunt Lillian's.

It was a good two-hour's hike from the 'sang patch to Aunt Lillian's. The return journey should have been quicker because more of it was downhill, but because of the little man, it ended up taking me a lot longer. I felt I had to be careful not to jostle him too much so I went slower than I normally would. Root would have gone mad at my pace. Every once in a while I stopped to make sure he was still breathing, then off I'd go again, wishing I was a crow and could fly straight back instead of tramping up one steep hill and down the other.

All in all, it was a disconcerting trip. I kept expecting an attack by whatever it was that had turned the little rootman into a pincushion. No matter how much I argued against it with myself, it made too much sense that his enemies would still be out here in the woods with us somewhere.

That was nerve-wracking all on its own, as you can imagine, but then from time to time, the little man would suddenly become nothing more than a heap of sticks and roots and whatnot in my arms. The first time it happened I pretty near dropped him. The bundle of twigs and leaves cried out—more at my tightening grip than the sudden movement, I guess—and then he returned, the bird's nest of debris in my arms changing back into a little rootman.

"I'm sorry," I said, but he'd already drifted off on me again.

It was kind of funny, if you think about it. For three years I'd been desperate to see one of the fairy people from those stories Aunt Lillian was always telling me. But now that I had, I couldn't wait to get back to her house and be done with it. I just hoped she could figure a way out of this mess I'd found myself in, because I sensed that my troubles had just begun.

2

It was closer to supper than lunch by the time I finally crossed the stream and started up the hill to Aunt Lillian's house.

"Oh, girl," Aunt Lillian said as I pushed the kitchen door open with my hip and came in. "What have you got us mixed up in now?"

Root lunged up from the floor but I blocked him with my leg and laid the little man down on the kitchen table.

"It's not like I did it on purpose," I said.

Aunt Lillian took charge like I'd been hoping she would. She got a swallow or two of her tonic in between his lips and rubbed his throat to make sure it went down, then wrapped the little man in a blanket and put him in a basket near the stove. Root was exiled outside the second time he came sniffing up to the basket, hoping to get him a decent look at the rootman.

"Tell me what happened," Aunt Lillian said.

We sat on either side of the basket while I explained how I'd come to be bringing the little man to her house in the first place.

"I didn't know what else to do," I said, finishing up. "I couldn't just leave him there."

Aunt Lillian had been studying the little man while I spoke. She looked up now.

"You did the right thing," she said. Her lips twitched with a smile. "Do you know what you've got here, girl?"

I shook my head.

"A 'sangman."

"You mean he's made of 'sang?"

"No. I mean he's one of the spirits we've been paying our respects to whenever we go harvesting. Looks like you finally got your wish and stepped into your own fairy story."

"I never wanted anybody to get hurt," I said.

Aunt Lillian nodded. "Guess there's always got to be some hurt to get the story started. In my own case, I got snakebit."

I knew that one by heart, how the snake bite led to her finally meeting the Apple Tree Man and all.

"Let's have a look at those arrows," Aunt Lillian said.

I fetched the makeshift envelope from my knapsack and carefully spilled the arrows onto the top of the kitchen table. Aunt Lillian lit a lantern and brought it over. It wasn't dusk yet, but the sun was on the other side of the house, so it was dark enough to need it here. With a pair of tweezers, she picked up one of the arrows and studied it in the light.

"Lord knows I'm no expert," she said, "but I'm guessing these are bee stings."

I gave her a blank look.

"They're also called fairy shots," she explained. "These ones here are what the bee fairies use on their enemies. They don't have stingers, so they can't exactly sting the way their bees do."

"He . . . the 'sangman said they were poison."

Aunt Lillian nodded. "I'm sure they are. And a lot more dangerous for the likes of me or you than to another fairy."

"Do you think he's going to die?"

"I don't 'spect so. If he's still breathing after—how many of those arrows did you take out of him?"

"A hundred and thirty-seven."

"I think he'll pull through. I'm more worried about you."

I gave her a startled look. "Why me?"

"Because you've done the one thing we're never supposed to do with the fairies, girl. You've gone and stepped smack into the middle of one of their differences of opinion."

"Was I supposed to leave him to die?"

"Not according to the 'sangmen, I'd say. But the bee fairies'll have a whole other take on the situation. They're the ones we've got to worry about now."

I didn't want to think about that. I stood up.

"I've got to go," I said. "Can I leave the 'sangman with you?"

"You can't go now," Aunt Lillian said.

"But I never told Mama I was staying overnight and she'll be worried."

"Which do you 'spect would trouble her more? To have you stay here tonight—which I'm guessing she'll figure out pretty quick, even if she does feel like giving you a licking when you do get back home—or to have you dead?"

"De . . . dead . . . ?"

"Think about it, girl."

"But bees don't come out at night."

"No, I don't suppose they do. But we don't know that bee fairies don't. 'Sides, I need you here for when we talk to the Apple Tree Man. We need advice from someone who's got himself an inside track on such things."

My eyes went big.

"We're going to talk to the Apple Tree Man?"

Aunt Lillian smiled. "Well, we're going to try."

3

The sun had set by the time we left the house and went out into the orchard.

"No point us going out until after dark," Aunt Lillian had said earlier. "Folks like the Apple Tree Man aren't particularly partial to us seeing them in the daylight, don't ask me why. So we might as well have us a bite to eat."

There was a half moon coming up over the hill behind the house as we walked through the apple trees to the oldest one in the orchard. According to Aunt Lillian, this was the Apple Tree Man's home. Unlike the other trees, she never trimmed this one. It grew in a rough tangle of gnarly limbs, surrounded by a thorn bush that was half the height of the tree. I'd wondered about it choking the Apple Man's Tree but Aunt Lillian assured me that while we might not be able to tell the difference, he kept its growth in check.

I always like being out at night. There's a quality to moon- and starlight that makes the commonplace bigger than life, like you're seeing everything for the first time, never mind how often you've seen it before. It was no different tonight, except for the added excitement of finally having me a look at this mysterious Apple Tree Man.

We'd brought a blanket with us and I spread it on the ground while Aunt Lillian had a one-sided conversation with the tree. Anybody watching us would have thought she was just as crazy as some folks already figured she was. I guess I might have had my own questions concerning the matter if I hadn't found that little man in the 'sang patch earlier in the day.

After a while Aunt Lillian sat down on the blanket beside me, slowly easing herself down.

"I guess he's not coming," I said when we'd been sitting there a time.

I didn't know if I was disappointed or relieved.

"Maybe, maybe not," Aunt Lillian said. "It's been a while since we spoke. Could be he's just mulling over what I told him."

I wanted to ask if he really lived in the tree, if she'd really ever talked to him, but I'd always taken her stories the way she told them to me—matter-of-fact and true—and didn't want to start in on questioning her now. 'Sides, it wasn't like I could pretend this kind of thing might not be real. Not after my own adventure.

"What are you going to do when you can't stay here by yourself anymore?" I asked when we'd been sitting there awhile longer. "Where will you go?"

I was thinking of the coming winter. Looking back, I realized I'd been doing more and more work around the homestead this past summer. Not just the heavy work, but easy tasks as well. What was Aunt Lillian going to do now that I had to go back to school during the week and couldn't come out here as often?

"I 'spect I'll go live with the Apple Tree Man—unless he's moved away. Is that what's happened?" she asked in a louder voice, directed at the tree. "Did you move away? Or do you just not have the time for an old friend anymore?"

"There's no quit in you, is there, Lily Kindred?" a strange raspy voice suddenly asked and I pretty near jumped out of my skin.

Aunt Lillian's teeth flashed in the moonlight.

"Just doing my neighborly duty," she said. "Sharing news and all."

He came out from the far side of the tree and if it hadn't been for the 'sangman I'd found, I'd have said he was the strangest man I'd ever seen. He was as gnarled and twisty as the limbs of his tree, long and lanky, a raggedy man with tattered clothes, bird's-nest hair and a stooped walk. It was hard to make out his features in the moonlight, but I got the sense that there wasn't a mean bone in his body—don't ask me why. I guess he just radiated a kind of goodness and charm. He acted like it was a chore, having to come out and talk to us, but I could tell he liked Aunt Lillian. Maybe missed her as much as she surely did him.

He sat down near the edge of the blanket and looked back and forth between us, gaze finally holding on Aunt Lillian.

"So is it true?" he asked. "You've found a 'sangman?"

"I wouldn't trouble you if it wasn't true. I know how you feel about your kind and mine mixing with each other."

He looked at me. "I don't know what she might have told you, miss, but—"

"My name's Sarah Jane," I told him. "Sarah Jane Dillard."

He sighed. "But the first thing should have been not to share your name with any stranger you might happen to meet in the woods."

"He's right about that," Aunt Lillian said.

"I've heard so much about you," I said, "I didn't think you were a stranger."

"No, he's a stranger, all right," Aunt Lillian corrected me. "That's what you call folks you never see."

"The point Lily and I keep circling around like two old dogs," he said, "is that it's dangerous for humans to be with fairies. It wakes things in you that can't be satisfied, leaving you with a hunger that lasts until the end of your days, a hunger for things you can't have, or be, that only grows stronger as the years pass. It wasn't always so, but our worlds have drifted apart since the long ago when magic was simply something that filled the air instead of what it's become now: a thing that's secret and rare."

"How he goes on," Aunt Lillian said.

There was no real anger in her voice. I couldn't recall a time when she'd ever seemed really angry about anything. But I knew this old argument that lay between the two of them was something that vexed her.

The Apple Tree Man ignored her.

"How do you feel, Sarah Jane?" he asked me.

I thought it an odd sort of a question until I started to consider it. How did I feel? Strange, for sure. It's disconcerting, to say the least, to find out that things you really only half-believed in turn out to be real. It starts this whole domino effect in your head where you end up questioning everything. If men can step out of trees, how do I know they won't come popping out of my salad bowl when I sit down to eat? I glanced up at the moon. For all I knew, it really was made of cheese with some round-faced old fellow living in the hollowed-out center.

Who was to say where the real world stopped and fairy tales began? Maybe anything was possible.

Just thinking that made the world feel too big, the smallest thing too complicated. The ground under the blanket seemed spongy, like we could slip right into the dirt, or maybe sideways, to some fairy place and we'd never return.

"I guess I feel different," I managed to say. "But I can't explain exactly how. It's like everything's changed and nothing has, all at the same time. Like I'm seeing two things at the same time, one on top of the other."

He nodded, but before he could say anything, Aunt Lillian spoke up.

"What do we do with the 'sangman?" she asked.

The Apple Tree Man turned in her direction.

"The night's full of listening ears," the Apple Tree Man said. "Perhaps we could take this indoors."

Aunt Lillian shrugged.

"You've always been welcome in my house," she said.

4

If it was odd just seeing the Apple Tree Man and knowing he existed, it was odder still to have him in Aunt Lillian's house. Inside, he seemed taller than he had in the orchard. Taller, thinner. And wilder. His bird's-nest hair looked twice the size it had been, with leaves and twigs and burrs and who knew what all caught up in it. He brought with him a strange feral scent. Mostly it was of apples, but underneath was a strong musk that made me feel twitchy. His knees were too tall to go under the kitchen table we all sat around, so he had to sit to the side, those long, twisty legs stretching out along the floor.

I went and got the 'sangman in his basket and set it on the table in front of the Apple Tree Man. The little man was still unconscious, but Aunt Lillian said he seemed to be sleeping now. The Apple Tree Man agreed with her.

"They're tough little fellows, no question," he said. "Have to be to survive—how many stings was it?"

I was about to answer when we heard a low, mournful howl from outside. That was Root, I thought. He really didn't appreciate being locked up in the barn with nothing but Aunt Lillian's cow Henny and a handful of half-wild cats for company.

"A hundred and thirty-seven," I said.

The Apple Tree Man nodded. "So I'm thinking he must have really ticked *somebody* off. Usually it's no more than a sting or two, just as a reminder that they're not friends, not no way, not no how."

"Why are they feuding?" I asked.

"It's like in the song."

"Aunt Lillian said there was a song but she couldn't remember it."

"A 'sangman fell for one of the bee fairies and took her away from her hive. Everybody used to know the chorus."

He began to sing softly:

> *Once he took her in his arms*
> *and kissed her long and true*
> *Once he took her in his arms*
> *wasn't nothing nobody could do*

Halfway through Aunt Lillian began to sing with him. I liked the way their voices blended. It was a natural sound, like when Laurel and Bess sing together.

"That does sound a lot like 'Shady Grove,'" I said.

The Apple Tree Man smiled. "The old tunes go around and around," he said. "You can't give any of them just the one name, or the one set of words."

"So why did 'sang and bee fairies get mad at each other?" I asked. "Falling in love's supposed to be a happy thing."

The Apple Tree Man glanced at Aunt Lillian, then looked back at me.

"The bee fairy that the 'sangman in the song stole away was a princess," he said, "and the bee folk didn't much cotton to one of their highborn ladies living in the dark woods, in a hole in the ground. They've been fighting about it ever since."

"Sounds like pretty much any feud in these hills," I said. "It starts with something small and then goes on until hardly anybody remembers the whyfor. They just know they don't like each other."

The Apple Tree Man nodded. "I suppose we're not so different from you in a lot of ways."

"You can certainly be as stubborn," Aunt Lillian said.

He gave her this look again, kind of sad, kind of moony, and it got me to wondering about the two of them. Aunt Lillian never made out like there was much of anything between them 'cept friendship, but they sounded a bit like the way it could get when Adie'd run into one of her old boyfriends.

If they'd ever been a couple, I guess he'd been the one to end it. I already knew that Aunt Lillian wasn't too happy about it, but now I got the sense that maybe he wasn't either. I thought about some of the things he'd been saying, then looked at the pair of them.

Old as she was with her own wrinkles and all, Aunt Lillian was probably more like an apple tree fairy now than she'd probably ever been in all the time he'd known her. Maybe the reason he'd been seeing less of her now than he used to wasn't so much because of what fairies can wake in a human, but because year by year she grew more attractive to him and he didn't trust himself around her. Figured they'd be happy for a time, but then she'd be gone, seeing's how our lives are so fleeting, while theirs go on forever. Maybe he just knew he couldn't bear the heartbreak.

And maybe I was just being a hopeless romantic and there wasn't any such thing going on between the pair of them.

"Can you take him with you?" Aunt Lillian was asking. "Let him finish his mending in your tree?"

"It's not him I'm worried about. It's you and Sarah Jane."

"Because of the bee fairies?"

The Apple Tree Man nodded. "There's no telling what they might do when they find out you've helped him. And they will find out. Not much goes on in the meadows or the woods that they don't know about."

I didn't like to hear that. I'd always found it a little creepy in Sunday school when we were told that God was always watching us. Then I decided I didn't believe in God—or at least not the way they talked about him—and I felt like I'd got my privacy back. Now I had fairies to think about.

"What can we do?" Aunt Lillian asked.

"We need to find you a safe place to stay for the next couple of days—just until we can see how the land lies. We need to find a way to tell the both the 'sangmen and the bee fairies that you weren't taking sides. You were just being neighborly, helping someone in their need."

"It's the truth," Aunt Lillian said.

The Apple Tree Man nodded. "But you know as well as I that sometimes the truth isn't enough."

I liked the sound of this even less.

"I can't just be going off without telling Mama where I'll be," I told them. "She's going to be mad enough I didn't come home tonight."

"I don't know what else to do," the Apple Tree Man said. "It's too dangerous for either of you to go anywhere right now and I doubt your mama would listen to the likes of me."

Just saying she believed her eyes in the first place, I thought.

The Apple Tree Man stood and picked up the basket with the 'sangman in it.

"Come with me," he said. "And don't bother bringing anything. You'll find whatever you need where we're going."

Aunt Lillian and I exchanged glances. When she finally shrugged and stood up, I joined her. I know the Apple Tree Man said I needn't bring anything with me, but I grabbed my knapsack by its strap and brought it along all the same.

We walked back through the garden, out into the orchard. The moon was all the way on the other side of the sky now, but still shining bright enough to light our way. I couldn't tell what Aunt Lillian was feeling, but I admit I was somewhat scared my own self. Right about then she took my hand and I felt a lot better.

I gave the thorn bush a dubious look when we reached the Apple Tree Man's tree.

"Just walk through with me," he said.

All Aunt Lillian and I could do was stare at him, the way you do when someone says something that particularly doesn't make sense.

"Don't worry," he added. "What you see as barriers are only there if you think they are. It might help to shut your eyes."

I couldn't decide which would be worse, seeing where I was going or not, but in the end I did close my eyes. I counted the steps and right about where I'd reckoned the bush would be I felt something feathery tickle every inch of my skin. I guess I could have been concerned about any number of things right then, from the danger we were in to what Mama was going to say when and if I ever got myself home, but the last thing I thought about as we passed out of this world and into some other was that we'd left Root in the barn. Who was going to look after him and Henny? Who was going to feed Aunt Lillian's chickens?

And then that got swallowed up by an even bigger question, one I hadn't even considered until now, when it was too late. I started thinking in on too many of Aunt Lillian's stories and the fear rose sharp and jittery inside me. How much time was going to pass in the world outside while we were hidden away in fairyland? I didn't want to spend a day or two here and come back to find Mama and my sisters twenty years older, or worse, all long dead and gone, like that artist Aunt Lillian had met once who'd spent a couple of days in fairyland only to find twenty years had passed back here in the world he'd left behind.

But it was too late for that now.

We'd already stepped outside the world, Aunt Lillian and me both, following a smooth-talking Apple Tree Man into his tree.

5

I opened my eyes to a buttery yellow light that seemed too bright after the dark night we'd left behind. I'd figured we'd end up right inside the tree and hadn't quite worked my mind around what it would be like, but instead of anything I might have imagined, we looked to be in somebody's house—a house that was a whole lot bigger than anything that could fit inside the trunk of any apple tree I'd ever seen. Back in the world we'd left behind, I could easily wrap my arms around its trunk, if I could get past the thorn tree protecting it. But here . . . here . . .

I was still holding hands with Aunt Lillian and we had us a look at each other, neither of us quite ready to believe what we were seeing, though there it was all the same, right in front of our noses.

"Welcome to my home," the Apple Tree Man said as he set the 'sangman's basket down by a stone hearth.

There wasn't any fire burning in it, but the big room we were in was cozy warm all the same. I looked around, trying to see where the light was coming from, but couldn't tell. It smelled like the

Apple Tree Man in here, of apples and wood, with that faint under-lying shiver of musk.

I guess we were in the living area of his house. The floor was polished wood with a thick, hooked rug in the center. There were a pair of battered armchairs in front of the hearth with a table between them. One wall was floor-to-ceiling books, like in a library, big, fat books, all bound in leather. Later I found out they were the annals of these here hills, written by the Apple Tree Man himself, some of them.

There were a couple of paintings and a handful of framed draw-ings on the other walls—familiar landscapes, I realized, as I recog-nized some of the subjects. Aunt Lillian got a funny look on her face when she spied them. She let go of my hand and walked over to give the nearest one a closer study.

Across from the hearth was a kitchen area that had a long wooden table running most of the length of the wall and all sorts of herbs and such hanging down from the rafters above it. Shelves held jars with dried mushrooms and tomatoes and I didn't know what all. There was a smaller wooden kitchen table set out a little from the longer one with a couple of ringback chairs around it. Over against another wall was a chest with clothes hooks above it. A coat as raggedy as the clothes the Apple Tree Man wore was tossed on top of the chest.

I saw two doors, but they were both closed, so I couldn't tell where they led.

"Where does the light come from?" I asked.

"Making light is one of the first things we learn," the Apple Tree Man said.

"And these paintings and drawings?" Aunt Lillian asked.

"They were gifts from a friend."

"Did you ever thank her for them?"

"I thought I did."

Aunt Lillian just made a kind of hrumphing sound.

I looked back and forth between them, sensing that undercurrent of old history again. I decided it was none of my business.

"When we get back," I asked. "How much time's going to have passed?"

Nobody answered for a long moment. Those two old folks, Aunt Lillian and the Apple Tree Man, just keep on looking at each other, a conversation happening in their eyes that only they could hear. The Apple Tree Man finally shifted his gaze to me.

"The same as passes here," he said. "Time runs at different speeds throughout the otherworld, but in this place you'll notice no difference."

That was a relief.

"What about Root?" I went on. "We left him in the barn. And Henny's going to need her milking."

"We'll worry about that in the morning. For now, have a seat by the hearth. I'll make us some tea."

"Aunt Lillian?" I said.

Maybe he was calm as all get out, but I had a hundred worries and questions running through my head, and sitting around drinking tea and not talking about any of them wasn't going to be the least help at all, so far as I could see.

"Not much else we can do right now," she said, moving away from the picture she'd been studying to take a seat in one of the two armchairs. "We might as well make ourselves comfortable."

I sighed and started to walk over to where she was sitting when a weird buzzing sound filled the air. I thought it was something of the Apple Tree Man's doing, but when I looked at him, he appeared as confused as Aunt Lillian and I were. The buzzing grew louder, turning into a deep rumbling drone. We all looked around, searching for its source.

"It's the 'sangman," Aunt Lillian said.

I glanced in his direction. The little man was still lying in his basket, his mouth open. I remember thinking, Is this what a 'sangman's snores sound like?, and then they came streaming out of his mouth, a yellow and black cloud of bees, thick as smoke, pouring out from between his lips like steam from a kettle.

"Down!" the Apple Tree Man cried. "Get down and lie still."

I knew what he meant. Elsie had told me about this before, how if you lay still on the ground, didn't so much as blink, bees that had been disturbed might just ignore you. So I did as the Apple Tree Man said and dropped to the floor. Aunt Lillian was already lying down—I never even saw her move, she must have done it so fast. The Apple Tree Man opened one of the two doors I'd seen earlier, then stretched out on the floor himself.

I tried not to even breathe as the buzzing cloud of bees circled the room at about the height of my head if I'd still been standing. They made a circuit of the room, once, twice, a third time, then they finally went streaming out of the door.

Long after they were gone and the Apple Tree Man had already stood up, I lay there on the floor, shivering and nervous, my heart beating way too fast.

"What in tarnation was that?" Aunt Lillian said.

I sat up then and gave the 'sangman a wary glance, waiting for more of the bees to come buzzing out of his mouth, but it looked like the stream of bugs was done coming out of him. The Apple Tree Man stood up and closed the door he'd opened earlier, but not before I caught a glimpse of what lay beyond.

There was a hillside meadow out there, not much different from the one that lay outside the apple tree in Aunt Lillian's orchard, 'cept everything about it was . . . I don't know how to put it. More, I guess. It was like the difference between a black-and-white movie and one you see in color. That hillside pulled at me like an ache in my heart. I didn't have me but the one peek at it, but I felt myself drawn to it like no piece of land had drawn me before. I was actually on my feet and making for the door, when the Apple Tree Man closed it shut.

"You don't want to go out there," the Apple Tree Man said, though we both knew that's *all* I wanted to do.

"I'd almost forgotten the ache that place can wake in a body," Aunt Lillian said.

She was looking at that closed door like her best friend had just walked out, never to return.

The Apple Tree Man shook his head. I thought it was because of what Aunt Lillian said, because of what he knew I wanted to do, but it turned out I was wrong.

"This is never going to work," he said.

"What's not?"

He looked at me. "I was going to take the two of you with me to the 'sangmen's hold. To bring the little rootman back to his kin and see if maybe they've got an idea or two that might get you out from the middle of this feud of theirs. But I can't bring you into that world. You'll never want to return. And when I do bring you back, you'll spend the rest of your lives heartsick for the wanting of it."

I didn't argue. That one glimpse I got me made me think what he was saying might well be true. But Aunt Lillian wasn't buying none of it.

"You need to give us a little more credit than you do," she said. "Sure, we've got the wanting to be in that place. And maybe, when we come back, we'll be pining for it. But we're stronger than you think. Everybody lives without things they figure they're desperate to have. That's just part of living. The sick person wants to be well. The rejected suitor can't stop thinking of the girl who turned him down. One person needs a fat bank account, another what that money might buy.

"We don't get what we want, life still goes on. We make do. We don't shut down and lie down in a corner and cry for the rest of our lives."

"Some do," the Apple Tree Man said. "Some people come back and they're never happy again."

"Maybe," Aunt Lillian replied. "But I'm not one of them. And I find it insulting how you keep on insisting I am—like somehow you know me better than I know my own self."

"I just think—"

"Too much sometimes," Aunt Lillian said. "No reason to be ashamed of it. It's a failing common to my people as well."

They stood there looking at each other, no give in either of them, until finally the Apple Tree Man gave a slow nod.

"My apologies," he said. "I should learn to take folks at their word."

"Would surely simplify a lot of things," Aunt Lillian agreed.

"And you?" the Apple Tree Man asked, turning to me.

I looked at Aunt Lillian, but she shook her head.

"I can't help you here, girl," she said. "This is one of those things that each of us needs to work out on our own. You understand what I mean?"

I nodded. I didn't like it, but I knew what she meant. I turned my attention to the Apple Tree Man.

"I guess the bees will be out there," I said.

"But they won't be concerned with us," he said. "Not unless we run into the bee fairies before we reach the 'sangmen's hold."

"How did they get to be inside the 'sangman in the first place?" I asked.

"It's part of the bee-sting magic. Their fairy shots are poison, through and through—there's no denying that. But they also give rise to new tribes of bees. What we saw coming out of the 'sangman was like a new hive—born in fairy blood and bee venom and now out swarming to make themselves a new home. They're going to be too busy to bother with the likes of us unless someone sets them on us."

"That's not where bees come from," I said.

I was always a good listener and I could remember any number of Elsie's stories about bees, from the old beegum hives that people used to make out of the hollowed sections of black gum tree trunks to how the best honey came from the nectar of sourwood tree blossoms.

"It's where these come from," the Apple Tree Man said. "If you hadn't pulled out all of those arrows, they would have consumed the 'sangman before they swarmed. As it is, there was just enough venom in him to make a small swarm, but not enough to harm him."

"But—"

"You're stalling," Aunt Lillian said.

I was. The truth was, I didn't know if I could do it. I didn't know if I was as strong as Aunt Lillian. I found myself remembering one of those stories of hers, the one about folks crossing over, how they came back either poets or crazy and I sure couldn't rhyme more than the odd verse or two of doggerel.

"You can wait for us here," the Apple Tree Man said.

I thought Aunt Lillian would take offense to that, considering how she'd been going on earlier about us being stronger than the Apple Tree Man gave us credit for. But she just gave me a kind look.

"There's no shame in staying behind," she said. "Considering all the stories about the trouble one can get into on the other side, maybe it makes more sense to stay clear of that land."

I could tell she meant it. That she wasn't going to think the less of me if I stayed behind. But that stubborn Dillard streak wouldn't let me off the hook as easily as Aunt Lillian would.

"No," I said, wondering if I'd live to regret it. "I've got to see this through now."

Nobody asked, was I sure?, or tried to argue me out of it. Aunt Lillian just gave me an encouraging smile. The Apple Tree Man picked up the 'sangman's basket, and off we went, through the door and away.

Awful Sharp Thing, A Bee Is
Adie and Elsie

"I'm starting to get worried," Mama said.

Adie shrugged, a gesture that was lost on her mother since Adie was lying on the couch, idly flipping through a magazine while watching some boy band on the music video channel with Laurel and Bess.

"Oh, you know Janey," she said. "She'll jump at any chance she can get to be up at that old woman's place."

"She didn't say she was staying overnight. I'm going to have words with that girl when you bring her back."

Adie sat up straight. "When *I* bring her back? Why do I have to go? Elsie's our nature girl. She'd jump at the chance to go into the woods."

"I'm sure she would. And you can certainly take Elsie or any of the other girls with you. But you're the oldest and if something happened to Sarah Jane on the way back from Lily's place, I'd feel better knowing you were there to deal with the problem."

Adie had to smile. That was Mama for you. Always making you feel like something you didn't much care for was actually something special that only you could do for her. Even at nineteen years old, and knowing this trick of Mama's, Adie couldn't quell the flicker of pride that rose up in her.

Closing her magazine, she got up to find her running shoes.

"And take this with you," Mama said when she had her shoes and coat on and was making for the door. "You can put it in a knapsack."

Adie sighed when she saw the jar of preserves and bag of muffins Mama was holding out to her. It seemed like you couldn't say hello to someone on the road around here without exchanging some kind of food or other. But she dutifully fetched a knapsack and loaded it up.

"And no dawdling," Mama said. "You tell Sarah Jane she's to come straight home."

Adie rolled her eyes. "There's nothing to dawdle over between here and Aunt Lillian's."

"Be that as it may . . ."

"See, this is why we need a cell phone. If we had one right now we could just call Janey and tell her to get her butt back home."

Mama smiled. "And you'd be happy with her taking it with her whenever she goes to see Lily?"

Adie thought about how often her sister went to the old woman's place and shook her head.

"I'll just go get her," she said.

She found Elsie in the pasture, carefully drawing a study of some little animal's skull she'd discovered in the grass. Mouse, vole—Adie couldn't tell. Elsie was still like a little kid in this. Fifteen years old and she'd just get all excited about finding a nest or a feather or some little animal's skeleton. But she knew more about what went on in the fields and woods around the farm than any of them. Adie supposed there was something to say about paying the kind of attention Elsie did to every little thing she came across in her wanderings.

"Come on, skinny knees," she said. "Mama says we've got to go look for Janey."

"Just a sec."

She waited while Elsie finished her drawing, made a notation under it and dated it, then carefully stowed away her pencil and journal in her own knapsack.

"How come we have to get her?" Elsie asked.

She stood up, brushing grass and dirt from the knees of her jeans.

"She never came home last night and Mama's worried."

"I just thought she was staying over."

"Well, she forgot to tell Mama that, so we're stuck fetching her back."

"You don't think anything's happened to her, do you?"

Adie thought of teasing her, but then realized that she was carrying around a little nag of worry herself.

"What could happen to her between here and there?" she asked.

She held up her hand as Elsie was about to answer. Elsie, being the family expert on everything that grew or lived in these hills, could probably come up with a hundred things that might have gone wrong.

"No," she said quickly. "I don't need to know. Everything's going to be fine. We'll find her and Aunt Lillian hoeing the garden or shucking peas or whatever it is that they do up at that place to keep themselves busy."

But they didn't.

It was strangely quiet around the Kindred homestead an hour or so later when they came into the last meadow and started up the hill to the house. The little nagging feeling in Adie's chest blossomed into real worry as they called ahead and got no answer. It grew stronger still when they heard Root barking from the barn. There was a frantic quality to his voice that made Adie's pulse beat way too fast.

The two girls ran to the barn, fumbling to unbar the door. When they finally got the bar off and the door open, Root bounded by them and took off up the hill, running into the orchard. Adie and Elsie exchanged worried glances, then hurried after him. They found him lying by an old apple tree half choked with thorn bushes, whining, his head on his paws as he stared at the tree.

"What is it, boy?" Adie asked. "What's wrong?"

"That's the Apple Tree Man," Elsie said.

"The what?"

"The Apple Tree Man. It's what Aunt Lillian calls the oldest tree in the orchard."

"And that means?"

Elsie shrugged. "I don't know. It's just what she calls it."

Adie looked away from the tree, back to the house. She didn't come up here very often. It wasn't that she disliked Aunt Lillian. She just found it too weird up here. You couldn't even use the washroom to have a pee because there wasn't one. There was only the outhouse where you *knew* there was a spider getting ready to climb onto your butt as soon as you sat down. Adie couldn't imagine living without electricity or running water—especially not on purpose.

"It's too quiet," she said.

"It's always quiet up here," Elsie said, but she sounded doubtful.

Adie knew just what she was thinking. There was something wrong, but neither of them wanted to say it aloud.

"I guess we should check the house," she said.

Elsie nodded.

Adie remembered what Mama'd said to get her to come up here.

You're the oldest and if something happened to Sarah Jane on the way back from Lily's place, I'd feel better knowing you were there to deal with the problem.

Maybe she was the oldest, but she didn't know where to start right now. She didn't feel at all capable. All she felt was panic.

She swallowed hard.

"They're just inside," she said, "where they can't hear us. That's all."

"Then why did they lock Root up in the barn?"

"I don't know, okay?"

Elsie looked like she was going to cry.

"I'm sorry," Adie said quickly. "I'm worried, too."

She took her sister's hand and started off toward the house.

"Come on, Root," she called over her shoulder.

But the dog wouldn't budge. All he did was stare at that stupid old tree and whine.

"Everything's going to be fine," she assured Elsie as they approached the house. "They're probably just gone off hunting berries or something."

Elsie nodded. "That's right. Janey said they were going out after 'sang yesterday. Maybe they went today instead."

"There. You see? There's nothing for us to worry about."

They both jumped at a sudden loud, moaning sound, then laughed when they saw it was just Aunt Lillian's cow having followed them up from the barn. Henny lowed again, long and mournfully.

"She sounds like she wants something," Adie said.

"Maybe she needs to be milked."

"But they would have done that before they left."

Elsie nodded.

They were on the porch now.

"Hello!" Adie called inside. "Is anybody home?"

They went inside, nervous again. They found no one on the ground floor and neither of them wanted to check the upstairs.

"This looks like last night's dinner dishes," Elsie said as they looked around the kitchen.

Adie dropped her knapsack by the door and nodded. "I guess we need to look upstairs."

Reluctantly, they went up the stairs, wincing at every creak the old wood made under their feet. The stairs took them into an open loft of a room. It had been where Aunt Lillian slept until her own Aunt Em passed away. Now it was just used for storage, though there was little enough of it. Some old books. Winter clothes hanging on a pole and draped in plastic. By the window there was a large trunk.

"There," Adie said, only barely keeping the relief out of her voice. "You see? There's no one here."

"What about the trunk?"

"You think someone's hiding in the trunk?"

Elsie shook her head. "But you could put a . . . you know . . ."

She didn't need to say the word. It sprang readily to Adie's mind. Yes, the trunk was big enough to hold a body.

Crossing the floor she went over to it, hesitated only a moment, then flung it open.

"Still nothing," she said. "And nobody, either. There's just a mess of drawings."

Elsie joined her by the open trunk and looked inside. She picked up the top drawings.

"These are really good. Who do you think did them?"

Adie shrugged. "Who knows. Maybe Aunt Lillian."

"I didn't know she could draw."

Elsie continued to explore the trunk while Adie used the vantage of a second floor window to see if she could spy any sign of Aunt Lillian or their missing sister.

Under the loose drawings Elsie found numerous sketchbooks, each page filled with sketches of the hills around the house. They were like what Elsie did in her own journal, cataloguing the flora and fauna, only the drawings were so much better than hers. Further in she found stacks of oil paintings on wood panels—color sketches done in the field in preparation of work that would be realized more fully in a studio. Under them were still more drawings and sketchbooks. Many of these had a childlike quality to them and were done on scraps of brown paper and cardboard.

She looked at the paintings again. There was something familiar about them. It was when she came to one depicting a black bear in a meadow clearing that she caught a sharp breath.

"What is it?" Adie asked.

"I've seen the finished painting this was done for. Or at least I've seen a picture of it in a magazine. The original's hanging in the Newford Museum of Art. But that means . . ."

She started looking more carefully through the paintings and drawings and began to recognize more of the sketches as studies for paintings she'd seen in various books and magazines. Then she found what she was looking for inside one of the earlier sketchbooks.

"Look at this," she said.

Adie gave the pages a quick study. From what she could tell somebody had been doodling various ways to write their initials.

"L.M.," she read. "What does that stand for do you think?"

"Lily McGlure."

"And she is?"

"Apparently the name that Aunt Lillian painted under," Elsie said.

"I thought she was a Kindred."

"I don't know about that. Maybe she changed her name. Maybe it's just a pen name. But this is amazing."

"Why?"

"*Why.*" Elsie repeated. "The Aunt Lillian we know is really Lily McGlure. What could be more amazing than that?"

"So?"

"So, she's famous. They often talk about her like she was one of the Newford Naturalists, even though her work was done a few decades after their heyday. But you can see why, when you look at her paintings."

Adie couldn't, really, but she didn't want to seem more ignorant than she probably already did, so she said nothing.

"She's supposed to have studied with both Milo Johnson and Frank Spain," Elsie went on, "though there's some dispute about that, considering how they disappeared at least twenty years before she started to paint seriously."

"How do you know all this stuff?"

"I don't know," Elsie said. "I read about it and watch the Discovery Channel. I just find it interesting, I guess."

Adie gave the trunk a thoughtful look.

"When you said these two artists disappeared," she said, "what did you mean?"

"Oh, it's one of the big mysteries of the Newford art world. They were out painting in the hills around here and they just vanished . . ."

Elsie's voice trailed off and she gave her sister an anguished look.

"We don't know that anything happened to Janey or Aunt Lillian," Adie said. "I'm sure it's just like we thought, they're just out hunting 'sang." She took the sketchbook from Elsie's hands and put it back in the trunk. "Come on. Let's close this up and go back outside."

Elsie nodded. She placed the drawings and paintings back on

top of the sketchbooks. Closing the trunk lid, she stood up and followed Adie back to the stairs.

"What do we do now?" she asked. "Do we stay? Do we go
looking for them? Do we go home?"

"See, this is why we really need a cell phone," Adie said. "Or
even two. We could call Mama right now and ask her what to do."

"But we can't."

"I know. Let me think a minute."

They stood out on the porch, looking out across the garden to
the orchard, where Root still kept his vigil by the old apple tree.

"We should put the cow back in the barn," Elsie said. "Or at
least in the pasture."

Right now the cow was in the garden, munching on the runner
beans that grew up a pair of homemade cedar trellises on the far
side of the corn.

Adie nodded and fell in step beside her sister.

"There sure seem to be a lot of bees around here today," she
said as they reached the garden.

Elsie grabbed the cow's halter and drew her away from the
beans.

"They're gathering the last of the nectar," she explained, "so
that they'll have enough honey to get them through the winter."

"I suppose," Adie said. "But these don't seem to be collecting
much nectar. It looks to me like they're just flying around."

Elsie studied the bees. Adie was right. The bees were ignoring
the last of the asters and such and seemed . . . well, they seemed to
be searching for something, but for what, Elsie couldn't tell.

"That's just weird," she said.

"Everything about this morning is weird," Adie said. "From the
way Root's acting and these bees, to how there's just nobody
around."

Elsie nodded. "I think we should put Henny back into the barn and go home. Mama will know what to do."

"I suppose."

Adie hated the idea of having to turn to their mother for help. She liked the idea that Mama was there, if they should need her, but she much preferred to solve her problems on her own.

They were halfway back to the barn when Adie suddenly put her hand on Elsie's arm.

"Do you hear that?" she asked.

She needn't have bothered. Elsie had already stopped and turned to look at the woods beyond the orchard herself.

"It sounds like bells," she said.

Adie nodded. Bells and the jingle of bridles. And now that they and the cow had stopped moving, they could also hear the faint hollow sound of hooves on the ground. Many hooves. Adie reached for Elsie's hand, to take comfort as well as give it, when the riders came into view.

They were like knights and great ladies out of some medieval storybook. The men weren't wearing armor, but they still had the look of knights in their yellow and black livery, with their plumed helmets and silvery shields. The women didn't ride sidesaddle, but they wore long flowing dresses that streamed down the flanks of their horses and trailed on the ground behind them. On either side of the riders ranged long-legged, golden-haired dogs with black markings—some cross between greyhounds and wolves.

Neither the riders nor their animals seemed quite right. They were all too tall, too lean, their features too sharp. A nimbus of shining golden light hung about them, unearthly and bright. The whole company—men and women, their mounts and all—were so handsome it was hard to look at them and not feel diminished. Adie and Elsie felt like poor country cousins invited to a palatial ballroom, standing awkwardly in the doorway, not wanting to come in.

"This can't be real," Adie said.

Elsie made no reply except to squeeze her hand.

The riders came down from the meadow, footmen running along behind, and circled around the two girls. The footmen notched arrows in their bows, aiming them at Adie and Elsie.

"Well, that was easy enough," said the woman who appeared to be leading them.

2

Laurel and Bess

It never made much sense to Laurel that they would still be weeding the garden in September when most of the vegetables had already been harvested. But that was the chore Mama had set her and Bess to while the younger twins were in charge of cleaning the house. Of course they weren't just weeding. They were also gathering errant potatoes and turnips and the like that had been missed during the earlier harvest, putting them in a basket to take inside later. When they were done weeding, they were supposed to turn the soil on the sections they'd weeded. After that, one or more of the other girls would spread compost over it all and that would be it until spring.

Mama liked a tidy garden, everything neat and ready for next year's planting.

"We should've gone with Adie and Elsie," Laurel said.

Bess shrugged. "This'd still be waiting for us when we got back."

"I know. But I'm bored. This whole weekend's just all too boring."

Last night's dance at the Corners had been cancelled, no one was exactly sure why. But there were rumors and gossip, as always.

Bess had heard from the postman that the building had become infested with rats and so the county had closed it down. Martin Spry, a fiddler who lived down the road from them, had told Laurel that someone had gotten themselves knifed at a stag the Friday night before and the police still had the building cordoned off for their investigation. But Mama said all of that was nonsense.

"Mrs. Timmons told me the Jacksons got called out of town," she said. "Something about one of their grandkids getting sick and by the time they heard, it was too late to get anyone to take over for the night. That's all."

Maybe, maybe not, Laurel thought. All she knew was that they hadn't got to play out since last weekend. Hadn't been playing, hadn't been dancing. It was just school—their last year, thank god; they'd turned eighteen a couple of months ago and would be graduating this June—chores, and watching interchangeable videos on the music channel.

Laurel leaned on her hoe. "I really wanted to play that medley of Ziggy Stardust tunes that we worked out—just to see the faces on the old fiddlers."

The twins loved the old tunes and songs, but they also had an inordinate fondness for music from the seventies and eighties which they kept trying to shoehorn into old-timey arrangements with varying degrees of success—everything from Pink Floyd to punk and disco.

"Instead," Laurel said, "all we have is boredom."

"Way too much, too," Bess agreed.

"If only something interesting could happen around here."

It was at precisely that moment, as though called up like an answered wish, that they heard the fiddle music come drifting down the hill and across the pastures to where they were working in the garden. The twins lifted their heads as one.

"Do you hear that?" Laurel asked.

"I'm not deaf."

"Who do you suppose it is?"

"Don't know," Bess said. "But it's not Marty."

Laurel nodded. "The tone's too sweet to be him."

"Doesn't sound like anyone we know," Bess added after they'd listened a little more.

Not only was the player unfamiliar, but so were the tunes. And that was irresistible.

Laurel laid down her hoe. "Are you thinking what I'm thinking?"

"Always."

Bess brushed her hands on her jeans and the two of them went into the house to collect their instruments.

3

Ruth and Grace

Ruth leaned on the windowsill she was supposed to be dusting and watched Laurel and Bess walk toward the woods with their instrument cases in hand.

"How come they get to blow off their chores while we're stuck in here?" she said.

Her thirteen-year-old twin Grace joined her at the window. "They just thought of it first, I guess."

"I guess. Hey, you know what would be funny? If we went down and put all those 'taters and such back in the ground."

Grace shook her head. "Too much work. You know what would be funnier?"

"What?"

"If someone hid their instruments and replaced them in their cases with stones wrapped up in T-shirts so the cases would still weigh the same."

Ruth turned to her twin with a grin. "You didn't."

"I'm not saying I did or didn't. I'm just saying it would be funny." She paused, then grinned as well. "But I sure thought they'd find out before now."

"If there'd been a dance last night," Ruth began.

Grace nodded. "And there they'd be, invited up on stage and opening their cases."

They started to giggle and slid down onto the floor with their backs to the wall, unable to stop, the one constantly setting the other off.

4

Laurel and Bess

"Mama's going to kill us," Bess said as they started across the pasture. She carried her banjo case with an easy familiarity to its weight.

"Only if she catches us," Laurel said. "I figure we've got two or three hours, maybe longer if she stops in to see Mrs. Runion."

Beth smiled. Mrs. Runion was a sweet old woman who lived on the edge of town and could talk your ear off if you gave her half the chance. Granny Burrell used to say that she'd been born talking, but Mama never seemed to mind. Mama was like Janey, in that she enjoyed visiting with old folks, saying, "All our history lives in those who've been around as long as Mrs. Runion. When we lose them, we lose a piece of our history unless we take the time to listen to what they've got to tell us."

Beth supposed she half-understood. She and Laurel felt the same about music and, while they weren't much for sitting around chatting with someone like Mrs. Runion, they saw nothing odd about making a two-mile hike up some bush road to spend the afternoon and evening listening to some old fellow scratch out tunes on his fiddle, or maybe rasp his way through one of the old ballads.

Music was something that needed to be passed along, too. Or at least the old songs and tunes did.

"She hasn't seen Mrs. Runion for a couple of weeks," Bess said, "so it's a good bet she'll stop in today."

Laurel nodded. "Will you listen to that fiddler play."

"I haven't heard a tune I know yet," Bess said.

"I just can't imagine who it would be, out in our woods like this."

Beth laughed. "Maybe it's one of Aunt Lillian's fairy people."

"You'd think Janey would have grown out of those stories by now."

"You'd think, but you'd be wrong."

They reached the woods and followed a deer trail that wound back and forth up the side of the hill. With each step they took, the fiddling grew louder and they marveled at the player's skill. The bass strings resonated, rich and full. The notes drawn from the high strings skirled up among the turning leaves into the autumn sky. There was so much rhythm in the playing that adding a guitar or a banjo wasn't even necessary.

Grinning at each other, they hurried forward. Finally they knew they were almost upon the fiddler and they vibrated with anticipation. The trail they followed took them into a clearing and there in the middle, where this path crossed another, stood the oddest little man. He was maybe three feet tall and looked like a walking shrub, a bark and leafy man playing a fiddle almost half the size of himself. They couldn't tell where the wood of his instrument ended and his limbs began. He seemed to have moss and leaves for hair, gnarly twigs for fingers—but oh how they pulled the tune from his fiddle.

He stopped playing at their sudden arrival and the three of them looked at each other for a long moment, none of them speaking, none of them moving or so much as even breathing.

This can't be right, Bess thought, but her head was too clouded and fuzzy for her to feel alarmed. She knew that such a fiddler couldn't possibly exist. How could he? But the cobwebs in her head didn't leave room for her to feel the least bit perturbed by his standing there in front of her all the same. Beside her, Laurel appeared to be just as spellbound.

It was something in the music, a faraway part of Bess's mind whispered. That, she was sure, was the source of the spell.

Belatedly, she was also aware that the spot where the two deer trails met might well be considered a crossroads, and there were any number of stories about the sorts of people you met at a crossroads. Like Old Bubba, ready to trade you the gift of music for your soul like he did with Robert Johnson. The fiddler didn't look like Old Bubba himself, but she wouldn't be surprised if a body came walking up and told her he was some kind of little devil man.

Oh, danger, danger, the little voice in her head whispered, but she couldn't seem to move, never mind run away.

"So you like music?" the little man said.

As soon as he spoke, Bess found she could breathe again. She didn't trust her legs to carry her far, but at least she could breathe.

"We love music," Laurel said.

"And play it, too, by the looks of those cases."

"We play some."

"Just exactly what are you?" Bess asked.

"A fiddler, what did you think? Get out your instruments and we'll play us a tune."

"I don't know that we should," Bess said softly to her sister as they laid their cases on the ground. "There's something not right here."

Laurel shrugged. "We're just seeing that Aunt Lillian didn't make up all those stories of hers that Janey keeps telling us."

"I figure we should be feeling a little more scared than I am."

"What? Of him? He's not much bigger than a minute."

"But he'll be magic. It was magic brought us here."

Laurel shook her head. "Wasn't magic brought me—it was music."

"Same difference," Bess said.

"I tell you what," the little man said, either ignoring their whispered conversation, or not hearing it. "Why don't we make us a bargain? If the two of you can play me a tune I've never heard before, I'll grant you one wish, whatever it is you want."

"And if we can't?" Laurel asked.

"Then you come away with me," the little man told them.

"How do we know you can deliver?" Laurel asked.

"What do you lose to find out? A bright pair of girls like you must know a thousand tunes."

Beth pulled at Laurel's arm when she realized that she was actually considering the little man's bet. Her sister had to be more deeply snared by his magic than she was to even think of agreeing to this.

"This is stupid," she said. "Nobody ever wins this sort of thing."

"It seems pretty straightforward to me," Laurel said.

"It is," the little man said. "But it has to be done here, and it has to be done now."

"Laurel," Bess began.

But her sister shook her head. "This is a sure thing. If we can't play him a tune he doesn't know, we deserve to be taken away." She turned to the little man. "You're on, mister. Get that wish ready."

She unbuckled the clasps of her fiddle case, lifted the lid, then shot an angry glance at that little man. All that was in her case were stones wrapped in a few T-shirts. Her fiddle was gone.

"That's cheating," she said.

Beth quickly opened her own case to find that her banjo was gone as well, replaced by similar stones wrapped in T-shirts.

"Forfeit," the little man said. "Now you come with me."

"No," Laurel said. "You cheated. What did you do with our instruments?"

"I did nothing to them."

"Then lend me yours."

"Of course."

He handed over his fiddle but there were so many little vines and twigs and leaves growing out of it that Laurel couldn't barely get a note out of a string by plucking it. Bowing was out of the question.

The little man snatched his instrument back and stowed it away in a bag that was lying on the ground by his feet. He put his bow in after, then tied up the sack and slung it over his shoulder.

"No more dawdling," he said. "Come along."

He held out a hand to each of them.

The twins began to back away, but he was quick and far stronger than he looked. He grabbed each by an arm.

"You're a lying cheat!" Laurel cried.

She aimed a kick at him but it hurt her toe more through her running shoe than it seemed to hurt him.

"I don't lie and I don't cheat," the little man said.

He said something else in a language neither girl could understand. They both grew dizzy, but before they could fall, the little man pulled them away, out of the world they knew and into his own. A moment later, all that remained at the crossroads were two open instrument cases, filled with stones.

5

Ruth and Grace

"Why'd they'd go into the woods?" Grace said, when she'd finally stopped laughing. "They could just as easily play around here."

"Because this way they won't have us bugging them."

"They think," Grace said.

"They dream."

"I can't wait to see their faces when they open those cases of theirs."

Ruth shot her a big grin.

Jumping to their feet, the pair ran downstairs and outside. Playing Indian scout as they followed the older twins was way more fun than cleaning house. They hid behind clumps of milkweed and tall grasses and Joe Pye weed, darting from one to the next, trying hard not to giggle too loud and give themselves away.

"There sure are a lot of hornets around today," Ruth said as they reached the deer trail their sisters had taken.

"Those aren't hornets, they're bees."

"Whatever."

"But you're right," Grace agreed. "There are lots of them. There's probably a nest nearby."

"Hive."

Grace stuck out her tongue. "What*ever*."

They'd heard a fiddle play the whole time they'd been crossing the fields. Here in the woods it was louder, but it didn't do the same for them as it did for Laurel and Bess. Pure, simple curiosity pulled them along the trail.

"Looks like they're planning to have a hooley in the woods," Ruth said.

Grace nodded. "Probably with a bunch of those old coots they're always playing with."

"Martin's not an old coot. I think he's handsome."

"But he plays the fiddle."

"Lots of nice people play the fiddle."

"Name one."

"Laurel."

"She doesn't count. She's our sister."

"Well, how about—"

"Shh!"

Ruth fell silent, realizing what Grace already had: They were too close to keep nattering on the way they were.

The fiddling had stopped and they could hear voices. They crept along the path until it opened into a small meadow and then they stood there with their mouths agape, staring at the little man with the fiddle that their older sisters had come to meet. Finally, Grace tugged on Ruth's arm, pulling her down, out of sight behind a bush. The two girls looked at each other, eyes wide.

"That . . . man," Ruth said in a voice that was barely a whisper. "He can't be real . . . can he?"

Grace shook her head.

"But there he is all the same," she said just as quietly.

"And Laurel and Bess know him. Came to meet him in the woods and all."

"I don't think they know him. Listen."

They heard Laurel make her bargain with the man. When she and Bess laid down their cases, Grace began to shiver.

"Oh no, oh no, oh no," she said, burrowing her face in Ruth's shoulder.

Ruth looked over her sister's head, understanding immediately. Playing that trick with the older twins' instruments wasn't funny anymore. It wasn't funny at all. And then . . . then the little man pulled them away into thin air; they were there one moment, the next gone as thought they'd all stepped behind an invisible curtain. She pressed her cheek against Grace's, trying hard not to cry because Grace was doing enough for the both of them.

She held Grace close, trying to breathe slow like Mama always said they should do when they felt upset. "People forget to breathe," she'd say, "and then they can't think straight anymore. They get mad, where they should be patient. Or do something stupid, when they could have been smart."

"Breathe, breathe," she said to Grace.

Slowly she could feel the panic ebb a little. She sat back and held Grace at arm's length to see that her sister was getting a hold of herself as well.

"That . . . that was real . . . wasn't it?" Grace finally said.

Ruth had to swallow before she replied. "Looks like."

"It's my fault. They could've played rings around that little man."

"You didn't know."

"It's still my fault."

"It doesn't matter anymore," Ruth said. "All that matters now is that we figure out a way to get them back."

Grace nodded. "I wish Janey was here."

"Me, too."

Janey wasn't the oldest, but she knew all the stories. She got them from Aunt Lillian and was happy to pass them along to anyone who wanted to listen, which, in the Dillard family, pretty much only meant their older sister Elsie, who liked them, and Mama, who always seemed to have the time to listen to anything any one of them had to say.

Ruth stood up. "Come on," she said. "We can at least look for clues."

"Clues? Suddenly we're detectives?"

"You know what I mean."

She walked into the meadow with Grace trailing after her. They touched the instrument cases with the toes of their shoes and walked all around the spot where the little man and their sisters had disappeared, but there was nothing to see.

"I guess we have to go home and get Mama to help," Ruth said.

Grace gave a glum nod.

They turned to the instrument cases, meaning to close them up and bring them along, when they realized that they were no longer alone. Right where the deer trail came out of the woods stood another little man, but where the one that had kidnapped their sisters had looked like a piece of a tree that decide to go for a walk, this one seemed more human. If you discounted his size. And the fact that he had virtually no neck—his round ball of a head seemed to sit directly on the round ball of his body. And then there were the wings—almost as big as him, fluttering rapidly at his back.

He looked, Ruth decided, a lot like a bee, what with the shape of his body and the wings and the fact that his shirt and trousers were all yellow and black stripes. She remembered all the bees they'd noticed on the way to this place. Were they *all* some kind of weird were-bees? She gave the meadow a quick study, but other than the fact that there seemed to be more bees than there should be, the little man appeared to be on his own.

"Well, now," the little man said. "The 'sangman got your sisters, and that made us even, but now we've got you, so we're ahead again."

Grace stooped and picked up one of the stones from Laurel's fiddle case.

Ruth quickly followed suit. Oddly enough, she didn't feel scared. She just felt angry now. Breathe, she started to tell herself, but then she realized she didn't really want to stop being angry.

"What?" she asked. "Are you on some kind of sick scavenger hunt?"

The bee man gave her a puzzled look.

"Because if you are," Grace said. "If you think you're taking us anywhere, we'll knock your brains right out of your head."

She hefted the stone she held to show him she meant business.

He held his hands up. "No, no. You can't do that. You're my captives."

"Not likely," Grace said.

But Ruth heard a buzzing and now Grace did, too. The bees that had been flying about the meadow earlier were all hovering nearby now. And not just a handful, but hundreds of them.

"I don't think we have enough stones," Ruth said. "Not to hit them all."

"Probably not," Grace replied. "But we can hit him."

"You don't want to do that," the bee man said. "Please. You need to calm down. No one will hurt you if you'll just come along quietly."

"We don't want to go anywhere," Ruth said.

"But you don't have any choice."

"Where do you want to take us?" Grace asked.

"Yeah, and why?" Ruth added.

"You're to be hostages, nothing more."

Ruth shook her head. "You don't want to mess with us," she said. "We've got a big brother, you know, and he's killed thirteen giants."

"No, you don't," the bee man said.

"Yes, we do," Grace said. "He's tall and fierce and he eats bees like candy. Eats them by the handful."

"He eats bee sandwiches," Ruth added. "And bee soup."

"Bee stew and deep fried bees."

"And he loves fat little bee men best of all."

"You don't have a brother," the bee man said. "Why would you pretend that you do?"

"Why are we supposed to be your hostages?" Grace asked.

"Yeah," Ruth said. "And what are we being hostaged for?"

"I don't think that's a word," Grace said.

"He knows what I mean."

"Your sister has the 'sangman prince," the bee man said, "and we need something to trade to her for him."

"So trade yourself."

"Or some of your bees," Grace added.

"And," the bee man went on, "if we didn't take you, the 'sangmen would. So you're actually safer with us."

"What are these 'sangmen?" Ruth asked. "Are they like the weird little guy that grabbed our sisters just now?"

The bee man nodded. "They're evil, rooty creatures."

"While you're just a bundle of sunshine and joy," Grace said.

"At least we don't take children of the light and put them in a dark hole."

"I think you're making this all up," Ruth said. "I think the two of you are in cahoots. You and this sing-song man."

" 'Sangman."

"Don't you start correcting me," Ruth told him. "You're not family."

"You're in danger," the bee man tried.

"Oh, right. Like we need to be protected from these sing-song men."

"Whatever they think they are," Grace put in.

"When what we really need is to be protected from you and your little buzzy friends."

"I think we should bop him with a stone and take our chances," Grace said.

"They've already stolen two of you," the bee man said, "and put a glamour on your sister so that she thinks she needs to help them."

"Which sister?" Ruth asked.

"Probably Els—"

Grace was cut off by the jab of Ruth's elbow in her side.

"Remember in the war movies," Ruth said. "Name, rank and serial number. That's all we're supposed to give the enemy."

Grace nodded and looked at the bee man.

"I'm Grace, daughter number six," she said.

Ruth shook her head. "You just love to rub in that you were born one minute earlier, don't you?"

"I'm not your enemy," the bee man said. "Please believe me."

"At least he's polite," Ruth said. "For a kidnapper and all."

"If you'll just come with me, the queen will explain everything."

"Oh, now he's got a queen," Grace said.

"Well, he is a bee man. I wonder what it's like to live in a hive?"

"Very noisy, I'd say."

"That's enough!" the bee man cried. "I don't know why I had to get picked for this stupid job, but I'm finishing it now."

He made a few odd movements with his hands and the bees swept in over the girls, covering their faces, necks and arms, leaving circles around their eyes and mouths.

"Don't move!" he warned them. "Don't even breathe, or my little cousins will give you a thousand stings and you'll like that even less than being captured."

Ruth stared at the bees covering her hands and then gasped. Riding each bee was a miniature version of the bee man who stood in front of them, each with a bow and a notched arrow. She turned her gaze to meet Grace's. They didn't have to speak. They each dropped the stone they were holding.

"That's better," the bee man said. "Now follow me."

He made another odd movement with his hands and the air began to shimmer, just as it had when the 'sangman had stolen away the older twins.

"I think we're in real trouble now," Grace said.

Ruth wanted to nod, but she was too scared to move in any way except for how the bee man told them to.

"We should have left a note for Mama," she said.

Then she and Grace followed the bee man into the shimmering air and the world they knew was gone.

6

Adie and Elsie

Deeper in the woods and higher up in the hills, there was no opportunity for Adie and Elsie to have any sort of a discussion with their captors. The bee man who had captured the younger twins was only a scout, and a reluctant one at that, happier to go about his own business without having to be involved in the various politics and machinations of the fairy court. The sooner he could be done with his duty and go back to his normal solitary ways, the better. Still, he wasn't mean, or even unfriendly, so he'd been willing to put up with a certain amount of the twins' comments and complaints before putting his foot down.

But Adie and Elsie had been captured by the main fairy court, led by a queen who had neither the interest nor patience for dialogue with her captives. As soon as Adie started to ask a question, the queen waved a long thin hand in her direction.

"Gag her," she said. "Gag them both and bind their wrists."

Footmen ran from behind the horses to immediately carry out her orders, carrying strips of cloth and ropes. Adie called out to the queen before they reached her and Elsie.

"Please," she said. "We'll be quiet. Don't gag us."

The queen studied her for a long moment, then gave a brisk nod.

"No gags," she told the footmen. "But bind their wrists and if they speak out of turn again, gag them."

Adie had a hundred things she wanted to know, but she kept quiet and held out her hands in front of her so that the footmen could tie them together, hoping that they wouldn't insist on tying them behind her back. This way, she'd feel more balanced and less likely to fall flat on her face on the uneven ground if they had a long march ahead of them. Happily, Elsie followed her lead and the footmen made quick work of their job.

The ropes the footmen used to bind their wrists seemed to be made from braided grasses, but they were no less strong for that. The sisters were led off under one of the big beech trees above Aunt Lillian's homestead, where they were kept under guard. The two girls sat down with their backs against the tree, leaning against each other as they listened to the conversation coming from where the queen and her court sat on their horses.

"Is there word on the girl yet?" the queen was saying. "The sooner we trade these sisters of hers for that wretched 'sangman, the happier I'll be."

"Not yet, madam," one of the other riders replied.

Before he could go on, a footman came running up.

"The 'sangmen have the older twins," he reported.

"Will she choose between the sisters?" the queen asked. "Does she fancy any above the others?"

"There's no way of telling."

"What about the younger twins?"

"We have scouts looking for them."

Elsie leaned closer to Adie, her mouth near her older sister's ear.

"Who are they talking about?" she asked, her voice quieter that a breath.

Adie shrugged. She cast a glance to their nearest captors. When she saw they weren't paying that close attention to them, she whispered in Elsie's ear.

"I don't know," she said. "But it's beginning to sound like Janey's got us all caught up in something we have no business being mixed up in."

"Do you know what 'sangmen are?"

"Haven't a clue. But I'd guess they have something to with 'sang."

"And Janey was going out to harvest some yesterday."

Adie gave a grim nod. "And it sounds as though these 'sangmen—whatever they are—have Laurel and Bess."

"What did she mean about choosing between sisters?"

"I guess they were hoping to trade us for someone Janey has, but now things have gotten complicated because the other side has the twins to trade."

"I don't get any of this. Janey would never hurt anyone, never mind capture someone the way these people have got us."

"I really don't think they're people," Adie said.

Elsie sighed. "I was afraid you'd say something like that."

They broke off when the queen glanced in their direction. Adie returned her glare with an innocent look and the queen's attention turned away from her once more.

"Look," Elsie whispered.

She nodded with her head to the apple tree that Root was still guarding. The fairies' dogs had formed a half-circle around him, effectively penning him in. But Root paid no attention to them. His gaze stayed fixed on the tree in front of him like there wasn't a fairy court behind him.

Oh, why didn't you run off, Adie thought. You'll be no match for that many dogs and who knows what magical powers they have.

But oddly enough, the fairy dogs showed no inclination of doing more than keeping Root penned up against the apple tree. Adie wondered why. Perhaps it was only because the fairy queen hadn't given the order for them to attack yet. Then she returned her attention to the conversation of the queen and her courtiers and the answer came.

"Has *anyone* tracked down the girl yet?" the queen was asking.

There was a moment of silence before one of her court replied.

"No, madam. We only know she's with the Apple Tree Man, but we can't reach them because the dog's barring the way through Applejack's door and no one knows where it opens on the other side."

"Then remove the dog."

That command drew another silence. Apparently, Adie realized, no one liked to deliver bad news to their cranky queen.

"We can't," one of the riders said. "It won't meet our gaze."

Adie and Elsie exchanged glances.

"Does that mean what I think it does?" Elsie whispered.

Adie shrugged. She wasn't sure, but what it seemed the fairies were saying was that you had to acknowledge their presence before they could interact with you. So maybe if they just concentrated on not believing the fairy court was here . . .

Before she could go any further with that, she was distracted by what what the queen was now saying.

"This should have been over long ago," the fairy queen complained. "We should have had a dead 'sangman by now and moved on to other matters."

"But the princess . . . your daughter. The 'sangmen still have her."

"She's no longer my daughter," the queen said. "Not after she's soiled herself by loving a 'sangman. Let her live in the dirt with them and see how she likes it."

Now that was harsh, Adie thought. She could remember when she was a little girl, reading fairy tales and watching Disney movies, how desperately she'd wanted to meet a fairy. She'd grown out of that, of course, unlike Janey, but she was happy now that she hadn't gotten her wish back then. And would have been happier still not to be experiencing this now. The fairy queen was too much like an evil stepmother. But she supposed that was what was to be expected, considering the kind of folklore that was prevalent in these hills. Many of Aunt Lillian's stories were downright gruesome.

She frowned, wishing she hadn't started this train of thought.

Elsie pressed against her and whispered, "I think we should try to follow Root's lead and, I don't know, disbelieve in these horrible people."

It was worth a try, Adie supposed. Though she could see it would be hard. Root might be able to focus entirely on one thing, but he was a dog and what did he know? Dogs already had a one-track mind. But she and Elsie had bound wrists to contend with. Noisy captors, jingling bridles.

She was about to close her eyes and give it a try, but the chance was gone.

A new commotion hubbubbed on the far side of the fairy court. Adie craned her neck to see what was happening and her heart sank. Their arms and faces might be covered in bees but she had no trouble recognizing that it was Grace and Ruth who were under all those buzzing insects.

"This just gets worse and worse," Elsie said from beside her.
Adie gave a slow nod.

7

Laurel and Bess

Laurel found herself wishing that she hadn't ignored Bess's common sense and simply left well enough alone. In fact, what she really wished was that they were back in the garden, doing their chores like they'd promised Mama they would. Even doing chores was way better than being here.

It was dark and damp in the place the little man had brought them. Underground, she assumed, since the floor was dirt, as were the walls. She hadn't been able to reach up far enough to touch the ceiling.

"Don't fret," the little tree man had said before leaving. "You won't be here long."

Easy enough for him to say.

She felt around in the dark until her fingers touched the sleeve of Bess's shirt.

"I'm sorry I didn't listen to you," she said.

"That's okay." Bess found Laurel's hand and gave it a squeeze. "I mean it's not okay being here, but it wasn't your fault."

"If I hadn't been so greedy with that contest business—"

"He would have just found some other way to get us here."

"But still . . ."

"Still, nothing," Bess said. "There was some kind of magic spell in that music of his. It made my head go all fuzzy and probably did the same to you."

Laurel thought about that. She did feel clearheaded, more so than she had in hours.

"What do you think they're going to do to us?" she asked.

"I'm trying not to think about it," Bess said.

"I wish I'd stuck some of that garlic from the garden in my pocket. Or maybe we could make a cross."

Bess actually laughed. The sound of it made Laurel feel better, like maybe the end of the world wasn't quite here yet.

"You're thinking of vampires," Bess said.

"Well, what don't little tree men like?"

"Who knows? Fire, probably."

"Do you have any matches?"

"Sure. Right here in my pocket with my corncob pipe."

Laurel sighed. "That's okay. We haven't got anything to burn anyway."

Bess gave her hand another squeeze.

"We just have to be patient," she said, "and wait for our chance."

"And then we kick ass."

"I know I'd like to kick something."

A Savage Grace

Sarah Jane

It was a funny thing about that world on the other side of the Apple Tree Man's door. You'd think, seeing the effect it had on Aunt Lillian and me after just a peek through at it, that once we got through into that world we'd have been overwhelmed. But it didn't happen that way. Sure, the place was a shock to our senses. Colors were more intense . . . oh, what am I saying? Everything was more intense. Colors, the air we breathed, the sharp edges of the blades of grass, the birdsong drifting down from the trees, the endless blue sky above. But I remembered what the Apple Tree Man had told us about coming to this place, how we'd never want to leave, and I didn't feel that way at all.

When I said as much, the Apple Tree Man gave me a funny look. I thought maybe I'd offended him, so I tried to explain.

"When I was a kid," I said, "we moved all the time, from one trailer park to another. It got so I never felt like I fit in, not anywhere we lived. I'm not blaming Mama and Daddy—that's just the way it was. Leastwise, it was until we moved to Granny Burrell's farm. Now I've lived there for pretty much as long as I've lived in all those other places put together, and you know what? I really like it.

"I like my familiar woods, watching the changes settle on them, season after season. I don't feel like a visitor anymore. I feel like a neighbor now. Like I belong. And pretty as this place is, I don't belong here. I can feel it like a buzz just under my skin. All over. It's saying, 'You've got another home.' "

"You could've took the words right out of my mouth," Aunt Lillian said. "I remember how scared I was of those woods around the homestead when I first came to live with my Aunt Em. But that feeling went away pretty quick and I've never wanted to leave them since. Even Paradise is going to seem wanting after living in those hills of ours."

The Apple Tree Man shook his head as he looked from her to me.

"I guess a body's never too old to be surprised," he said, "but I have to tell you, I had no idea you were so strong."

"Strong?" I said.

He nodded. "To resist the enchantments of this place so effortlessly."

"Makes you think, doesn't it?" Aunt Lillian said. "'Bout wasted years and all."

He nodded again, slower this time. I guess it finally hit him that he didn't have to keep Aunt Lillian at a distance—didn't have to, never had to. He got this hangdog look in his eyes that made me want to tell a joke or something, just to cheer him up.

"I just didn't know," he said.

"It's the red hair that makes them strong, Applejack," a voice said from above. "Why else do you think we cherish it so?"

Aunt Lillian and I pretty much jumped out of our skins. We looked up and saw what we thought was a cat sitting up there on a branch, looking back down at us. Except it wasn't really a cat. It was more like a little man, or a monkey, with a long tail and all covered with black fur and catlike features. It had fingers like me, but a cat's retracting claws that protruded at the moment as he cleaned them with a bright pink tongue.

"How come fairy creatures always talk to me from out of trees?" Aunt Lillian said.

"What do you mean?" I asked.

"Nothing," she said. "It's an old story."

The cat man laid out along his branch, head propped up on one hand. He looked to be about twice the height of our little unconscious 'sangman but that still only made him a couple of feet tall.

"Oh, do tell," he said.

But Aunt Lillian had already looked away, her attention now on the Apple Tree Man.

"He called you Applejack," she said. "Is that your real name—the one you never told me?"

"It's a name," the Apple Tree Man said. "The one by which I'm known in this place, just like I'm the Apple Tree Man in your world."

"So what *is* your name?" I asked.

"Well, when he's drunk," the cat man said, "we call him Billy Cider."

"We don't have names the way you do," the Apple Tree Man said. "We don't have any need for them. All we have are what people call us."

"Like sometimes," the cat man said, "people call me Li'l Pater." He waited a beat, then added, "You know, because I could be a smaller version of the Father of Cats."

Aunt Lillian looked back up at him and smiled. "A *much* smaller version," she said. "And not nearly as fierce."

"It's just what some people call me."

I got the feeling that this was something he tried out on every new person he met, hoping that they'd think maybe he really was kin to that big old black panther that Aunt Lillian had met when she was younger than me.

"We can call you that," I said.

"What are you doing here?" the Apple Tree Man asked.

Li'l Pater smiled. "I came to see the fireworks and oh my, they should be something."

"Fireworks?" I asked.

"He doesn't mean real fireworks," the Apple Tree Man explained.

"You do know that the bee queen's really not happy with you?" Li'l Pater asked.

The Apple Tree Man shrugged. He glanced at Aunt Lillian and said, "Let her get in line."

"I'm not mad at you," Aunt Lillian told him. "Just disappointed you never took the chance."

"Why's the bee queen mad?" I asked.

"When isn't she mad?" Li'l Pater replied. "But this time it's because that little 'sangman you've got stowed away in a basket stole away her daughter and you got in the middle of her settling her debt with him."

I looked at the Apple Tree Man. "I thought that happened ages ago."

"It did," Li'l Pater said before the Apple Tree Man could speak. "The first time. But this is the seventh daughter of hers that's gone off and wed a 'sangman. She really thought the sixth would be the last. But just to be sure, this one she kept in a hive as tall as a tree, locked up in a little room way up top with only a window to look out of."

"Like Rapunzel."

"Don't know her. What court is she from?"

"It's in a storybook."

"This isn't a story," Li'l Pater said.

"What I don't understand," Aunt Lillian said, "is why these daughters of hers keep running off to marry 'sangmen. You say there've been seven now?"

"Just like me and my sisters," I said.

"You've all married 'sangmen?" Li'l Pater asked.

"No, I just meant there's seven of us, too."

Li'l Pater nodded. "Lucky number. 'Specially when you add in the red hair."

"What's so special about red hair?"

"Everything. A fairy can't hardly resist a red-haired human. It's as much a reason for them to be kidnapping your sisters as to make a bargain with you."

"Wait a minute. What do you mean kidnapping my sisters?"

Li'l Pater regarded them with surprise. "You didn't know? The 'sangmen have two while the bee court has the other four."

I thought my heart would stop in my chest and gave Aunt Lillian and the Apple Tree Man an anguished look.

"Why . . . why are they doing this?" I asked.

"For barter," Li'l Pater said. "They want to trade your sisters for the 'sangman in your basket."

"But we were already *bringing* him back."

"They didn't know that."

"And if both sides have my . . . my sisters . . . what am I supposed to do? Choose between which I'll save and which I'll sacrifice?" I looked down at the 'sangman. "For somebody I don't even know?"

"Should have thought of that before you got involved in all of this," Li'l Pater said.

I nodded glumly. Aunt Lillian had warned me often enough. The one sure road to trouble, she'd say, is to get mixed up in the middle of a fairy quarrel.

"That doesn't matter now," I said. "All that's important is that we rescue my sisters, and for that, we need a plan."

"This should be good," Li'l Pater said.

"And to start with," I went on, "I don't want you around when I'm making it."

"What did I ever—"

"I don't know you," I told him. "And right now I can't take the chance of trusting you." I turned to the Apple Tree Man. "And come to think of it, who's to say that I can trust you either?"

"Now, Sarah Jane," Aunt Lillian said. "The Apple Tree Man might be a lot of things, but—"

I shook my head, not letting her finish. "He may be your friend, but I wouldn't call him a very good one. And he certainly hasn't said or done anything to prove that he's mine. I can't take the chance of trusting any fairy—not with my sisters' lives at stake."

Before anyone could protest, I stepped over to where the Apple Tree Man had set down the basket with the 'sangman still sleeping in it. I picked up the basket.

"I may have my own disappointments with the Apple Tree Man," Aunt Lillian said, "but I'd trust him with my life."

"What about the lives of my sisters?"

She regarded me for a long moment, then shook her head.

"That's something you can only decide for yourself," she said.

I don't know where this fierce feeling had come from—probably something locked in the Dillard genes. We were the kind of folks who depended on ourselves. But I guess it could have just been blind panic, born out of the shock of learning that my sisters were all in danger and it was my fault. My fault, but fairy were caught up in every which part of it.

The thing that swayed me was how the Apple Tree Man didn't try to change my mind. Li'l Pater sat up on his branch, muttering about I don't know what all. I wasn't listening to him. But the Apple Tree Man stood still as a tree, waiting for me to make up my own mind.

And I guess the other thing that swayed me was I didn't have the first clue how to go about doing anything. I didn't know where the 'sangmen lived—leastways not in this world. I didn't know what to do when I found them. I didn't know anything about these bee fairies and how to go about rescuing anyone from them either. I pretty much didn't know anything.

So I took a breath and looked at the Apple Tree Man.

"I'm sorry," I said. "I guess if Aunt Lillian trusts you as much as she does, I should be able to do the same. I'm just so worried about my sisters."

"I understand," he said.

"And what about me?" Li'l Pater asked. "Are you going to let me help?" He spread his fingers and his cat claws popped out from the end of each of them. "I can be fierce as the Father himself."

Having accepted the Apple Tree Man's help, I looked to him for guidance on this. He gave Li'l Pater a stern look.

"You'll only help?" he asked. "No tricks, no jokes?"

Li'l Pater nodded.

"You swear on the fangs of the Father?"

He nodded again.

The Apple Tree Man turned back to me.

"By that oath," he said, "you can trust him."

"So what do we do?" I asked.

I was anxious. I didn't know what the fairies were doing to my sisters, but every moment they were with them was too long for me.

"First we'll follow our original plan," the Apple Tree Man said. "We'll see the 'sangmen and free the sisters they have. When they see we're returning their little prince, they'll be honor-bound to let your sisters go and help us."

"And the bee fairies?" Aunt Lillian asked.

"I have an idea how to deal with them as well, though it will depend on Sarah Jane's courage."

The very idea of bees made my knees knock together, but I knew I'd try whatever was needed to be done.

2

Adie and Elsie

Except for being covered in bees, the twins didn't seem to otherwise be hurt just yet, so Adie turned her attention to Elsie's knapsack. The fairies had left it on her back, either because they didn't know what it was, or they didn't care. After all, what could a couple of teenage girls do, hands bound and with such a host to stand against them?

"What do you use to sharpen those pencils of yours?" Adie asked.

"Just this old jackknife that George gave me," Elsie said.

"Is it sharp?"

"Well, sure it is. It has to be to cut the wood properly . . ." Her voice trailed off and she gave Adie a quick look. "What are you planning to do with it?"

"Whatever it takes to get us all out of here."

The attention of the whole fairy court, including their guards, was on the tubby little man who'd arrived with the twins in tow. If she was ever going to have a chance, this was going to be it.

"Turn around so I can get at your knapsack," she said.

"I don't like this," Elsie said, but she did as she'd been asked. "There's too many of them, Adie."

"I only need to get to the queen," Adie replied.

With her hands bound together, Adie had trouble getting the fastenings undone, but she finally got the last one loose and was able to reach in. She dug around among Elsie's sketchbooks and the various roots and twigs and whatnots that Elsie picked up on her walks until she felt the handle of the knife and pulled it out. Laying it on the ground, she took the time to close up the knapsack again before trying to open the knife. After a lot of fussing and one broken nail, she managed to pull the blade out of the handle and began the awkward process of sawing through the grass rope. Luckily, Elsie hadn't been exaggerating. The blade was sharp and easily sliced through the tightly-woven rope.

"This is only asking for more trouble," Elsie said.

"They brought it on."

"So you're just going to stab one of them?"

"Look," Adie said. "They're not even people, okay? They're bugs. And the thing you do with bugs when they start annoying you is you squash them."

"But—"

"No one threatens my sisters, Elsie. That's the bottom line."

After checking to make sure that they were still unobserved, she cut through Elsie's ropes.

"Make sure you hold your hands like they're still tied," Adie said.

Elsie nodded. Her gaze went to where the twins were being brought up to the fairy bee queen.

"Look what they've done to our Ruthie and Grace," Elsie said.

"I know. They may be brats, but they're *our* brats." Adie touched Elsie's shoulder to get her to turn around. "I'm going to slip off into the woods. What I need you to do is create a diversion in about, oh, say, five minutes."

"I think we should try the disbelieving business first."

Adie shook her head. "I think it's way too late for that so far as we're concerned. I mean, we *know* they're here, right?"

"I suppose."

"Trust me on this," Adie said.

Before Elsie could think of something else to try to get her to stay, Adie slipped off behind the tree and into the woods.

3

Laurel and Bess

"I think I hate the dark," Laurel said.

"This is the first I've heard of it."

"Maybe I've always hated it, but I just didn't know till now because I was never anyplace so dark before."

Normally, all Laurel had to do was close her eyes and she could call up Bess's features in her mind's eye. But here, where it was just as black whether she had her eyes open or not, she couldn't do it. There was only the unending dark and it was beginning to get to her.

"If we were Girl Scouts," she went on, "we'd have come prepared with a flashlight."

She couldn't see Bess's smile, but she could feel it.

"Or at least candle and matches," Bess said.

"Exactly. And maybe a bag of chips or some cookies."

"Except if we were Girl Scouts," Bess said, "we'd still be working in the garden, because Girl Scouts do what they say they'll do. They don't go off chasing after fiddlers in the woods."

"So we'd be lousy Girl Scouts from the get-go."

"Pretty much."

Laurel sighed. "I guess we should have been looking out for some old lady to help on our way into the woods. Or a talking spoon. Or a lion with a thorn in his paw or something."

"What for?"

"Well, you know. In the stories they always come back to help you when you get in a pickle."

"I hate stories like that," Bess said. "People should help each other for the sake of doing a kind deed—not because they're scared not to, or for some reward."

"You mean like Sarah Jane helps Aunt Lillian."

Now it was Bess's turn to sigh. "And we're always teasing her about it. I guess you're right. We should have been looking for talking spoons and the like."

"Nobody even knows we're here, do they?" Laurel said.

"Except for the little man who dumped us here."

Neither said anything for a long moment.

"Did I mention how much I hate the dark?" Laurel finally asked.

"Maybe once."

Laurel squeezed Bess's hand. If she had to be stuck in a place like this, there was no one else she'd rather be with. This was how they came into the world, the two of them, together in the dark womb. Perhaps they were going to go out in the darkness as well. That made her think about her life and what she'd done with it. Sarah Jane had a few years' worth of good deeds in her favor. What did she have?

"So do you think we're shallow people?" she asked.

"No," Bess said. "We're passionate about music, aren't we? I don't think that shallow people are passionate about anything."

"Music. That's what got us here in the first place. There was some kind of magic in that fiddling, wasn't there? You knew right away, didn't you?"

"I didn't know exactly," Bess said. "But I knew there was something not right." Laurel thought Bess was finished, but after a moment Bess added, "Maybe we should make our own music magic."

"With what? We don't have any instruments."

"We could lilt a tune."

"And do what with it?" Laurel asked. "If you've been taking magic lessons, this is the first I've heard of it."

"Well, at least it would help to pass the time."

"That's true."

They both fell quiet until Laurel finally said, "I can't think of a single tune."

"This from the girl who was ready to have a tune contest with a woody fairy man."

"I can't believe I was so stupid."

"You weren't stupid," Bess said. "You were enchanted. It's not the same thing."

"I suppose. Oh, I know. We could try that version of 'Walk Like an Egyptian' that we never got to play at the dance last night."

"I don't know. I think it'd be too hard without my banjo. How about 'Sourwood Mountain' instead?"

"Okay."

Bess started to hum the tune. When Laurel came in with a nasal "diddly-diddly" lilting, Bess joined her, the two of them taking turns harmonizing on the melody. They went from tune to tune, sticking with those that were associated with the Stanley Brothers, since that was how they'd started, and it was like they were sitting in on a session with their instruments in hand. Everything went away, except for the music. It didn't particularly help them in their present situation, but at least it made them feel a lot better.

4

Sarah Jane

I let Aunt Lillian and the Apple Tree Man take the lead and followed along behind with Li'l Pater at my side. The little cat man still seemed put out that I hadn't wanted to include him in our party and wasn't talking to me, but that was okay. I didn't really want to talk to anybody. I didn't want to talk, didn't want to think. I just wanted my sisters to be safe again.

The only thing that made any of this even remotely bearable was seeing how well Aunt Lillian and the Apple Tree Man were getting along. She seemed younger than I ever remembered her to be—her back was straighter, she was sprier and giggling. Maybe it was something in the air of this place, but I think it was the fact that the Apple Tree Man was finally back in her life.

Personally, I don't know what she saw in him. I won't say he was butt-ugly, but he sure wasn't going to win himself any prizes for handsomeness either. I guess it's that he just wasn't human, not with his gnarly limbs and that barky skin with all those twigs and leaves and such growing out of him every which where. I'd have thought that maybe at Aunt Lillian's age, it wasn't a physical thing, that courting wasn't so important anymore, but she was acting just like Adie or the older twins do when they're flirting with some fellow.

It got me to wondering if I was ever going to know what it felt like. I decided that since it hadn't happened yet—and here I was about as old as Adie when she took off with Johnny Garland—it probably never would.

That just made me glummer.

Then I realized what I was doing—worrying about my love life, or more to the point, the fact that I didn't have even the slightest promise of one—while the only thing that should have been on my mind was the trouble I'd put my sisters in.

That totally depressed me.

"How come you're so mad at me?" Li'l Pater said.

I turned to him. "What?"

"Well, you must be, the way you're giving me the silent treatment and all."

I didn't really want to be talking about this with him, but I suppose it was better than listening to the conversation inside my own head.

"I'm not mad at you," I said. "I don't even know you."

"And that's why you don't want my help."

"Look," I told him. "The Apple Tree Man vouches for you, and Aunt Lillian vouches for him, so here you are."

"But you don't want me to be here, do you?"

"I just want my sisters to be safe."

"We'll rescue them," he said with a confidence I didn't feel. "We're in the middle of a story now and since we're the heroes, it has to all come out right for us in the end. You'll see."

"Except in their minds, the bee fairies and 'sangmen are the heroes. Who's to say that the story won't go their way?"

"I never thought about that."

"Well, don't," I told him, already regretting that I'd put the question in his head. Mama often said that putting bad thoughts into the air by speaking them aloud was a sure way to call bad luck to you. "I like the way you think it'll all work out, way better than I do the worries in my own head."

I was so busy talking to Li'l Pater that I bumped right into the Apple Tree Man, never having realized that he and Aunt Lillian had come to a stop.

"What is it?" I asked.

But I guessed pretty quick by the stony ground underfoot and the thick canopy of poplar and beech and oak. We were on familiar ground, standing at the top of a slope running down into a 'sang field, the plants growing thick and tall below us. We could have been in the same one as I found the 'sangman in yesterday. I suppose some places aren't that much different from one world to the other.

"I'm going to call the 'sangmen to us," the Apple Tree Man said. "Unless they ask you a question directly, let me do the talking."

I gave him a reluctant nod, still not trusting him as much as Aunt Lillian did.

"And if you do have to answer a question," he added, "give them the answer and nothing more."

"Do you know these people?" I asked.

"We've met, but I've never spent a lot of time with them. I don't much cotton to the whole idea of courts and royalty and all the way some of the fairy do."

"Why not?"

"Well, the trouble with courts," the Apple Tree Man said, "is you're stuck with a king or a queen and they almost always think that the whole world turns around them."

I knew a few folks like that back in our own world.

"I like to go my own way," he added, "and not be beholden to anyone else."

I knew a bunch of folks like that, too, starting with pretty much my whole family.

"I'll follow your lead," I told him.

He called out, making a sound that was like a cross between the nasal *yank-yank* of a nuthatch and a fox's bark. I gave Aunt Lillian a look, but she was studying the land below. When I turned to have my own look at the 'sang field, I saw them come popping up all over the patch, little 'sangmen and women, all gnarled and rooty like the wounded fellow I'd rescued, the one that got us all into this mess in the first place.

It was eerie to watch. One minute there was just the 'sang, growing taller and with more prongs than I ever saw back in our own world, and the next we had a whole mess of these little people in among the 'sang, and not much taller than the plants, looking up at us. It was like they'd come right up out of the ground, and for all I know, that's exactly what they did.

But what concerned me right about now was how there wasn't the one of them was wearing what I'd call a friendly expression. I looked to the Apple Tree Man and didn't take much comfort from the fact that he didn't seem near so worried as I was feeling my own self. I started to say something, but then I remembered his warning. So I just stood there and kept my mouth shut, waiting along with the others as those 'sangfolk came up the slope towards us.

Oh, it was a strange sight. A goodly number of them were taller than the little man I'd found—two or three times his one-foot height, some of them. But if a lot of them were bigger, they looked pretty much the same, more tree than man. They were like walking bushes with bark for skin and rooty hair and twigs and leaves and every such growing up out of them every which place you might look.

The one in front was near four feet high, but he gave off something that made him seem bigger still. I can't tell you exactly what it was. I guess maybe it was the fact that he was the boss, which was something I found out as soon as he and the Apple Tree Man began to talk.

"So, Applejack," this big 'sangman said. "Have you come to trade my boy's life for the girls?"

The Apple Tree Man shook his head. When he spoke, his voice was mild, with just the smallest hint of a rebuke in it.

"We were only bringing him back to you," he said. "Doing what any good neighbor would do, he sees someone in trouble."

I felt Li'l Pater stiffen at my side and knew what he'd be thinking. The Apple Tree Man was just up and giving away our bargaining chip. But I figured I knew what he was about and I guess I'd have done the same. There's no time when it's right to trade in people's lives, no ifs and buts about it. Though if you want to look for a silver lining, I suppose it's always better to have somebody be beholden to you than not.

But I still held my breath, waiting for that 'sangman king to answer. After all, these were my sisters we were talking about.

"Looks like I owe you an apology," the king finally said. "I'd been told you were ready to trade him to the bee court, but I should have known better."

The Apple Tree Man didn't reply. He just handed over that basket as easy as you please. A 'sangwoman come up from behind the king and plucked the boy out of the basket. The way she held him so close to her chest, I figured she had to be his mother. 'Bout then I also noticed this pretty little thing, as different from the 'sangmen as

I am from a crow. She was pale-skinned and golden-haired, her features fine and sharp, and fluttering at her back were a pair of honest-to-goodness little wings. She came sidling up and the 'sang-woman included her in her embrace.

"Someone bring up those red-haired girls," the king said over his shoulder.

One of the other bigger 'sangmen popped out of sight and before you could say Jimmy-had-a-penny, he was back with Laurel and Bess in tow. The two of them stood blinking in the sun, Bess brushing dirt from her jeans.

Soon as I saw them, I didn't mind me either the Apple Tree Man's advice, or the worry of maybe upsetting 'sangmen. I just ran forward and hugged them both, as happy to see them, I reckon, as the 'sang queen was to get her own boy back.

While we were still in the middle of all of that was when the king started in with the tall tales, covering up for how he hadn't taken the time to trust that the Apple Tree Man, at least, would do right by him and his people. I guess royalty in fairyland isn't all that much different from the politicians in ours. Folks in charge just can't seem to actually admit to making a mistake and you can't really call them on their lies because, as soon as the words leave their mouth, it's gospel, so far as they're concerned.

"We aren't like the bee queen," he said. "We took the girls, sure, but it was only to protect them. When we heard that the bees had captured two of your young miss's sisters, I sent my forester to watch over the others and bring them here if they should happen to come into the forest.

"Two did, and he brought them safe. But when he got back to watching for the others, it was to find that they'd already been taken by the bees."

I led the twins back to where Aunt Lillian was standing with the Apple Tree Man. They gave Li'l Pater a curious look, but by then they must have been getting as used to fairy-tale people as I was, and they were more interested in what the king was saying. Laurel hadn't heard the Apple Tree Man's warning about letting him do the talking, and I guess, being who she was, she probably wouldn't have listened anyway.

"He wasn't just watching anything," she said. "He pulled us right into the forest with his fiddle playing."

"What else was I supposed to do?" the forester said.

I recognized him as the 'sangman who'd brought the twins up from wherever it was they'd been kept, and was surprised to find myself starting to tell the difference between them, because when they first came popping up all over the 'sang field, I'd have said they all looked the same.

"You try sitting in a meadow for hour after hour," he went on, "waiting on the chance that somebody might or might not take it into their head to come rambling up in the woods."

"So instead you put some kind of spell on us with your music."

He shook his head. "I was just passing the time."

"And your 'contest'?"

"I thought it a good way to bring you back without having to get into all the whys and wherefores that you probably wouldn't have believed anyway."

"Right. So then you stole our instruments and—"

"Now that's just a plain lie!"

"Now everybody hold on here," the king said. "Maybe we didn't choose the best way to bring you here—"

"Not to mention that the accommodations sucked big time," Laurel muttered.

"But we meant well."

I didn't care if that was the way he wanted to see it. He could tell any kind of story at all so far as I was concerned, just so long as the twins were safe. But my sisters weren't ready to let it go just yet.

"Then who stole our instruments?" Bess asked.

"Maybe we can worry on that some other time," the Apple Tree Man said. "Right now we should be making plans to rescue your other sisters."

"Just say the word," the king said. "We can't field the same numbers as the bee court, but we'll fight beside you until we win, or there's none of us left standing."

"I was hoping to find a more peaceful way to settle this," the Apple Tree Man said.

I was ready to go along with that, but the king shook his head.

"The bees only know one kind of argument," he told us. "And that's who's stronger."

"Maybe so," the Apple Tree Man said, "and I don't mind having you to fall back on if things don't go right. But I've got something else I'd like to try first."

I guess we were pretty much all in disagreement with his plan when he was done telling it, except for Li'l Pater, who I still wasn't sure was really on our side. I could understand the Apple Tree Man helping us on account of Aunt Lillian, and the 'sangmen because they might feel beholden to us, but Li'l Pater was still a mystery.

"You've trusted me so far," the Apple Tree Man said. "Trust me just a little longer."

"And if it doesn't work?" I asked, not wanting to think of what might happen to my sisters, but I couldn't not think about it either.

"No one will be hurt," he said.

"Can you promise me that?"

He hesitated for a long moment, then slowly shook his head. "Can't anybody promise you that."

"It'll work," Li'l Pater assured us, which didn't help much so far as I was concerned. "The one thing fairies can't resist is a mystery."

I agreed in the end. I didn't feel like I had any other choice. By all accounts, the bee court far outnumbered the 'sangmen. Adding in the Apple Tree Man, an old woman, three girls, and some kind of little cat man didn't seem to change the odds much in our favor. And since no one was coming up with a better idea, we were stuck with this one, for better or worse.

"You're not doing this alone, Janey," Bess said.

Laurel nodded an agreement.

"But—"

"They're our sisters, too."

I looked to Aunt Lillian and the Apple Tree Man for help, but didn't find any.

"If there are three of you, it'll work more in your favor," he said. "Especially since you're all red-haired."

"What's that got to do with anything?" Bess asked.

"Redheads are sacred to the Father of Cats," Li'l Pater explained. "Most fairies won't harm them."

"So we don't really have anything to worry about," I said, happy now to have endured all those years of being called "Carrot-head," "Freckleface," and the like in the schoolyard.

The Apple Tree Man got an uncomfortable look.

"I said 'most,'" Li'l Pater told us.

"And there are many ways to hurt a person," the king of the 'sangmen added, "without actually killing them."

"Great," Laurel said.

Bess nodded unhappily. "Yes, that's really comforting to hear."

The thought of anything bad happening to my sisters was too much for me to be able to hold in my head for long without going crazy.

"Let's just do this," I said.

5

Ruth and Grace

The worst thing, Grace thought, about having bees all over your face and arms was how much they tickled. But you didn't dare do a thing about it. All you could do was feel the way your skin squirmed under all those fuzzy little bee feet and try to remember not to swat at them and their tiny riders. It was a horrible feeling. Even when the cloud of them finally lifted from her and Ruth, she could still feel thousands of little feet carpeting her skin. It was like the way you imagined cobwebs staying on you after you've brushed them away. Even though you know they're gone, a ghostly veil of them still clings to your skin.

"Grace . . . ?" Ruth said at her side.

Instead of rubbing at her face and arms the way Grace was, she was looking past Grace, farther up the slope, her face pale. Grace slowly turned to see what had caught her sister's attention.

She almost wished she hadn't.

Bee fairies, it seemed, could come in any size. From the tiny ones that had covered them on the journey to get here and the fat bumblebee man who'd captured them, to these terrifying lords and lady with their grim faces, sitting tall and straight-backed on horses that didn't seem quite right. But then the riders weren't quite right, either. They were almost people, but their features were all too sharp and they had a cold light in their eyes like no normal person Grace had ever seen. There were footmen, too. A lot of them. Armed with bows and arrows, rapiers, and slender spears with barbed tips.

Her own heart sank.

"So," she said in a small voice, her hand reaching for and finding Ruth's. "Tell me again why we left the house today, when we could have been safely doing housework, which, I have to tell you now, I would just love to be doing because it'd sure beat being here."

"Anything would beat being here," Ruth said.

"You wouldn't happen to have any firecrackers in your pocket, would you? Or a pistol, say?"

"No, but . . . but would a can of Raid do?"

Grace squeezed her hand and found a weak smile. "Never let them see you're scared," she remembered Adie telling them once when she and Ruth were being picked on by some kids at school. "That only eggs them on like they're a pack of dogs. Just stand up and take the licking, and try to give back as good as you get. You might get hurt, but they're going to know you're not easy targets and next time they'll think twice before they come after you."

And it had worked, too—a couple of black eyes and a few dozen scrapes and bruises later. They'd only ever had to fight twice, standing back to back as the bullies ganged up on them. They might only have been ten years old at the time, but after that, even the older kids left them alone.

"A can of Raid would be perfect," she told Ruth now.

"If only."

"And it would have to be humongous. How big a pocket do you have anyway?"

"Be still!" the only woman in the group told them.

She looked to be their leader—the queen bee, Grace supposed. They all had a hardness, a mean, savage air about them, but from the look of her, she could have invented the very idea of meanness. Which was sad for a whole bunch of reasons, but one was that she could have been so pretty if she hadn't let that cruelty twist her features.

Grace swallowed hard. No fear, she told herself. Or at least don't show it.

"Oh, shut up, yourself," she said. "Who do you think you are—our mother?"

Ruth tugged at her sleeve with her free hand. "You know, maybe we shouldn't be quite so—"

"I am hardly your mother," the woman interrupted, her voice like ice. "I am no one's mother. Not any longer."

"Big surprise there," Grace said. "No boyfriend either, I'm guessing. Not with that personality."

"May . . . maybe you should think about a makeover," Ruth said.

That was the spirit, Grace thought.

"Oh sure," she added. "Mama says they can make you feel like a whole new woman, which with you, would be a big improvement."

The woman smiled, which somehow made her scarier than when she was just looking mean.

If she could have, Grace would have taken off right then. Just run off with Ruth, as fast and as far away from here as they could. But they couldn't outrun horses. Or those strange dogs she now spied, six or seven of them crouched in a half-circle. She blinked, realizing that the dogs had Root penned up against the trunk of some old apple tree, though Root didn't appear to be taking much notice of them.

Turning back to the woman, she caught a glimpse of red hair farther up the slope. Staring harder, she realized it was Elsie, sitting on the ground under a big beech tree, her hands tied in front of her.

Did that mean they had Adie, too? And Janey?

"I don't know if you're brave or simply half-witted," the woman said, "and frankly, I don't really care. But you are an annoyance."

"Shall we bind them and put them with the others?" one of the footmen standing by her horse asked.

"Well, now," the queen said. "We certainly don't need all four of these wretched girls to bargain with. All we need is one more than the dirt-eaters have."

"Should I take the other back to their world?" the fat little man who'd captured them asked.

"Why bother? Just kill one of them—the rude one who talks too much—and put the other with her sisters."

"But, madam," the little man began, obviously as shocked as Grace was with the queen's offhand order for her execution. "They are red-haired . . ."

The queen gave him a long cold look. "Are you arguing with me?"

"No, but . . . the Father of Cats says such mortals are sacred."

The queen made a sharp motion with her hand and one of the footmen stepped forward, notched an arrow and let fly. All Grace's bravery fled. She winced, but the arrow wasn't meant for her. It struck the little man in the throat and he went down, knees buckling under him. He gasped, tearing at the arrow with his fingers. Blood streamed over his hands and down his chest before he toppled over onto the ground.

Grace thought she was going to throw up. Ruth's sudden tight grip on her hand would have hurt if she wasn't already gripping Ruth's hand just as fiercely.

"Thank you," the queen told her footman. She turned to regard her court. "Does anyone else have something they wish to discuss?"

It had been quiet in the meadow before this. Now the silence was utter. Not even the horses moved.

The queen returned her gaze to the twins, that terrible smile twitching the corners of her mouth.

"That's better," she said. "Now if someone would deal with these little wretches . . . ?"

The bowman notched another arrow.

6

Adie

Creeping through the underbrush, Adie heard none of the twins' exchange with the queen. She was too busy sneaking up on one of the queen's footmen—a scout or a guard, she wasn't sure which. It didn't matter. All she knew was she didn't want him behind her when she went for the queen with Elsie's little jackknife.

She didn't really think she'd succeed. Or if she did, she didn't think she'd survive. But the jackknife was made of steel, so it had iron in it, and all the fairy tales said iron was deadly to fairies, so there was the chance she'd be able to do some damage. And while she might not survive, perhaps at least her sisters might get away in the confusion.

That was all that really mattered. That they were safe.

Right now the jackknife was folded up and in the pocket of her jeans. In her hands was a three-foot-long branch that she'd picked up from the debris under the trees. It hadn't been her first choice. She'd kept picking up and hefting various branches as she continued to sneak up on the bee fairy until she finally found one with some weight to it that didn't feel as though it would break the first time she used it.

It was hard to stay quiet. If this part of the wood hadn't been sprucey-pine, she probably wouldn't have gotten as far as she did. But the ground was thick with a carpet of needles, spongy and silent underfoot. Every time she did make some noise—stepped on a twig, pushed through the occasional bush—she stopped dead and crouched low, not daring to breathe, hoping the bee fairy would think it was only a squirrel or bird.

Maybe it was true that they had some Indian blood in them from their father's side, she thought, as she managed to creep almost up on the footman without his noticing her.

Okay, this was it.

She straightened up, took a long, deep breath, and stepped forward, swinging the branch. The footman grunted when the branch connected with the back of his head and toppled forward, his spear falling from his hand. The force of the blow stung the palms of Adie's hands enough so that she almost lost her grip on the branch. The footman landed on his hands, down but not out.

They're not people, Adie reminded herself. They're bugs. It's hurt them or be hurt *by* them.

She swung the branch again, just as the footman was half-rising and turning in her direction. The blow caught him in the temple and this time he went down and stayed there.

Adie dropped the branch and had to go down on one knee. She was shaking so badly she didn't think she could stand and felt she might throw up. But she made herself take a few steadying breaths until the queasiness passed and she was able to get back to her feet. Picking up her stick, she held it ready and nudged the footman with her foot. He didn't move. She tried again. When he still didn't move, she traded her branch for his spear and began to work her way back to the meadow where the fairy court held her sisters captive.

She arrived just in time to see one of the queen's footmen kill a fat little man that looked like a bumblebee, then turn his bow in Grace's direction.

7

Elsie

As soon as the twins began to mouth off to the fairy queen, Elsie shook her head. She couldn't believe that they were being their usual incorrigible selves at a time like this. Didn't they realize that they were just making things worse?

And speaking of things getting worse, any moment the bee fairies were going to notice that Adie was gone.

Making sure that nobody was looking in her direction, she got to her feet and looked around for something she could use as a weapon. She wished her legs didn't feel like jelly, that her heartbeat wasn't drumming double-time in her chest. That she could at least take one deep breath.

Why couldn't she be as brave as Adie, just getting up and doing what needed to be done?

She glanced back at the fairy court, then stood rooted in place, watching in horror as the queen had the fat little man standing by the twins shot by one of her footmen. He notched another arrow and aimed it at Grace.

Her protective instincts sent a surge of adrenaline through her and she could move again. There was no time to worry if Adie was in position or not. Now was the time for the diversion. But while she was trying to decide between running around shrieking like a madwoman, or picking up a stick and attacking her captors, someone else provided the diversion for her.

Wide-eyed, she watched Sarah Jane, Laurel and Bess come dancing into the glade, paying no attention to the gathering of bee fairies.

8

Sarah Jane

I felt like a guerrilla soldier as we made our way to where the bee fairy court was holding my sisters captive. Li'l Pater led the way—something which didn't particularly thrill me, but both the Apple Tree Man and the 'sangmen deferred to him in this, explaining that moving between the worlds could be tricky. The Apple Tree Man only went back and forth through his tree, while the 'sangmen usually only crossed in between their 'sang patches in either world. So without someone like Li'l Pater, we could end up miles from where we needed to be, or at a disadvantage as we all tried to sneak out of the Apple Tree Man's tree without being seen.

Li'l Pater brought us out of the fairies' world and back into our own right in the woods just above Aunt Lillian's orchard. At one point he held up a hand for us all to stop while he crept ahead. When he finally waved at us to come along, I spied one of the bee fairies unconscious behind a tree, trussed up with grass ropes. It seemed he was a little fiercer than you'd think from the little size of him. And then I saw the bee court and my sisters below and realized he'd played us fair in this as well.

"I guess I misjudged you," I told him.

He was pretty gracious about it, except for the little smirk in one corner of his mouth.

"Oh, that's all right," he said. "I know that's just the way you big folks are."

"Yes, well, it's not like we—"

"You'll be careful," Aunt Lillian said, crouching beside us.

I nodded, wondering if she'd interrupted to stop me and Li'l Pater from getting into another argument. Probably. Not much got past Aunt Lillian. And while I was trying my best not to get started again, Li'l Pater didn't make it easy and I could feel it happening all the same.

I turned from them to stare out at the bee fairies. I guess they were more like the way I'd always pictured fairies in my head—sort of special and scary, all at the same time. Instead of being all rooty and earthy like the 'sangmen, they were bright and shining, sharp-featured and tall. Some rode horses and they had a pack of lean dogs that had Root penned up against the Apple Tree Man's tree. Root wasn't paying any attention to them. He was just staring at that tree—waiting for us to come back out again, I guess.

Looking back at the fairy court, I picked out the red heads of my sisters. Grace and Ruth were easy to spot—they looked like they'd just been brought in and were the center of everybody's attention. It took me a little longer to find Elsie, way over by a tree. I couldn't find Adie and my heart started beating too quick. I had to hope she was just lying down in the grass, out of sight.

While I was studying the fairy court, the 'sangmen slipped away from us, taking up positions all along the edge of the woods close to where we'd arrived. They carried stout cudgels and spears, knives and short bows with arrows made of some kind of dark wood and fletched with what looked like owl feathers. The 'sangmen were supposed to be our backup in case the Apple Tree Man's plan didn't work out. Seeing the size of the bee court, I was surely hoping it wouldn't come to a fight. There were *way* too many of the bee fairies for my liking.

Taking a steadying breath, I turned to the twins.

"Remember," I warned them as we were about to leave our hidey-hole on the edge of the meadow. "No matter what happens, not a word."

Bess mimed a zipper closing from one corner of her mouth to the other.

"Our lips are sealed," she said.

Laurel grinned. "Good one. The Go-Go's, right?"

" 'Fraid so. I know they're completely passé."

"Nope, they're doing a reunion tour, remember?"

"I always liked the Bangles better."

"This is serious," I told them.

"We know that, Janey," Bess said, putting her hand on my arm. "But we're scared and this is the only way we know how to deal with it."

"Hey," Laurel asked the Apple Tree Man. "Is it okay if we hum while we're doing this?"

"I don't see why not," he told them.

"And we could dance, too," Bess said, "till we get up close."

Laurel nodded. "But something slow. I vote for 'Shenandoah.' "

"Incongruous dancing is an excellent way to get their attention," the Apple Tree Man assured them.

"What do you think, Janey?" Laurel asked, turning to me.

"Why not?" I said.

Nothing seemed real, anyway.

I looked away from them, back out to where the bee court was holding my other sisters captive. The queen looked angry. She said something that I couldn't quite hear from where we were. But then she waved her arm and one of her footmen just up and put an arrow into the throat of this fat little man standing by the twins. My stomach did a flip as he dropped to the ground, blood pouring out of his neck. The next thing I knew he had another arrow nocked and was aiming it straight at Grace.

"Oh god," I said. "We don't have any more time."

I turned to Laurel and Bess. All their tomfoolery had drained away, along with the blood in their faces. We were all pale-faced and feeling a little shaky as we came dancing our way out of the trees, Laurel and Bess humming that old tune in two-part harmony, all of us with handfuls of grass in one hand, the pieces cut to lengths of six or seven inches.

Please, please, please, I was praying to whoever'd listen. Let this work. Don't let them shoot Grace like they did that little man.

A murmur rose from the bee court when they saw us coming, but I didn't dare look at them. I just concentrated on what we were doing. I wasn't nearly so nimble on my feet as the twins, but I did my best. Laurel and Bess got right into it, but then they're used to being on stage, performing in front of an audience, though I guess they'd never been in front of one this strange before. I just felt like a complete idiot. But I could take the embarrassment if it rescued my sisters.

About halfway between the trees and the bee court, we started laying down our blades of grass. We did it with deliberation, like it had meaning, just the way the Apple Tree Man had told us.

"Doesn't matter *what* it is you do," he'd told us, "just so long as it's long past curious and you do it with conviction. And don't answer them when they ask what you're doing, just keep at it."

"But what if they get mad at us?"

"Oh, they'll get mad all right. But so long as you keep at it, they won't be able to help themselves. They'll just have to know what you're doing. Maybe they'll threaten you, maybe they'll threaten your sisters, but you stick it out. There'll come a point when they'll start bribing you with anything and everything you might imagine."

"I've got a pretty good imagination," Laurel said.

Bess poked her in the side, but she smiled.

"You hold on," the Apple Tree Man told us, "until they offer you a boon—that's the only time you stop and look straight at them."

So that's what we did. I could feel a terrible twitch up between my shoulder blades. I guess I was just expecting that bowman to turn from Grace and shoot his arrow at one of us instead.

Anywise, like I said, halfway between them and the woods, we started making patterns with the blades of grass, laying them on the ground, carefully studying what we'd done, then laying another. Nothing that made sense, but we acted like it was the most important thing in the world and I guess, considering what all was at stake, maybe it was.

I know. It seemed crazy, but then I suppose lots of things in the stories Aunt Lillian's told me seemed that way when you first heard them, but they worked out okay in the end. I was just going to have to trust the Apple Tree Man that this would, as well.

I didn't look at the bee court, but I could hear them murmuring as I laid another blade of grass down, looked at it for a moment, changed its position, then did this slow soft-step to the side where I put two more down. Laurel and Bess were doing the same—I thought with their usual self-assurance until I noticed Bess's hand was trembling as she worked on the pattern she was building.

"What are they doing?" I heard someone ask.

It was a woman's voice—imperious and sharp. It had to be the queen.

Another voice murmured something apologetic that I couldn't make out.

"Well, then find out," the queen said.

I saw a footman approach Laurel. He poked her in the back with the end of his bow.

"You there," he said. "What are you doing?"

Her humming faltered, then died, leaving Bess to do a harmony on her own until she, too, stopped. Laurel turned to look at the footman and gave him a sweet smile that only me being her sister let me know she was a half-step away from blowing her top.

Don't, don't, I thought. Don't talk to them. Don't tell them what we're doing.

But she didn't give in, though I guess being Laurel, she had to ad lib some.

"Cabbages need their kings, too," she said, then went back to what she was doing.

"What is that supposed to mean?" the queen asked.

The footman poked Laurel again, but this time she completely ignored him. He turned his attention to me.

"You heard our queen," he said.

I thought I was ready for his poke, but I was in the middle of bending down and it made me lose my balance all the same. I went down on one shaking knee, expecting him to hit me or shoot me or I don't know what, but I made a point of laying out two more blades of grass, carefully arranging them, before getting back to my feet again.

"This is a trick of some kind," the queen said.

Of course it was. And I guess others in the court thought the same from the glimpses I snatched of them. But I could also see that the Apple Tree Man had been right: They were mesmerized by what we were doing, trying to figure it all out.

"Just shoot one of them," the queen ordered.

I forgot to breathe then. The twitch between my shoulder blades intensified. I knew the 'sangmen were ready to come charging out of the woods to help us, but at least one of us would die before they could do anything.

The fat little man who'd been standing with Ruth and Grace returned to my mind's eye.

The way the arrow went into his throat.

The blood.

Seconds slipped by and I dared a glance at the bee fairies,

quickly laying another blade of grass as I did. None of them had an arrow nocked and aimed at any of us. They'd just come closer, trying to get a better look at what we were doing.

"You!" the queen cried to one of the footmen near me. "Shoot her."

But the footman wasn't paying any attention to her.

I did another dancy side step, even though Laurel and Bess weren't humming their tune anymore, and carefully laid down three more blades of grass in a triangular pattern.

The queen addressed another of her footmen, then one of the riders who had dismounted to come closer. They all ignored her.

"Then I'll do it myself," the queen said.

She stepped to the footman standing closest to her and reached for his bow.

I don't know what would have happened then. But before the queen could grab a bow, there came this godawful cry from the woods where we'd left the 'sangmen. Anybody lives in these hills for a time knows that sound. It's the scream of a panther. You don't see them much at all, but time to time you'll hear that terrible cry of theirs, like a woman or child wailing in pain.

The cry was repeated, this time followed by a weird, quiet *pit-a-pat* sound that was loud in the sudden stillness. I tried to figure out what it was. Then I remembered Aunt Lillian's stories about the Father of Cats and the sound his tail made as it patted the ground.

The sound stopped everybody dead in their tracks, including the queen.

"The Father of Cats," I heard one of the fairies closest to me say.

The queen shook off her paralysis and reached for the bow again, but the footman stepped back, pulling it out of her reach.

"I . . . I'm sorry, madam," he said. "But the Father of Cats has spoken."

I figured for sure she'd blow her stack at that. Instead, she sighed and walked over to me.

"Very well," she said. She stood in my way. "Let's end this nonsense, child. Tell me what you're doing and I'll give you the gift of your sisters' lives."

I ignored her, just as the Apple Tree Man had told me to, though I was surely tempted. But getting away from the bee fairies this time wasn't enough. What was to stop them from coming after us again?

"You want more?" the queen asked. "What? Treasure? A long life? Good luck in love? A cure for your miserable freckles?"

I laid blades of grass at her feet, making a shape that started by her toe and then moved away till it looked like a fan.

"Answer me," the queen said.

I started to hum "Shenandoah," but I never could hold much of a tune. Luckily first Bess, and then Laurel picked it up, replacing my weak voice with their strong harmonies. I moved away from the queen to lay down more grass.

"Child," the queen said, her voice hard.

I took a pebble from my pocket and laid it on the ground, then balanced a blade of grass upon it.

"Offer her a boon," one of the other fairies said.

"Perhaps I'll change her into a toad," the queen replied. "We'll see how well she dances and sings and lays down those damnable blades of grass then."

Could she even do that? Probably. She was magic, after all.

I heard a buzzing and saw that some of the bee fairies were tinier than I thought possible. I'd never noticed them before, though I had noticed the bees they were riding. I just hadn't realized there were little people on them until a few of them flew right under my nose, trying to get a closer look at what I was doing.

"Offer her a boon," either the same bee fairy or another repeated.

"A boon, a boon," more of them took up.

The queen said nothing for such a long time that I finally had to sneak a peek at her.

"Well, child?" she said. "Is that what it will take to unravel this mystery for us?"

I laid down one more blade of grass, then straightened up until I was facing her. She stood a full head taller than me, imperious and threatening. I gave a quick nod.

"Then ask your boon," she said. "But remember this: if you've played us for fools, if all this game of dancing and blades of grass is only so much nonsense, the bargain will be undone."

I let the last of my grass fall to the ground and clasped my hands in front of me.

"What are the limits of the boon you will grant?" I asked, repeating what the Apple Tree Man had told me to say when it came to this moment.

The queen's eyes narrowed and I knew that she realized I'd been coached, but I guess there wasn't a whole lot she could do about it at this point.

"No harm can come to us or any under our protection," she said, reluctantly it seemed.

It was pretty much the answer that the Apple Tree Man told us she'd have to give.

"Nothing else?" I asked.

"Nothing else."

"Then this is the boon I ask," I said. "That you harm no one here, nor in any way cause harm to another for the rest of your days."

There was fury in the queen's eyes now. The Apple Tree Man had warned us about that as well. But I guess we had her right in a corner because she gave a unwilling nod.

"The boon is granted," she said, her voice tight. "Now tell us what you were doing."

"A spell."

"That was no spell."

The Apple Tree Man had expected this as well.

I shrugged. "We were told it was a spell. We were told that only music and dancing and the pattern of the grass would rescue my sisters from you. We don't know much about magic, but we had to give it a try because we didn't know what else to do."

"Who told you this?"

"It doesn't matter," I said, though I guess to her it mattered plenty.

I beckoned to Ruth and Grace then. Laurel called out to Elsie. I was about to ask after Adie, but she came out of the trees behind the fairy court's horses, carrying a spear. I guess she'd been planning to make her own try at a rescue.

"It's time you were going," I told the bee queen.

She shook her head. "No. You didn't play fair."

She made a gesture with her hand and before we could do a thing we were all gone from that field by Aunt Lillian's orchard and back in the otherworld again.

"You lied about what you were doing."

"No, we—"

"Kill them!" the queen cried. "Kill them all. Then go back into their world and kill their mother. Kill all of their friends and their friends' families. Burn down their homes. Salt their fields."

There was a crazy look in her eyes, but I suppose it didn't much matter. Crazy or not, she was the queen and there was nothing we could do to stop her—not with only the seven of us and the fairy court in this world and our friends left behind in the other.

Guess I was right, always to be so scared of bees. Some part of me must have known that one day they'd kill me.

I saw Adie lift her spear. I stepped in front of Ruth and Grace. Laurel and Bess came to stand beside me, though what the three of us could do to protect the younger twins, I didn't know. Elsie was halfway from the tree where she'd been standing to where we were. She stopped dead with bee fairies all around her.

An ugly murmur went through the court. The bees carrying the tiny fairies buzzed angrily in the air all around us. All I wanted to do was close my eyes and have it be done with, but I couldn't do it. I had to go down swatting them bees, do what I could to keep my sisters as safe as I could before the bees finally brought me down.

Turned out it wasn't necessary.

The bee fairies weren't mad at us. They were mad at their queen.

One of the tall riders stepped up to her and before she could stop him, he got hold of this pendant she was wearing and gave it a tug. The chain broke, and he stepped back with the pendant in his hand just before she took a swing at him. Before she could try again, he pointed a finger at her.

"We've put up with your angers and feuds for too long as it is," he said. "But when you break a solemn oath, you go too far."

The queen fixed him with a cold look. "Don't you dare judge me. I am your queen and so long as I—"

"Queen no longer," he broke in.

He lifted a hand and I don't know how many of those bee-riding fairies came swarming. Thousands, I figure. Each with a bow and their tiny venomed arrows.

"When you broke your oath," he said, "you forfeited your royalty. You've lost your place in this court."

He cut downward with his hand and all those little bee fairies let loose with their arrows.

I didn't much like that queen. Truth be told, the way she threatened my sisters, I wouldn't have cried to find out she'd up and died somewhere, somehow. But when I saw her killed, right there in front of my eyes, all I felt was sick.

She dropped to the ground with I don't know how many thousands of those little arrows sticking out of her like she was a pincushion, writhing and crying from the pain of the venom. I actually started to step forward, wanting to do something to ease her pain, but Bess caught hold of my arm.

"Wait," the bee fairy who'd given the order to have her killed said to me.

The bees carrying the tiny archers had all landed now, most on the ground, some on the horses or the taller fairies. It was so quiet in the meadow that the queen's dying gasp echoed for what seemed like forever.

I looked at the new leader of the fairy court.

"Wait," he repeated.

And then I heard it—the same sound I'd heard in the Apple Tree Man's house. The rumbling drone of a bee swarm coming from inside the dead queen. I guess she got shot so many times, the process was all that much quicker. My sisters on either side gasped as the newborn bees came swarming up out of the queen's mouth.

There were a lot of them—a lot more than had come out of the little 'sangman. So many that, for a long moment, we couldn't even see the bee queen. Then they went spiraling up and away, this dark buzzing swarm of bees, like a storm cloud driven afore the wind. All that was left of the queen was the shape of her, made up of what looked like old dried honeycombs, gray and papery.

The new leader looked like he was about to say something to me, but just then we heard a commotion at the far end of the court. The bee's dogs started up barking as out of the woods came an army of 'sangmen, led by their king and queen. The 'sangman I'd rescued walked beside them, hand-in-hand with the last daughter of the bee queen. In amongst the crowd of 'sangmen I spied Aunt Lillian, the

Apple Tree Man, and Li'l Pater, who, I found out later, was the one who brought them all over to this part of the otherworld where we were.

"Hold!" the leader of the bee fairies cried to the court as they started nocking arrows and readying their spears.

He walked through the court to meet the 'sangmen. After glancing at each other, my sisters and I trailed along behind him, Adie and Elsie joining us so that we were all seven of us together. The 'sangmen awaited the bee fairy's approach. They were purely outnumbered, no question about it, but they looked ready to fight all the same and damn the consequences.

But there wasn't going to be a fight, it appeared. The bee man went down on one knee in front of the princess and offered her the pendant that he'd torn from her mother's neck. She hesitated for a long moment, then took it. The court erupted into cheers, all these bee fairies grinning at each other, gone in the blink of an eye from these grim, dangerous creatures to folks just looking for an excuse to have a party.

My sisters and I exchanged puzzled looks, but I was feeling hopeful that maybe all our troubles were done.

The princess—I guess I should call her the queen now—signaled the bee man to rise, then had him lead her to us. There was a happy laugh sitting there in her eyes, but when she spoke, it was like the exchange I'd had with her mother, serious like a ceremony.

"Your boon was fairly asked and just," she said. "We have no quarrel with you, nor with any other. Will you promise us the same?"

"Well, sure," I said. "We never wanted any trouble in the first place."

She sighed. "I know. But my mother . . . she . . ."

"Wasn't exactly easy to get along with."

She nodded.

"Still . . . it seems harsh, what happened to her." When she gave me a puzzled look, I added, "You know, killing her and all. If it was my mama . . ." I didn't finish. I guess our situations were too different to set one up against the other.

"Did your mother lock you in a tower for most of your life?" she asked. "Did she never have a kind word for you?"

"It's okay," I said. "You don't have to explain. I know things were different for you."

She gave a slow nod. "They were." She waited a beat, then added, "But she wasn't killed. She was changed into a new tribe. This is her chance to begin again and make amends for the wrongs she did in this life."

That all sounded fine and dandy, but it put a big question in my head. I didn't know quite how to ask, but I had to know.

"Is there . . . any chance she could get it into her head to come after us again?" I asked.

"No. You'll be safe now. You and your sisters and anyone under your protection. You have my word on that."

"Thanks for that," I said.

"No. Thank you," she said. "All of you," she added, looking around to take in my sisters and the 'sangmen as well.

She held out her hand and the little 'sangman prince left his parents' side to come stand by her.

"We both thank you," she said.

There was a moment's silence, then the fairy court cheered again. This time the 'sangmen joined in.

I guess this is where the fairy tales always end. Trouble was, we still had to get home.

9

"Did you hear me roar like the Father of Cats?" Li'l Pater asked me.

"That was you?"

He nodded, then whapped his tail on the ground to make that *pit-a-pat* sound we'd heard after the panther's scream.

"Guess you saved the day," I told him.

"Bet you're glad I came along now."

"Better than glad," I said and I meant it.

Both fairy courts were gone and we were alone in the meadow now, just Aunt Lillian and us Dillard girls, the Apple Tree Man and Li'l Pater. My sisters didn't know what to make of this pair of fairy people, but they were taking it in good stride. I guess with everything they'd already seen today, spending time with a little cat man and a fellow who looked more like a tree than a man was pretty tame. Heck, Grace and Ruth were already tussling in the grass with Li'l Pater like he was some long-lost friend of theirs, paying no mind to the rest of us.

But while I was grateful for the help the pair of them had given us, I was pretty much done with fairylands and the people in them. I went over to where the Apple Tree Man and Aunt Lillian were talking.

"I want to go home," I told him. "I purely hate it here."

"Of course," the Apple Tree Man said. "But you know you've only seen the worst this place has to offer. There is far more laughter and glory in this land than could ever be represented by feuding fairy courts."

What happened to how dangerous it was for ordinary folks to cross over here? I wondered. But I didn't press him on it. I got the sense he wasn't talking to me anyway, but to Aunt Lillian. I don't know why I didn't see this coming, but I knew as soon as she put her hand on his arm that she'd be staying.

"I won't be coming back," she said.

"I guess I knew that," I said, "but that don't make it any easier."

"I know. But I've got a chance here . . ." She shot a girlish glance at the Apple Tree Man—like Adie at her worst—and I had to smile. "I guess I just need to take it."

I didn't know what to say. It wasn't my place to steal this moment of happiness, but I was going to miss her something terrible.

"I've already made arrangements with my lawyer," she went on. "I wanted everything to go to you. I was thinking of it as an inheritance, but now . . . I suppose it's a gift. You're the only one I know that will take care of all I hold dear. I just have to come back and stop by his office to sign it over to you to make it official."

Now I really didn't know what to say.

"What?" Laurel asked. "You mean you're giving her that ramshackle old homestead?"

Bess elbowed her in the side.

"Sorry," Laurel muttered.

But Aunt Lillian didn't take offense.

"The homestead," she said. "Yes. But also the hills. I'm not sure how much land's involved. Something in the neighborhood of a hundred square miles, I reckon. The lawyer will know for sure."

"You own all that land behind our farm?" Adie asked.

"No one owns the land," Aunt Lillian told her. "But I guess I hold the paper on it."

"But you . . ."

Aunt Lillian grinned. "Live plain and simple and poor as a churchmouse?"

"Something like that."

"Maybe she doesn't have any money," Elsie said, "but I'm guessing Lily McGlure has more than enough."

"Who's Lily McGlure?" Laurel asked.

"Famous artist," Adie told her. "Loads of money."

I wondered how Adie'd come to know something like that, but it got explained pretty quick.

"I'm sorry," Elsie was saying to Aunt Lillian. "I know we shouldn't have looked in that chest with all your paintings and sketchbooks, but we got scared when we couldn't find you or Janey. So then we got thinking about bodies and where you could hide them . . ."

"That's all right, girl," Aunt Lillian said. "It's nothing I'm ashamed of. I just always kept my distance from being Lily McGlure on account of once folks know you got money, they come hounding you for it and you never do get no peace. Folks always knew me as Lily Kindred, living with her aunt, Em Kindred, though I was born Lillian McGlure. It was just plain happenstance that the McGlure name got used on my art at the first, but when I saw the advantage of it, well, I just left it that way."

"You're a famous artist?" I asked. "When did that happen?"

"Oh, a long time ago," Aunt Lillian said. "I started in on drawing when I was younger than you and I guess I did pretty well because, after a time, I had me all these folks in Newford, and even further off, falling over themselves to buy what I was doing. Got me an agent and everything, selling both the originals as well as prints and the like. Aunt Em and me, well, we didn't need more than we had—and didn't want it neither. So first off, I bought all this land to keep it safe from the developers and the mining and logging companies and such, and then I had any other money coming my way put into a trust fund to take care of taxes and all.

"A body could get richer'n hell, selling off the land and using the money in that fund, I reckon."

"I would never do that," I told her.

She smiled. "I know. Why do you thinking I'm leaving it to you, girl? But you ever find you need some money, maybe to get you an education, or for one of your sisters, don't you be shy about selling off some of that old artwork of mine. And you'll find a treat or two, down at the bottom of that chest. I got me three color studies by Milo Johnson, any one of which'd fetch top dollar at an auction."

Elsie's eyes went wide, but the rest of us didn't much know who she was talking about.

"Probably another famous artist," Laurel said.

"Only the most famous to paint in these hills," Elsie said, "after Lily McGlure."

"Now you're embarrassing me, girl," Aunt Lillian said, but I could see she was pleased with the compliment all the same.

"Why did you stop painting?" Elsie asked.

Aunt Lillian shrugged. "I don't know. I got old and my fingers got stiff. And I said pretty much all I had to say with my paints, I reckon, though I've still been drawing in one of my sketchbooks from time to time. The thing is, you do a thing long enough, don't matter how much you love it, it can start to wear some and you want to turn to something else. Gets so you look at what could be the perfect picture and you just want to hold it in your head and appreciate it for what it is, 'stead of trying to capture it on canvas.

"And then once Aunt Em died, I didn't really have the time no more."

She turned to me.

"You remember this, girl," she said. "You don't have to be no spinster to live out on that old homestead and do it right. Don't you be afraid to go into town from time to time, maybe find yourself a boyfriend."

I just shrugged. That didn't seem even close to likely, but I didn't see no point in arguing the fact.

"There's just one more thing," Aunt Lillian said. "I'm leaving you with a lot of benefits, I guess, though truth to tell, it just lets my heart rest easy knowing that everything I got's passing into such good and capable hands. But I've got to leave you with an unpaid debt as well."

"What's that?"

"Well, that Father of Cats that Li'l Pater and the fairies were talking about—that's the same old black panther in those stories I told you 'bout when I was a girl. You 'member them?"

I gave a slow nod.

"Well then, I reckon you remember how I owe him. That debt's supposed to pass on to my children and their children after. But I never had me a child. I guess the closest I've come is you, so I'm asking you to take that on as well."

"What . . . what's he going to ask me to do?"

I knew I couldn't say no to Aunt Lillian, but I was remembering how even those fierce bee fairies had seemed a little nervous when they thought the Father of Cats was taking an interest in their affairs. And if he scared *them* . . .

"I don't rightly know," Aunt Lillian said. "But I told him I'd only do whatever it was if no one would be hurt by it."

"The Father of Cats is an honorable being," the Apple Tree Man said. "What he asks of you might be hard, but it won't be wrong."

I nodded. "Okay," I said. "I'll take on that debt for you, Aunt Lillian." I turned to the Apple Tree Man, adding, "And I guess I owe you an apology just like I did Li'l Pater. I should have just trusted you."

He smiled. "Nothing wrong with someone needing to earn your trust. I'm just happy it all worked out the way it did. You were very brave out there with the bee fairies."

"I didn't feel brave. I just felt stupid."

"Oh, I know," Bess said. "And scared, too. I was sure they'd hear my knees knocking against each other from one end of the meadow to the other."

I just looked at her for a long moment.

"But you and Laurel," I finally said. "You're always doing stuff in front of people. Playing and singing and dancing."

"Well, I get nervous doing that sometimes, too," Bess said. "Laurel's the one that's not scared of anything."

Laurel laughed. "What's the worst that can happen? You make a fool of yourself, but life goes on."

"Except here we could've got ourselves shot like the queen did," I said.

Laurel went quiet pretty fast.

"There's that," she said.

I turned back to the Apple Tree Man.

"It's time we were going," I said.

I'd told the truth before, about not wanting to be in this place. But right now I didn't want to go because it meant leaving Aunt Lillian behind. I figured I'd probably see her from time to time, but nothing was going to be the same anymore. I was happy to look after that place of hers for her, but I was thinking how that could be a lonely way to live, what with her being gone and all.

I guess she knew what I was thinking. She came up and put her arms around me and just held me for a time.

"You'll do fine, girl," she said. "I don't expect nothing less from you."

I held on tight to her for a moment longer, then we gathered up Grace and Ruth from across the meadow where they were still playing with Li'l Pater and we all made our way back to where the door into the Apple Tree Man's house opened out on this world.

10

I guess Root pretty much thought he'd died and gone to heaven when me and all my sisters came traipsing out of the Apple Tree Man's tree. He jumped up and barked and ran around in circles, not knowing who to greet first. But he finally settled on me, jumped up and put his paws on my stomach, looking at me like I was the best thing he could ever find in this world which, I suppose, from his point of view I was, seeing's how I'm the one that first found him and does most of the looking after for him. But he was a dog full of love, and after I'd fussed some with him, he went and visited everybody else, full of wet kisses, that tail of his wagging so hard you'd think it was going to come off.

"Well, some things don't change," Adie said as she took Root's paws in her hands and pushed him away from her. "I swear that dog's got double his quota of loving enthusiasm."

"He just missed us," Ruth said, bending down and not minding Root's sloppy kisses all over her face.

Adie pulled her to her feet.

"Don't let him do that," she said. "He's just putting germs all over your face."

"Is that true?" Ruth asked Elsie, the Dillard expert in all things natural.

Elsie shrugged. "Probably."

"Just think where that tongue of his has been," Adie said.

"Yeah," Laurel put in. "You forget what he uses to lick his butt?"

I guess we were pretty much home and settling right back into our usual sisterly ways.

"Anybody know what time it is?" Adie asked.

None of us had a watch, but I checked the position of the sun.

"Four," I said. "Maybe four-thirty."

"We should get a move on," Adie said. "Mama's going to kill us and don't think for a minute she's going to buy the story of what really happened to us today."

"I just need to get Henny back into the barn and feed the chickens," I said.

"We can help," Grace and Ruth said in the same breath.

"And we have to have one more look in that chest of Aunt Lillian's," Elsie said.

Adie started to shake her head, but as soon as Elsie brought it up, we were all of us interested.

"What's another half hour," Bess asked, "when we're already as late as we are?"

"Yeah," Laurel said. "You've already had a peek at all of those pictures of hers."

I don't suppose Adie had any real choice in the matter, not with all of us determined. Laurel and Elsie rounded up Henny and put her back into the barn, milking her and making sure that she had water and feed, while the younger twins and I saw to the chickens. We threw out extra feed for them, in case I was late getting back up tomorrow, and made sure Henny had plenty of water and food, too. Then we all trooped into the house and up the stairs to the second floor.

I guess with Aunt Lillian having been this famous artist I should have expected her work to be good, but I was still surprised when I got an actual look at all those drawings and paintings that filled the chest.

"They're not paintings," Elsie explained, when Laurel wondered aloud why the wooden panels Aunt Lillian had used weren't hanging in some museum. "They're what you call studies, something you do in preparation of the real painting."

Ruth picked one up and held it closer to her face. "They look like real paintings to me."

"Sure do," Grace said. "They look good enough to hang in a museum to me." She turned to her twin. "Remember that school trip we took to the museum in Tyson? These pictures are better than half the stuff we saw in there."

Ruth nodded. "Yeah, at least these are about something."

"Any museum would pay top dollar to own these," Elsie said.

Laurel grinned. "I guess that means you're rich, Janey."

"Only if she sells them," Elsie reminded us. "She might not want to do that."

"I've got to think on it," I said.

Truth was, I was feeling a little overwhelmed. It was strange enough, knowing I'd be holding paper on the homestead and all the hills around us, without taking into account all these paintings and sketchbooks and all. All I really wanted was to have Aunt Lillian back and for things to be the way they'd been before. I already missed her something terrible.

"You could probably afford to put in electricity and a phone line," Adie said.

Laurel laughed. "Why's she got to do that? She could just buy herself a big old house in town—have cable and everything."

"That's not the point of all of this," I said.

Adie shook her head. "So what is? To live hard and never have the time to enjoy life a little?"

"I don't know that it's something I can explain," I said. "I know I felt the same way as you do when I first came up here and saw how Aunt Lillian was living. But the more I helped out and the more I learned, the more I came to understand that easy's not necessarily better. When you do pretty much everything for yourself, you appreciate the things you've got a lot more than if someone just up and hands it to you, or you buy it off the shelf in some store."

Adie looked at me for a long moment and I knew she still didn't get it. But she wasn't going to argue with me neither.

"We should go," she said. "Mama's going to be back by now and worried sick."

I nodded in agreement and was ready to go, but just then Elsie pulled some more paintings from the bottom of the chest.

"Here they are," she said.

"Are these paintings or—what do did you call them—studies?" Ruth wanted to know.

"They were done as studies, the same as those of Aunt Lillian, but I guess they're paintings, too."

There were three of them and even I could tell right off that they'd been done by somebody else.

The first was of the staircase waterfall where the creek took a sudden tumble before heading on again at a quieter pace. The second was of that old deserted homestead up a side valley of the hollow, the tin roof sagging, the rotting walls falling inward. The last one could have been painted anywhere in this forest but it was easy to imagine it had been done down by the creek, looking up the slope into a view of yellow birches, beech and sprucey-pines growing thick and dense, with a burst of light coming through a break in the canopy.

I guess I don't know much about art, but I liked these paintings a lot. They were kind of rough—not a whole lot of detail—but I could recognize where they'd been done, and they were about as good as a picture gets. Not better than Aunt Lillian's, just different. But Elsie got more excited than I'd seen her in a long time.

"These are the ones by Milo Johnson," she said.

"The other famous artist," Adie said. "One of the two fellows who disappeared in these woods back in the twenties or something that you were telling me about."

Elsie nodded. "And I guess we know where they ended up."

None of us said much for a time. We just sat there by the chest, thinking about the day we'd had.

"Any of you got a bad urge to go back across?" I asked.

Adie and the older twins shook their heads. The younger twins looked primed and ready, but I think that had more to do with the fun they'd been having at the end with Li'l Pater. Only Elsie got this kind of dreamy look that put a deep worry in me.

"You won't try to go back," I said to her.

She blinked, then looked at me. "I don't know. Everything was so much more *there* than it is here. I hated all the business with those fairy courts, but I've got to admit, that if the chance came up, I'd probably go."

"Promise me you won't unless you talk to me first."

She met my gaze, then gave a slow nod.

"You've got that promise," she said.

"We have *got* to go," Adie said.

We put everything back into the chest except I kept out one of the sketchbooks, filled with drawings and little handwritten descriptions of various plants and such to bring home with me. I put it in the backpack that Adie'd used to bring up some preserves for Aunt Lillian, then I closed the door on her house—no, it's my house now, I realized—and we headed for home, stopping only to collect Laurel's and Bess's instrument cases along the way.

Grace and Ruth played innocent but there wasn't one of us didn't figure we knew who'd played that trick of filling them with stones. I guess the only thing that saved them from getting a licking from the older twins was how close we'd all come to dying today. Thing like that puts everything into a different perspective, that's for sure.

11

There was a thunderstorm in Mama's eyes when we come trailing out of the woods and crossed the pasture to home. She didn't even acknowledge Root's happy greeting, just stood there with her hands on her hips as we came up to her.

"Now remember," Adie had warned when we were on the path coming home. "We lost track of time and we'll just take what Mama gives us in punishment. No talk about fairy courts and otherworlds or we'll all be looking at a licking."

Everybody'd agreed with her, though none of us felt real happy about telling Mama a lie as big as the one we'd be telling her now. And then we still had to figure out a way to explain how Aunt Lillian had come to leave all her property and lands to me.

But agreeing's one thing, doing's another, and the younger twins were just too excited by it all to remember to keep it to themselves.

"Mama! Mama!" Grace cried as she broke from us and ran toward her. "You're not going to believe the story we have to tell you."

For as Long a Time as Distance
Sarah Jane

Mama took it better than I'd ever have thought she would.

Once Grace started into the whole story, we couldn't just leave her hanging, so we all filled in our parts. We started talking in the field behind the house and ended up sitting around the picnic table in the backyard, Mama looking from one to the other of us, waiting for one of us to admit we were just pulling her leg.

"You know what this sounds like, don't you?" she said when we were finally done.

I just pushed the sketchbook across the table to her. It didn't really prove anything, except that Aunt Lillian was quite the artist. There was nothing in the book to confirm bee fairies and 'sangmen and otherworlds and any of it. There was only our word.

Mama looked up from the sketchbook.

"Well, I've heard stranger stories," she said. "But that was late at night when folks were spinning yarns and maybe we'd partook of a jar or two of 'shine."

"We weren't drinking," Ruth assured her.

Mama laughed. "No, I don't suppose you were."

"But you believe us, don't you?" Grace said.

I could see that she didn't want to. It was a hard, strange story to swallow. But I knew what she was thinking. We were her own girls, and maybe we'd told a fib or two in our time, trying to get out of a chore or go someplace that maybe we shouldn't, like some of the dances Laurel and Bess went to, but we'd never lied to her about nothing important. It just wasn't something we'd do. So maybe what we'd told her sounded too much like some old storyteller's crazy yarn, but come down to the crunch, she didn't have much choice.

"I suppose I have to," she said with a slow nod.

I guess it helped when Aunt Lillian came by a couple of days later and took Mama and me into town to see her lawyer. I think what I liked best was that Mama never came right out and asked Aunt Lillian about the strange story we'd told her. Once she'd taken us at our word, it wasn't something she needed to have anybody confirm.

But the business we conducted with the lawyer allowed her to see that this much of the story we'd told was true, without her having to go asking anybody about it.

"Are you sure about what you're doing here?" she asked Aunt Lillian as we drove into town.

" 'Bout as sure as a body can be about a thing they don't know is right or wrong, they just feel it's something they've got to do. For as long a time as distance I've been steady, doing what I should do. I reckon maybe it's time I took me a chance."

I saw the corner of Mama's mouth twitch with a smile.

"I know that feeling," Mama said.

"We all do, girl," Aunt Lillian told her. "It's what makes us human."

As the months went by, our adventures in that otherworld pretty much started to seem like a dream. But I had the homestead and the maps of the hills marking off my property that the lawyer gave me to prove that it really did happen, and we talked about it among ourselves, my sisters and me.

My schooling never did progress. I moved out to Aunt Lillian's homestead not long after we got back and there was nothing no one could say or do to make me change my mind. I'm a Dillard woman, through and through, headstrong as any in my family. I guess Mama knew that, and maybe she also knew that I was a woman out of time, that I was always going to be more comfortable on the homestead than I'd ever be in the modern world.

"Least this way we can still see each other from time to time," she said. " 'Stead of having you run off somewhere and never knowing where you are or how you're doing."

She'd come up once in a while and I always made a point of stopping by the farm whenever I went to town. And I had all my supplies delivered there instead of to the Welches' like Aunt Lillian used to have done.

I sold those three Milo Johnson paintings and we got more money for them than I thought it was possible to get for a thing. I divided that money in eight equal portions for Mama and the seven of us girls. Mine I just gave to the foundation that had been looking after Aunt Lillian's money for all those years.

I didn't sell any of Aunt Lillian's work, but through the foundation I donated all of what Elsie called the color studies and field paintings to the Newford Museum of Art, and they were pretty pleased as they were just starting in on a retrospective of her work. They tried to get in touch with me or Aunt Lillian through the foundation, but the foundation wasn't giving out my name or whereabouts and I got left in peace.

The money changed things—not who we were, just our circumstances. Mama paid off the mortgage on the farm. If she'd wanted to live simple like me, she didn't need to work anymore, but she liked the going into town and staying busy that holding her job entailed, though she went from full-time to part-time. Mornings she'd be at her work— dispatch in the sheriff's office. Afternoons she'd visit old folks like Mrs. Runion or do charity work at the hospital in Tyson, or at the old folks' home in town.

Adie didn't get married, but she had herself a child, a little red-haired girl that she named Lily. She and Lily lived with Mama on the farm and Adie squirreled away her share of what we got from the paintings in a college fund for Lily.

I remember thinking sometimes how she'd seemed lonely, even with six sisters and all those boyfriends she always had. After Lily came along, she never seemed like that to me again.

Laurel and Bess took the money and made themselves a CD which is doing pretty good, they say, but it's old-timey music, so you're not about to hear it on the radio anytime soon. Especially not since in among all those old tunes and songs, they did a few covers of stuff by the Clash, Barry White, and a funny version of "Blue Suede Shoes" with the chorus line changed to "don't you step on my blue-grass shoes."

They're traveling all the time, playing music festivals across the country in the summer, then touring in Europe during the winter. Seems like folks over there in places like Germany and Italy and such appreciate their kind of music more'n folks do here at home.

Elsie came to live with me, but not right away. She finished high school, then went on to study art at Butler University in Newford before she finally moved in with me. She was kind of a throwback there, the same way I've been ever since that day Root and I first met Aunt Lillian. Instead of slapping any old thing down on a canvas and finding something smart to say about it, she was drawing from life, sketching and cataloguing what she saw in the city the same way she'd done in the woods and around the homestead.

She loved to go through Aunt Lillian's journals, comparing how Aunt Lillian took to a subject to how she herself put it down on paper. But most of her time she spent out in the woods, summer and winter, painting and drawing. We fixed up a big studio for her in the barn with good northern light and a potbellied old woodstove for the colder weather. She didn't paint at night—we still didn't have electricity or running water, and not much interest in getting either. Evenings we'd spend on the porch in the summer, just soaking in the night music of the hills. In the winter we'd read by oil lamps and candles in the parlor, or sitting at the kitchen table. Sometimes we'd just talk the whole of the night away.

About our only concession to the modern world was getting a cell phone. We kept it charged using a twelve-volt, but it was a pain hauling that old car battery back and forth through the woods for it to get charged. The only place we could get that phone to work is from the top of the hill, up back of the house.

I asked her once after she'd moved in with me if, given the chance, she'd still go back into that otherworld.

"Only if I knew I could come back here," she said.

Not long after we had our adventure, Grace and Ruth got themselves a new friend, this fourteen-year-old boy named Peter Little. They were always talking about him, visiting with him, or he'd be at the farm with them. It was a few months before I finally got to meet him and when I did, I took him aside.

"You look different," I said.

He was a little taller than me, maybe sixteen, a wiry teenager with crow-black hair and dark blue eyes that were sort of almond-shaped.

"Better or worse?" Li'l Pater asked.

I shook my head. "Not much of either. Just different. The girls know who you are?"

He hesitated for a moment, then nodded.

"You actually have a place you're living?"

"Just the woods."

"You're not going to hurt them in any way, are you?"

He gave me a shocked look that told me more than any words

he could have used. It just come up on him sudden, before he could even start to speak, and I held up a hand.

"I just had to ask," I said. "They're my sisters."

"And I know how protective you are about them."

"I guess you do." I cocked my head and gave him a considering look. "So what are the three of you doing all the time?"

"I'm . . . teaching them about magic."

"Nothing dangerous, I hope."

I was thinking of the mischief that pair could get into all on their own without adding spells and what-have-you into the equation.

He shook his head.

"And what about you?" I asked. "What are you getting out of it?"

"I'm learning what it's like to be human."

I guess you're wondering about what I was doing, how my life got changed by the adventure and all that money. Well, the truth is, it didn't make a whole lot of difference one way or the other. I missed Aunt Lillian something awful, but looking after the homestead kept me busy. I loved living up there full-time, just me and Root, and I never really got lonely. If I did, it was just a short ramble along the creek and I'd be back at the farm with Mama and my sisters.

I did try my hand at drawing like Elsie and Aunt Lillian, but it wasn't something I could ever get the hang of, don't ask me why. But I took to writing pretty well. It's not like I have the language I read in the books Mama gets for me from the library. But I find I like to put things down on paper. The stories Aunt Lillian told me. Things I see in the fields and woods around the homestead. Thoughts and dreams and such.

Elsie wants us to do a book together, a kind of field guide or collection of essays about these hills of ours. I'd write the words and she'd draw the pictures. I'm thinking on it, though I'm not sure that I want to write something that any old body could just pick up and read. Elsie says I just need to learn to let the words go once I've put them down on paper, but I don't know.

Anywise, my life wasn't changed too much by the adventure or the money or even living up here on Aunt Lillian's homestead—not inside me. Not who I am. That came from a whole different direction, one I wasn't even close to expecting.

I was splitting wood and putting it up in the woodshed for the winter when Root gave a warning bark. I set down the ax and turned to see what had caught his attention. With Root it could be anything from crows in the corn to a groundhog getting too bold for his britches—just saying a groundhog wore britches.

For a second I didn't see anything. Then this fellow came out of the woods on the far side of the trees, moving so smooth and easy it was like he'd just appeared there. I had a moment's worry, thinking maybe this was some more business with the fairies, but as he got closer, I could see he was human. Leastwise he looked human, though handsomer than most boys I've run across.

He was maybe eighteen, wearing hiking boots, jeans and a white T-shirt with a buckskin jacket over top, and carrying an ax. His hair was black as a starless night under a baseball cap turned backwards. His broad features had a coppery cast to them so I figured he was probably from the rez. Even with that jacket on you could tell he was strong as well as graceful.

My pulse started to quicken and I told it to hold up there. Whatever reason this boy had to come here, it wasn't to court me. But my heart wouldn't listen.

"Hey," he said. "Is Lily around?"

My mouth felt too dry to talk so I just shook my head.

He smiled. "I see you're doing my job."

"Your . . . job?" I managed.

"Putting in the winter wood."

He held out a hand so that Root could give it a sniff, then bent and ruffled his fur. Standing up again, he came over and offered me his hand, too—to shake, not smell.

"I'm Oliver," he said. "Oliver Creek."

"Sarah Jane Dillard."

His palm was dry and a little rough and my pulse just started going quicker. I let go of his hand and took a step back. I didn't know what was the matter with me. I was feeling so hot I figured I must have a fever.

"Are you always this quiet, Sarah Jane?" he asked.

I shook my head.

"My granddad's a friend of Lily's," he went on. "We help her out with some of the heavier work around here."

"Like chopping wood."

He held up his ax and nodded. "You want a hand?"

"Sure. Thanks."

We didn't talk much as we worked. Oliver was better at chopping and splitting than I was, so I let him go to it and spent most of my time stacking the stove-lengths in the woodshed. After a couple of hours, we took a break and sat on stumps by the wood pile, sipping iced tea.

"So where's Lily?" Oliver asked. "Out hunting and gathering?"

I smiled and shook my head. "She's . . . gone away."

He gave me a sharp look and I realized what that had sounded like.

"No, she's not dead or anything," I quickly said. "She's just moved . . ." I sighed. "It's complicated."

"She's gone into the otherworld," Oliver said.

Now it was my turn to look hard at him.

"You know about all of that?" I asked.

He shrugged. "My mother's got sixteen sisters and they're all medicine women, so all I've ever heard since I was a kid was about the manitou and *manidò-akì*—the spiritworld. Never been there myself, though. Never seen a spirit either, but I guess I believe they're out there."

"So what makes you think Aunt Lillian went over there?"

"Well, Granddad's told me about this friendship she's got with some tree spirit in the orchard and how every time he used to come up here he'd half-expect her to have gone off into *manidò-akì* with him."

"John Creek," I said. "That's who your grandfather is, right?"

It was coming back to me now.

He smiled. "That's right. And I'm still Oliver."

"Aunt Lillian's told me about you."

"All good, I hope."

I don't know why it came over me, but I had to duck my head to hide a blush.

"Well, that's where she went," I said, hiding behind my hair and pretending to look at something on the ground. "Into that otherworld with the Apple Tree Man."

"She leave the place in your care?"

I nodded.

"So you mind if I come by from time to time?" he asked.

I looked up at him. "You don't have to. I'm not as old as Aunt Lillian—at least not yet. I can do the heavy work."

"I wasn't offering to do work," he said, "though I'm happy to lend a hand. I was thinking more of just coming by to visit."

"Why would you want to do that?"

I don't know why that came out the way it did. I was just too nervous, I guess. And now I figured I'd just insulted him or something. But he only smiled.

"Because I like you, Sarah Jane," he said. "And I'd like to get to know you better."

He got up then and fetched his ax from where he'd stuck it in the chopping stump.

"I've got to go," he said. "I promised Granddad I'd come by and give him a hand mending his traps before it got dark."

I stood up and didn't know what to do with my hands.

"Thanks for all your help," I said. "I would've been at this all day if you hadn't come by."

"No problem. You busy tomorrow?"

I thought about a hundred things I still had to do, from chores to getting the place ready for winter, and almost said so when I realized what he was really asking.

"No," I said and then I got real brave. "Would you like to come for dinner?"

"I'll count the minutes," he said with a grin.

He gave Root a quick pat, tapped his index finger against his temple and pointed it at me, then headed off, back across the field. I just stood there watching him go until he disappeared in among the trees, then sat back down on the stump and hugged my knees.

"You hear that, Root?" I said. "He said he liked me."

So I guess that's my story.

If you want to know more about Aunt Lillian and the Apple Tree Man, or if the Father of Cats ever came to see me, or even what kind of mischief Ruth and Grace got into with Li'l Pater—those are all stories for another time.

Anything else . . . well, it's nobody's business but my own.